MW01487439

ANOTHER GIRL LOST

"A masterpiece of the suspense/thriller genre, *Another Girl Lost* by experienced and talented novelist Mary Burton is a simply riveting read from cover to cover. Original, compelling, expertly crafted, and highly recommended."

—*Midwest Book Review*

THE LIES I TOLD

"Burton's intriguing suspense novel puts readers in a quandary of interpreting reality from illusion."

—Bookreporter

DON'T LOOK NOW

"With plenty of possible suspects, Burton's latest will appeal to readers who want light romance and heavy suspense."

—*Library Journal*

BURN YOU TWICE

"Burton does a good job balancing gentle romance with high-tension suspense."

—*Publishers Weekly*

"Scorching action. The twists and turns keep the reader on the edge of their seat as they will not want to put the novel down."

—*Crimespree Magazine*

HIDE AND SEEK

"Burton delivers an irresistible, tension-filled plot with plenty of twists . . . Lovers of romantic thrillers won't be disappointed."

—*Publishers Weekly*

CUT AND RUN

"Burton can always be counted on for her smart heroines and tightly woven plots."

—*For the Love of Books*

"Must-read romantic suspense . . . Burton is a bona fide suspense superstar. And her books may be peppered with enough twists and turns to give you whiplash, but the simmering romance she builds makes for such a compelling, well-rounded story."

—*USA Today's Happy Ever After*

THE SHARK

"This romantic thriller is tense, sexy, and pleasingly complex."

—*Publishers Weekly*

"Precise storytelling complete with strong conflict and heightened tension are the highlights of Burton's latest. With a tough, vulnerable heroine in Riley at the story's center, Burton's novel is a well-crafted, suspenseful mystery with a ruthless villain who would put any reader on edge. A thrilling read."

—*RT Book Reviews* (4 stars)

WHAT SHE SAW

ALSO BY MARY BURTON

The Forgotten Files

WHAT SHE SAW

MARY BURTON

Montlake

Text copyright © 2025 by Mary Burton
All rights reserved.

Published by Montlake, Seattle

www.apub.com

Amazon, the Amazon logo, and Montlake are trademarks of Amazon.com, Inc., or its affiliates.

EU product safety contact:
Amazon Media EU S. à r.l.
38, avenue John F. Kennedy, L-1855 Luxembourg
amazonpublishing-gpsr@amazon.com

ISBN-13: 9781662516047 (paperback)
ISBN-13: 9781662516054 (digital)

Cover design by Ploy Siripant
Cover image: © Stephen Mulcahey / ArcAngel Images;
© Chipmunk131 / Shutterstock

Printed in the United States of America

WHAT SHE SAW

Prologue

Rafe Colton

Thursday, July 31, 2025, 11:00 a.m.
Red Onion State Prison, Pound, Virginia

In prison, I learned to appreciate the little things. Cracks in a wall. A bug scurrying along the floor. Underlined words in a dog-eared prison library book. Or when a prisoner's smile turned feral. Cells didn't offer me the big picture, but they taught me focus.

Front and center in my mind were the lumpy mattress in the prison hospital bed, the IVs running from my arms, and a machine beeping in time to my slow and sloppy heartbeat. The doctors said my cancer was worse. I would be dead in a year or two. Some said I should be relieved—this disease would end three decades in prison. But I liked living. And I wanted to squeeze out all I could of what was left.

A female nurse sat across the room, reading charts. Mousy brown hair was secured in a tight bun. She was younger than me, mid-thirties to early forties. Her skin still had some life in it, but it wasn't glassy smooth like a teenager's. A few lines had etched into creases around her eyes, marking a lifetime of disappointments. Half glasses reminded me of a librarian I'd had in middle school. Mrs. Davenport. Alone at night,

I've dreamed about the nurse. What did she look like in her teen years? Was that hair silken? Were her curves tight and hot? Was her skin soft?

I rubbed my fingers against the coarse prison sheets and tried to remember the feel of a young woman's smooth skin. Memories were too distant to grab.

Sighing, I curled my fingers into a fist. Time hadn't been kind to me either. But it isn't charitable to most of us.

"Darlin', could you do me a favor?" I asked.

The nurse looked up.

"I sure could use a drink of water, darlin'." My lips slid into a slight grin.

The nurse's expression softened. Time hadn't robbed me of all my charms. When I was younger, I enjoyed many appreciative glances from females. Now I missed the way their eyes glistened, and their lips parted as they watched me move.

She filled a cup with water and carried it to my bedside. I took the plastic, careful to brush my fingers against hers. The V of her scrubs dipped low, as if she wanted me to see the curve of her breasts. Her boxy top didn't hide her narrow waist and rounded hips. And I bet her calves had a nice shape despite the comfortable black shoes.

She didn't wear perfume, and her skin carried the scent of a sensible soap. Once I was surrounded by young women who smelled like mountain flowers and sex.

I sipped the water, letting the cool liquid roll down my dry throat. "Thank you, darlin'. I appreciate you."

Her face remained neutral, but her eyes grew expectant. Her head tilted. She wanted to smile, but she didn't.

I liked knowing I could charm a woman with a grin. I was old and dying, but still vain.

The door buzzer chimed. The moment broke. The nurse took the cup back and crossed to the security door. She opened it to a man dressed in a dark suit, white shirt, and sensible shoes. A cop. There's no missing a law enforcement officer's demeanor. The good ones are always tense, anticipating trouble and ready to spring. This guy was a tiger coiled, prepared to pounce.

We'd met twice before. Sergeant Grant McKenna.

He hadn't shared much of his own past, but he'd questioned me about the crimes that earned me a life sentence. The papers and the cops called me the Mountain Music Festival Killer and dubbed my so-called victims the Festival Four. Not the coolest monikers, but they stuck.

The powers-that-be tried and convicted me of four murders three decades ago. To this day, I still professed my innocence. I was framed. The cops had never found the bodies. And I argued the commonwealth's case was based on physical evidence planted in my barn.

A prison guard stepped inside the clinic and stationed himself by the door.

I sat straighter, wincing as I adjusted the pillow behind my bony back. The handcuffs that bound my left wrist to the bed dug into my fragile skin.

Grant knew the basic facts about me and had a working knowledge of my case. I didn't know how deep he'd dived into the finer points, but he knew enough. I was flattered he was there. I hadn't had many visitors in recent years, though there was a time when the Mountain Music Festival Killer eclipsed Charles Manson, Ted Bundy, and John Wayne Gacy.

According to the cops and press, my rampage spanned not years but a six-hour window. Psychologists assumed I would have killed more women if the cops hadn't stopped me. My splash in the headlines was intense and brief. No one remembered me now. I wasn't even a footnote. All that kept me relevant was the missing bodies.

"Sergeant," I said.

"Mr. Colton." He extended his hand to me.

I took it, disarmed by this very human gesture. I was amazed the guard allowed it. "How's retirement?"

"Can't complain." Grant withdrew his hand and pulled up a chair.

"Washington, DC, right? Homicide?"

"Good memory."

"Living on the pension now?"

Grant leveled his gaze on mine. "Basically."

"Why aren't you enjoying retirement?"

"Guys like you and me never really leave the game, do we?"

Many cops were filled with unspoken rage. Past traumas, unsolved cases, killers who got away—it all haunted them. They came here hoping that if they found the Mountain Music Festival bodies, they would find salvation.

However, the good cops hid their emotions well. And I'd established that Grant was one of the good ones.

Grant watched me closely. "I hear you're up for another parole hearing. Your chances look good this time."

"I'm no threat to anyone," I said. "Finishing out my days in the mountains isn't too much to ask, is it?"

He regarded me for a beat. "You want to return to Dawson?"

"Yes."

Grant never brought a notepad or file. But I suspected his memory was laser sharp. "The parole board will be reviewing your case next month. Compassionate releases are popular."

Release. I'd heard the word before, but after too many disappointments, I didn't dare allow any emotion. I crossed my fingers. "From your lips to God's ears."

Grant folded his arms over his chest. He was fit. Lifted weights. A runner. We'd made small talk about workouts during his last visit. I exercised any chance I got. It paid to be strong in here.

"I spoke at a conference a few weeks ago," Grant said.

No small talk today. "About me, I hope?"

"Your case among others."

"What was the theme?"

"Convictions without bodies."

"Interesting. You get a lot of cases like that?"

"Enough."

"Must be frustrating for the police and the families. No closure. And the judges and juries struggle to justify convictions like mine. How many of them wonder if they put away an innocent man like me?"

"I don't know." Grant sat back, unbuttoning his jacket. I appreciated that he dressed the part of a professional lawman.

"I bet a lot of them worry and wonder if they made the right call."

"You willing to tell me where you buried those bodies?" Grant asked.

"No foreplay today?" I chuckled. "Direct. To the point. But girls like a little warm-up before the big event."

Years ago, the police and prosecutors had dangled a reduced sentence if I told them where the bodies were. Even if I had known, I wouldn't have told. Cops can lie, and I don't trust them.

Plus, I'd grown to enjoy the mystery of this unfinished story. All humans chase attention. We pursue it in different ways. Some get on the stage. Some publish. Others get tattooed or choose the perfect personalized license plate. Anyone who says they don't want to be noticed doesn't know how to escape the shadows.

My silence kept me center stage. Maybe it wasn't the attention I'd once craved, but visits like this broke up the monotony of prison life. Beggars couldn't be choosers.

"I'm-an-innocent-man." I'd made this statement so many times, the words had conjoined.

"You've said that."

"The Mountain Music Festival and the Festival Four victims are ancient history."

"Not everyone has forgotten."

"I bet you can count those that remember on one hand."

"I'm driving to Dawson," Grant said.

My memories of Dawson relied now on pictures I'd clipped from articles about the Festival Four. Those images were black and white and at least a decade old. They didn't capture the vivid blue skies, the rolling green mountains, or the scent of honeysuckle in spring.

"It's a small, middle-of-nowhere town."

"I consider that an asset."

His southern accent was faint but strengthened as he spoke about Dawson. I'd bet it was his hometown, or it reminded him of home. "You're going to Dawson for peace and quiet?"

"There's a writer working this story. I've met her. She's sharp. Tenacious. She's headed to Dawson."

He was teasing me. Dawson. The case. A woman. "You think she'll do what cops and thirty-one years couldn't do?"

"She might."

"Is she writing a book about me and all those missing women?"

"I don't know. Maybe."

Talking about a woman who was thinking about me was tantalizing. "You have a hard-on for her?"

He didn't answer. Ah, a good southern gentleman.

I pressed, sensing a tender spot. "Are you trying to woo her with my deep dark confession?"

Grant shifted, smoothing a wrinkle from his suit jacket with long, tanned fingers. "Men have jumped through hoops for a pretty woman since Adam and Eve. I'm no different."

Ah, this was the part where he pretended that he was my pal. My buddy. "What we won't do for a woman."

"You have a few words of wisdom?" Grant asked. "You were always good with the ladies."

"It's been thirty-one years. I'm out of practice." But riding a woman came naturally, and I bet I'd have no problem if I ever had the chance again. "You overestimate me."

He grinned. "I don't think so."

Grant was good. He was baiting a hook. And I shouldn't have taken the bite, but I couldn't resist. "Tell me more about this woman. Blond? Brunette? Tall? Short?" My mind ran wild with possibilities. "Does she have a name?"

"Her name is Sloane Grayson. Dark hair. Very attractive." The cop's voice softened just a fraction. Grant liked Sloane Grayson's look.

"I don't get to read too much true crime in prison. Is she a good writer?"

"She is." Grant's gaze and face remained relaxed. But his fingers opened and closed once into a fist.

"Tell Ms. Grayson I don't know where the Festival Four are. A polygraph proved that."

"I bet you run circles around a polygraph."

Talk of Dawson and Sloane Grayson stirred a longing I'd suppressed for years. "If I don't get out in time to join you in Dawson, keep me posted. I'd like to see what you unearth." A smile tipped my lips. "Excuse the bad pun. I find amusement where I can."

Chapter One

Joe Keller

Friday, May 20, 1994, 8:00 a.m.
10 Hours Until the Festival

Stardom. Joe Keller knew the young woman beside him spent her days dreaming of fame. She was a sweet little thing with blond hair and big brown eyes. Had tits a man could get lost in.

Like all the others, she saw herself standing on a stage with bright lights shining down as she strummed long fingers over her guitar. Her kind went to bed at night hearing the cheering crowds. He'd crossed paths with a lot of girls like her in his days as a guitarist and roadie.

Joe took a right off the main road. Once he'd dreamed of having assistants who'd take care of his needs. They'd drive him everywhere, stock his dressing room with his favorite hamburgers and lines of coke. And they'd shine his collection of guitars. Everyone kissed your ass at the top. That's what he'd wanted when he was her age.

"You with one of the bands?" he asked.

She shifted, balancing her blue guitar case between her legs. "No. But I'm hoping to get some playing time onstage. Are you in a band?"

"I used to play guitar." It was hard not to stare at her face. "You're dreaming about being a star?"

"Yeah. Who doesn't?" She wanted new outfits, hair and makeup assistants, and costumes that glittered with rhinestones. She wanted everyone to know—*know*—she was a star. One day, she'd be impossible to ignore. If he had a nickel for all the girls like this one.

She gripped her guitar case again as he took another turn onto a smaller mountain road. He downshifted, knowing the hills required the engine to grip harder.

Her blue guitar case was beat-up and covered with stickers naming cities that he'd bet she'd never seen.

"Nice case," he said, hoping to draw her out. The bright-blue case had caught his attention as she walked down the road by Dawson's bus station. Didn't take a detective to know she had her sights set on the big music festival scheduled to kick off later today. She couldn't have been more than eighteen or nineteen. "You're too young to have a history like that."

She glanced at a tattered Nashville sticker. "I bought it used. I like its history."

"You hear any stories about the case?"

She tucked a blond curl behind her ear. "The pawn shop owner told me the woman who'd owned it played with the Rolling Stones in the sixties. I hope to have those kinds of experiences."

"Don't hurry your life." He'd done his share of rushing, and he'd made a lot of mistakes. "I'm Joe, by the way."

"Laurie."

The truck's engine groaned loudly as he drove up the steepening hill. The split plastic seat crackled under his ass as he shifted. A fine sheen of cigarette ash covered his dashboard. When he was alone, he didn't care, but with Laurie, he wished it were cleaner.

"What brings you here?" Joe asked.

"I was working in a diner in Waynesboro. Then a guy came in for coffee. He had a Kurt Cobain vibe. He was lean, and his dark glasses accentuated his chiseled features. After his coffee, he asked if he could hang a few posters. My boss said yes, and 'Kurt' taped flyers in the front window as well as the men's and women's bathrooms. I offered him a soda. He said yes, and he told me about the festival. He made it sound so huge."

She'd described the festival promoter, Rafe Colton. Rafe had always been fast and loose with the truth. "It's going to be something."

"What are you doing at the festival?"

"Delivering equipment. Stages, lighting, and rigging. All the unsexy stuff that makes a show work. And I'll play a few sets with the Terrible Tuesdays."

Her eyes brightened with interest. "So, you're going to get onstage."

"No guarantees. Right now, I'm a delivery driver with a guitar. I drop my deliveries, and I might get to play a few sets. Nothing fancy."

"The promoter is looking for new artists. They have these kinds of events in the big cities, like Nashville, but never in Dawson. I'm lucky."

"And you took the bus to Dawson?"

"I'd planned to drive, but my car gave out three days ago. I hoped the bus would drop me off closer. More walking than I figured."

"And then I came along."

She grinned. "Lucky me."

Joe rubbed his hand over his scraggly beard. He looked older than forty, but he liked to think he still had game. The tattoos that covered his arms showed life experiences like Laurie's guitar case.

"You'll wow the crowds," he said.

"You think so? You haven't heard me play."

"You have an energy. A vibe. The producers call it the 'it' vibe."

"Thanks. I'm hoping to wow the crowds."

"Anyone willing to walk down a road with a guitar in this heat wants fame."

"It's all I've wanted since I was a little girl," she said.

"You ever been onstage before?"

"A few times. None of my gigs have been much to brag about. Coffee shops, high school talent shows, and a small church festival. But you got to start small, right?"

11

"Yeah, you do."

Joe slowed the van. Laurie looked toward the trucks hauling stage equipment as he nosed the truck toward the festival entrance, which funneled into an open field. She shifted in her seat, tightening her grip on the guitar.

Joe took a right turn into the main entrance. The setting for the festival was beautiful. A bright-blue sky provided a backdrop to rolling hills. An old gray farmhouse sat nestled among a collection of oak trees, and beyond the house, plump gray clouds lurked as if trying to decide whether rain was worth the effort.

The truck rolled and belched as it moved down the dusty road. Joe rounded a corner away from the farmhouse. Ahead were more trucks and workmen hoisting the lights of a fifty-foot stage outfitted with sound equipment. He parked next to a collection of vans and small trucks. All were open and being unloaded.

"There's so much happening," she said.

"Controlled chaos. This is the calm before the storm."

She sat a little straighter. "I can't wait."

He rested his massive, inked forearms on the steering wheel. He stared at the people unloading boxes, setting up vending stands, and hanging Mountain Music Festival T-shirts and posters. "In the light of day, it always looks like a bright, shiny penny. But night is coming. So be careful, Laurie."

"My dad split when I was ten. I learned how to handle myself. I'll be fine, Joe. Not my first rodeo."

"A regular sage," he quipped.

"I'm young, but I'm not stupid."

"That's good. Keep your thinking hat on, Laurie. I've worked Rafe Colton events before. They always get crazy." He wasn't sure why he felt the need to caution her. "I've seen girls like you get eaten up."

Her smile told him his warning flew right past her. "Thanks, Joe. I promise to be careful."

"There's a hamburger vendor setting up," he said. "I bet you could pick up a few hours of work, and they'll feed you if you're hungry."

"Thanks. I'll do that."

He reached for a rumpled receipt on the seat and scribbled a number on it. "This is my number. After the festival, if you have questions, give me a call."

She stared at the bold numbers as she reached for the door handle. "Why do you look so worried, Joe?"

"Like I said, I've worked this kind of event before."

"You're a nice man."

He drew in a breath until the full expanse of his chest pressed against his T-shirt. "Not so nice. And there are going to be worse than me out there over the next eighteen hours."

She opened the door and gripped the handle of her guitar case in her right hand. Her stomach grumbled. She laughed. "A burger would be nice."

"Best of luck."

She waved to Joe and walked toward the crowd. When she reached the first food vendor, she glanced back and caught his gaze. She smiled, then introduced herself to the young woman setting up the burger station.

A horn honked, drawing Joe's attention back to the job at hand. He had some pull with a few of the bands. He'd find a way to give her a show-business break, and maybe, who knows, maybe they could find a quiet spot and she could thank him properly.

Chapter Two

SLOANE

Friday, August 15, 2025, 12:00 p.m.
Dawson, Virginia

It wasn't the first time I'd visited the small town of Dawson, nestled in the mountains of Central Virginia. Located twenty miles northeast of Interstate 64, between Charlottesville and Waynesboro, Dawson was a favorite stop for history buffs, wine enthusiasts, sightseers, or anyone looking for a burger or a bathroom break.

The town's year-round residents hovered around five thousand. But during the summer and fall tourist seasons, when visitors filled rental properties tucked in the hills and valleys, the population swelled to four times that.

I'd arrived during a "shoulder" week. Summer vacationers had left because public schools and colleges were back in session. And it would be two weeks before Labor Day, when the fall hikers arrived. Basically, rents were lower right now.

I'd rented a mountain cottage so far off the beaten path that, even in high season, few wanted it. My budget liked small, rustic cabins in hard-to-reach places.

I found the rental office on Main Street and parked my Jeep in front. Midday was slow in Dawson, but the pace would pick up a little around the dinner rush.

Out of the Jeep, I shouldered my backpack and crossed to the rental office. Agencies usually sent me an entry code, so I didn't have to bother with check-in. But when I'd rented the place, I was told there was no electronic lock on the cabin. Too much trouble to change the batteries. Okay. Not ideal, but I was here to work, not play.

Bells jingled as I pushed open the door to an office. Two empty desks greeted me. The walls were covered in images of homes far nicer than I could ever afford. My little cabin wasn't featured in any framed print.

I walked up to the front desk and rapped my knuckles against faux wood. "Hello?"

Footsteps shifted and a toilet flushed. Seconds later, a woman in her late forties emerged from a restroom, drying her hands. Her blond hair was styled into a ponytail, and makeup enhanced handsome features. She wasn't tall, and her figure looked as if it were carrying a few extra pounds under a cotton top that skimmed over designer jeans narrowing to custom boots.

I had interacted with rich folks when I'd been hired for a couple of ghostwriting gigs. With rich people, it's not the clothes or cars that are the tell, but the attitude. One woman who came from old tobacco money wanted her life story told but didn't "like worrying over the details." Another trust funder who looked homeless wanted his vision for the future enshrined on the page. I could have told them both their stories wouldn't sell. But I didn't because the money was good. Both had liked my final product, but to my knowledge, neither book had been published.

"Well, hello there," the woman said. She tossed her paper towel into a trash can and extended her hand. "I'm Bailey Briggs Jones. What can I do for you?"

In the weeks after the concert, Sheriff CJ Taggart had interviewed Bailey Briggs, who'd been seen at the concert with one of the Festival Four victims, Debra Jackson. Bailey had admitted under oath that she'd seen Debra at the concert, and they'd chatted about high school. She'd been very calm when she testified that she'd left the concert via the fire road around 1:00 a.m. and hitchhiked home.

"I'm Sloane Grayson." I hoisted my backpack higher on my shoulder. "I rented a cabin and need to pick up the keys."

"Pick up the keys!" Bailey laughed. "That's a blast from the past. We have two rentals like that now. Seeing as the Sawyer place is already rented, you must be after the Taggart cabin."

"Taggart, that's right."

"We haven't had much interest in that cabin for a while, and his great-nephew is on the verge of selling it." She opened a drawer at the first desk and removed a set of three old keys on a ring. "The locks are old, but they work."

"I'm sure it'll be fine."

Bailey gripped the keys in manicured hands before she dropped them in my calloused palm. "You're here for two weeks?"

"That's what I've paid for, but who knows? Is the cabin rented after my stay?"

"Lord, no. You could keep it all September."

"Good to know."

"Why would a young gal like you want to hide away in an old cabin in the woods?"

"A quiet place to work. And I'm on a deadline."

"Are you one of those true crime writers?"

"Why would you ask that?"

"The only people who've ever had any real interest in Taggart's cabin were into solving crimes."

If I feigned ignorance, I learned more. People loved to talk and prove they were in the know. "What crime?"

"Taggart was the sheriff in Dawson for over twenty years. He investigated the Mountain Music Festival murders." She spoke as if the facts were ingrained.

"I read something about that."

"Who are you writing for?"

"I have a contract with a magazine. Circulation isn't huge."

"Why come here?" She shook her head. "We see hikers and mountain bikers in Dawson. Not writers."

"Easier to concentrate if I don't have interruptions."

"You won't get any at the cabin. It doesn't have Wi-Fi. Or cell service. You'll have to drive down the mountain to get your phone to work. The coffee maker is an automatic drip, so buy a bag of ground coffee. Clean sheets and towels are in the storage closet. There's a television and VHS player. Taggart liked his westerns and old war movies."

"Sounds perfect."

"And how did you find our agency?" Bailey's voice rose with the question.

"Dawson made the Top 10 list for 'Out-of-the-Way Haunted Mountain Locations.' Your agency is one of two in town."

She nodded. "We had a ghost hunter stay at the cabin about two years ago. He didn't stay but a couple of nights."

"Is the house haunted?"

"Depends. Are you scared of ghosts?"

The dead never bothered me. Trouble tended to follow the living. "No. I figure once you've crossed over, you're no real threat to me."

"That's very brave of you. I'm not so courageous. I'm sure the dead are watching, and I don't like it."

"Why are ghosts watching you?"

Gold beaded bracelets on her wrist rattled as she brushed back a wisp of dyed blond hair. "Unfinished business."

Bailey's smooth skin had the look of Botox and fillers, but her eyes reflected a distance that belied her pleasant expression. But I imagined when she was younger, she was stunning. "Fair enough. The living have their share of it, too."

"Either way, I don't like being around anything spooky. You're one brave woman."

"Ghosts, dogs, and I get along fine."

She laughed. "Well, Sloane, enjoy your stay. Remember, no Wi-Fi or cell phone service, but if you need a signal or anything else, the convenience store at the bottom of the mountain is the place to go."

"Thanks, Bailey."

I'd learned long ago to play along, smile. Sooner or later, they'd figure out what I was about, but for now, I wasn't interested in baring all.

"The cabin isn't on my GPS," I said.

"No, it wouldn't be. As far as the satellites are concerned, that part of the world doesn't exist." She reached for a phone in a rhinestone case and texted me a PDF. "Follow those directions, and you'll find it. Download it now."

I selected the attachment. "Will do."

"Make sure you're gassed up and have your groceries. It's a thirty-minute drive to the cabin. And that's in good weather."

"I'll stop on the way out of town."

Her head tilted as she stared at me. "Well, I hope you enjoy your stay, Sloane Grayson." She hesitated. "Grayson? You have family in the area?"

"No. Thanks, Bailey. I'm sure I'll see you around."

Out the front door, I settled in the Jeep and hooked the cabin keys on my ring. I drove down Main Street, absorbing the feel of Dawson.

What had initially put the place on the map was the railroad. In its heyday, the old farm town shipped produce to restaurants as far north as Washington, DC, and New York City. Some visitors had come to Dawson looking for healing springs promising cures for a variety of ailments. Others had come in search of gold in mines that were quickly played out.

Little old Dawson had enjoyed good times for about forty years. And then the interstate was built, and goods shifted from rail to tractor trailers.

The town hit hard times in the late '80s and early '90s. Dawson leaders had hoped to turn their hamlet into a hub for music festivals. They'd enjoyed a little success. Then the mayor had booked the Mountain Music Festival thirty-one years ago. That event was supposed to cement Dawson's reputation.

And it did. But not as anyone expected.

As bands played through the night, four women vanished from the festival.

Almost immediately, expected profits evaporated. And the town was gripped with worry and fear as the sheriff searched for the killer. The killer was caught. But the women were never found. Not a win-win, but justice had been satisfied.

Still, even after the sheriff arrested his man, vendors stayed away from Dawson for at least fifteen years. Restaurants and inns closed. Many Main Street businesses shuttered.

And the only tourism came in the form of reporters and thrill seekers drawn to the newest "Murder Capital of the South."

The locals made peace with their dark past. And everyone agreed to keep it buried along with the women. Memories faded, and the names of the missing were forgotten.

Discount real estate prices attracted investors, vineyards, and a new wave of festival events. Having fun and making money trumped old fears. For the last five years, music festivals had become a major moneymaker for Dawson. The town had thrived.

Now the little town's two-hundred-year-old buildings were fit for any tourism brochure. Brick establishments that had serviced failed gold mine offices, railroads, banks, and feed stores now housed tony clothing boutiques, cafés, and bars. At the end of Main Street was the Depot Diner. Untouched since the '50s, the Depot was the lone holdout to change.

I parked in front of the grocery store, grabbed my backpack, and hurried inside. I somehow picked the one cart with a bad wheel that turned backward as I moved up the center aisle. Mac and cheese, cookies, soups, luncheon meats, coffee, and Stove Top stuffing were my go-to travel work foods. I always argued that carbs fueled my brain when I was pulling a lot of facts together. I grabbed a box of strawberry Pop-Tarts and a six-pack of soda.

At checkout, the clerk rang up my purchases. She was in her mid-fifties and had pulled her gray hair back in a ponytail, unable to contain all the flyaway hairs. "You have any coupons?"

"No coupons."

She looked up at me. She'd pegged me as a tourist. I expected no privacy in a small town. If this lady didn't ask questions about me, Bailey would.

"If you come back on Thursday, we have a five-percent discount."

"Great. I'll keep that in mind." I swiped my credit card and said a small prayer that I'd not hit the limit.

The transaction went through, and she handed me my receipt. "Where are you staying?"

"Up the road."

"One of the old properties or a new one?"

"Old." Before she could ask anything else, I grabbed my groceries and left the store. Maybe if I'd come during the high season, I'd have blended better, but the shoulder-week rates were hard to beat.

With Bailey's directions pulled up on my phone, I drove west toward the mountains. I passed the convenience store and took the right up the mountain road. But I almost missed the blue TAGGART CABIN sign. My tires kicked up dirt as I stopped and took a right onto a narrower road.

For another mile I wound up the road curving around the mountain. The pitch grew steeper, and in several spots the shoulder half slid off the mountain. It didn't take many guesses to figure out why someone who had no interest in people chose this location. No one ever dropped by here by accident.

As my Jeep engine strained up the hill, the red light on my gas gauge caught my attention. Bailey had told me to tank up, but I'd calculated I had another fifty miles of driving. If I didn't press too hard, I could still make it if I coasted downhill back toward town tomorrow.

I spotted the last blue arrow and took another left. Minutes later, the narrow road opened to a small field with a log cabin in the center. Gravel popped under my tires as I drew closer to the porch, which looked as if a strong wind would topple it. I shut off the engine, knowing I didn't have the gas to waste.

I reached into the back seat and grabbed my groceries. My stomach grumbled, and I fished out the box of Pop-Tarts and unwrapped a sleeve. I took a few bites, then climbed the three stairs to the porch.

I fumbled with the key and shoved it in the old lock. Door hinges groaned as I kicked open the door. The cabin was dark. The remaining daylight leaked through the thick canopy of trees and smudged windows. Bags slid to the floor, and I fumbled around the wall until I found the light switch.

The overhead bulbs didn't give off much light. But it was enough to see a large stone fireplace, recliner, couch, TV/VCR, small round dining table, and galley kitchen beyond. Off to the left was a bedroom with a small double bed.

I set the groceries on the yellow countertop and finished off my Pop-Tart. I drew in a breath as the sugar, fat, and chemicals hit my stomach and brain. Whatever vague promises I'd made last week about clean eating were too much of a reach now. As soon as I settled, I'd order eggs and whole wheat toast at the Depot. Protein was brain food, right?

The refrigerator was working and the interior clean. I unloaded the carton of milk, deli meat, and bread before lining up the rest of the nonperishables on the counter. As a kid, I'd liked the look of a full refrigerator. The sight had eased the faint anxiety always in my belly. A full fridge promised that tomorrow was going to be a good day.

I moved from lamp to lamp, turning all five on. The extra light didn't chase away the gloom, but there were fewer shadows for the ghosts.

Outside, I opened the Jeep's tailgate and unloaded a single box filled with color-coded files. Most of my work was in the cloud. But I still made paper copies because when the dots didn't connect, I pinned the papers on a wall, and the different perspective always revealed something new. From the glove box, I retrieved my holstered handgun, an accessory I always traveled with.

I set the box near the recliner. The kitchen table wasn't large, but I dragged it to the center of the room. It would be my makeshift desk.

My life had been crazy when I was a child, and it hadn't changed much since. To combat the chaos, I kept my physical world very organized. Because I traveled constantly for work, my life often narrowed to my desk and laptop. My happy place was sharpened pencils and a sunrise screen saver.

I closed and locked the front door and sat in the recliner.

Silence settled over the room. City life was filled with everyday sounds, but up here, there was nothing except the rustle of leaves and the chirp of birds. It was Taggart's decompression pod.

Sheriff Charles James "CJ" Taggart had taken the job as Dawson sheriff in the spring of 1994. When he was hired, he'd recently left the marines, where he'd worked twenty-seven years as military police. Civilian law enforcement would have been a natural choice. He'd said in several interviews that he'd expected his duties would shift among speeding tickets, barking dogs, and the occasional drunk in town. He'd been looking forward to a slower pace because the work he'd done on the bases included rapes, assaults, and murders. Drunk marines found trouble easily.

When he'd first accepted the job as sheriff, he'd rented a house in town near the police station. From what I'd read, he'd adapted with ease. Originally from the area, he loved rural, small-town living.

The town council had approved the Mountain Music Festival six weeks before he'd taken the job. Mayor Mike Briggs, a tall, imposing man, made his money in construction and real estate. He had painted the festival as a well-organized, family-friendly event during Taggart's job interview. The promoter, Rafe Colton, had a long, solid history of event planning. Taggart had told the sheriff's search committee that he'd looked forward to working the event.

And a week after he was on the job, shit went sideways.

And his life was fucked forever.

Chapter Three

CJ Taggart

Friday, May 20, 1994, 9:00 a.m.
9 Hours Until

Sheriff CJ Taggart was already pissed. And his day hadn't started.

He backed his Crown Vic into his reserved spot at the Dawson sheriff's office. He shoved the gear into park and shut off the engine. He didn't like to start the day mad. And he'd thought leaving the marines and moving back east would solve that. It hadn't.

He pushed out a breath, climbed from the car, and grabbed his hat and settled it on his flattop haircut. As he crossed the cracked asphalt, he fumbled with his keys and found the one that opened the station's back door. The door open, he heard the slow, steady voice of Deputy Sean Duke, who worked the night shift. He'd been with the department for fifteen years and manned the phones and jail.

Taggart passed the framed photos of the five other men who'd served as Dawson's sheriff. They all had a stern, rigid stance that reminded him of himself. Law enforcement attracted a personality type.

The dispatcher was trying to reason with a caller complaining about a noisy neighbor. Taggart didn't need to hear the caller to know: loud music, partying, fast cars cutting doughnuts on a dirt road. Standard small-town stuff that he now wanted in his day.

The Mountain Music Festival loomed today. Despite assurances that this was a family-friendly event, the festival had been tossing out warning signs. The festival proposal had been thin on details. As soon as he'd read it, Taggart had called Mayor Briggs and talked about pulling the plug on the event.

Briggs shot down Taggart's objections over the poor security, limited venue entries and exits, and minimal toilet facilities. If his worries played out, too many people were going to descend onto Dawson tonight.

He'd thought civilian life would be different from the military. He'd thought guys who'd never worn a uniform would be more adept at making decisions. He'd assumed that outside of the military, civilians made more logical choices. But guys like Mayor Briggs proved him wrong. Incompetent higher-ups existed in all walks of life.

Taggart and Deputy Jed Paxton were the only LEOs available to work the festival's security tonight. Despite assurances from the mayor, he worried this event was an accident waiting to happen.

"What could go wrong?" the mayor had asked.

Taggart had forbidden that question among his long-range recon team when they were in North Vietnam. Anyone stupid enough to tempt Fate found himself isolated by the unit and exposed to land mines, stray bullets, or a fall off a cliff. Fate had no problem punishing the naive or stupid.

He moved into his office and hung his hat on a peg behind his desk, which had a pile of pink message slips on it. He'd already learned that most calls were mundane. But to assume there were no issues would irritate Fate.

"Sheriff."

Taggart met his deputy's gaze. Jed Paxton was twenty-two and had been with the department a year. Paxton had been born in Dawson, and his father had once been mayor of the town. Paxton was tall, with big shoulders and thick black hair. He had been the star of the local football team, and women still flirted with him because he'd always be the high school hero.

By the same age, Taggart had been a marine for five years, been shot in Vietnam, and completed a sixty-day rehab stint in a Tokyo military hospital. For Taggart's twenty-second birthday, Uncle Sam had ordered him to Okinawa as a military police officer.

"What do you need, Deputy?" Taggart asked.

"Mayor Briggs is on his way. He wants to talk to you about the music festival."

"Is there an issue?" He'd written a detailed critique of the festival proposal.

"He's not happy with your security recommendations."

No surprise that the mayor had not liked Taggart's memo. The top brass, civilian or military, rarely listened to common sense.

"Anything else?" Taggart asked.

"No, sir."

"When's he stopping by?" The pink messages reported noise complaints, a missing dog, and gunshots near the Nelson farm.

"Now."

Taggart glanced at the clock: 9:00 a.m. This amounted to a surprise inspection. He singled out a pink slip. "Who called in the report of gunshots near the Nelson farm?"

"Mrs. Nelson. She thinks the Crawford boys are target shooting in the woods again."

That section of the county was wooded, and the land was billy-goat steep. "Remind me. Who are the Crawford boys?"

"Zeke and Sammy. They live on the mountain across from the Nelson farm in a small cabin. They've lived up there since they were born and know the mountains like the backs of their hands. They like to target shoot and hunt."

"It's out of season."

"They don't recognize the government. They hunt when they want to. Getting them off the mountain would require an army."

"Are they a threat?"

Paxton hitched his thumb to his gun belt. "Beyond not paying the fifteen-dollar hunting license fee and growing weed, no. They keep to themselves."

For now, Taggart had bigger issues than hunting licenses. In the outer office, the door opened and closed. He ran his hand along his tie and straightened his shoulders, straining the starched creases of his uniform. Mayor Briggs appeared in the doorway.

Taggart didn't extend his hand. "What can I do for you, Mayor Briggs?"

Mayor Briggs glanced at Paxton. "Hey, Jed. Tell your dad I'm looking forward to our tee time tomorrow."

"Will do, sir." Paxton moved toward the door. "Can I get you a coffee?"

"No, thank you. Close the door on the way out."

Paxton nodded, not glancing in Taggart's direction, and closed the door.

Taggart motioned toward a set of two chairs angled in front of his desk. "Would you like to have a seat?"

They'd attended the same high school, but Taggart had been five years ahead of Briggs. Whereas Briggs took summer vacations during his high school years, Taggart had been changing oil, spark plugs, or transmission fluid in his stepfather's garage.

"I won't be here that long."

"What can I do for you?"

"Your evaluation of the festival has a few of the council members worried."

"I have real concerns. I want to cancel it until Colton addresses the issues."

"We're not shutting it down. Canceling now would be like leaving the bride at the altar. We got to go through with it."

"I sent a request to the state police for officers to work the music festival. This job is too much for Paxton and me to cover."

"The promoter has promised to hire private security."

"I've reached out to Mr. Colton twice, and he's not called me back."

Briggs cleared his throat. "I'm in an election year, Sheriff Taggart. The locals aren't fond of state government. And they won't appreciate seeing state police patrolling their festival. Besides, we can't afford the extra manpower."

Frustration scraped under his skin. "The extra patrols are for everyone's own safety."

"They won't see it that way. And like I said, we can't afford the state guys."

"I've seen the lineup of the bands. They're not family friendly. Estimates put festival attendance at five hundred people. That's too much humanity for three men to police. And what if the crowd size surges?"

"We won't see a surge. We'll be lucky to get the five hundred. This is a small regional concert with second-rate bands. Mr. Colton has assured me that he's hired extra security."

Rafe Colton made a lot of promises, but the follow-ups never happened. Taggart worried this could be a problem. "I need him to call me back and tell me how many extra men he's hired."

"Security is his problem. It says so in his contract. You're there to be the town's representative."

Five hundred people was still five hundred potential problems. "If the festival gets out of control, it lands on me. Once night falls, people change. They get drunk, horny, and start thinking they can get away with more. And if you pack them into a small space, the chance of trouble goes up."

Briggs shook his head. "You keep assuming that there won't be enough security."

"Colton has not given me any solid numbers."

"Let me worry about Colton."

Taggart's relationship with Briggs was new and untested. But he had always struggled to keep his opinion to himself. "Colton is cutting corners."

"You're in the civilian world now, CJ," he said. "Time to be more flexible."

Taggart nodded even as his jaw pulsed.

"I've heard your concerns, but I'm telling you, this event is going to be fine."

Tension sliced up Taggart's spine, but too many years of respecting the chain of command kept him silent. "Roger that."

Mayor Briggs's frown flipped into a quick, easy grin of even white teeth. "Excellent. I appreciate you're trying to keep on top of this, but it's going to be fine. The Depot is poised to make a nice fee off their food stand at the festival. And the T-shirt vendor has invested too much in the festival inventory. The economy is still soft, and they've all taken a hit in the last few years. This is their chance to get ahead."

Main Street had several boarded-up businesses. Last year, the pharmacy and the bank had moved thirty miles east to Charlottesville. The few remaining businesses didn't get the traffic they had five years ago. The local furniture factory had shuttered, and though tourism was a moneymaker, it wasn't enough. The school budget was getting cut, and whatever forensic supplies Taggart's department needed remained on a wish list.

The mayor and town council were eager for new business. They offered tax credits like candy, but so far, no bites. And until they filled the abandoned factory, tourism would have to make up the difference. Festival posters peppered the store windows, and folks were excited about its earning potential.

After walking Briggs to the front door, Taggart rubbed the back of his neck as he moved to the break room and poured himself a cup of coffee. He sipped, reminding himself this wasn't war, and no one was shooting at him. Dawson was a quiet town. A couple of decades had shrunk his past problems with the town down to almost invisible. He hoped they stayed small. "Little problems going forward."

The muscles along his neck coiled tight and tense. He wanted to ease off the throttle and not worry, not push. He'd lost big while he was in the service because he'd pressed too hard. But old habits died hard. Like it or not, he couldn't shake the sense that trouble was circling.

Chapter Four

SLOANE

Friday, August 15, 2025, 2:00 p.m.

After my desk was set up, I dumped a can of tomato soup into a small clean, dented pot. I switched on the propane burner. As the soup heated, I opened a sleeve of crackers and nibbled. The cabinets had four bowls and four plates. In the drawers, an equal number of forks, knives, and spoons. Taggart was a kindred soul.

I sat at the table and opened my laptop. Gusts of wind whipped outside, rattling the shingles and smacking the shutters against the house. The air was ripe with moisture, signaling a storm.

I was used to solitude, but I was also used to Wi-Fi to stay connected to the world. The old Timex on my wrist was more sentimental than functional.

Now, as I glanced at no bars on my phone, I reminded myself that I wanted to be here. To disconnect. But no bars meant no control. No access. That realization didn't ease the panic clenching in my chest.

I crumbled crackers into my soup. The first few bites were hot, but the tomato-carb combo settled my stomach, and by the end, I felt more human. My stomach had been queasy for a few days. I'd ignored whatever illness it was and willed it away.

I opened my file on Sheriff CJ Taggart, the investigating officer for the Mountain Music Festival case.

Born in 1944, Taggart was a throwback to a different generation. His father had died on the beaches of Anzio, Italy, and while his mother had married again, CJ and his stepfather never got along. At seventeen, he convinced his mother to sign a waiver allowing him to join the marines. He'd served in Vietnam and been injured near Da Nang in 1965. According to his medical reports, bullets struck his right arm, left leg, and belly. Medics airlifted him to a field hospital and later to Japan to recover. After his release from the hospital in 1966, he joined the military police force in Okinawa, where he worked until 1993.

At the age of forty-nine, he'd been investigating the murder of a female soldier who'd been having an affair with a colonel. Taggart suspected the colonel. The brass told him to back down. Which he hadn't done. The colonel kept his job, and Taggart left the marines.

After separating from the marines, he'd traveled a bit, but eventually he grew bored and started looking for a job in civilian police work.

A red glow warmed the inside of the cabin. I looked out the window to see the sun setting toward the mountains. I walked outside to the front porch and watched as the red glow sank lower until it vanished behind the mountain. Lightning streaked across the sky.

Taggart had lived in this cabin for ten years. How many nights had he sat out here and watched the sunset? Or had he been so lost in his own troubles he didn't care to look?

A phone rang, startling me. Staring at the flickering bar on my cell, I realized it wasn't mine. It was the yellow wall mount in the kitchen. I crossed to the phone, hesitating as my hand rested on the receiver. Weird not to know who was calling.

I lifted the receiver to my ear. "Hello."

"Sloane." The familiar, deep voice belonged to Grant McKenna. I pictured a tall, lean guy who wore a dark suit with a black tie. Sunglasses would have made him a perfect cast member for *Men in Black*.

We'd met at a crime conference six weeks ago. I'd been speaking about my recently published article in *The Washington Post*. I'd investigated the murder of Suzanne Malone. Susie, as she was known to her friends, was thirteen when she went for a bike ride near dusk. She didn't come home, and her parents called the police. Anyone who could helped search for her.

Her body was found three days later, but her killer was never caught. Grant had been speaking earlier about murder convictions without a body. When I finished my presentation, he caught me as I was exiting the dais. He'd had several pointed questions about my presentation. He'd been paying close attention. I didn't understand his interest, and then he'd mentioned an upcoming parole hearing for Rafe Colton. My ears perked.

I'd offered to buy him a drink. We'd huddled in the bar over beers and then dinner as I drilled him for information about Colton. After we shut down the bar, we ended up in my room.

I remember the heady scent of desire and his rough hands reaching for the button on my jeans. I'd jerked off my shirt and he'd kissed the mounds of my breasts.

My jeans had dropped with one yank, and I'd kicked them off. Seconds later, he'd pushed into me, shoving my back against the wall. I'd wrapped my legs around him, pulling him in as deeply as I could. Talking about the Malone case always left me agitated, and sex with Grant was the least dangerous way for me to let off steam.

The sex had been urgent, exciting, and intoxicating. After the conference, we went our separate ways. We'd traded a few texts over the last six weeks but hadn't spoken. If Grant had stuck to his plan, he'd seen Colton a week or two ago.

"You've arrived in Dawson?" His logical, steady voice was relaxed, measured.

"I was standing on Taggart's porch. Sunsets guaranteed to wow any tourist. How did you get the landline number?"

"Doesn't take a detective to figure out where you'd stay in Dawson. I made a call or two and got the number."

"Aren't you clever."

"I don't picture you lounging in the woods."

I remembered how much I enjoyed talking to him. "No. I was rereading my files. I'm headed into town tomorrow to talk to Sheriff Paxton."

"Good start. He had a ringside seat at the festival, during the investigation, and at the trial," Grant said.

"Hoping it shakes loose a different perspective."

I tried to picture Grant. He'd said he had an office in a historic brick building in downtown Charlottesville. But he'd never quite explained what he did beyond collecting a retirement check.

"I'm sure you'll find a way to get his attention."

"Attention-getting is my superpower."

"Be careful," he warned. "Don't assume everyone will be thrilled about you digging into a case marked 'closed.'"

"I'll tread lightly. How did your meeting with Colton go?"

"As all the others. He's charming. Loves the attention. Offers no answers."

"His parole board meeting is still a go?"

"It is."

"What do you think are his chances of getting out?"

"Better than fifty-fifty. Unless you find those bodies."

"I'm doing what I can."

"Keep me posted."

"Will do."

I ended the call and returned to the front porch. Tree branches rustled. A creature darted through the woods. An owl hooted. The darkness was restless. I thought back to our night at the conference and tried to define how I'd felt. He'd been exciting. I'd enjoyed his company. Yet when we went our separate ways, I didn't miss a beat.

I felt basic emotions such as sadness, anger, and sometimes happiness. But my feelings hovered near the low end of any emotional scale. I knew more intense feelings existed, but I couldn't grasp them.

Sometimes my limited emotional bandwidth was a gift. And sometimes it wasn't. Unprocessed feelings created tension in my body that sooner or later needed an outlet. At times like that, my muscles cramped. Deep, watery breaths tightened my chest, and I felt as if I were drowning.

When I was working on a Susie Malone–type article, negative physical side effects were common. Headaches, stomach pains, pressure in my chest.

I let off steam by driving too fast on the interstate at night, breaking and entering, or having sex.

I reentered the house, locked the front door, and returned to my makeshift desk. A glance at my phone revealed no bars. If I wanted to talk on the phone, it would have to be the landline.

I'd seen many shady places since I'd decided freelance writing suited my unwillingness to hold a regular job. I worked all the time. I could take a day off, but I rarely did. Work was my therapy. My way of dealing with all the crap that had been shadowing me since I was a kid.

I sat in the recliner that must have been Taggart's. The cracked leather smelled of lemon, and I could imagine Bailey spritzing it with Febreze to mask any musty scent. The wear patterns on the arms told me the old sheriff had pushed his hands back and forth as he ruminated on the past. Was he pleased or haunted when he looked back?

I glanced at the collection of ten VHS tapes on the boxy television. Westerns. Clint Eastwood.

I hoped Taggart's cabin was haunted. I hoped he understood that, despite an arrest and conviction, the families had no resolution. Four women had vanished on the night of May 20, 1994. Though everyone believed the women were dead, I needed to find them.

Thunder cracked and lightning flashed across the sky outside, pulling me from my thoughts. Drawing in a breath, I rubbed my hands over the worn leather.

I wanted to dig into Taggart's mind and follow in his steps. But he was dead. So I'd make do with the new sheriff, the victims' families, and the few remaining witnesses. There were missing pieces to this case. And I would find them. I would fill in the blank spaces and find the victims' bodies.

Neither the answers nor the bones would transform me into a normal woman able to grieve the loss of her mother, who'd been one of the victims. But it was a step in the right direction.

Chapter Five

CJ TAGGART

Friday, May 20, 1994, 10:00 a.m.
8 Hours Until

The festival was going to be a shit show.

Briggs had told him, again, not to worry. It would all be fine. *Fine.* Taggart hated that word. It always foreshadowed disaster.

He took the turnoff to the Nelson farm and wound his way up the road toward the venue. He'd been out to the farm a few days earlier. He'd walked the site and surveyed the entrance and exit locations. Beyond the main road, a rough-cut dirt service lane arrowed up the back of the property. It had been built for firefighting crews but hadn't been used in years. According to the farm's owner, fallen trees had made it impassable to vehicles. If there was an emergency, this site was a bottleneck. Taggart had ordered two guys from public works to clear a path yesterday. This new escape route was rough, but it was better than nothing.

Trucks and crews had arrived, and a large center stage had been constructed with the green mountains behind it. Workers hoisted lights up onto the rigging as other crews off-loaded large speakers. Trucks with trailers were parked at angles to make room for others coming and going. Even with the limited number of vehicles present, it was difficult to maneuver. His worries doubled.

Colton had picked this location for its spectacular Woodstock-type views. And right now, it looked stunning and reinforced all Colton's promises.

A split rail fence ringed the farm, and beyond it stood a thick stand of trees. There was no security fencing to control anyone ready to slip in unnoticed. Five hundred people. Why did that number sound like Colton had pulled it out of his ass?

Taggart drove over grass crushed flat by a dozen other vehicles. He passed the first aid trailer and parked near the Depot's food tent. Inside the Depot tent were prep tables, grills, and boxes of buns and condiments. The gal setting up the stations, Patty, worked the counter most breakfasts at the Depot. She was tall and lean and had tied back her ink-black hair in a ponytail. She couldn't be more than nineteen and already had a kid. In the last week, the Depot had become a regular stop for him before work. Always friendly, Patty would fill his coffee cup before he settled on a counter stool.

Another gal worked beside Patty in the tent. He didn't recognize her. She was young and blond and wore her hair in braids woven with strands of beads. She listened as Patty pointed to all the stations in the tent. No doubt she was here for the festival.

A rumbling multicolored VW van pulled in behind his car. The van hearkened back to the summer of '60, right before he shipped out to Saigon. During that long, hot summer, he'd yet to enter the marines, and he'd been dating a girl who'd driven a VW van. Kelly. She hadn't been his first, but she'd made him feel things he never dreamed possible. He still looked back on their weekend fondly.

A tall man rose out of this van. He had long dark hair that skimmed his shoulders, and a dark-blue Mountain Music Festival T-shirt stretched over his muscled chest. His jeans and boots were worn, and his deeply tanned skin looked more suited for sunny beaches than cloudy mountains. Rafe Colton, the festival promoter.

Taggart moved toward Colton. "Mr. Colton."

Colton's lips spread into a wide, disarming grin. His eyes twinkled with excitement. "Sheriff, call me Rafe." He made a grimace. "My dad is Mr. Colton."

"Right."

"How's your day so far?"

"Well, it was good until I walked up here."

Colton's smile remained warm as his gaze turned curious. "Why is that? It's all coming together perfectly." He surveyed the stage. "This place is going to be alive with people, music, and love in less than eight hours."

"How are ticket sales going?" Taggart asked.

"Steady. About half sold."

"Which means two hundred and fifty bodies?"

"Exactly right. We'll sell more at the gate, but I doubt we'll move all five hundred tickets. This concert won't make anyone rich, but it's going to be beautiful, spiritual. The music, the open air, and good energy. It never gets better."

"I'm less worried about energy than I am the bodies." Taggart glanced toward the overcast sky.

"I appreciate your concern," Colton said. "You're a man who knows his job." Black beads rattled on his wrist as he pressed his hand to his heart. "I'll be on-site during the entire event, and I'm here to help you. Stop worrying."

Taggart had known a supply officer on Okinawa who had been a carbon copy of Colton. A wheeler-dealer, Sergeant Ken Jefferson could find anything for anyone—for a price. Everyone loved Sarge. Taggart had busted him for cocaine distribution, a move that was not popular with many. "It's supposed to rain this weekend."

Colton's grin widened. "Maybe. Maybe not. It's still fifty-fifty. Be positive." He leaned forward a fraction. "I'm a glass-half-full kind of guy, if you hadn't noticed."

Taggart had known a lot of soldiers who'd been convinced they were bulletproof. Most were dead now. "How much extra security have you hired?"

"We've got twenty guys showing up before we open the gates. Also, their team is installing a few cameras."

"That security proposal never hit my desk. What's the name of the company?"

"Sorry. I forgot. Security will be handled by Woodward Security. They're a solid firm. I've used them before."

There was a lot Taggart didn't know about this event.

"You started, what, last week?" Colton asked.

When Taggart had run the military police department, he'd had more control. You walked onto his base, and he owned you. But out here in the civilian world, he had more restrictions and less authority. His inexperience in this world now felt like a weakness. But he never let anyone get a whiff of his doubts.

"I've been in policing for twenty-seven years. Soldiers and civilians aren't that different."

"I bet the soldiers are tougher. They all carry guns, right?"

"People are people."

"What can I do to erase your worries, Sheriff Taggart?" Colton asked. "I don't like seeing you so troubled."

"Cancel the festival."

Colton laughed. "In too deep now. What else can I do?"

"Make sure that security shows, control your perimeter, and keep the lights on after sunset."

"All top of my list, Sheriff Taggart." Colton clasped his hands together. "I appreciate your concern."

Colton had all the right answers. Slick, smooth, and pursued by trouble. "My deputy and I'll be on-site an hour before the gates open."

"Terrific. You're amazing." A truck driver honked his horn, catching Colton's attention. When he looked past Taggart toward the stage, his smile faded a fraction. "Duty calls."

"Sure, don't let me stop you."

"It's going to be fine." Colton pointed at him.

Colton's easy smile vanished. He was no longer the salesman, and his expression turned direct. The driver jabbed his finger toward the stage, and Colton followed him toward the platform as another vendor hoisted more lights to the metal framework above.

"Sheriff!"

Taggart turned toward the woman's voice and spotted Patty headed in his direction. His blood pressure eased. "Patty."

She brushed a strand of hair off her forehead as she smiled. "Ready for the big festival?"

Something about her had a way of softening his mood. "Ready or not, it's happening."

She scrunched up her face in a mock frown. "You sound so negative. It's going to be great."

More tension melted from his muscles. "That so?"

"It is so," she said. "I've already made fifty bucks making burgers for the work crews. That's going to buy a lot of diapers."

"How old is your baby?"

"She'll be a year this summer. Cutting a tooth and already walking. She'll run the world one day. You have kids?"

"No. Never been married."

"Never too late."

He laughed. "Too set in my ways."

The second gal working the tent called out to Patty, drawing her attention. "Be right there." She turned back around and smiled at Taggart.

"Looks like you have help."

"That's Laurie. She's here for the festival. She's a singer. Hey, Laurie, this is Sheriff Taggart."

Laurie looked up and waved. "Hey!"

"She's trying to make a few bucks before the bands take the stage."

"A little extra dough never hurts." As Laurie moved toward them, her gaze sparkled with an enticing youthful excitement.

Taggart nodded. "I'm sure the help is appreciated."

"It is." Patty picked up a box of supplies. "Grills are cool again, but we'll fire them up in a couple of hours. We'll hook you up with a burger."

"Thanks."

Her grin was infectious. "Do you always look worried?"

"I do." He watched her explain to Laurie how to set up the station.

Taggart drew in a breath. He wanted to believe that it was all going to be fine. Shit, one of his ex-girlfriends had accused him of negativity enough damn times. But experience told him there were too many factors that said otherwise.

He strode back to his Crown Vic and slid behind the wheel. Angling out of the festival lot took a minute or two of maneuvering. An incoming truck inched through the entrance, forcing him to wait as it passed. When it was all clear, he drove down the road.

A half hour later, he was parking in his spot at the sheriff's office. He unlocked the back entrance and closed the door behind him. His footsteps blended with the ringing of phones and conversations in the front reception area. In his office, he hung up his hat and flipped on his Toshiba computer. As the machine booted up and the screen flickered to life, Deputy Paxton appeared in his doorway.

"What do you need, Deputy?" Taggart asked.

"I'm going to run home for an hour or two. It's going to be a long weekend, and I'd like to take a load off while I eat lunch."

"Sure, go ahead. Where's Sean?"

"Not feeling well. At home, but says he'll be good to go by showtime."

"I've got the desk covered. We need to be back at the festival site by four."

"Will do."

As Paxton turned, Taggart asked, "What do you know about Woodward Security?"

Paxton considered the name. "Never heard of them. You check the Yellow Pages?"

"Colton says they're sending twenty security guards. I hoped to learn more about them other than their address and phone number."

"All the festival planning was done after the old sheriff left and before you arrived. I wasn't included in any meetings with the mayor and festival promoter, but I can call my buddies in Roanoke."

"Do that." It was too late to make any changes, but at least he'd know who he was dealing with.

"I'll get right on it."

"After you do, take that break. It's going to be a long night."

Chapter Six

SLOANE

Saturday, August 16, 2025, 7:30 a.m.

I shoved my gun back in the glove box and slammed it closed, then turned the key in the ignition and headed into town. As I coasted down the mountain, the road felt more familiar. I stopped at the convenience store and filled my tank. Inside the store, I walked past the coffee to the soda fridge.

I paid for the gas and a ginger ale, then drove toward Dawson. I was two hours ahead of schedule. I'd never been a great sleeper, and it turned out total darkness and quiet didn't help.

Bottom line, insomnia left me with two hours to kill. I parked in front of the Depot. The red neon sign in the front window blinked OPEN, and I could see several of the booths were full of customers. I crossed to the front door. I hesitated a moment and then opened the door as bells jingled above my head. I found a seat at the bar and watched a waitress serve coffee to a group of young hikers.

I'd spent a few weeks digging into every detail about the town, the victims, and the killer. I had done a detailed background check on the Festival Four. They all shared one truth: Dawson was the last town they ever saw.

The victim foremost in my mind was Patty Reed. She'd shown up in Dawson thirty-two years ago. Eighteen years old and pregnant, she'd been fleeing an abusive boyfriend. She'd wanted a better life for herself and her baby when she'd taken a job at this diner. She'd worked until the day she gave birth. And two weeks later, she returned to work with her baby strapped to her chest.

Patty. Patty Reed.

My mother.

Taggart's file contained interviews with people who had known Patty. Buddy, the Depot owner, had offered her 25 percent of the total food sales if she worked the tent at the festival. Despite Colton's attendance estimates, she'd told Buddy she expected at least a thousand people at the event. She'd been hearing the buzz in town for weeks and sensed a large crowd.

Patty's 25 percent would have amounted to about $3,500. A real nice chunk of change in 1994. The money would have paid past-due bills and tuition for an accounting class at the community college. She'd wanted more for herself and for me.

As I settled on a barstool, a heavyset man in his fifties walked up to me with a pot of coffee in hand. Without a word, he filled the stoneware mug in front of me. Most who worked the breakfast shift had been up by 4:00 or 5:00 a.m. and had few words. "Cream? Sugar?"

The sugar and fat sounded good. "Yes to both."

He glanced at me, paused, then left me with cream, sugar, and a menu. The man returned minutes later, no pad or pencil in hand. "Made a choice?"

"Whole wheat toast, butter on the side, and berries."

"Coming right up." He glanced back at me. "Do I know you?"

"I've made a few short trips to Dawson, but I've never been here."

He shook his head. "I could swear we'd met."

My grandmother, Sara, had told me that I looked like Patty. Sara had precious few pictures of Patty, and the ones she'd had were grainy or out of focus. "I have one of those faces."

"Oh, I know faces and names. I never forget any of them."

"Don't know what to tell you."

He shrugged, put my order in, and got caught up in a rush of new arrivals at the bar. Ten minutes later, he set the plain wheat toast and blueberries in front of me.

"Do you have family in the area?"

"Not anymore."

His eyes widened. "So you did have family in the area?"

"A long time ago. I was a baby."

He hesitated, tapping his large fingers on the counter as if flushing out a memory.

"You look like someone I knew once."

"Really?" I reached for a dry piece of toast, opened a strawberry jelly packet, and spread it.

"We were about the same age. I was learning the ropes from my old man, and she was a waitress. She was one of the hardest-working people I knew."

"What happened to her?" I knew the answer, but I liked to watch people when they responded to questions like this.

Disappointment tightened his face. "That's a long story."

"I got a little time." I wrapped chilled fingers around the warm mug, drawing in the heat.

"You ever hear of the Mountain Music Festival?" He asked as if he expected me not to know. For most it was ancient history. And few cared about history anymore.

"Sure. Who hasn't? It was a big case back in the day."

Surprise wrinkled his brow. "Most people don't know about it. Which is a good thing. Tourists were afraid of Dawson for a long time after that."

I bit into the toast, willing my stomach to settle. "Time papers over a lot of the facts."

"I never thought anyone would forget that festival. It was the worst thing that could have happened to Dawson. After the furniture factory closed, we needed to bolster tourism. But the festival shut all that down."

"I read about the factory. It employed fifty people."

"My brothers worked there." The guy nodded as he wiped his hands on his apron. "You don't act like her."

Silent, I mixed more cream into my coffee, hoping it would soften the bitterness, before asking, "Do I know you?"

"I'm Buddy. I own this place."

I nodded. "Who's my twin?"

"Patty Reed. She worked here thirty-two years ago."

"That's awesome recall after all that time."

He drew in a breath. "Hard to forget Patty."

I picked up a triangle of toast. "Why?"

"She was one of the Mountain Music Festival victims."

That was the final detail in Patty's brief biography. Patty Reed, nineteen, last seen at the Mountain Music Festival. Presumed dead. But those few words didn't paint an accurate portrait of a woman who had been a force. "Tell me about her."

He shook his head. "Why do you care?"

"You brought her up, not me. I'm making conversation now."

Wagging a finger at me, he asked, "Are you related to Patty?"

"Do you have a picture of her?" Good interviewers deflected back to the inquirer.

"I do, as a matter of fact."

"Can I see it?"

"Why?"

"Curious."

"Let me fill a few orders, and then I'll be back."

I nibbled on toast as Buddy filled more coffee cups. He set several breakfast plates down on the counter and rang up tabs. I kept eating, unsure if my stomach felt unsettled because I'd not eaten since the tomato soup, or if my body was reacting to the case. As I'd gotten closer to Dawson, I'd felt sicker.

Most of the victims I wrote about weren't saints. Some were, but most had crossed a line. They'd slept with or sold themselves to the wrong guy. They'd taken drugs, wandered into a sketchy bar, or blindly trusted a predator. None of these victims had deserved what happened to them.

"I keep this posted in my office," Buddy said. "I should have taken it down a long time ago, but I couldn't bring myself to do it. Didn't want her forgotten." He handed the image to me.

The rumpled color photo had a torn corner and a coffee ring stain. The background was this diner. There were a few folks sitting at the bar. A gal with permed blond hair wore a loose-fitting pink-and-white-striped sweater. A guy sported a bushy mustache and a black Bon Jovi T-shirt. In the background there was a pay phone.

The photo's details faded from view as I studied a young woman with a bright smile who stood closer to the camera. Her thick black hair was like mine, and our vivid blue eyes were the same shade. My gaze narrowed into a tunnel as I searched inside myself for a flicker of love or regret. If anything on this planet could ignite feelings inside me, it would be a picture like this. I suspected most people would have felt sadness, outrage, or fury. But I felt nothing. I angled my phone over the picture and snapped.

"You look like Patty," Buddy said.

I lifted my gaze. "You said Patty vanished at the festival."

"That's right." Buddy tapped the counter as he stared at me. "Patty had a kid. A daughter. And she'd be about thirty-two now."

"Yeah."

"Are you Sloane Reed?"

"I am, but the last name is Grayson."

Buddy's gaze grew distant—as if he'd been transported back three decades. A customer summoned him, but he didn't respond. Finally, he cleared his throat. "Why is your last name different?"

"I took my grandmother's surname. Reed was my grandmother's first husband, and Grayson was her second or third."

"Why are you here?"

I glanced into the face of the young, vibrant, hopeful woman in the photo. She looked nothing like the woman described by the media.

Many reporters focused on Patty's relationship with her ex-boyfriend, Larry, who had several assault charges filed against him. They also mentioned Patty's underage drug charge and her out-of-wedlock child. They'd all painted her as a troubled woman living on the edge. The general tone hinted that good girls were safe from danger, and bad girls got what they deserved.

"I'm writing about the Mountain Music Festival victims."

"It's been thirty-one years. The killer is rotting in prison."

"And the bodies were never recovered. There's no closure for the families."

"You think a collection of bones will help anyone now?"

"It might. And all those women deserve to be found."

A patron held up an empty cup, but Buddy ignored him. "I liked Patty. She was a ray of sunshine. Never had a frown on her face or a sour word. After you were born, she brought you to work and waited tables with you strapped to her chest. You were fat and had no hair."

My grandmother had plenty of pictures of me when I was a baby but only one image of Patty holding me. When I was seven, I found it in her bedroom drawer and took it. I reached in my wallet, pulled out the cracked photo, and laid it on the counter.

A smile lifted Buddy's lips. "Yeah, I remember you."

In both images, Patty's hair was in a ponytail, but I wondered what it had looked like down. I wondered if she had a signature scent. If her hands were soft or calloused. Did she have a favorite song?

"When was the last time you saw her?" I asked.

"The time I remember most was earlier in the day. We were boxing up supplies for the booth at the festival. Her sitter had canceled, and she'd brought you to work for a few hours."

"What happened that morning?"

"I kept a playpen in the back for you and anyone else's kid who needed a temporary place to land. You didn't like the pen. You hated naps. That morning you were playing with a few wooden spoons and a bowl. I always figured you'd be happier with a blowtorch and a knife. Never a dull moment with you."

He wasn't far off the mark. I'd not been a normal kid. I didn't care about birthdays, dolls, or games. I was more interested in looking through my grandmother's dresser drawers, purse, or the glove box in her car. And after I'd searched every inch of our house, I broke into my neighbors' homes.

"What were you discussing?"

"Hamburger buns," he said more to himself. "She wanted to stock more. I was worried about getting stuck with too much inventory. She was right, of course."

Later it would come out in testimony that Buddy and Patty had been having an affair. Grainy security footage caught Buddy pulling Patty into a supply closet while I'd played in that playpen with my kitchen supplies.

Patty had resisted, but Buddy had kept tugging. Patty had glanced back toward me. Finally, she'd relented. Fifteen minutes later, they'd emerged. He was smiling. She looked stressed. I was beating the spoon against the bowl.

Patty had wanted to end it with Buddy, other employees of the diner had said. But a woman with a child had to weigh her choices carefully, especially when she was one paycheck away from being homeless. The older I grew, the more I admired how she'd handled her tough journey.

"You arrived at the festival around ten p.m.?"

"To bring Patty more buns and to clean out the cashbox. She had been right. That festival was a real moneymaker."

"How did she look?"

"Fine. She was tired. Another girl who was helping Patty was getting ready to play on the stage."

"Laurie Carr."

"That's right. Had a blue guitar case covered in old travel stickers."

She became known in the press as the Blue Guitar Girl. Later, that blue guitar's strap would play a pivotal role at trial.

"Laurie leaves, and you help Patty with the booth for a couple of hours. Then she takes a bathroom break."

Thirty-one years had etched deep lines into his face. "Yeah. That's right. She left. I thought she'd be right back. But I never saw her again."

"Did you love her?" I asked.

"I did. I wanted to marry her. But she wouldn't say yes."

"Why not?"

His shoulders slumped under decades of disappointment. "She wanted to take you and leave Dawson."

"Why?"

A sigh and then the distress vanished. He straightened. "She wanted a different life, I guess."

"Taggart suspected you," I said. "He mentioned you in his notes."

Buddy's mouth flattened. Annoyance and bitterness radiated from him. He coughed. "He suspected everyone at first. And then the other missing person reports rolled in. He couldn't tie me to any of the other missing women, and he had to hunt elsewhere."

Everyone assumed the same person had murdered all the women. But I was open-minded enough to wonder if the killer had help.

Chapter Seven

Sloane

Saturday, August 16, 2025, 9:00 a.m.

I parked in front of the Dawson Sheriff's Department. It was a simple brick building with small windows and solid doors. It mirrored hundreds of other municipal structures across the country. I'd been in dozens of police departments over the last decade, and I'd come to wonder if the same guy had sold all the jurisdictions the exact same blueprint.

I grabbed my backpack, got out of the car, and crossed the sidewalk to the front door. Inside, I faced a glass wall that separated the working office from the public waiting area. The walls were covered with community event flyers, lost-dog announcements, wanted posters, and local ordinances. The navy-blue walls had been refreshed with a coat of paint in recent years, and the upholstered chairs had new coverings. Law enforcement administrations didn't embrace change. Redecorating, like justice, was rarely swift.

Behind the thick pane of glass sat a stocky woman with graying brown hair and wire-rimmed glasses. She cradled a phone under her chin as she took notes on a pink message slip.

The receptionist set the phone down and looked up. I moved closer to the speaker nestled in the thick glass. "I have an appointment with Sheriff Paxton. My name is Sloane Grayson. And you are?"

"Jennifer Watts." She leaned forward a fraction. "You're the writer?"

News traveled fast. "Yes."

"Right." Jennifer studied me through the glass as she pressed an intercom button and announced my arrival.

I turned from the window, finding her curiosity annoying. Most in her world didn't like people like me. I was the disrupter, the finder of secrets, the troublemaker.

While I waited, I surveyed a flyer detailing upcoming community events. Next Friday, there was a band playing '70s music in the town square pavilion.

A side door opened, and a short man dressed in a uniform appeared. He'd shaved his head but sported a big mustache. For a moment I wondered if they'd sent the wrong man out to see me and then realized it was Paxton. All the images I'd seen of him were at least twenty years old, and back in the day he'd been muscular but trim. The muscle had softened to fat. In his mid-fifties now, he'd run for sheriff after Taggart died. During his campaign, he'd never mentioned the Mountain Music Festival's missing victims. His unwillingness to dredge up the past had won him the election.

"Sheriff Paxton?" I extended my hand.

He accepted it. "Sloane?"

"One and the same."

"Come on back to my office. We can have a little chat."

"Great."

Jennifer buzzed us back in. I followed him down a long, painted cinder block hallway. It was covered in formal images of the sheriffs who'd served the town of Dawson. I paused when I passed Taggart's portrait. Judging by his dark hair, the photo had been taken shortly after he'd arrived on the job.

"Taggart left some big shoes to fill." Paxton paused at his office door.

Taggart's vivid gray eyes glared, as if daring the world to contradict Paxton. I pulled my gaze away and produced what should have passed for a friendly smile. I decided Paxton had had his fill of comparisons to the last sheriff. "A complicated legacy, from what I've read."

"That's what some say." His gruff voice was stuffed with emotions.

Though still in Taggart's shadow, Paxton was the sheriff. I needed to highlight that distinction often.

I followed him into his office. More white cinder block walls with photos of Paxton with state and local officials. Bookshelves included awards from local businesses and the state association. They reminded me of participation ribbons that parents gave to kids when they finished dead last in a swim meet.

He motioned toward two olive-green chairs angled in front of his desk. As I sat, he moved around to the chair behind his desk. A classic power move that always amused me.

I didn't reach for my notebook because it tended to make people nervous. They were inclined to talk if they believed their words were unrecorded and could be forgotten. Lucky for me, I had one hell of a memory.

"Quite the operation you have here," I said. "Looks like you run a tight ship."

His chair squeaked as he leaned back a fraction. "I like to think so."

"You've been sheriff for five years now?"

"I have."

"What made you want the job?" I asked.

"I've been with the department since I was twenty-one. No one knows this county better than me."

"Nice for the business owners to know who they can call if they need help. Not a 9-1-1 number but a name and face on the other end."

"Exactly. Dawson is a close-knit community."

"One big happy family?"

He chuckled. "Like all families, sometimes we get along and sometimes we don't."

"Crime can't be that bad in this area." That was the image the tourism bureau promoted in all their posts.

"You didn't come here to talk about crime statistics." He threaded his fingers over his rounded belly. "You said in your email that you're doing a piece on the Mountain Music Festival in 1994."

He'd broken the ice. Good. Small talk annoyed me. "That's right. It's been thirty-one years, and cold cases are always of interest to readers."

He steepled his fingers. "It's not a cold case. We caught the killer."

"I was thinking about the bodies. They were never found."

"Not for lack of trying."

"It's a mystery. A missing piece of the puzzle. The human brain likes pieces in their rightful place."

"Think anyone cares now? Most folks have bigger fish to fry. How many millions of people have died or gone missing in the last thirty-one years? The price of gas or groceries trumps this story."

"I disagree. Stories like this tend to distract people from their everyday world."

"You write to remind people that someone else has it worse off than them?"

"Something like that."

"There's not much I can do for you, Sloane. It's been thirty-one years, and the chance of finding any traces of those bodies is slim to none." His voice wrapped me in a patronizing, fluffy ball.

"Time can shake loose facts and confessions. New information can solve cold cases."

"I don't know who you'd talk to."

"You're my first. I was hoping you could tell me a little about that weekend. You were right there at ground zero."

"I was there."

"From what I read you were a big help to Sheriff Taggart." There was no rule that said I had to tell the truth.

"I was. Sheriff Taggart and I worked as a team."

"You weren't looped into the festival planning?"

"No. The old sheriff did the bulk of it. It was a done deal when Taggart accepted the job. The planning committee was more worried about posters and concessions than security."

"Can you tell me about the first few hours of the festival?"

"They were the easiest. Weather was warm and the skies clear. The bands and vendors were arriving, but it was orderly at that point."

"But . . ."

"Taggart wanted to make a last-minute request to the state police for extra men. But Mayor Briggs was a cheap son of a bitch, and he would nickel-and-dime the event to the very end."

"What about Woodward Security?"

"I made calls for hours about Woodward. They were a new outfit and had no track record. Their rates were the cheapest in the state. When I arrived, I didn't see any of their guys."

"When you testified at the trial, you said Tristan Fletcher was the first victim you saw at the festival."

"She was issuing wristbands to staff and attendees."

"What do you remember about her?"

"She wore cutoff jeans and a halter top. I didn't recognize her, and it wasn't till later that I realized she would be one of the missing."

I'd seen pictures taken of Tristan that day. The cutoff jeans hugged her butt, and the halter top put her breasts on full display. "I've seen pictures of her. Terrific figure."

He stilled, as if imagining that tight body swaying. "She was pretty."

"Lots of good-looking girls at the festival."

"Yeah."

I'd seen hundreds of festival pictures. One captured Paxton in uniform along with a couple of young girls passing him. The girls were wearing shorts and ripped T-shirts that skimmed full breasts. In the image, a tall blonde was looking back at him and smiling. Paxton's gaze was locked on her breasts—or, as he said in court, the long line of her neck.

"Who approved the tents?" At least a dozen campers had set up pup tents on the edge of the field. Most were patched and covered in dirt, as if they'd seen their share of camping trips.

"I'm not sure. Taggart and I didn't."

"The tent owners insist that they'd pitched the tents for the purpose of sleeping."

He shook his head. "They weren't fooling anyone."

"Several women who filed assault complaints said they'd been pulled in one of those tents."

"The tents were a pain in the ass. We should have pulled them down as they went up."

"Did you see Patty?"

"Yeah."

"What were your impressions of her?"

"I liked Patty. Even considered taking her out."

"But she had a kid."

He nodded. "I didn't need that kind of complication in my life." His face flushed as if he remembered. "Sorry. You're Patty Reed's kid?"

"I am." A half smile tipped my lips. "And for the record, I'm not sure I'd date anyone with kids. My work is my life."

He studied my face as if searching for more traces of Patty. "I was totally into my job," he said finally. "My plan was to work in Dawson a few years and then move on to a bigger department. I dreamed of being a city homicide detective."

But he'd stayed in Dawson. Big dreams faded, and his life hadn't changed much. "Why didn't you?"

"In the end, I couldn't leave Dawson. More ingrained in me than I'd imagined."

"You also crossed paths with Laurie Carr," I said.

"Yeah."

"I've seen pictures taken of her. Hot."

He cleared his throat. "Yeah."

In a different era or maybe if I were a guy, he could have made a few off-color jokes about hot chicks. But he was careful now to watch his words.

"You said you saw Taggart arguing with Colton at about seven that night."

"They were standing toe to toe by the stage. Taggart didn't look happy, but Colton was relaxed and smiling. I guessed they were discussing security."

"You didn't approach?"

"No. I walked toward the stage, which already had hundreds of people clustered around. The guitar player grinned at one of the girls standing close to the stage. He said something only she could hear, and she tossed back her head and laughed."

Thirty-one years ago, Paxton's comments had been more forthcoming. *"Guys in bands get all the pussy,"* he'd told a reporter. *"I reckon Colton had all he could handle. I should take up guitar again. I was pretty good at it at one point."*

"About that time there was a woman by the tents who was in trouble," I prompted.

"Which one? That festival walked hand in hand with booze, drugs, and sexual assault."

"She was young. About seventeen, eighteen."

"Right. Bailey Briggs." She'd been lying face down in the grass beyond the tents. Her arms and legs were spread eagle. But her jeans and peasant top appeared intact.

He'd testified that he'd knelt by Bailey and rolled her on her back. Her thick blond hair was swept over her face, and he hadn't recognized her immediately. She'd breathed in and out slowly, and he'd pressed his fingers to her throat, searching for a heartbeat. He'd studied the silken hair framing the freckled, pale face and realized who she was.

"The mayor's daughter."

She was a senior in high school, and she'd had her troubles with the law. The last sheriff had fixed several tickets for her.

"I escorted her to the first aid trailer. She didn't have any idea where she was. She said she was fine and then she threw up on the ground. Moments like that were why I'd set my sights on homicide in a bigger city. The dead stayed where you left them, and they sure as shit didn't barf."

"You left her at the first aid trailer?"

"Yeah. I thought she'd be fine."

"But you lost track of her."

"I couldn't remember which trip to the first aid station it was when I realized Bailey had vanished."

"But she didn't leave the festival. She hooked up with one of the victims, Debra Jackson, also a local high school student." All the girls had been young and pretty.

"I didn't find that out until later."

Chapter Eight

SLOANE

Saturday, August 16, 2025, 9:30 a.m.

"When did you realize the concert was going south?" I asked Paxton.

He drew in a breath and shifted in his chair. Thirty-one years and the question seemed to still annoy him. "I've been asked that question so many times."

"It irritates you," I said.

"It does. Reporters are Monday-morning quarterbacks. None of you were on the field making calls and dealing with the mayhem."

"You have a point. All of us have twenty-twenty vision in retrospect." I wasn't here to piss him off and shut him down. "I'm not judging. I'm trying to see the scene as you did."

"No matter how long we talk, you never will." His eyes narrowed. "What's your angle?"

"No angle. I want to find the victims' bodies."

That softened his frown a fraction. "Thirty-one years in these mountains is a lifetime. You'll never find them now."

"The earth never completely swallows everything. There's always a trace or a clue."

The black leather of his chair creaked as he leaned back. "That's a nice thought, but the world is a big place."

"No one noticed that the women had disappeared."

"No wonder. By midnight, people had packed the field. It was shoulder to shoulder. Rafe Colton said there'd be a few hundred people, but there had to be two thousand or more. People had hiked up the fire road and slipped into the venue through the woods. The music kept amping up the crowd. The promised large security turned out to be just three guys in black security T-shirts who didn't arrive until eleven. We were all in over their heads. Honest to God, I was never so glad to see the sun rise. Unless you had someone watching your back, anyone could've been swallowed up by that mess."

"Taggart made multiple statements to that effect. He said halfway through the night he couldn't find Rafe Colton."

"That's right. He was impossible to find for a couple of hours."

"Could he have driven off the mountain?"

"No way. The roads were jammed."

"And the mayor? Where was he?"

Paxton shook his head. His mouth tightened. I suspected he was chewing on a few choice words. But politics got the better of candor. "Mayor Briggs was a good man. He wanted the best for this town. Dawson was hurting financially then. Folks were out of work, and he wanted to help."

"He thought the festival would be a success," I said.

"He did. He thought it would be over and done with before anything bad happened."

On the fifth anniversary of the festival, Mayor Briggs had shot and killed himself. He was found lying in his backyard, a .45 by his right hand and a bottle of Jack Daniel's by his left. The concert that was supposed to solve so many problems condemned the small town to fifteen years of purgatory.

"Bailey Briggs Jones took over the family business." I'd not asked Bailey about the concert yet, but that would come soon.

"That's right." He leaned forward, threading meaty fingers. "You're on a fool's errand, Sloane. You're going to stir a lot of bad memories, get a few clicks, and then you'll move on. You won't be around to see the wreckage."

"The wreckage has followed me ever since." I drew in a breath and met his gaze. "I've spent my entire life wondering if she's dead, alive, suffering, or living a better life without her child."

Paxton sat back in his chair. "I'd think this would be the last place you'd ever want to be."

"I tend to run toward trouble."

"There's no trouble here," he said. "Dawson is a peaceful town."

"It looks very serene." Not all murder scenes were dark alleys. Some were nice homes. They were places of work, favorite neighborhood parks, or tree-lined jogging trails. Murderers didn't need to set the stage to do their thing. Anytime, anywhere.

He settled his elbows on his desk. "How long are you going to be in town?"

"A week or two. I want to get to know Dawson and talk to the folks who were at the festival thirty-one years ago."

"They aren't as easy to find."

"I've found a few."

"I heard someone rented Sheriff Taggart's cabin." Sharp-eyed and a little flushed, he seemed annoyed. "Was that you?"

I focused on an award behind him on a credenza. A service award from the Rotary Club. The year was 2022. There was a framed image of a football team. 1988. I suspected Paxton was in the cluster of boys somewhere. He was as much a part of this town as the roads and bridges. "That was me."

"Why? Sheriff Taggart's been dead five years."

"Thought I'd get a little insight into him. Maybe I'll catch some of his vibe."

"You know he shot himself in that cabin. He sat on the front porch and put a revolver to the side of his head."

"That explains why the place is haunted, right?"

Paxton shook his head. "I'm not giving you access to the sheriff's case files."

"I'd be surprised if you did," I said. "Most jurisdictions don't welcome me." My research often began with one cop who'd never been able to forget a case.

Paxton rose. "Thanks for coming, Sloane. But I think we're finished here."

I stood, taking a moment to settle my bag on my shoulder. "Thanks for your time, Sheriff Paxton."

"Best of luck to you," he said. "Don't speed in my town."

As I made my way down the hallway, I caught Paxton's reflection in a framed picture in front of me. He had stepped out into the hallway, and he watched as I reached for the security door. It was locked, trapping me inside.

I glanced to Jennifer, but she didn't meet my gaze. Irritated, I stared at her as I rattled the door. When she set down the receiver, she exhaled a breath and pressed the buzzer.

I crossed the lobby and stepped outside. The sun was bright and the sky clear. The mountains, now my temporary home, skidded across the skyline. The distance didn't feel that far as I stared at the ridge. But as I drove out of town, I realized how isolated I was in Taggart's cabin.

Chapter Nine

CJ Taggart

Friday, May 20, 1994, 6:00 p.m.
The concert begins

The air was thick with the scent of booze, sweaty bodies, and rain. Taggart glared up at the three-quarter slice of the moon. It spilled what light it could through thick clouds. Thunder and lightning could give him an excuse to shut this nightmare down. But so far all he got was thick gray clouds ripe with rain.

The country music band onstage was covering Journey's "Don't Stop Believin'." The crowd jumped up and down as they pumped their fists in the air. It wasn't the best cover he'd heard. But the energy remained positive and upbeat except for a few fights he and Paxton had broken up. The first aid trailer was already treating cases of intoxication, scrapes, and bruises. Nothing critical. So far so good.

The crowd had well exceeded five hundred. There must be two or three times that number of people here. The masses still had a positive aura, but the energy of a large crowd could change on a dime. The next band up was a hard rock group, and their music would stir the crowd.

He spotted Colton standing by the stage, smiling, and waving his arms as if he were a member of the audience. He'd finally reappeared from wherever he'd been. If he was worried about weather or overcrowding, he gave no sign of it. Several young girls approached Colton and swarmed around him. One brunette leaned in close and whispered in his ear. He laughed. Her body jiggled with excitement. Another woman in cutoffs and a cropped T-shirt danced in front of him, and he watched but wouldn't join her. He was the king, and this was his court. He wasn't worried about their argument over security. This festival was now underway, and if it became a runaway train, there wasn't much Taggart could do to stop it.

He turned toward the food tent and saw Patty handing out burgers. Even after hours of setup and cooking, she had a smile on her face. When a couple of drunk guys approached her tent, her expression grew guarded. They ordered burgers, and when she was ready to serve, they began searching for money. One tried to reach for his order, but she snatched it back. That bright smile had vanished.

Taggart strolled toward the tent, coming up behind the guy as he reached over the counter for the bag. Taggart clamped his hand on the guy's shoulder, startling and pissing him off with the one move.

The man whirled around. His fist was half-cocked when he realized he was staring at a cop. The uniform tamped down some of his anger, but the guy wasn't going to let it go easy.

The offender was in his early twenties. He had full sweeping bangs that no self-respecting man would allow. Taggart guessed he'd wrapped up university finals or was headed into a summer session. Frat boy. Rich.

"Is there a problem?" Taggart asked.

Frat Boy shrugged. "She won't give me my order."

"You pay for it?"

"I did." Frat Boy had a straight face, as if lying were an entitlement.

"Got a receipt?" Taggart asked.

"It's a burger tent at a concert. They don't do receipts here."

"He didn't pay," Patty said.

Frat Boy didn't bother a glance in her direction. "She's lying. I paid her twenty bucks."

"For a five-dollar burger?" she asked. "That was generous."

"She owes me change," Frat Boy challenged.

"He didn't give me anything," Patty said.

Taggart didn't need convincing. "I was standing behind you when you tried to snatch the burger out of her hands. Now you can pay her five bucks or move along."

"I paid."

"Don't press me," Taggart said.

The band guitarist dived into a long riff. It was hard to hear over the noise. He hoped Frat Boy would push back. He could think of nothing better than tossing this guy to the ground and cuffing him. It would be a major pain in his ass to haul him to jail, but he'd make the sacrifice.

Frat Boy glared at him and then at Patty. The young man looked pissed, as if Taggart had crossed the line between the rich and working poor. Taggart flexed his fingers.

Fishing a crumpled five from his jeans pocket, Frat Boy tossed the bill over the counter. It sailed past Patty onto the dusty ground.

As she reached down to pick up the money, Frat Boy tried to grab his burger. Taggart stopped him. "Wait for the lady to say you can take it."

Frat Boy fumed but waited until Patty pushed the burger toward him. He grabbed it, and as he stalked off, he tossed a glare back at her. He wouldn't forget this townie's slight. Taggart lingered around the hamburger tent until Frat Boy vanished into the crowd. "If he bothers you, let me know."

"Par for the course, Sheriff," Patty said. "He's not the first tough customer I've dealt with."

"Other than him, how's it going?"

The growing line behind him didn't seem to rattle or rush her. "It's fine." A few raindrops hit the top of the tent. She glanced up toward the sky. "Weatherman said fifty percent chance of rain."

Droplets splashed his hat and starched shirt.

The guitar player's fingers must have been moving at a thousand miles an hour as the singer hit a high, sharp note. The crowd cheered, and he could feel the energy ratchet up several notches.

Two more gals stepped up to Patty's table. Both were young, dressed in those damn jean cutoffs. They swayed until they noticed him, then stiffened as if they were focusing on not looking buzzed. They each ordered burgers. Good. Food in their belly would at least soak up some of the booze.

Taggart tossed a ten-dollar bill on the table and ordered one burger. She handed it to him and reached in the cash register for change.

"Keep it," he said.

"Thanks, Sheriff."

"Food supplies going to hold out?" Hungry concertgoers always ginned up trouble.

"We might. I radioed Buddy and told him to bring more, but he's so worried about overordering. I'll sell until I'm out."

"Call if you need backup."

Her genuine grin softened all the night's frustrations. "Will do."

As he took his first bite of the burger, the raindrops plopped slow and unsteady. He moved to the edge of the crowd by the main gate and took another bite. He demolished the burger in three mouthfuls. He'd learned as a young marine to eat chow quick if it was hot.

The sky was quiet, no signs of thunder or lightning. Fat droplets hit the dry dirt.

The band didn't break stride and rolled right into "Any Way You Want It." The audience remained jazzed, as if they'd never heard this song before. Shouts of excitement rolled over the crowds.

He moved to his car and pulled a poncho from the trunk. He slipped it on, hoping the rain wouldn't come.

By 11:00 p.m., the rain picked up speed. At first, the cooler air was a relief. But as the water pounded and soaked his poncho, his irritation doubled. Damp fabric chafed skin and chilled skin to the bone.

But no one here realized that yet. It was still fun and games. Cool rain. Plenty of food to be had. Booze. Maybe a dry tent or two for now.

But none of it was going to last. Cars filled the limited parking at the edges of the field, and the overflow snaked halfway down the mountain's main and service roads. Getting out of here now was damn near impossible. These folks were trapped.

Chapter Ten

Sloane

Saturday, August 16, 2025, 11:00 a.m.

As I drove past the real estate office, I saw Bailey unlocking her front door. I'd not been candid with her when I'd checked in because I wasn't ready to dive into my questions. I knew she'd gotten drunk and landed in the first aid trailer. She'd sobered up enough to sneak out of the tent by 10:00 p.m., and she'd been spotted with Debra Jackson around midnight. Debra had vanished soon after.

In May 1994, Bailey Briggs had been a popular high school senior. She'd liked to party. And when the remorseless girl got into trouble, her father made the consequences go away. For what it was worth, her parents confirmed Bailey arrived home at 4:00 in the morning.

I parked across the street from Briggs Realty and crossed. Bailey had begun working at the agency after she'd dropped out of college. And when her father took his own life three years later, she'd taken it over. To everyone's surprise, she'd made the business work.

Bailey had gotten to know Rafe Colton when her father was negotiating the festival dates with him. She'd admitted she thought Colton was hot and charming.

I opened the agency's front door. Bells jingled above my head. Bailey had not turned on the lights, and she was nowhere in sight. Easy to assume the place wasn't open yet.

I walked up to her desk and picked up the brass nameplate that read "Bailey Briggs Jones." When she'd dropped out of college, she'd married her college sweetheart, Danny Jones. Her lack of a wedding band suggested they'd divorced.

Divorce was a tough place to land at any stage of life. My mother never married, and I didn't plan on taking that path, either. Marriage and dependence on anyone were not in the cards for me. You can't miss what you never had.

Setting the nameplate down, I spotted several pens that read "Briggs Realty." I grabbed two and slipped them in my backpack. They were advertising, right? And I always needed a pen.

The files on her desk were property records. I straightened the edges until they were a neat stack. Judging by the height of the pile, whatever slump Dawson had suffered in the 1990s and early 2000s was in the past. Rentals appeared to be booming, as was new construction. Bailey was riding high.

Like Bailey, I'd acted out as a teenager. I didn't get blind drunk, but I liked to break things. A tipped-over potted plant in an abusive vice principal's office. "DICK" scratched in the high school bully's car. A body check against a guy who hadn't given his seat to an older woman on a bus.

Bailey had done nothing to me. But she annoyed me. Maybe I saw myself in her. Or more likely she'd been Dawson's princess, whereas Patty had been on Team Outcast.

I placed my hand on the stack and eased it closer to the edge of the desk. I imagined the flutter of papers scattering all over the carpeted floor.

"Hello?" Bailey called from the back room.

I curled my fingers, drawing my hand back. "Hey, it's Sloane. The renter of the house in the woods."

Bailey came out of the back room holding a steaming cup of coffee. The Briggs Realty logo was embossed on the mug. I wondered if she had logos on her underwear. "Oh, hey."

"Sorry to bother you." I tossed on my best smile.

"Everything okay with the cabin?" she asked.

"It's great. No complaints." While some people might have been freaked out by the isolation, I liked it. I did my best thinking in the quiet. Even if there were ghosts.

"Can I get you a cup of coffee?" She raised her mug.

"Thanks. But no. I stopped by the Depot and had several," I lied.

"The Depot's coffee will put hair on your chest."

I smiled. "I believe that."

"What can I do for ya?"

"I'm looking for a family that used to live near town, and I figured no one knows the area and the families like you do."

A half smile tugged her lips. "Not much gets past me."

"Great. I'm looking for Monica Carr. She was a friend of my mother's." Very possible they'd crossed paths but not likely they were friends.

Bailey's gaze glanced upward, as if she were accessing a data bank of families in her brain. And then her smile softened, and she shook her head. "You said Monica was your mother's friend?"

"They went to school together and corresponded for many years. Thought I'd say hi, but her number isn't listed."

"Your family is from the area?" Her head tilted.

"My mother and grandmother weren't here very long."

"Grayson. You remind me of Patty Reed. Was she your mother?"

"That's right."

"And Patty was friends with Monica? I don't see how."

"Not super close," I lied. To my knowledge the two women had never met. "But they liked each other. Did you know my mother?"

A detached emotion passed over Bailey's face. "I saw Patty working at the diner all the time. But we never hung out."

No, I doubt the town princess would have hung out with the diner waitress with a bastard kid. "I get it."

Bailey cleared her throat. "I didn't realize Monica hung out with Patty."

"They did."

Bailey's face tightened as if she were looking back in time. "Monica keeps to herself. She's not fond of surprises."

"I'm not a fan of them, either. Do you have a number for her? I'll text her and give her a heads-up I'm in the area."

"I can't give out client information."

"Oh, I didn't realize she was a client."

"I mean, it's been fifteen years, but I sold her mother's place after Monica inherited it."

"Oh. Okay." Sometimes a curious expression was enough to coax more information.

"Monica had it tough. Her husband left her. Her only daughter died of cancer. And, well, her niece Laurie vanished. And she was barely nineteen."

"Like Patty."

"Yes."

"Damn. Monica could use a friendly face and good news from an old friend."

Bailey seemed to enjoy holding secrets. "I can't give you her number, but I can tell you she spends her Saturdays volunteering at the senior center. She hangs around until about three."

"That's great. Where's the center?"

"A few miles from here." She rattled off an address.

"Got it. Thanks."

"Sure."

"I picked up a little gossip today," I said. "I hear the town's former sheriff shot himself at the cabin where I'm staying."

"It was a tragic event. It was over two weeks before he was found."

"Wow. I guess that explains the ghost hunters."

That startled a laugh. "Seen any ghosts?"

"Not yet. But I'll keep you posted."

"Are you going to write about the Mountain Music Festival?"

"Maybe."

"Do everyone a favor and don't. The mid-nineties weren't the best of times for this town. And no one wants to remember."

"Four women vanished. Don't they deserve a little space in our memories?"

Her face flushed. "Of course, we need to honor them. But rehashing the case will do no one any good."

"Even if rehashing means we find them?"

Bailey went silent, as if realizing arguing with one of the victim's children was a tactical error. "I'm sorry about Patty. She seemed nice."

Bailey smiled but I sensed she had nothing else to say to me. "Thanks." I tacked on the word, and it dangled like a frayed afterthought.

Keys in my hand, I left the shop and crossed to my Jeep. Behind the steering wheel, I glanced back toward the agency. Bailey stood at the office's main window. She sipped her coffee as she stared at me. As she turned, she brushed past the files hovering near the desk's edge. The stack fell to the floor.

I started the engine and drove toward the senior center. Monica would be getting off in a couple of hours. Better to catch her at the end of the day, when she was tired and thinking about heading home. She'd have let her guard down.

As much as Bailey annoyed me, I felt a kinship with Monica. The way I saw it, we were on the same team. After the Mountain Music Festival ended, both our lives had changed for the worse.

The handful of people damaged by the festival amounted to about two dozen. No one important in the grand scheme. Not enough people to warrant digging up the past. But even if the world had forgotten them, I had not.

My grandmother had never thought of herself as a grandmother and had trained me to call her by her given name, Sara.

Sara and I didn't talk about Mom often. I didn't bring the topic up much when I was little because I didn't think about the mother I didn't remember. In kindergarten, I began to have questions. Most kids had moms and dads, and some were raised by grandparents like me. Some parents were divorced, a few in jail, a couple dead. But my classmates knew where their parents were. When I asked Sara, she could never tell me exactly where Patty was. And even at five, unanswered questions irritated me.

Around my seventh birthday, Sara's drinking had gotten worse. I'd wait until she was on her third G&T before asking for anything.

"Where's my mom?" I asked.

"What?" Ice clinked in her glass as she drained the last of it.

"My mom. All the kids at school know where their mothers are. Gina's mother is dead, but she has a grave and can visit her and lay flowers. Billy's mom lives in Vegas and is a dancer. Where is my mother?"

"I don't know." Ice cubes clanked. Sara took another long drink.

"How could you not know? She's your daughter. You always know where I am."

"That's because you're little. I knew where your mom was when she was your age." She looked in the empty glass, rose, and walked toward the kitchen. "But she grew up, and it got harder to keep up with her."

I followed, unsatisfied. "Why was it hard?"

She unscrewed the top of the gin bottle. "She fell in love with a bad man."

"My father?" All kids had a mom and dad somewhere.

"That's right."

"Where's my dad?"

She drained the last of the clear liquid. "Prison. He's in a big time-out."

My time-outs were frequent but rarely lasted more than an hour. "For how long?"

"For the rest of his life."

"Wow. Was he really bad?"

Sara's eyes grew watery, and the lines around her mouth deepened with her frown. "He was."

"Does he know where Mommy is?"

"He says he doesn't." She filled the glass with gin and dropped in a couple of fresh ice cubes. The clear liquid sloshed around the edges of the glass. "No one knows where your mom is, Sloane. We looked everywhere, but we couldn't find her."

"You didn't look everywhere, or you'd have found her."

I was good at pushing aside memories like this. I didn't like to think about my grandmother, but she had a way of finding her way into my present.

Shrugging off the unease, I arrived at the Dawson senior center, I saw the elderly residents moving in slow motion. My mind wandered to Patty and the missing. Police and volunteers had searched all areas within fifty miles of the festival. This included fields, ravines, buildings, and forests. They'd sent scuba divers into the quarry lake, searched barns, basements, and ditches. Yet Patty and the others remained lost.

Bodies could be burned, chopped up, or buried deep, but they didn't disappear. Even the smallest haystack needles were somewhere.

And I hoped the last thirty-one years had shaken loose a few truths. Because someone knew where the Festival Four were.

Chapter Eleven

CJ Taggart

Friday, May 20, 1994, 11:00 p.m.
5 Hours Into

It was pissing down rain. What had started as a cooling mist had turned into a downpour that would not let up. The bands were under cover. And without any cracks of lightning, they couldn't stop without forfeiting their pay.

The crowd was growing larger. The air was cooling, and he half hoped that it would turn frigid and chase everyone off the site. The fewer bodies here, the better.

To his right, a young guy cocked back his fist and drove it toward a second guy's head. The blow clipped the second guy's cheek. Pain registered on his face and, seconds later, rage. The second man barreled into his attacker. The two fell through the thick rush of bodies and slammed into the mud. The crowd parted, ringing the two men as they threw fists at each other.

Taggart pushed through the crowd and pulled the top guy back as he cocked his fist, ready to strike again. Taggart wrenched his arm behind his back and reached for the cuffs on his belt. As he secured the cuffs around the guy's wrists, he looked toward the second guy covered in mud and blood. He reached for his walkie and called Paxton. "Yeah, get to the northwest quadrant. Got a man down."

"Roger."

A girl moved close to Taggart. She was in her late teens, had long black hair, wore faded jean shorts and a halter top that the rain had plastered to erect nipples. He could swear she'd been onstage about a half hour ago.

"What's the deal?" As the girl spoke, the thick scent of pot and beer wafted off her.

"Back off," Taggart ordered.

"Why? I'm asking a question. Can't I ask questions?"

"I'll have you transported to the station, and you can ask all the questions you want from inside a jail cell."

She held up her hands, revealing the impression of a henna tattoo on the underside of her right wrist. "You don't have to get all ugly with me."

Rain dripped from his cap as the crowd pressed in closer. An uneasy anger rolled through the crush of people. It would take little to set them off.

"Let me go, man," his detainee shouted to the crowd.

"Be quiet." To make his point, Taggart tightened the cuffs.

The crowd around him began to chant: "No. No. No."

"They're going to eat you alive," his prisoner said, grinning.

"Maybe," Taggart said. The chants grew louder. "But they'll get a chunk out of your hide, too."

"I'm not the cops."

"When a crowd turns and grows wild, they don't care who they hurt or what they destroy," Taggart growled. "You're going to be my shield."

"Fuck you, man."

Paxton pushed through the crowd toward Taggart. The deputy surmised the situation, lifted the injured man out of the mud, steadied him, and pushed him forward out of the crowd. Someone threw a plastic water bottle. It struck Taggart on the shoulder.

Taggart shoved his man forward, his hand slipping to the grip of his gun. When they reached the edge of the crowd, he glanced back, ready to draw on anyone who challenged him. The girl with the long dark hair stared at them. He couldn't tell if she was high or curious.

Taggart deposited the injured man in the first aid trailer and then loaded his cuffed detainee in a paddy wagon on-site. It wasn't the most comfortable place to wait, but he'd have water and fresh air. In the morning, Taggart would take him to jail.

Paxton glanced at the woman before joining Taggart at the tent.

"Do you know the one with the dark hair?" Taggart watched the girl melt into the crowd.

"I met her earlier. Name is Tristan. She was handing out wristbands. She's a dancer."

"Right." Taggart shifted his attention to Paxton. "Have you seen Colton?"

"He's not up by the stage?"

"Not for the last few hours. Guy keeps vanishing."

"Check by the trailers near the woods. I saw him headed that way earlier in the evening."

Rain thrummed on his jacket, dripping down his arms and legs. "Any sign of the security team?"

"Nope."

"I'm headed to the trailers." As he moved around the edge of the crowd, he glanced toward the hamburger tent. Patty was handing out burgers and collecting money. She was smiling but looked exhausted. The world was full of hardworking Pattys. These women sacrificed their youth and beauty in the hopes they'd crawl out of poverty. A few made it out of the hole, but most would spend their lives chasing enough money to make rent.

The collection of six festival trailers was located at the edge of the venue. This area should have been off-limits, but the crowds had spilled beyond the rope marking the area for staff. He passed the two tractor trailers that had brought in the large equipment. Under both were couples huddled together, wrapped in soaked blankets, and sleeping bags. The ground was muddy, but the trailers stopped the bulk of the direct rainfall.

The next three trucks were smaller. They had transported in A/V equipment for the different bands. He checked each cab to ensure the front and back doors were secure. They were. The final vehicle was an RV that Colton used as his office.

The interior of the trailer was dark, and there were no signs of movement. He pounded on the door with his fist. There was no answer, but when he tried the door handle, he discovered it was unlocked. He twisted and opened the door.

"Sheriff CJ Taggart. Is anyone here?"

There was no answer. He stepped inside and stopped to swipe his muddy boots on a mat already covered with dirt. Water dripped from his hat and rain jacket to the floor. "Colton. It's Sheriff Taggart."

Silence echoed from the cabin. The light switch didn't work. He unhooked his flashlight from under his rain jacket and shined it around the cabin onto a small sofa and a simple white bra and panties on the floor. A coffee table sported a glass ashtray, which held a discarded cigarette still smelling of smoke.

Outside the music kicked up into the band's final, violent notes. The crowd roared and cheered like a bellowing giant.

Five more bands were set to take the stage before sunrise. But the seven hours remaining felt like a lifetime.

As he turned, he spotted Colton moving toward the trailer. He was rain soaked. Head bowed, he was at the trailer when he looked up and saw Taggart.

"Sheriff, is there a problem?"

Taggart blocked the man's entrance into his own place. "Where's my extra security?" he demanded.

"They just arrived," Colton said. "I've been on the walkie for the last hour, trying to find more guards here. There was a paperwork mix-up."

"Your crowd could go feral any minute. Two men cannot keep them under control if it goes sideways."

"I know. And I appreciate how hard you and your deputy are working. I'm going to see you both get a bonus."

"I don't want a bonus. I want to keep this event from going sideways."

"I've done concerts before. It always gets a little dicey about this time." He motioned for Taggart to step aside. "Mind if I go in my trailer? I need a change of clothes before I head back out there."

Taggart shifted to the right but didn't leave the trailer. "Sure. Make yourself at home."

Colton grinned. "That's nice of you."

He watched Colton walk by the discarded underwear as if it were par for the course. Colton didn't bother to close the folding door as he stripped off a wet sweater. He tossed it into the small bathroom. The garment hit the floor with a loud *plop*. Next came the jeans, and soon he was standing naked, rummaging through a pile of clothes on an unmade bed.

Colton yanked on a new sweatshirt and jeans. Shoving hands through his dark, wet hair, he grinned. "That helps a lot. You and your deputy are welcome to stop here if you need to change or need a quiet moment."

"I'll worry about both after the concert." He nodded toward the bra, which had a small pink flower on the right cup. The garment reminded him of something a young girl would wear. "Where's your guest?"

Colton glanced at the undergarments. "Back to the concert, I guess. She was sleeping when I left."

"Didn't take her clothes?"

"She was soaked to the bone. I told her to take one of my shirts. She's out there somewhere now, I guess. Or she left. She didn't like the rain."

"What's her name?"

"I didn't catch it."

"How old was she?"

"I didn't check her ID." He brushed past Taggart. "Look, Sheriff, these events can get raw once the sun goes down. Girls are here for two reasons. They want to get on the stage, hoping for a break. We're a small festival, so they assume they'll get noticed easier. And then the others are looking to party hard and explore their darker sides. On nights like this, good and bad girls are all the same. And if I can have some fun along the way, then no harm and no foul."

Taggart didn't believe Colton, but there was no way of proving he was lying. This guy was not what he presented to be. And if he had any kind of complaints or evidence against him, Taggart would haul his ass into jail now. But he had nothing other than a damp set of women's underwear.

Taggart turned and reached for the door handle.

"You don't like me very much, do you?" Colton asked.

"Not my job to like or not like. I keep the peace."

But Colton had hit the nail on the head. Taggart didn't like Colton. He created perfect storms like tonight so he could watch them spin out of control and soak up the chaos.

"I like you. I appreciate how you care about those drunken slobs out there."

"That's what you think of them?"

A brow arched. "Am I wrong?"

Taggart stared at him a long moment. "Radio me if there's any trouble."

"Will do."

Out in the rain, Taggart braced against the cold and the wet. The previous band had finished its set and the next was setting up equipment. These lulls were good for about thirty minutes. The latrines and food tents would be swamped. And anyone who'd brought a tent or had a car parked nearby would have retreated to dry off.

A feeling of helplessness washed over him as he stared at the crowd. The odds had been stacked against him in the past. And when disaster unfolded, he cleaned up the mess later. It was like that now.

Head bowed, rain pelting his hat, he moved toward the crowd. A group of three men dressed in security guard uniforms moved toward him. He hoped this was not the team Colton had mentioned.

He greeted the first man to reach him with an outstretched hand. "Glad to have the assist."

"Sorry we're late," he said. "The dispatcher sent us to the wrong location. I'm Kevin Pascal and this is Ben and Roger. We've got more men coming, but it'll be another hour."

Taggart swallowed a curse. "Get into the crowd and do your best to keep the peace. A lot of drunks and drug use. Don't focus on detaining anyone unless it's dire." The complaints would start rolling in tomorrow. He could already imagine calls for robbery and sexual assault.

"We're armed with Tasers and nightsticks," Kevin said.

"That works best in conditions like this. We have a security wagon by the main entrance. There are extra zip ties if you need them."

"We have a few dozen each. But we'll get more if necessary."

The new band onstage struck up a chord, and the lead singer sauntered up to the microphone and shouted, "Hello, Dawson, you dirty motherfuckers!"

The crowd roared to life, fists pumping in the air as bodies jumped up and down. More guitar chords blared out from the stage.

Four songs in, a young female singer drifted to the edges of the stage. When the lead singer beckoned her forward, she strode toward him. She was tall and lean, with blond hair that skimmed her waist. She wore a halter top and jeans that rode low on her gently rounded hips. She crossed the stage, her blue guitar slung over her body, and stepped up to the microphone. The girl from the hamburger tent. Laurie.

As the lead singer began a cover of Tina Turner's "Better Be Good to Me," Laurie moved toward him, smiling as she strummed her guitar.

She looked a little nervous as she belted out a few solid notes. The crowd cheered. And by the second refrain, she was smiling. When the song ended, the singer shouted, "Give it up for the superhot Laurie!"

Laurie waved. She grinned from ear to ear as she left the stage. Her moment in the spotlight had ended as fast as it started.

Chapter Twelve

SLOANE

Saturday, August 16, 2025, 3:00 p.m.

Smiling, I walked up to the senior center's reception desk. I hoped the news of my arrival had not reached the center yet. "Hey, I'm here to see Monica Carr. She's been so amazing with my mother, and I want to thank her."

The mid-forties receptionist had black hair tied back into a ponytail. She wore aqua glasses attached to a silver chain around her neck. "You missed her."

I set a gift bag on the counter. "Darn, I had a present for her."

"You can leave it with me."

"It's cake. It should be refrigerated."

"Oh, well, she'll be back in a few days."

I shoved out a sigh, trying to strike a balance between sadness and frustration. "I can run it by her house. She's on the way toward Mom's house."

"I'm sure she'd be fine with that."

I opened my phone. "She's on Craig Road, right?"

"No, Jones Road."

I searched the street. It looked rural. "That's right. End of the road on the right?"

"Left."

"Okay."

"Number 2020."

"Perfect. Thank you," I said.

As I walked back to my car, I caught my reflection in the window of a storefront. Dark hair draped down my Rolling Stones T-shirt. Worn jeans skimmed my long legs. I slid into the car and tossed the bag in the back seat.

I plugged Jones Road into my phone and drove east. It took me a good thirty minutes before I made the left down a small gravel road.

I'd made a career interviewing victims. Sure, some of them didn't always get the story right. But most had a handle on the offender, even if they didn't remember all the details. There was something about being face-to-face with a killer or rapist that imprinted impressions on a body that even a mind didn't recall.

I'd spent countless hours reading Taggart's police records. But there was no replacing interviews with the victims and their families. Most victims of crime weren't wealthy. And cops and reporters tended to discount them if their home situation was dysfunctional.

I couldn't write a book on parenting or family bonding, but I understood even the most messed up of us had something to offer.

My GPS led me off another secondary highway onto the graveled and tarred Jones Road. The trees on either side were thick, and long branches draped over the road. Several scraped against the side of my car as I searched for a house at the end of the road on the left.

I spotted a rusted mailbox that rested cockeyed on a leaning post. The name "Carr" was visible, but the two *R*'s looked more like *I*'s. I turned down a narrow, rutted driveway that arched in front of a brick rancher. The grass around the house looked freshly cut. But the edges of the yard were ragged, as if weed eating were a bridge too far. I got it.

Homes, as a rule, were a pain in the ass. I was happy living on the road and operating off my laptop and a post office box in Charlottesville.

I pulled around the arch and nosed my car toward the end of the driveway. I'd not called ahead, which was a huge risk. Even when I notified a contact I was coming, I was cautious. I was a stranger, and my interviews stirred up bad old memories for people that could go sideways.

That had been the case last year when I'd interviewed the father of a murdered girl. The victim had been one of six girls killed by a man who'd lived five houses down from the family. It was a lower-middle-income neighborhood outside of Baltimore. The slain girl's father was devastated. He'd tried to start a nonprofit for missing kids, but it had never gained enough traction. He'd lost his job, and his wife left him.

As I'd pulled into his driveway, the father had staggered outside. He'd been drunk and brandishing a .45 caliber handgun. He'd fired two bullets at my Jeep. I'd shoved the car's gear into reverse and hit the accelerator. I took out two clay planters as I raced out of the driveway. I'd not pressed charges, but I also hadn't approached him again. After that day, I parked on the street.

I walked along the cracked cement sidewalk and, seeing no doorbell, knocked hard. A glance at the untrimmed shrubs brought to mind an old cop's joke about 1970s porn snatch.

The door opened to a woman who was a few inches shorter than me. Her thinning gray hair was scraped back into a ponytail, and her face was lined. Her T-shirt and jeans were clean but old and threadbare.

"I'm Sloane Grayson. I'm writing an article about the Mountain Music Festival."

"I heard there was a reporter in town." She studied me.

"Already? News travels fast."

"Edna at the grocery store and I are friends, and she knows Bailey. Why are you here? Why care about a case that's thirty-one years old?"

"I don't want people to forget about those women." I avoided the word *victim*. The term dehumanized the women and made them faceless.

"You'll make a small splash, but no one will care for long."

"I don't make small splashes. Mine are big and messy."

That prompted a small smile.

"I'd like to think my articles matter."

She sighed and stared at me a long moment before unlatching the hook on the screened door. "Come on in."

I followed her into the dimly lit house. It had low ceilings and white walls that needed a fresh coat of paint about a decade ago. On those walls were dozens of pictures of a young blond girl. In all the photos, she was holding a guitar and smiling.

"That kid came out of the womb singing. And she was playing her daddy's guitar by the time she was four. Such talent. She was convinced she'd be a big success."

The girl was Laurie Carr, later known as Blue Guitar Girl. From what I'd learned about Laurie, she'd been nineteen when she vanished. She'd made several demo tapes and wanted to sing in Nashville. She'd thought the festival would be her big break. She'd sung a duet onstage with the lead singer of the Terrible Tuesdays, a five-man rock band. The band had done well on festival circuits for about five years but disbanded by 2000. A local news station had been filming, and they'd captured Laurie and Joe Keller's set. Laurie had been good and maybe could have gotten a contract. Maybe.

I followed Ms. Carr. The sofa was threadbare, the coffee table covered in old magazines, the carpet shag. The avocado-green kitchen dated back to the 1980s.

"I made lemonade this morning," Ms. Carr said. "Care for a glass?"

"Sounds great."

She pulled out two mason jars from a dark-grain wooden cabinet and a pitcher of lemonade. The bright yellow wasn't found in nature, but I wasn't going to argue.

She set two glasses on a round kitchen table and motioned for me to sit. I lowered to the chair, letting my backpack drop to the ground. The lemonade was tart and made my lips pucker.

"It'll put hair on your chest," she said.

"Like the Depot coffee?"

"Better. Vodka adds a bite to the sweetness, if you need a little."

"No, this is fine." I set the glass down. "Again, thank you for seeing me."

She rattled the ice in her glass. "Nobody ever asks me about Laurie anymore."

"I've seen a video of her singing at the festival. As rough as the tape is, you can't miss she was great."

"She was special."

"What prompted her to go to the Mountain Music Festival?"

"It was a chance to sing. My brother, her father, didn't have money for fancy lessons, but that never stopped her. Then she saw the poster for the festival in the Waynesboro shop where she worked. The day of the festival, her car was in the shop, so she took the bus to Dawson and then started walking toward the site. Finally, one of the band guys picked her up."

"Joe Keller."

"Joe told me he'd warned my girl to be careful, but she was so sure that she had life figured out."

"She couldn't have known."

"She would've loved playing for a big crowd. I can't imagine how good that must have felt for her." She rose and grabbed a bottle of vodka from the freezer. Unscrewing the top, she offered me a sip, but I declined. She put a healthy dose in her lemonade.

"I understand you helped raise Laurie."

"Her mama ran off when she was five, so I stepped in to help."

The similarities among Laurie, Patty, and me weren't hard to miss. "You reported Laurie missing, right?"

"I called the station on Saturday afternoon. Not enough time had passed for the police to take a report. But Laurie had promised she'd check in by Saturday afternoon. And she was always good to her word. When she didn't call, I called the sheriff's office. The dispatcher told me to give it time. When she didn't come on Sunday, I called first thing on Monday. The lady on the phone said the sheriff was investigating other complaints about the concert."

Given the numbers, I suspected so many crimes hadn't been reported. "What did he say when you told him your niece was missing?"

"He reminded me she was over eighteen, and that young girls sometimes took off longer than they said."

"And?"

"And that pissed me off. I *knew* my girl. I knew she wouldn't run off and not call home. That wasn't Laurie. I told him." She took a long pull on her lemonade. "He called me back that afternoon and asked me to come to the station. I thought they'd found her body. When I got there, there was another woman. She said her daughter was missing."

"Do you remember the missing woman's name?"

"Patty. The woman was her mother, Sara." She shook her head. "All these years and I can't forget the names."

"You remember Patty after all this time?"

"Patty's mother and I sat together in the waiting room for several hours. Didn't take long to realize why we were both there."

"That's not standard police procedure."

"I didn't know what was proper or what wasn't. By the time I left, I was worried. My Laurie was missing and so was Patty. Both were young and pretty."

"Witnesses later said that Laurie worked the hamburger stand with Patty."

"Made sense to me. Laurie always found a way to make a few bucks. My girl was resourceful. She had the talent and the work ethic for going the distance in Nashville."

Who knew if Laurie would have been a star. Death had a way of whitewashing away faults and highlighting strengths. Either way, she'd deserved to live her life. "Did you keep up with Sara?"

"You know a lot about this case."

"I do."

"Sara and I talked on the phone. We were frustrated that the cops couldn't find their bodies."

"When did you learn there were two other missing girls?"

"A week after the concert. The sheriff had a third missing person report but didn't announce it until his press conference."

"Debra Jackson."

"That's right." She sipped her lemonade. "After the press conference, another family called in a report."

"Tristan Fletcher's family."

"The dancer."

"And after that the story went national."

She sipped her lemonade. "Reporters showed up at my door. They didn't call ahead."

"Neither did I."

"But you're polite. Most of them weren't. One pounded on my door at midnight. I damn near shot him."

"Joe was questioned."

"He'd done time in jail when he was younger. Assault. And they held it against him at first."

"He acknowledged his record in his interviews."

"We all make mistakes. He'd gotten on with his life. And he was nice to me. Didn't look down on me like some of those reporters looking for a reason to discredit me. I wasn't Laurie's mama, and I'd had a child that had died. Some tried to link all that to Laurie's death." She shook her head. "I can't even say if my girl is dead or not. Without a body to bury, I can't even grieve for her."

I understood the irritation of unanswered questions. When I was a kid, I'd pretended that my mother wasn't dead. *She was traveling. She was making movies in Hollywood.* Those lies came back to bite me, so I fabricated better ones. *Yes,* I'd admit, *my mother was dead, but it had been a terrible car accident when I was a baby. She was buried in a distant city.* By the time I was fifteen, I didn't mix with my peers very much, which meant fewer questions to deal with. I'd also stopped wondering if she'd show up at the mall, school, or my doorstep. I knew she was dead. But my grandmother never gave up hope. Until the day Sara died, whenever she drank too much, which was often, she insisted that my mother was alive. I found it annoying. We'd argue. She died two days after my eighteenth birthday. My first thought was that she was with Patty. Sara was at peace. And so was I. For a little while.

"Did you go to the trial?" I asked.

"I couldn't afford the time off from work, and I didn't want to see Rafe Colton. I worried that I'd shoot him where he sat."

Courtroom sketches portrayed a smiling, relaxed defendant sitting next to his attorneys. "Was Laurie dating anyone?"

"She had a few guys that followed her like puppy dogs but nothing serious."

"You have any names?"

"David Green was the most attached to her. He still lives near Dawson. He's married and has three grown kids." She shook her head. "He's been married longer than Laurie was alive. Hell, she'd be fifty now."

"Yeah."

"Why are you doing all this? And don't tell me because you want people to remember." She shook her head. "People have the memory spans of gnats."

A quiet rage rubbed against the underside of my chest. "My mother was Patty Reed. I want to know where he put them in the ground."

Monica studied me. "You think you can find them? The police had no luck."

"Time can loosen up facts once held close. And cops follow the rules. I don't."

A slight smile tipped the old woman's lips. "Do me a favor and break every fucking rule. Smash them all to bits."

"That's what I do best."

Chapter Thirteen

SLOANE

Saturday, August 16, 2025, 5:00 p.m.

When I left Monica Carr's house, stress pounded in my head. I wanted to feel sadness or even anger, but I didn't. However, my body sensed something was off. A knot was wound so tight in me that I thought the cord would snap.

Whenever one of my articles dropped, a big switch tripped like a breaker. And then the pressure hissed away. There was no better feeling than when the spotlight shifted to a killer who'd thought he'd gotten away with murder.

I loved watching their stages of grief. Denial when the cops arrested them. Anger in the interview phase. Bargaining with their attorney. A few accepted their fate, but many never did. I hoped depression overtook them all when the cell door closed behind them.

But until an article was finished, I was dangerous. And this article wasn't even close to complete.

The pressure inside my head was growing, and I needed to find a release. I'd promised myself that I'd avoid any risk-taking misadventures. No stealing, no breaking and entering, no high-speed driving. If Grant were around, we'd have sex. But with no Grant, I had to find a way to walk the straight and narrow. No missteps. No misdeeds.

I reached for my cell and dialed a familiar number. Grant picked up on the third ring, making me wonder what had taken him so long.

"Sloane. This is a surprise." A door closed.

"Thought I'd touch base."

"What's wrong?"

"Why do you ask?"

"You aren't the type to call and chat."

"Nothing's really wrong."

"But."

"I interviewed Laurie Carr's aunt." I didn't need to fill in the pieces. He knew the case almost as well as I did.

He didn't offer an opinion. "And?"

"Ms. Carr has never gotten past her niece's death. She's a lot like Sara."

"And you?"

"How can I feel loss? I never knew my mother." I pulled onto the highway.

"Still, the idea of her mattered. Every girl needs a mother."

I laughed. "I'm not a regular girl, Grant. I don't feel any loss for Patty or Sara. I don't experience normal emotions."

"What do you mean?"

I pressed my foot on the accelerator and passed a truck in the right lane. "I have never processed feelings like regular people. Love, hate, guilt all elude me."

"Sounds like a sociopath."

"That's what Sara said. She asked a friend of a friend about why I never cried or never feared consequences."

I'd never bothered with honesty before. But for some reason I needed him to see the worst of me.

"You're unique, but I don't think that's a bad thing."

"Some of my ways are bad."

"How bad?"

"I've never hurt anyone who didn't deserve it."

His voice dropped. "Have you hurt anyone?"

"Not badly."

"What was the worst?"

"A guy who killed his stepdaughters. He reported them missing. I followed him for weeks. He was hard to nail down, and then he fell down a flight of stairs. He was easier to talk to with two broken legs."

A beat of silence. "People trip."

A truck ahead of me in the left lane was going too slow. This was the fast lane. I pressed the accelerator and edged up closer to his bumper. "I want to meet Rafe Colton."

"Seeing you could shake something loose from him."

"Maybe."

The truck driver tapped his brakes, and his lights popped on, but I didn't slow. He glanced in his rearview mirror and flipped me off. I kept riding his tail. If Grant weren't on the line, I'd have leaned on the horn by now. He cut to the right, and I raced past him, not bothering a glance.

"What are you doing?" he asked.

"Speeding."

I pressed the accelerator, watching my speed climb to ninety. I caught up to the next dumbass in the left lane. The male driver operated a Mercedes. Such a great muscle car, and he drove like an old woman.

"Slow down."

"Okay."

"I mean it. You're not good to anyone dead."

"Such sweet words. Let me know when you have a meeting set up."

I ended the call, and I laid on the horn. The man driving the Mercedes slowed ahead of me. Our cars approached a semi in the right lane. I was unable to pass, so I rode the Mercedes's tail, gripping the wheel as the space around the car shrank to inches in the front and to the right. The driver shot me the bird.

When we passed the truck, I cut into the right lane and zoomed past the Mercedes. I cut left and slowed. He slammed on his brakes and swerved in his lane. His driver's-side wheels went off the road before he righted his car. I tossed him a grin and accelerated.

My heart raced as adrenaline shot through my body. Games like this were pointless and dangerous. I was going to get myself hurt or killed one day. And I was getting a little old for stupid choices. Still, the snarl inside me stopped twisting tighter. I felt better. I could manage now.

Time to focus on the article.

Laurie had worked the hamburger stand with Patty. She'd also crossed paths with Buddy, Sheriff Taggart, and Paxton. Buddy testified that he'd dropped off extra burgers and buns and cleaned out the cashbox about 10:00 p.m. on Friday night. He'd met Laurie but couldn't remember her name.

I had hoped talking to Monica Carr would give some more insight into Laurie. But like the other women, the festival had swallowed her whole. Buddy's impression of Laurie would be different.

Twenty-five minutes later I parked in front of the Depot. I felt better. And I was hungry.

When I glanced through the window, I saw Bailey sitting at the bar eating cherry pie. Never one to avoid trouble, I entered the diner, sat beside her, and smiled. "Hey."

Her Realtor smile flickered to life. "Did you find Monica?"

"I did."

She arched a brow. "How did it go? You get something to use for your article?"

The news was spreading fast. "Sad. She's never gotten over her niece's loss."

Bailey lifted a shoulder and let it drop. "I still miss my dad." The words sounded rote, like they'd been rehearsed too much.

"It's not the same. You know how he died, and where he's buried."

Her grip on the fork tightened. "I hear you're asking a lot of questions in town."

"It's the only way to learn."

"Why didn't you ask me questions earlier?"

"Still getting my feet wet. But you're on the list."

She stabbed a cherry. "Have you written anything I would have read?"

"If true crime is your thing."

"I don't care for that. The violence is unsettling."

"Ignoring it or pretending it never happens isn't a good plan, either."

"How do you do it? Doesn't it bother you?"

"Sure, sometimes." That was a lie. I could absorb the violent details and testimony with dispassion. But that level of detachment exacted a price, as my highway adventure today proved.

"I can't watch dog rescue videos on YouTube. Reading about people would be too much."

"Then you won't like my stuff," I said.

I caught the waitress's gaze, and when she approached the bar, I ordered a soda, fries, and a hamburger. Her name badge read "Callie." "Thanks, Callie."

"Sure thing."

Bailey's smile wasn't as bright as it had been this morning.

"The story explains why you wanted the Taggart property," she said.

"I was hoping for inspiration."

Callie set the soda in front of me, and I sipped, grateful for the cool liquid.

"Did you see Patty with Laurie Carr at the festival? The two worked the hamburger tent together."

She set her fork down. "I don't want to talk about that day."

"Why not?"

"It wasn't a positive experience for me. I made stupid mistakes."

"You were, what, seventeen or eighteen? Kids that age make mistakes."

She picked her fork back up and stabbed a plump cherry nestled between the crust. "Yeah. But most kids aren't related to the town mayor."

"I read Taggart's notes. He escorted you to the first aid station. When he came back later, you were gone."

"That's right."

"Where did you go?"

"I left the festival."

"When?"

"I don't know. About ten."

"In your testimony you stated you didn't get home until four a.m."

"I left through the woods because the main entrance was blocked," she said. "It took hours to get out."

"You walked off the mountain?"

"That's right."

"It's twenty miles to town."

"I was younger, fitter in those days, and at the bottom of the mountain, I hitched a ride back to town."

I stabbed my straw in the crushed ice floating in the soda. "Who gave you the ride?"

Bailey giggled like a child. "You sound like a cop."

"I'm not a cop. I'm a writer, and I'm trying to find the bodies of four missing, likely dead women."

"Likely? There's no *likely* about it. They can't be alive after all this time."

"Their stories need to be told."

She leaned closer and whispered, "No one cares. That festival is ancient history."

Her slight discomfort was amusing. "You knew Rafe Colton, right? He worked with your father to plan the festival."

"I met him once or twice. But we weren't friends."

I liked ripping open scabbed wounds filled with rot and infection. "He was hot and charming. He must have noticed you."

"Sure, he did. But that was that."

"Is he why you snuck out and went to the festival?"

She tapped her fork against her plate. "No."

"Some theorize Colton had help."

"I don't have all afternoon to sit here and listen to this crap." She dropped her fork, letting it fall on the half-eaten piece of cherry pie. "You have no idea how hard it was for us all after the festival. We were all terrified until he was arrested. I didn't sleep for weeks."

"You were worried for your personal safety?"

She stood and grabbed her purse. "Leave me alone."

"See you around?"

Her smile was as sweet as artificial syrup. "Not if I can help it." She tossed ten bucks on the counter and left.

Buddy came out, glanced at the half-eaten pie, and set the burger and fries in front of me. "That's not like Bailey. She looks pissed."

I had that effect on people sometimes. "She said she had work." I sipped my soda and then plucked up a hot, salty fry. "Do you remember Laurie Carr working your burger stand at the festival?"

He picked up Bailey's plate and wiped the counter with a rag. "You're still on that?"

"Did you see Bailey at the concert?"

"I saw her about nine. She was buying a burger." The words sounded automatic, as if the repeated words were etched into his brain.

"How did she seem?"

"Distracted by the bands and the crowds."

"When's the last time you saw Bailey that night?"

"About midnight."

"She said she left before then."

He shook his head. "Yeah, she says a lot of things."

"Thirty-one years ago, I bet Bailey was hot and got lots of attention."

"She was smoking. And high-maintenance. Never worth the trouble, as far as I was concerned."

High-strung and privileged. Not much had changed with Bailey. "Did you see Laurie at the tent?"

"Sure. For a little while. Then she left to go sing onstage."

"That would've been about eleven p.m.?"

"That's right."

"How long did you work the tent with Patty?"

"A couple of hours. Then Patty said she needed a quick break, so I hung around a little longer."

"Were you surprised Patty didn't return to the tent?"

"Pissed mostly. By two a.m., I was tired and running out of food. So I shut the stand down and went looking for her. I thought I'd find her near the toilets or the woods getting high."

"She used drugs?"

"Everyone that night was. I could see her needing a line or two to keep her energy up."

"Did she use coke often?"

"No. But that night was hard. I figured she'd gotten a boost and lost track of time."

Buddy had created this story about Patty to justify his inaction for over two hours. "When did you tell this story to Taggart?"

"After Sara called in her missing person report, he came looking for me."

"Anyone else I should be talking to about Laurie?"

He scratched the back of his neck. "I got nothing for you."

Taggart had talked to all the band members during his investigation. They had all been busy getting on with the show. In my files and papers, I had a list of the band members and the road crews. No one had noticed her leaving after her set.

The forensic investigators found a set of partial prints on the guitar. But none were linked to anyone in the national fingerprint database. One partial print belonged to a Terrible Tuesdays band member. But video footage showed him touching the guitar onstage as she sang. Taggart had also run fingerprint searches against all the men associated with the case.

"There's a theory that Rafe Colton was working with someone. What do you think?"

"I didn't know the guy that well. When he brought his posters in the diner and was hanging them, we shot the shit. He was fun. Had great jokes. But I never saw him with anyone else."

"Did he flirt with Bailey?"

"Sure. She loved it."

Buddy returned to his kitchen. I took several bites of the burger. It tasted good, but my stomach quickly filled. I never could eat much when I had a problem I couldn't solve.

The sun dipped toward the mountains. The light shone into the diner and reflected off mirrors behind the bar. I had maybe two hours of sunlight left. The dark never scared me, and I wanted to see the site of the festival after the sun had set. I wanted to see what the concertgoers had seen. Yes, they'd had some light from the stages and the temporary lights near the first aid trailer, but large pockets of the field had been dark.

I tossed a ten-dollar bill on the bar and left. In my car, I cranked the radio, and I drove the ten miles west toward the Nelson farm, the site of the festival. The old woman who'd leased the land to the festival had died fifteen years ago. Records showed that her grandson had inherited the house and the land. He lived in Washington, DC, and didn't visit the property often.

I spotted the black, rusted mailbox. Despite its dilapidated state, I recognized it from Taggart's file, which the old sheriff had shipped to me days before he died. Not hard to figure why he'd picked me to take up the mantle. I'd sat on the files for a few years before I couldn't ignore them any longer. I'd spent the last two years embedding all the case details into my brain.

A set of headlights crested the hill ahead, so I slowed, wanting the driver to pass me. The driver didn't pass by until I reached the mailbox. Cursing, I kept driving until I reached the top of the hill and turned my car around.

With no one on the road, I turned left into the long dirt driveway. My headlights skimmed the bumpy road. Several times I had to veer hard to the right or left to avoid getting stuck in ruts carved in the dirt by gushes of rain. Ahead I saw a large oak tree that had appeared in the crime scene photos. Thirty-one years had added at least ten feet to the tree and gnarled and thickened the bark.

I knew the concert field was to the left. I pulled to the side of the road and shut off the car. Without the headlights, the night grew heavy. The quarter moon spit out a little light but not enough. I grabbed a flashlight from the car's glove box.

In 1994, the field had been freshly cut and the hedges around it trimmed. Now the grass was as tall as my thighs and the hedge thick with thorns.

I walked along the shrubbery until I found a small opening. I slid through, irritated when thorns caught my jeans and scratched my skin. When I stumbled onto the field, I decided that if I returned, I'd bring bolt cutters and carve out an easy path.

The grass brushed my jeans as I moved toward the center. I'd stared at so many pictures of the festival. But thirty-one years of growth and change had thrown off what I expected to see. The trees at the edges of the field were taller, thicker. And the old split rail fence had collapsed.

My gaze trailed the fence north. I rotated until I faced the spot where the stage had been. I opened a playlist on my phone. I hit play, and Laurie's grainy festival recording of "Better Be Good to Me" echoed in the night. Her voice had a rough edge as she emphasized the word *meeee*.

I shut off the flashlight and allowed the darkness to wrap around me. Laurie's voice faded in and out as she moved away from the microphone, which caught the crowd's cheers. A breeze brushed my face. I imagined I was Laurie, standing onstage, staring at the crowd that had swollen to over two thousand. The rush of cheers and clapping must have reverberated in her chest. The high would have been incredible. She'd known, *known*, singing was going to be her life's work. I understood that kind of wanting. I chased my articles with a similar intensity.

I turned toward the spot where Patty had sold her burgers. I wondered if her soul and those of the others were chained to the land. I'd seen a movie once about five airmen stranded in the African desert near the ruins of their downed plane. They'd seemed normal. Regular guys frustrated by the crash and trying to get home. And then one by one, the men had vanished. It turned out, they'd died in the crash days earlier. They'd been dead all along. But they couldn't go to heaven or hell until their bones were found.

I reset the audio, closed my eyes, and listened as the gritty recording replayed. Were those four women swirling around me, begging me to see them? *Find me! Find me!*

"I'm doing my best, ladies. I'm doing my best."

I shut off the recording, letting the silence give my mother space to talk to me, to whisper a secret in my ear. But I heard only the winds and the hoot of an owl in a distant tree.

Lowering to the ground, I lay back on the dry grass. I shifted until the bristles flattened into a cushion. The sky was clear and the stars bright as the last of the sun vanished behind the mountains. My eyes drifted closed as I tried to be in my mother's shoes. How desperate had she been in those days? Her boyfriend had ditched her, and though he worked in a garage near Dawson, he never gave her money or bothered to visit us.

When Larry was convicted of murder and sent to prison, my grandmother never took me to visit him. And I was fine with that. He'd ignored Patty and me, so I wasn't going out of my way to see him. No one mentioned Larry unless I got into trouble in school. When I landed in the principal's office and my grandmother was called, she took her time getting to the school. I guessed she thought making me stew was its own form of punishment.

When my grandmother finally picked me up from school, she said, "You look like her, but you're not her. You're him. He could never control himself, either."

"I can control myself," I said.

102

"You hit that boy today with that rock on purpose."

Billy Johnson had been teasing another girl. So I'd slammed a rock into the center of his back, tipping him forward onto his knees. He'd screamed like I'd done something drastic, like cut off a finger or toe. "He was being mean to another kid. I told him to leave her alone, but he laughed."

"His knees required fifteen stitches to close the gash, Sloane. You hurt him."

I felt no shame or guilt. He was a bully and had gotten a taste of his own medicine. "He deserved it."

My grandmother had sunk into a sullen silence. When we'd arrived home, she'd cracked a beer and sat in front of the afternoon game shows. She'd ignored me for the rest of the day. I'd grabbed a bag of chips and a cola and gone to my room. We were happiest when we weren't pretending that we loved each other.

In the distance a car engine rumbled, and the headlights turned down the long driveway. I sat up and watched as a car pulled up behind mine. A large man got out, his flashlight cutting into the darkness.

I sat up, brushed the grass from my pants, and crossed the field to the hole in the hedge. My eyes had adjusted to the darkness, and I didn't need the flashlight to show the way as I walked toward the car's burning headlights. Spatial awareness in the dark was kind of a superpower for me.

As the man circled my car, I approached him, knowing he'd not heard me. "Can I help you?"

His hand dropped to a holstered gun on his belt as he whirled and shined the light onto my face. I shielded my dilated eyes.

"Who are you?" I demanded.

Tension rippled through his wide shoulders. "Grant."

"What are you doing here?"

"Better question for you."

"I asked first," I said.

"I own this property."

The light made it harder to see his face. "Since when?"

"Since my grandmother died fifteen years ago."

I knew he'd been a cop. I'd always sensed the easy smile hid a steel determination. I'd witnessed his excellent memory in action. But I really didn't know Grant. And I sure didn't work with anyone. Irritation scratched under my skin. "The grandson in the DC area. Is that why you were so interested in this case?"

"The case has always been on my radar. And then I heard you were investigating the case now."

"You could have told me," I said.

He lowered his hand from the gun's grip. "We're still in the get-to-know-you stage. I don't want to be a part of any article you write."

"I'd have honored any off-the-record request." I thought back to the hotel room, when he was dressing. Several times I'd sensed he wanted to say something. I could have pressed but didn't care enough to ask.

His shrug and grin likely deflected most challenges. "Once a cop, always a cop."

I wasn't distracted. "Do you live in Dawson?"

"Considering it. I have contractors coming to look at the house next week. We'll see how much renovations cost."

"Small world."

"It gets smaller every day."

This was business for him, and I'd keep it that way. "How's my appointment with Colton going?"

He stepped toward me. "Working on it."

"Don't give him the impression I'm anxious. I'm not. Never have been."

"I won't." He studied me. "Why are you out here in the dark?"

"I was lying in the grass in the spot where my mother worked her hamburger stand. I was hoping her ghost would reach out and tell me what happened. But no luck."

His brow furrowed with more curiosity than annoyance. "Do you often channel ghosts when you work on your articles?"

"I'll listen to anyone who'll give me an angle on the story."

"You'll have better luck with the living."

"I'm open to suggestions."

"There's a café in Waynesboro," Grant said.

"That's about fifteen miles west of Dawson, right?"

"Yes. It's not a big café, but they have live music every Saturday. Check out the singer. He's pretty good."

"The man got a name?"

"Joe Keller."

"The guy who gave Laurie her ride into the festival and sang a duet with her."

"The very one."

"No one I've talked to in town mentioned he was playing."

"Have you alienated the entire town yet?"

I had a reputation for upsetting apple carts. "Not everyone. But I'm working on it. Thanks for the lead, Grant. I appreciate it."

"Do me a favor and limit your trespassing to the daylight. In the country, interlopers get shot."

But I did my best work in the dark. Tonight was no exception. "I'll keep that in mind."

Chapter Fourteen

SLOANE

Saturday, August 16, 2025, 9:00 p.m.

The café in Waynesboro was on Main Street near the South River. Once a junction between two railroads, the city was now a tourist stop along I-81 south and home to a few factories.

The bar was trimmed in shiplap siding and a rough-edge laminated wooden top. Behind the bar was a collection of liquor bottles, beer taps, and an opening to a small kitchen in the back. The floor area was packed with twenty small cocktail rounds, each stocked with four chairs. All were full.

The center stage was small, covered with an Oriental rug and an empty barstool. An acoustic guitar leaned next to a microphone. The entire setup took up almost all the stage's space. I glanced around the crowd, looking for an older musician.

When I didn't see him, I caught the bartender's attention. In her early twenties, she had swept up her purple-streaked dark hair into a thick ponytail. An intricate tattooed sleeve covered her right arm from her bicep down to the middle of her forearm.

"What can I get you?" she asked.

"Ginger ale. Is there going to be live music tonight?"

She popped the top of a ginger ale can and poured it over a glass filled with ice. "Yeah, he's on break. Back in the alley having a cigarette."

"I hear he's pretty good." I fished a ten-dollar bill from my back pocket.

She set the soda in front of me. "He's decent. I hear back in the day he was on the rise."

And now he was here. "There's got to be a story there."

She grinned. "Always is."

I took a long sip. "How long before the set begins?"

"Ten minutes."

"Excellent. Thanks."

I drained the soda. Lying in that field had made me so thirsty. I headed to the back exit. Outside, the warm air rushed me as I stepped out under a back porch light. I looked around but didn't see anyone, and then by a dumpster, I spotted a lean guy with long gray hair bound into a ponytail. He stepped out from behind the dumpster and checked his zipper to make sure he was put back together.

When he looked up and saw me, he stopped midstep and looked startled.

"Sorry," I said. "I didn't mean to interrupt."

"I've pissed behind my share of dumpsters, trees, and bushes in my career. You won't be the first to surprise me."

"The bartender said you were on a break."

He fished a rumpled pack of cigarettes and red plastic lighter from his back pocket. "That's right."

"I'm Sloane Grayson. In full disclosure, I'm a writer working on a piece about the Mountain Music Festival."

"Haven't heard about the festival in over a decade." The lighter flared, and he pressed it to the tip of his cigarette. Smoke rose past his squinting gaze. "I'm Joe Keller."

"Most people see it as ancient history. They don't want to talk about it."

"I don't mind talking." He inhaled and allowed the smoke to trickle over his lips. As he stepped forward into the light, shadows deepened the lines of his face. He looked like a thinner version of Bob Dylan.

I edged a little closer. "Do you remember Laurie Carr?"

"Blue Guitar. Sweet kid. I told her to be careful. We sang a duet onstage."

"How did you end up driving her to the venue?"

"She was walking along the side of a dirt road with her blue guitar case slung over her shoulder. The sunlight was hitting her blond hair and her tanned body. I offered her a ride, and she was glad to have it. She told me right off she wanted on the stage."

"And you helped her get her shot."

"When I saw her serving burgers, I told her to meet me at the stage about eleven. Right on the dot, she was there, so I waved her onstage. I wasn't sure how it would go, but I had to give the kid her due. She delivered. I got chills."

"I was listening to the tape tonight. She was good."

"She had talent, looks, and the 'it' factor."

"You had some strong vocal chops yourself."

"I had moves back in the day."

It was hard to accept that Laurie was dead when her voice hit and held such high notes like a pro. "No one saw her vanish."

"The world eats up good people all the time," he said. "If she'd lived, she'd have had a hard road ahead of her. The music industry destroys girls like her."

"She deserved the chance."

"I didn't say she didn't. Look at me. I was an experienced singer and guitar player, and it ate me up and spit me out."

"How?"

"Signed my rights away. I was so hungry for the short-term gain I didn't see the future. I never would've saw myself here now."

His career path didn't interest me, but for the sake of bonding, I asked, "So why keep at it?"

"It's in the blood. Won't let me go."

"The café looks packed. You must still have some moves."

"I didn't say I wasn't good. Had the business sense of a rock."

"After Laurie's set, it was the end of the Terrible Tuesdays' performance, right?"

"Yep."

"She must have been jazzed and not ready to leave."

"The bug bit her good. Euphoria is high when a set goes well. It was the band's ninth show in eight days, but they were juiced. I had to hustle to keep up."

"What did you and the guys do after your set?"

"Broke down the equipment with the road crew and loaded up the van. Laurie stuck around to help."

"And after?"

"I saw her walk off toward the toilets by the woods."

"And then what?"

"I would've followed her if I could. She was amazing."

"But you didn't."

"I had to pack up so the next band could get onstage. I didn't think about her for several more hours. And by then she was gone."

"But you stayed at the festival?"

"Everyone could see getting out was going to be tough. The main and fire roads, even to foot traffic, approached gridlock. We found a small clearing near the farmhouse. Most guys in the bands pitched tents and spent the rest of the night partying. I hoped Laurie would find us, but she didn't."

"This was about one a.m.?"

"Yes."

"Was it raining then?"

"It had been most of the evening."

The farmhouse fields were ringed with woods. If a young woman had gotten too close to the trees, someone could have lured her into those woods. Darkness and rain would've made it even harder to find them. Later Taggart and others searched those woods. They'd found Laurie's blue guitar case.

"Anyone else show interest in Laurie?"

"We all thought she was hot. Any one of us would've tapped that. That's half the reason most of those guys were in the band. If she'd offered, I'd have gone for it." A bitter smile twisted his lips. "I have a picture of Laurie and me taken backstage after our set."

"Do you still have it?"

He reached in his wallet and removed a rumpled picture. He handed it to me.

I studied the smiling faces, barely recognizing Joe. Laurie was radiant. "A great moment. Can I take a picture of this?"

"Keep it. I've carried it long enough."

"Why did you?"

"Someone needed to remember her. Now you can."

I understood the obsession to remember. "You're performing so close to the concert location. Do you ever go back to the festival site?"

"I went back about fifteen years ago. I tried to remember the large crowds and the cheers. But you can't catch lightning in a bottle."

"Any theories about the whereabouts of the victims?"

"A million places to hide a body in this area. And once these mountains swallow you up, it's next to impossible to find you."

"The mountain didn't swallow them up. A human disposed of them."

"Yeah."

"What did you think about Rafe Colton?"

"Smooth as silk," he said. "I met a lot of guys like him in the industry, but he was one of the best salesmen I ever met. He believed his bullshit."

"The commonwealth's attorney got his murder conviction against Colton without the bodies. No one in court stepped up and said they saw Colton grabbing one of the women, driving a truck off-site, or digging a hole. That led some to believe he was working with someone else. Someone who helped him hide the bodies."

"I heard that."

"Any theories?"

"He could convince anyone to do anything. He had a million-dollar smile. His festivals had their own tribe of groupies."

"Any one of his followers stand out?"

"Why don't you talk to Rafe Colton? I hear he's easy to find."

"He's insisted he's innocent for thirty-one years. And without the bodies, he'll make parole next month."

"Like I said, he can make anyone believe anything." His tone was filled with bitterness.

"Okay, thanks, Joe."

Smoke circled around his head. "You going to see him?"

"Eventually."

"And why are you so special? Why will he talk to you?"

"Men like Colton hate to be ignored. And I can be entertaining when I try."

His lips twisted with a crooked smile. "And you think your showing up is fun for him?"

"I do."

"And he'll string you along with empty phrases and leads, like the music executives did with me."

"That's a risk. But I'm betting his upcoming parole hearing will put him on edge. Freedom is almost in his grasp, and he's getting cocky. Pride is steps ahead of a fall, right?"

He shook his head. "He was a slippery son of a bitch."

"Any angle I can use with him?"

"He still owes me five hundred dollars for that concert. Stiffed everybody who worked that event." A long ash dangled from the edge of his cigarette. "Rafe Colton was all talk. And that couldn't have changed."

"Good to know, Joe. Thanks for talking to me."

"For what it's worth, I hope you find them. Laurie deserved better."

"Thanks." I walked down the back alley, bypassing the crowded bar. I wasn't in the mood for people or loud noises. Already I craved the quiet darkness that surrounded Taggart's cabin.

As I moved toward my car, I spotted Grant McKenna walking toward me. "The show is inside, not in the alley," he said.

"I went inside. Joe Keller was out back taking a smoke break."

"And?"

"He was happy to talk. But I still have a lot of random pieces, and the full picture escapes me." I handed him the old photo of Joe and Laurie.

He studied it, shaking his head, before he handed it back to me. "Did you dig up any leads on possible accomplices for Colton? Taggart didn't spend much time on the theory after Colton's arrest."

"I've looked. There were plenty who loved and followed Colton like a religious leader," I said.

"The concert music was loud, and the sound would've given him cover to subdue and kill the women."

"But no one heard or saw anything. Feels like a stretch. Unless another person lured them to a secluded location."

The shadows deepened beneath his unshaven jaw. "Makes sense. But what happened to the bodies? The entire concert area was searched multiple times."

"Maybe that same person loaded the bodies into a truck or trailer and drove it off the property after the concert ended."

A restless pause, saturated with curiosity, settled between us. "How is it up at Taggart's cabin?"

"Quiet. The man lived like a monk."

"Cell service is for shit up there."

"You've been there before?"

"Once or twice."

I could imagine him in the living room, small kitchen, or bedroom. The area suited him. "Are you going to renovate the farmhouse?" I asked.

"Or tear it down. I'm more interested in the land."

"It's a couple of hundred acres, right?"

"Give or take."

What we'd shared six weeks ago added some weight to the space around us. We'd had sex, but we weren't lovers or friends. As tempting as it was to invite him back to the cabin, I didn't need the distraction. "Stay out of trouble."

"Watch the trespassing." He paused. "I'll be in the motel in Dawson."

"Good to know."

I slid behind the wheel. As I drove off, it wasn't quite 11:00 p.m. It felt too early to go home. I wasn't into the bar crowds these days, but I wasn't ready to self-isolate at the cabin. I'd not yet seen the inside of the Nelson farmhouse. And I wanted to.

Chapter Fifteen

SLOANE

Saturday, August 16, 2025, 11:00 p.m.

I retraced my journey back to the farmhouse. I was careful not to take the turnoff toward the Nelson property, just in case Grant was tailing me. I drove an additional two miles down the road, and when I was sure no one was behind me, I made a U-turn. As I approached the farm entrance, I cut my headlights. Moonlight dripped on the driveway as I drove toward the house.

I parked off to the side under the drooping branches of an overgrown oak tree. I reached in my glove box past the gun for a small lockpicking kit I always carried.

Out of the car, I didn't approach the front door but walked through thick brush and tall grass ringing the house. Sliding on the gloves, I brushed my hips past grass and shrubs as I walked. Thorns grabbed at the leather of my gloves.

Up the back stairs, I tugged on a metal screened door and braced it with my backside. I pulled out my lockpick. The lock was old and rusted, and it took less than thirty seconds to open it. I tucked the picks back in the case. I'd learned long ago to put my equipment back in place, so I didn't lose track of anything. Once, an owner had startled me. I'd dropped my pick. I'd been forced to leave it behind as I dashed out the back door as the woman shouted at me.

Colton had not chosen this farm site randomly. He'd built a relationship with the owner, Harriet Nelson, over several years. She'd say later how charming he was, how much he reminded her of her grandson, and how creative his ideas were. I wasn't sure if that grandson was Grant or someone else. Grant always struck me as the straight-and-narrow kind of guy. He was the type who worked two jobs to put himself through college and helped his mother on weekends.

When Colton had asked about using Mrs. Nelson's farmland, she'd agreed. He'd promised to leave the land as he found it, and if she thought he was like Grant, she assumed he would. But Colton had left her with devastation and notoriety that followed her for years.

The kitchen was frozen in time. The yellow plaid wallpaper, a small square Frigidaire, a propane stove, and a cracked tan linoleum floor dated to the '60s. The counters had once been wiped clean but now were covered in a thick coat of dust. I opened several cabinets. They were empty except for mouse droppings.

On the refrigerator was a cherry-shaped magnet holding up a faded picture. The edges curled in slightly. The image featured five smiling boys. All were in their early to mid teens. Their bodies were tanned, and their toned arms wrapped around one another, forming a chain. This was what a normal kid in an ordinary childhood looked like.

The shot had been taken in the field outside. And if I wasn't mistaken, Grant was the tallest boy in the center. He must have been about fourteen or fifteen. I removed the picture, sticky and brittle, and glanced at the back. The faded date read "May 1994." Grant had been at the farm shortly before the festival. I snapped an image of the picture and replaced it.

I moved into the living room. The two couches, coffee table, and lamps were covered in plastic. A mirror on a wall caught my reflection, and I realized how out of place I looked.

Up the small staircase, I stepped into the bedroom that faced the concert site. Mrs. Nelson had left her farm during the festival and gone to visit her sister. From this window, she would've had a clear view of a large toolshed as well as the entire venue. I tried to imagine the crowds crushing toward the stage as they danced, shouted, and sang.

Colton had insisted he had never returned to this house during the event. But the house or toolshed would have been good places to stash a body for a short time. There were also wells and ravines nearby, all perfect hiding spots for a dead body. Taggart and his volunteers had searched every inch of this farmland. No one found anything.

But I'd always believed the best answers were the simplest.

I moved to the bed and smoothed my hand over the white sheet covering the patchwork quilt. I sat. Springs groaned and squeaked.

My phone rang, cutting through the silence. I glanced at the display: Grant McKenna. I rose, angling my body away from the window.

"Grant," I said.

"Making sure you made it home safe."

"Why?"

"Those back roads can be dangerous."

"I'm fine. Is that the reason you called?"

"You have a reputation for unconventional methods. Wondering what you're up to."

"Nothing exciting."

"I doubt that."

"Thanks for the checkup." I hung up the phone and moved to the windows, peeking between the curtains. I could see my Jeep tucked in the shadows, but there was no sign of Grant.

A surge of excitement rushed my system. The possibility of discovery always made treks like these interesting. Instead of hurrying outside to my Jeep, I lingered by the window, waiting, watching.

As silence settled around me and the darkness calmed my heightened nerves, I grew bored. Down the stairs, I walked through the kitchen and left through the back door, taking the time to lock it. Inside my Jeep, I started the engine. I didn't turn on the headlights until I reached the main road.

Chapter Sixteen

CJ Taggart

Saturday, May 21, 1994, 1:00 a.m.
7 Hours Into

The rain had stopped, and the air had warmed. The mud was thick, and most of the concertgoers were soaked to the bone. Drier air sent a sudden rush of warmth through the crowd. One of the last bands took the stage, and people who had been weary and worn down perked up. The first electric guitar chord telegraphed heavy metal. The lead singer's deep, gravelly voice blended with pulsing guitar riffs that breathed life into the crowd.

Taggart spotted a man pulling a woman through the crowd. She tugged against his grip, digging her heels in as she tripped forward. Fatigue pulsed through Taggart's body as he caught up to the couple. "What's going on?"

The man pretended not to hear. The woman yanked against his grip.

"Let her go," Taggart shouted.

The man's jaw was set, but the tendons in his arm slackened. The woman slipped free, turned, and pushed through the crowd. The mass of humans swallowed her whole. Taggart motioned for the man to move to the edge of the crowd as the crush of bodies pressed against him. The man pivoted and melted into the crowd.

Taggart didn't go after him. There'd been a thousand moments like this over the course of the night, and no doubt there were dozens of women he hadn't saved. This entire event was a cluster, and the best he could do was save who he could as he counted the minutes to sunrise.

A long line stretched from the burger stand, and a few folks in line were shouting for service. He strode toward the tent and found no one behind the counter. Piles of burgers wrapped and ready to sell, and the griddle was still hot.

Buddy stood at the till, dishing out cash as another man shouted an order at him. He grabbed two burgers and tossed them on the table. There was no sign of Patty.

Taggart moved around the table past Buddy, searching for Patty. He half expected to see her lying on the ground from exhaustion. But she wasn't in the tent.

He turned to Buddy, who was serving a young woman with damp dark hair and a soaked Grateful Dead T-shirt. "What happened? Where's Patty?"

Buddy didn't glance back. "She took a break an hour ago. I want to go look for her, but I can't get away. The line is endless."

"Which direction did she go?"

"Toward the toilets by the woods."

"Can I get a burger?" another girl shouted.

He'd known Patty two weeks, but each time he'd seen her in the diner, she was hustling. Always had a smile on her face and seemed to take her responsibilities seriously.

"She sure isn't going to get paid for the burgers I sold," Buddy grumbled.

The revenue from this stand was money in her pocket. "I'll go look for her."

When the next person stepped up to the stand, Buddy held out a burger. "That would be great. I need her back here."

Taggart glanced at the supply of burgers. They were dwindling. Buddy and Patty had planned for five hundred people at the festival. But there'd been at least two to three thousand. When the burgers were gone, the grumbling, cold, wet, tired people would grow more restless.

Deputy Paxton pushed through the crowd. Dark circles hung under his eyes. He was breathless when he said, "This can't end fast enough."

"No, it cannot," Taggart said.

"Where's Patty?" Paxton asked.

"Last seen headed to the latrines about an hour ago."

"That's not like her," Paxton said.

"No, it's not." He could cut the power to the stage and order the band to wrap. But the pent-up energy of the masses could ignite into a riot if they didn't keep the music going. Wet, cold, hungry. This crowd was ready to erupt. But the band did need to slow its pace and bring the energy down. "Hang out here for a few minutes and contact me if Patty shows up."

He shoved his way through the crowd, past wet, sweaty bodies that smelled of pot, booze, and desperation. When he made it to the side of the stage, he caught the band manager's attention. "I need to talk to Rafe Colton. Is he up there?"

"He got back a few minutes ago. He's on the east side of the stage."

Taggart ducked under the security chain, then walked around the stage and up a back staircase. The music slammed his head as he stepped over cords and black travel cases.

He spotted Colton standing off to the right, rocking his body. He didn't bother to strike up a conversation but grabbed Colton by the arm and pulled him toward the exit. Colton's grin vanished, but he followed Taggart off the stage and to a quieter spot.

"Hey, man, are you okay? What's going on?" Colton asked.

"You need to order this band to slow its roll. The crowd is getting too amped up," Taggart said.

"But the guys are in the flow. They're hitting their stride, and the people are loving it."

"Tell the band to wind it down."

"Why? This crazy music is why we're all here."

"The people out there are strung tight. It won't take much to make them snap."

"Man, I've done events like this before." He grinned and laid his hand on Taggart's shoulder. "They are amped, but trust me, it's going to be fine."

Taggart glanced at Colton's hand, streaked with red scratches. "Tell the band to wind it down or I'm cutting the electricity to the entire area."

Colton lowered his hand. "And what will happen if you do that? That mob will get angry."

"It's bedlam either way. I don't care if it's now or an hour from now. Ramp it down."

Colton shook his head. "I'll lose money if we stop now. Christ, can you imagine the complaints and lawsuits. I'll breach my contract with the town."

Taggart faced the stage and searched for the cables connected to a generator. He wasn't sure which to pull, but he'd yank them all until the music stopped.

Hands landed on his shoulders, and his fingers balled into a fist as he turned toward Colton's contrite expression. He was ready to beat the piss out of the man. He'd lose his job, but right now he didn't care.

Colton held up his hands. "I'll talk to the band."

The veins in Taggart's neck bulged. He clenched his fists. "Do it now."

Colton climbed up on the stage and spoke to the manager. Immediately, the two began arguing as Colton pointed toward Taggart. It didn't take sound to hear the string of curses. But the manager held up his hand. When the band reached the end of the song, he moved onstage and spoke to the lead singer and guitarist.

No one in the band looked happy, and Taggart knew he'd catch hell for this. The guitarist strummed his chords slower and softer, and the drummer soon joined him. Boos and shouts rose from the crowd as fists pumped, but the lead singer grabbed the mic and told an off-color joke to the crowd. Hints of laughter rumbled over the masses. The energy held steady.

The band members looked at each other but kept playing. Taggart climbed up on the stage, watching the crowd. The slower music had the opposite effect. It triggered waves of restless energy.

The singer, sensing the negative shift, picked up the tempo of his song. His band joined him, and the energy rose. The new version of the song teetered between heavy metal and the attempted ballad. Taggart hoped they'd found a shaky balance. He needed five more hours, and then the sun would rise and this nightmare would end.

At the edge of the crowd, the flickers of the first flames caught in a pile of trash. The red haze rose. By the time Taggart was off the stage and pushing toward the fire, it had jumped to the undergrowth.

Chapter Seventeen

Sloane

Sunday, August 17, 2025, 1:00 a.m.

When I reached the cabin, my body was drained of the energy that had been snapping through me for days. I stepped through the front door, switched on the lamp, which spit out enough light to be annoying. I dropped my pack in a chair, made my way to the kitchen, and filled a mason jar with water.

Tomorrow I'd track down the family of Debra Jackson, known as "Victim #3" by the media.

I lowered into Taggart's recliner, pulled the handle on the side, and raised the footrest. The chair groaned as I leaned back and closed my eyes.

I wasn't sure how long I had slept when I heard a loud thud. Something had hit the side of the cabin. I startled upright and blinked, staring into the shadows and then out the windows. I reached for my gun and realized I'd left it in the Jeep. Stupid. I rose and moved toward the front door. I unlatched it and looked outside. Lying on the porch was a baseball-size rock. Whoever had hurled it had taken a chunk out of the wood siding.

I'd not drawn the curtains when I'd arrived back, giving whoever was in the woods a chance to look inside. I'd left the light on. I'd been in a display case. Off-the-grid places like this were ideal for anarchists, meth dealers, and brothers like Zeke and Sammy Crawford, who didn't like the government.

I picked up the rock and hefted it in my hand. It was heavy, and whoever had tossed it had a serious arm. I crossed to the Jeep. I was relieved to find my gun in the glove box. "Hey, whoever is out there. I'm doing my thing here. I don't want trouble. And I sure don't care about what you're doing."

Wind teased the trees and an owl hooted. I waited, tightening my fingers around the gun's grip. My heartbeat slowed. Rock in hand, I went back inside and locked the door.

Tempting as it was to close the curtains, I didn't. I moved to the kitchen and glanced at an almost accurate stove clock. Three o'clock in the morning. This was the in-between time. Too early to get up, not enough time to fall back to sleep. I had the choice of ninety extra minutes of bad sleep or running out of steam later today. I set up the coffeepot and pressed the brew button.

I peed, showered, and put on clean clothes that didn't smell like field dirt, a smoky bar, or an old lady's home.

After I drained the hot water from the shower, I toweled off and dressed. With no Wi-Fi or cell service, I couldn't check comments on my latest article, now live on *The Washington Post*'s website.

In *The Post*'s coverage of Susie Malone's cold case, I'd pointed out the cops had a few suspects. But they had never been able to prove that their number one man, a local pastor of a two-thousand-person church, had killed the girl.

When I'd interviewed the chief detective, Bob Watson, he was convinced the pastor was the killer. But there'd been witnesses from his church who'd testified that he'd been with them at the time the girl vanished from an evening bike ride.

"If you're so convinced, why don't you do something?" I demanded of Bob.

Anger circled around, suffocating me. Susie's parents were divorced and both worked full time. She didn't have many friends but liked to ride her bike.

Bob glanced at a thirty-year-old Timex watch. He cleared his throat, as if unclogging a persistent anger that was forever lodged in him. He met my gaze. "I did all that the law would allow."

I stared into blue, watery eyes encircled by deep wrinkles. "What are things you can't do?" I asked.

He tapped his watch as his jaw tightened. "I can't follow him because that's stalking. I can't wiretap his house or phones. I can't beat a confession out of him."

"Beaten confessions are often false. And I only care about the truth."

My frankness softened the hard lines around his mouth. "I gave up on court a long time ago."

Phone tapping sounded cumbersome. But stalking the good pastor or breaking into his home was my wheelhouse. If there was evidence, I would find it. "Let me see what I can do, Bob."

"Take your best shot."

It took me six months of following the pastor, who'd established a very routine schedule. To keep tabs on him when I had another article to write, I placed a tracker on his car. At the six-week mark, I was growing impatient. The guy did nothing out of the ordinary. We could keep this up for years, but I didn't have the patience to play that long. I called Bob and asked if he could contact the pastor and tell him a new investigative team was looking into the case. Bob was more than happy to comply.

Two days later the pastor broke his routine and, after an evening prayer session, drove sixty miles to a small town near his. Following him that far was tricky, and several times I veered off and caught up to him a few miles later.

He parked at a storage facility and hurried inside the building. He was inside for almost an hour, and when he emerged, he was smiling.

Of course, the pastor's name was not on any lease agreement with any storage unit. I tugged on rubber gloves and proceeded to break into and search the twenty storage units. Number 19 was the winner. The unit was bare except for a chair and a plastic storage box in the back. In the box, I found mementos, including a charm bracelet, a necklace, and a set of young girl's panties. Guys like the pastor liked to keep trinkets reminding them of their deeds. I could picture the pastor laying out each item, sitting in the chair, and masturbating.

I took pictures of it all and then put each item back exactly how I'd found them. On the way out, I opened storage unit number 20 for giggles and swiped an empty travel bag that looked like it could come in handy. Then I posted a camera outside to monitor the entrance for me.

Two days later, Bob and I met for coffee at a diner a mile from the storage unit. "Do you want a few incriminating tips, or do you want it straight?"

Bob raised his coffee cup to his lips, hesitating before he said, "We're both adults here. Serve it up."

"The Blue Mountain Storage Facility is one mile from here. You'll like what you find in unit number 19."

He didn't admonish me or recite some law-and-order speech. "Okay."

"Tonight, there's going to be a wicked fire in unit number 18. And don't worry, it's full of bad patio furniture and a few nasty white couches. The owner will be grateful."

Bob sipped his coffee, nodding. "So close to number 19, the fire department will have to open 19 in case the fire has spread."

"That would be my play."

He set his cup down and checked his watch. "Okay."

"I want an exclusive interview."

"You got it."

Fast-forward a year and the pastor was in jail, three cold case murders had been closed, and my article was now live. The headline was way larger than my name, which was okay because it was an excellent hook. **Pedophile Pastor Pleads.** Even before the article had dropped, many of the pastor's parishioners had sent threatening emails—they didn't like my questioning the faith of their spiritual leader. A few had mentioned biblical retribution.

I turned from the window. Woodland snoopers or zealots—it didn't matter. "Bring it."

I filled a large mug to the brim. I raised the cup to my lips and sipped. For whatever reason, the java still wasn't agreeing with me.

From my file box, I removed the manila folder for Debra Jackson. She'd been eighteen when she'd vanished. Debra, like Patty, had lived locally. She'd worked at a dry cleaner. She was a straight A high school student and lived in a trailer a few doors down from Patty after her mother had thrown her out of the family home.

Debra had a younger sister, Marsha Sullivan, who now lived in Roanoke, about an hour away. I wasn't crazy about another drive but counted myself lucky that Marsha had agreed to see me.

I spent the next couple of hours reading case notes on Debra. The more I read, the more I realized she'd have been right at home on Team Outcast.

Chapter Eighteen

SLOANE

Sunday, August 17, 2025, 2:00 p.m.

Marsha Sullivan was in her garden yanking weeds when I pulled into her driveway. The house was a brick rancher with a long, narrow porch that stretched across the front. Baskets filled with ferns dangled as a rocker dipped back and forth as if someone had just risen out of it.

I shifted my sunglasses to the top of my head and grabbed my notebook and pencil. I'd spoken to Marsha a few days ago and told her about my project. It had taken some convincing to get her to agree to see me.

"Ms. Sullivan?"

She pressed the back of a garden-gloved hand to her forehead and rose. When she faced me, it took me a moment to determine if I had the right person. This woman, with graying hair and shoulders ripe with fatigue, didn't look like the outraged teenager who'd advocated for the victims at the trial thirty-one years ago.

I'd read several profiles on Marsha. Almost all the headlines sounded something like, **"Where Are Our Girls?"**

"I'm Marsha Sullivan. And you must be Sloane Grayson."

I extended my hand, finding a small smile and doing my best to appear approachable. "Thank you for seeing me."

Sweat glistened on her brow as she nodded for me to follow her to the porch. On a small table between the two rockers were a pitcher of lemonade and two glasses. "I'm surprised. No one talks about the festival anymore or the girls."

"That's why I'm writing about it."

"I heard your mother was Patty Reed?"

News traveled fast. "That's right." We both sat, and she filled two glasses with lemonade.

"You look like her." She handed me a glass.

"You knew my mother?"

"We weren't friends, but I saw her at the diner when I came in for breakfast before school. My mother wasn't a morning person and didn't like cooking breakfast. I also saw her with you at the trailer park. I think you were crying."

"Sounds like me."

"Babies cry."

Sara used to complain I took crying to a new level. "What was Patty like?" My curiosity for my mother was a constant itch I'd never been able to scratch.

"Always had a smile on her face. She was a year older than Debra, and she was the one that encouraged Debra to leave home."

Patty had left her mother's home when she'd started dating Larry. When my mother got pregnant, my grandmother had forbidden her to see Larry again. Patty had refused. But as soon as Larry found out about me, he'd cut ties. My sweet, loyal mother had gotten herself pregnant by a psychopath who would slaughter three random people in a bar fight two years later.

Larry's genes swam in my body, and my grandmother blamed all my quirks on him. I never hurt anyone like Larry had, unless they attacked a member of Team Outcast first. And even then, my revenge was nothing super violent. I wasn't the sweet, kind, or vulnerable girl my mother had been. Nor was I a crazed psychopath like my father. I was somewhere in between.

"Why did Debra move out?" I asked.

"My mother married a guy who could be a real jerk. I went along to get along, but not Debra. She didn't like Frank and never held back. Mom didn't want to lose Frank, so she told Debra to move out. And she did."

"How long did she live on her own?"

"Ten months." As she sipped her lemonade, the muscles of her neck moved as if her throat hurt. "When she left the house, it all changed. Mom got weirder and Frank meaner. I spent my time hiding at friends' homes or my bedroom."

"Did you see Debra often?"

"At first yes. I'd stop by the dry cleaner's after school. I'd bring us peanut butter and jelly sandwiches, and we'd talk. It was nice."

"But that changed?"

"She got busy. Supporting herself, applying to colleges, and trying to be a teenager took all her time."

"Debra dated a guy named Kevin, right?" Stored details from Taggart's case notes rushed to the front of my brain.

"Kevin Pascal." She set the glass down and rolled her shoulders as if shedding an old grudge.

"I'm assuming he wasn't Prince Charming."

"He wasn't bad. He was attractive. Bought her flowers. Even flirted with me in a way that made me feel special."

"Why did she break up with him?"

"Kevin didn't like her spending so much free time on schoolwork. He got annoyed when she talked about going to college. He wanted a simple hometown girl who wouldn't achieve much and thought the sun rose and set around him."

"A witness testified that Debra and Kevin showed up at the concert together." I didn't need to reference my notes. "He was wearing his security guard uniform. They were seen going their separate ways."

"She was meeting me at the festival. But her boss told her she had to close the store at the last minute. She called and said she'd get there when she could. I went ahead with friends. Kevin happened by the dry cleaner's and offered her a ride."

"Nice guy."

"He liked to be the knight in shining armor." A halting breath filled her lungs.

"You made it your business later to talk to everyone who saw Debra at the festival."

"I did. I wanted to account for every second. I wanted to find her. But piecing together the evening was easier said than done. Booze, crowds, and chaos swallowed up my memory."

The value of original sources could never be underestimated. "What didn't you tell Taggart that you thought wasn't important at the time?"

She drew in a steadying breath as if still carrying a weight. "I hooked up with Kevin at the festival."

That was a new tidbit that had never been discussed. "Can you expand on that?" I made sure she saw no judgment. I didn't care that she'd slept with her sister's ex. What I cared about was how new information would get me to my goal.

She held my gaze for a moment and then said, "I was near the stage, off to the side. He saw me and came over and said hi. I was wasted. And Kevin was Kevin, always charming. He took my hand in his and asked if we could go to a quieter place to talk. He'd missed seeing me."

Kevin had seen an opportunity and taken it. "And?"

"We walked away from the crowds toward the farmhouse."

"Did you go inside?"

"There was a large shed in the backyard."

I'd stared at that shed from the kitchen window when I'd been in the house last night. "I've seen the pictures of it."

"The shed wasn't as bad as anyone would think. Or I was too drunk to notice." She ran fingers through her graying hair. "He was gentle. Maybe because he knew me or because I was young. It wasn't terrible."

But he'd known she was young and drunk. She was Debra's little sister. He'd taken advantage. "What happened after?"

"He said he had to get back to work. I stayed in the shed and lay there for a while. Then I went back to the concert."

"I don't mean to be weird, but I'm going to ask indelicate questions."

"It's okay."

"Did he talk while having sex?"

"He called me Debra once. Later, after she was gone, I thought back on that and wondered why."

"No violence?"

"It was uncomfortable, but I didn't know what I was doing."

She might not have been a virgin, but she wasn't super experienced. "And you never told this to Taggart?"

"When I sobered up after the festival, it felt like a dream. For a few days, I convinced myself it didn't happen. But you know the harder you try to forget something, the realer it becomes."

"You were at the trial almost every day. The prosecution called Kevin as a witness to establish timelines. Did you two speak before or after the trial?"

"No. I was ashamed, and he was nervous. He sensed he could be a suspect."

"Taggart questioned him hard. But the sheriff couldn't prove Kevin had anything to do with anyone's disappearance."

"Kevin's big crime was that he was a shitty security guard. For all his talk of wanting to be a cop, he was afraid of conflict."

"He failed the police entrance exams twice."

She smiled. "Yeah, he never tested well."

I sipped my lemonade, finding it too sweet for my taste. "This is great. Thank you."

"I like sugar too much."

"It's delicious." To prove it, I took another gulp. "Where's Kevin these days?"

"After the trial, he left the area for over twenty years. And then about ten years ago, he moved back to Dawson. He works as a security guard for the computer company that located here a couple of years ago."

"What's the name of the company?"

"PH Puckett Computers."

"Have you seen Kevin since his return?"

"From a distance. I sometimes check up on him."

Stalking? My kind of girl. "Why?"

"I heard killers sometimes visit spaces that remind them of their victims."

She was right about that. Killers often experienced sexual excitement when they revisited the burial site. "Do you think he killed Debra?"

"I have no proof. But if he wanted to, the concert would've been the perfect place to do it."

"Why kill the other women?"

She shrugged.

"Does Kevin have a favorite place to visit?" I asked.

"No. But he does like to drive at night."

"Any consistent destinations?"

"Every time I've followed, he goes northeast of town. Turns east before reaching the festival site."

"And PH Puckett. When was the Puckett Computer building built?"

"Fifteen years ago. It was a large vacant tract of land in 1994."

"How close to the concert?"

"Ten miles south of the venue and ten miles north of town." She hesitated as pieces of a puzzle connected. "All that land was out of the way thirty-one years ago. Unless you were farming or poking around the old gold mines, there was no reason to go up that way."

"Gold mines?"

"Not really gold. A hundred years ago, some fool thought he'd found gold. It was pyrite."

"Fool's gold."

"Yep. The mines collapsed in on themselves before any of us were born."

"Why does Kevin still return to that area?"

She shook her head. "Do you think Kevin got a job on the very site where the women are buried?"

"Maybe. He wouldn't be the first killer to obsess over unmarked graves. Any other construction that happened after the concert?"

She leaned forward, her eyes sharper with interest. "Sure. Half the town has been built in the last fifteen years. We have a lot of folks moving here to retire. Dawson was voted one of the best retirement communities in the US."

A hidden ravine on the mountaintop was almost as inaccessible as tons of concrete. "Where does Kevin live?"

"Fieldstone Apartments. It's a two-hundred-unit complex outside of Dawson." She recited his address as if it were etched in her heart. "It was built ten years ago."

I scribbled it down. "Do you think Kevin is a killer?"

"I thought Kevin murdered Debra. But then Taggart made his arrest. So I guess I was wrong."

"How well did Kevin know Rafe Colton?"

"I always thought they met at the concert," she said.

"Could they have been working together?" I asked. "I'm convinced Colton had help. I just don't know who."

"Why are you so sure?"

"Colton was popular. His festivals had groupies. He was MIA a few times during the event, but someone could always place him somewhere."

"Several girls testified they were having sex with him in the farmhouse or in a tent."

"I don't think he got off that mountain until sunrise, like everyone else."

"Colton was seen driving his truck off the site about nine on Saturday morning. No place to hide bodies."

"Correct."

She sat back, her gaze a mixture of hope and fear. "I want you to find them."

"I'm doing my best."

"If you need anything, give me a call. I don't mind creating a little trouble."

"I'll let you know." Marsha's passion for this case, her history with Kevin, and her guilt made her an unreliable helper. She was too connected. So was I, but I wasn't emotionally attached like she was.

"What do you think the chances are?"

"For finding the girls? I'm not sure. I'm doing my best to shake a lot of bushes. That tends to make people nervous. And nervous people make mistakes."

"Do me a favor and make Kevin nervous."

I couldn't resist a smile. "He's on my list."

Fieldstone Apartments was located twelve miles outside of Dawson. When I parked in a visitor parking lot, I was struck by how ordinary the complex looked. Its light-brown siding and faux brick entrances all created a welcoming mountain-community vibe. If I were into signing leases and stability, I'd give it a second look. But I wasn't. My Jeep was about as permanent as it got.

I parked at the end of the lot, several buildings away from Kevin's section. I sat for ten minutes, watching the flow of people in and out of the parking lot. This time of day, it was quiet. Most people were still at work.

Out of my car, I wasn't nervous or rushed. I moved down the sidewalk, not worried about who saw me. Later people might remember seeing a woman with dark hair. Maybe they'd remember a blue shirt, but most eyewitnesses had terrible recall. Best case, most would remember I was female, but they'd argue if I was short or tall, young or old.

I crossed the lot toward the entrance to his building. His apartment was located on the first floor, which was good. If I had to leave by a balcony or window, I could escape without risking a broken bone.

From my back pocket I pulled my lockpicking kit. One. Two. Three. *Click.* I pocketed the set and opened the door. I listened for signs that I wasn't alone. Feet hit the floor, and I tensed as I hovered by the door. Out of the bedroom came a mixed-breed dog that looked part lab and shepherd. He wagged his tail and, head bowed, moved toward me.

I knelt. "Hey, guy."

I scratched him behind the ears. "You're such a good dog."

People, I could take or leave, but I had a softness for animals. When I was growing up, my grandmother hadn't allowed pets in the house, but the neighbors had a collie named Vince. I'd often hopped the fence and slipped into my neighbors' house. I'd grab fresh luncheon meat from the refrigerator. I'd sit in the kitchen and share it with Vince.

"So, what do I need to look for?" I asked the dog. "Does Kevin have any trinkets?" The dog nudged my hand, so I kept rubbing. I moved to the refrigerator, found a container with cooked hamburger. Removing the top, I set it on the floor for the pup.

The dog dropped his nose into the bowl, gobbling the contents.

I moved down the hallway to the unit's one bedroom. Kevin kept his place clean and organized. The bed was made, and the pillows fluffed. The coins on his dresser were arranged in a neat pile. Aftershave and a brush stood at right angles to each other.

The bathroom was as clean. The sink sparkled, his toothbrush stood upright in a cup, and the towels were hung.

I opened the medicine cabinet. It contained aspirin, vitamins, a prescription for a mood stabilizer, and sunscreen.

Taggart's records had noted that Kevin had been diagnosed with mood swings before the women vanished. He'd broken up with Debra and had gotten into a fight with a cop. The incident had landed him in jail for sixty days. He'd been released two weeks before the concert. Woodward shouldn't have hired him, but they'd been short-staffed when Colton made the Friday morning call for security. Turned out Colton had never finalized festival security details with them.

I closed the cabinet and moved to the living room. The dog had eaten the meat and was now licking the container's corners.

I sat on a leather sofa and glanced at the three piles of magazines lined side by side. One pile contained guns and ammo magazines, the next news, and the last porn.

"Charming, Kevin."

I opened the end table drawers and searched a small desk nudged into a corner. Nothing here that piqued my interest. The dog joined me, and I rubbed his head. I filled his water bowl, and as he drank, I replaced the top on the meat container and put it back in the refrigerator.

I was tempted to push the magazines on the floor, but Kevin might blame the dog. Instead, I turned each pile 180 degrees, so their mastheads faced away from the couch. The magazines, along with the missing meat, would catch Kevin's attention.

On the faux mantel, I spotted a framed picture. I rose and crossed to it and studied the image. It was a decades-old picture of Kevin and Debra. She wore a blue sundress, and he had donned his security guard uniform. In the background was the Mountain Music Festival banner. It would have been one of the last images taken of Debra.

"Why hang on to this?"

Did he still mourn Debra? Or was the picture a token of the night? Mementos. Sometimes they linked to sexual stimulation and satisfaction.

I removed the picture from the frame and glanced at the back. Someone had scribbled "1994" in the upper right-hand corner. I took several pictures with my phone before replacing the image in the frame. Using the hem of my T-shirt, I wiped my fingerprints from the frame and glass.

I scratched the dog on the head, left through the front door, and locked it behind me. I moved across the lot. As I sat in my car, my phone rang. Grant's name flashed on the screen. His timing was unsettling.

"Hello, Grant."

"Sloane. What are you up to?"

I started the car's engine. "Breaking and entering. How about you?"

He chuckled. "Really?"

"Of course."

"Breaking and entering and I guess trespassing, too. Any other infractions?"

I laughed. "A few. Why the call?"

"I read your article. I called Bob Watson and congratulated him on the arrest. He speaks well of you."

"How's Bob? I like him." I had a genuine affection for a cop who never gave up.

"Doing well. Sends his regards. Find anything against Colton?"

I glanced up at Kevin's apartment building. "Still trying to figure out if a second person was involved."

"If you had to bet on that?"

"I'd say yes."

"How about dinner?" he asked.

Kevin's truck pulled into the parking lot. He parked in front of his unit. Out of the truck, he moved to the bank of post office boxes. He grabbed his mail and trotted to his apartment. Seconds later he appeared with his dog. The dog walked at his side, staying in step with Kevin. His tail wasn't wagging. Kevin liked discipline more than the dog did.

Kevin couldn't have noticed the magazines or missing meat yet. I wished I could be around to see the confusion on his face. "I can always eat," I said.

"Meet me in town at the Bistro at seven."

As Kevin vanished back into his building with the dog, I put my Jeep in drive. The wheels rolled, and I angled the car toward the exit.

"How are you doing?" Grant asked.

His concern was perplexing. "I'm fine. Why do you ask?"

"One of the victims was your mother."

I pulled off the road and into a small parking lot. A glance in the rearview mirror told me no one was behind me. "I'm dealing just fine."

"I used to say that when I worked a tough case."

"I suspect you're nicer than me," I said.

He chuckled. "See you at seven?"

"Looking forward to it." I hung up and tossed the phone in my console.

Behind me an engine rumbled. My rearview mirror caught Kevin's truck roaring down the road. I switched on my dash cam and then ducked down until I heard his car whoosh past. I counted to three and then rose. Jeep in gear, I drove. And when his truck crested a hill, I hung back, far enough away not to be seen and close enough to catch the top of his cab on each hill.

Kevin crossed over the hill and slowed. To the right was an old barn. It was gray, weathered, and falling in on itself. It was at least a hundred years old. As he slowed toward a stop sign, I pulled off to the side of the road. He lingered at the sign, taking time to look right and then left. There was no traffic coming from either direction, but still he paused. Was he checking his phone? Grabbing a stick of gum or adjusting the radio? I couldn't tell, but I made a note of the spot.

He was on his way soon, and anyone who wasn't watching him wouldn't have noticed the hesitation. Traffic picked up on the next stretch, allowing me to fall back. The rest of the route was straight road and fed into the Puckett parking lot.

I drove past the gate and continued west. When I approached a turnaround, I pulled off and angled my Jeep back to where I'd been. I retraced Kevin's trip, and when I reached the stop sign and the old barn, I parked on the side of the road. I got out of my Jeep.

I crossed the road and walked up to a split rail fence. I hopped it and moved into the field. This location was ten miles from the Nelson farm. It was close enough for convenience's sake but not so close that anyone moving around here would be noticed. A van could've fit in the barn. With the cover of shiplap and beams, anyone could have off-loaded the bodies. They could have been stored here temporarily or buried in the nearby woods. The van could've slipped away after dark unnoticed. This area hadn't been covered in the searches.

I stood in the center of the barn, staring up at the softening sunlight trickling through open patches in the roof. I closed my eyes and listened. I half hoped someone would reach beyond the veil and tell me something important. Of course, they did not. I'd found the dead mutinously silent. It would be up to me to force the living to speak.

Beams above creaked and groaned as the wind whistled through the barn rafters.

I knelt and ran fingertips over the soft soil. Thirty-one years ago, there might have been tire tracks from the van. But those remnants were long gone.

Colton had been convicted of four murders. There'd been witnesses who'd seen him talking to the victims, but there'd been no red flags. But late into the evening, someone had lured, drugged, or coerced the women away from the crowds. None had ever been seen again. The commonwealth's attorney argued Colton had been the person who'd enticed the women into the shadows and murdered them.

But kidnapping healthy, young women required time and energy. Colton had vanished for a few hours, but taking four women in that time frame would've been tough.

And Colton left the site in a vehicle that wasn't big enough to store four bodies. I believed someone, like a devoted groupie, had helped him transport the victims off the festival site. Any van or truck leaving during the mass exodus would have blended into the parade of vehicles rolling down the mountain.

Kevin had picked up Debra at her dry-cleaning shop about 10:00 p.m. on Friday night. The grainy old security film showed Debra smiling when she opened the shop door. Kevin wasn't wearing his security guard uniform but jeans and a flannel shirt. He'd leaned in for a kiss, and she'd shifted so his lips landed on her cheek. He'd looked young and very strong. She'd handed him a dry-cleaning order, and he'd stepped behind a changing curtain. He emerged in his uniform.

The couple had been in the dry cleaner's for ten minutes. Then Debra unhooked a key from her ring, hid her purse behind the counter, and exited the front door. She'd locked the door and tucked the key behind the mailbox. After she'd climbed into his 1980 Ford truck with a camper top, they'd left for the festival.

The truck's back windows had been covered with interior curtains. Kevin said that was because he often took the truck camping, and he liked his privacy. The truck's bed would have been big enough to transport four bodies. But Taggart had searched Kevin's freshly washed truck. Kevin said he liked a super-clean truck and detailed it a couple of times a week. The sheriff had had a state forensic team comb the cab and bed for evidence. There'd been no signs of the victims' blood, hair, or clothing.

Even the best detail job didn't clean the cracks and crevices, where bodily fluids could drip, trickle, and slide. Even single hair fibers could attach to the underside of a seat or a floor mat.

My gaze scanned the tall grass in the field. I'd have to double-check Taggart's notes, but I was certain this area had not been combed extensively.

Many of the 1994 searches had focused on the land north of the festival. The primary tipster had been Hazel Miller. She'd been in her eighties. She'd called after Taggart's press conference. She'd sworn she'd seen a shadowy figure digging a hole in her fallow field. She was certain that had to be bodies.

Taggart and his group of growing volunteers had searched the north side of the mountain as Ms. Miller had indicated. They'd found graves, but they'd been for the remains of two deer poached out of season. When Taggart had explained to Ms. Miller what he'd found, she'd not been convinced. And when the crowds and attention drifted away from her, she'd called Taggart again. At least a dozen more times. A second, smaller crew was dispatched, but this time they found nothing.

Despite Ms. Miller's mistakes, her calls had biased everyone. All eyes tended to look north. No one had searched this far south.

Nothing in the barn caught my attention. Maybe Kevin had just stopped to stretch his shoulders or scratch his balls. Or maybe he was savoring handiwork that had gone unnoticed for thirty-one years.

Chapter Nineteen

CJ Taggart

Saturday, May 21, 1994, 6:00 a.m.
Sunrise

Taggart stared at the scorched edges of the field. It had taken him fifteen minutes to stomp out the blaze.

The concertgoers were trickling out of the muddy, ruined field. The line of cars and vans stretched at least a mile. Those who'd secured parking spots down the mountain and left had gotten out. But the rest at the top were trapped in a bottleneck that would take hours to unwind.

He looked toward the food tent. Buddy was packing up what little supplies remained. There was still no sign of Patty.

"Buddy, have you seen Patty?" Taggart asked.

"No. I think she's flaked on me."

Taggart glanced at overturned tables. The griddle that had run cold when the propane went dry hours ago. The cashbox lay on the ground, now dented and muddy. A few scattered coins lay beside it, but all the bills were gone. "Why would she do that?"

"She's pissed at me." Dark circles smudged under Buddy's eyes.

"Are you sure she didn't have an emergency?"

"Hell if I know. I'll ask her when she shows up at work on Monday. Then I'm going to fire her."

Taggart's gaze lingered on the carnage inside the tent. A square shape caught his attention, and he moved toward it. From the muck he pulled out an ID badge. It belonged to Patty Reed. He smoothed the dirt from her smiling face. "You're not worried about her? She could be hurt."

"She's not hurt. She's a scrapper. She decided she needed a break. I bet she thinks she's teaching me a lesson."

"Why would she do that?"

"We had an argument yesterday morning. She wanted a raise, and I said no. I tried to tell her the diner is barely getting by, but she didn't believe me."

"You sound pretty sure about her."

"I know her well, if you know what I mean. She's been moody. Always going out of her way to pick a fight with me."

"Why is that?"

"Who knows? Chicks, right?"

"Are you sleeping with her?"

Buddy's face flushed. "How does that matter?"

"I'll take that as a yes."

"It's not like that. I asked her to marry me."

"And you had a fight."

"I love her, man."

Taggart knew how thin the line between love and rage could be. "Buddy, tell Patty to give me a call when she shows up."

"Yeah, sure."

Taggart surveyed the field littered with beer cans, trash, and discarded clothes. Under the oak tree, two young men were slumped forward. Their eyes were closed and their mouths open. He walked up to the teenagers and nudged each with his muddied boot. When neither responded, he kicked them in the feet. The first was a redhead with a sunburned face. The other was covered in mud.

"Boys, get up. Time to go home. Party is over."

The young men looked up at him. Each blinked slowly and yawned. The redhead sniffed and stood. He swayed and reached for the tree for balance.

The second kid stood. He looked at his body. "What happened?"

"I don't know," the redhead said.

"Start moving toward the exit," Taggart said. "Time to return to the real world."

Taggart watched them stumble toward the mountain road. He'd made a few dumb moves when he was that age. Shit. He was lucky to be alive.

A loud bang pulled his attention toward the stage. A boom that held the lights had fallen and hit the stage hard. He hurried toward the crash. He didn't release his breath until he confirmed no one had been crushed. He wanted to think that no one had been hurt all night. But he couldn't claim that until everyone had left and he'd searched the property and the woods around it.

Colton stood by the stage. He didn't look upset, stressed, or tired as the crew dismantled the boom. He looked relaxed, given the carnage around him.

Taggart walked up to Colton. "The rest of your security team never arrived."

Rafe looked shocked. "The company screwed me. I paid for twenty guys. I got three."

Taggart remembered Kevin. And he'd seen the two other guards from a distance after midnight. "It was chaos last night."

"Everyone was rocking out and having a great time. Crazy success, wasn't it?"

Police reports would start rolling in today. He almost didn't want to return to the office. Colton had better have a good attorney. "And your cleanup crews?"

"On the way, Sheriff. They radioed me about fifteen minutes ago." Behind him, a truck pulled a white trailer toward the fire road that snaked up the back side of the property.

"Do you have any reported injuries?" Taggart asked.

"Just the usual at the first aid tent. That's all been shut down, and those people have been shuttled off the mountain. Relax, Sheriff, the festival went off without a hitch."

Taggart shook his head. "You've destroyed the field."

"The rain was heavier than I expected. Christ, the mud was incredible, wasn't it?"

Taggart glanced at his own coated boots. His uniform was wet and splashed with muck. "Make sure you answer your phone if I call. It'll be a miracle if there are no police reports."

"Hey, I'm easy to find."

If Taggart found a reason to arrest the man, he'd do it. Festival complaints would be snowballing soon. And given Colton's background, he was a flight risk.

"Sheriff?"

He turned. An exhausted Deputy Paxton strode toward him. Dark stubble covered his chin.

"We have a problem," Paxton said.

"What?"

"A girl. In the tent city. She's beat up pretty good. I've cuffed her boyfriend to a tree and called the medics."

Taggart's jaw tightened. He glared at Colton. "Like I said, don't go far."

"I'm at your disposal."

Taggart followed Paxton through the sloppy, sucking mire. Most of the tent city was gone. The remaining abandoned shelters reminded him of deflated, crumpled balloons.

They arrived at a blue tent at the edge of the woods. The boyfriend was handcuffed to a tree. He wore no shirt, and a scruffy beard dusted his chin. His jeans were coated with dried, cracked mud. His feet were bare.

"Would you tell Barney Fife to unlock these cuffs!" the man shouted.

Taggart opened the tent flap and peered in. A young woman lay on her side. She wore a Depot T-shirt that looked a lot like the one Patty had worn. Underwear but no pants. "Ma'am?"

Her legs were covered with bruises. Some looked fresh and others older. "What is your name?" Taggart asked.

"I'm fine," she said. "I just need a minute."

She wasn't okay. And she'd need more than sixty seconds. Taggart softened his tone. "Did your boyfriend hurt you?"

She sniffed as she shook her head. "No. I fell."

Taggart bet she'd told that story to the cops before. "We're sending in medics."

Her eyes widened with panic. "No. I'm fine. I don't need help." She attempted to sit up but winced and lay back down.

"Okay." He didn't know what she'd taken, but she was high. "You don't have to do anything you don't want to. What's your name?"

She relaxed. "Amy."

"Where did you get that T-shirt, Amy?" he asked.

She glanced at the shirt. Confusion cleared. "I found it in the woods."

"You found it?"

"I didn't steal it," Amy insisted.

"Where in the woods?"

"On a tree branch."

"Did you see the woman who was wearing it?"

"No. It was just there."

"Can you let me go?" the boyfriend demanded.

In the military police force, Taggart had seen his share of domestic abuse in the base housing. Those cases left a sour taste in his mouth. A home was supposed to be a safe place.

Taggart straightened and turned to the man handcuffed to the tree. "What's your name?"

The man rattled the cuffs. "Let me go."

Taggart shook his head. "You're in my world now. You answer my questions."

"Let me go!"

Paxton reached in his pockets. "I can't find the key."

Taggart shrugged. "Looks like you're stuck, pal. Now give me your name."

The man rattled the cuffs, scraping the metal against the wet bark. "Billy Walton."

"You have identification?"

"In the tent somewhere or maybe my car."

"Where's your car?"

"Parked on the hill, I think."

"Who is the woman in the tent?" Taggart was exhausted and holding on to his patience was a struggle.

"Amy Wheeler." Billy rubbed the cuffs against the bark as if they'd somehow break. "She's my girlfriend. She got drunk, and some guy tried to take advantage. I saved her. I didn't hurt her."

Taggart had heard a hundred versions of this story before. "Who tried to take her?"

"I don't know. Some guy who was creeping around in the woods. I heard her scream, and I went running. I found her like this."

"And the torn T-shirt?"

"I don't know."

Taggart sensed he was lying, and until Amy could tell him more about the mystery man, Billy would wait it out in jail. "Paxton, uncuff him from the tree, but secure his hands behind his back."

"What the fuck!" Billy shouted.

"I'm arresting you for assault," Taggart said.

"I didn't hurt her. I told you I saved her."

Whatever the truth was, Taggart wasn't hopeful Amy would file charges against Billy. The couple likely operated in a circle of violence that wouldn't end until Amy left or died.

The medics arrived at the tent. As the techs spoke to Amy, Paxton led Billy to the waiting police van. It took another half hour to get the young woman out of the tent. She didn't want to leave, and when they strapped her to a gurney, she screamed.

This wasn't Colton's doing, but he'd set the stage for this disaster. Taggart noticed Colton speaking to a truck driver and jogged over to the vehicle. The driver was Kevin, one of last night's security guards.

"Where's he going?" Taggart demanded.

"He's helping the road crews move the equipment out. I'll be back." Colton nodded toward Billy. "What's the deal with that?"

"Guy says a man tried to hurt his girlfriend."

Colton shook his head. "Guys like that always blame someone else." His brow furrowed. "This festival was supposed to be about peace and love and togetherness."

That would have been the case if he'd had more security. "You didn't get any other complaints of attempted attacks?"

"Nope. But I'll ask the crew if they heard about anything like that." Colton banged the flat of his hand on the top of the truck.

Kevin slipped the gear into first and punched the accelerator. The wheels spun in the mud. He put the truck in reverse, backed up a fraction, and then shifted back into first. He gunned the engine. Tires spun. Mud spit out. He repeated this seesaw back and forth for a couple of minutes until the truck and trailer popped out of the sloppy rut.

Colton stood back, his hands in his pockets. He watched the truck and trailer move toward the fire road. He didn't take his gaze off it until it vanished down the road.

Colton looked pleased with himself. Despite the chaos surrounding him, he was happy. That happiness wasn't going to last. If he'd made money on this event, he'd better hang on to it. The lawsuits were going to eat him alive.

Chapter Twenty

SLOANE

Sunday, August 17, 2025, 5:00 p.m.

Amy Wheeler lived an hour west, near Staunton. When Taggart had found her in the tent, she'd been disoriented. He'd assumed she was high, but she'd been suffering from a concussion. Later, he'd interviewed her in the hospital. But she didn't remember what happened or how she'd ended up with the Depot T-shirt that was later confirmed to have been Patty's.

Amy had broken it off with Billy almost thirty-one years ago. And Billy had died in 2020 of a heart attack. At the time of his death, he'd been high on meth and lying on a lounge chair in his backyard. Bob Marley had been playing on his phone and burgers sizzled on the grill.

Taggart had questioned Amy again about the T-shirt and the man who'd tried to hurt her. She'd never been able to provide specifics. And as other leads had rolled into his office, Amy had been forgotten. No one had interviewed her since.

I hoped thirty-one years had helped Amy's memory.

I pulled up in front of the garden shop located on a rural route. The entrance had a fantasy kind of vibe, with vines snaking over a tall arch. I drove past water features and potted trees toward the large greenhouse.

Out of the car, I surveyed the lush greenery. I liked plants. But they didn't like me. They tended to die when they came into my orbit. I could almost hear the last plant I'd owned screaming for help as I carried it out of the plant shop.

Shifting my sunglasses on top of my head, I crossed the graveled lot into the greenhouse. The woman behind the register had long gray hair tied back with a red bandanna. She wore overalls and a black T-shirt covered in small words. I thought I made out the word *Peace* on one of the sleeves. The last thirty-one years hadn't been so hard on Amy that I couldn't recognize her.

I picked up a plant and studied its delicate flowers. "Don't worry," I whispered. "I'm not buying you."

I moved toward the register. "Hey, can I ask you a question?"

The woman looked up and smiled. "Sure."

"You look like you know plants."

"I own the place."

"How long?"

"Twenty years."

"How delicate is this plant?" I set the plastic pot on the counter.

"Very. It requires watering and the right amount of sun."

"So, if I ignore it for a week or two . . . ?"

She laughed. "It'll die."

I held up my thumbs. "They're both brown."

"We do have cactus plants, but they still need care."

"Do they need water?"

"Sometimes. How about a dream catcher? We have several dozen to choose from."

"Perfect."

She came around the counter. "Let me show you."

I followed her down a narrow path lined with lush, thick foliage. Amy had been an addict and covered in bruises when she'd attended the music festival with Billy. But she'd turned it around.

She stopped at a collection of circular dream catchers hanging from a vine-wrapped pergola. "They're all made locally. I know the artist, and she has good energy."

I grabbed the catcher closest to me. "I like this one."

"We have more if you want to keep looking."

"No. This one will do the trick."

"Okay. That was easy. Let me ring you up."

I followed Amy into the greenhouse and to the register. She rang up the purchase, and I dug my credit card out of my wallet. Fingers crossed it wasn't maxed out. A bad credit card didn't help build relationships. The transaction went through.

"Would you like a bag?" Amy asked.

"No. I'll take it as is."

"Great."

When I approached a person cold, it was always tricky. "Can I ask you another question?"

"Sure."

I ran my finger along the thin rope wrapped around the dream catcher. "This one is about the Mountain Music Festival."

Her shoulders pulled back. "That happened thirty-one years ago."

"I know. It hasn't gotten much attention in the last decade."

"Why are you asking?"

"My mother was one of the women who vanished. Her name was Patty. She was selling hamburgers that night. Taggart found you wearing her Depot T-shirt."

Amy was silent for a moment. "I remember her at the burger tent. I didn't have enough money for a burger, and she gave me one anyway. She was a kind soul."

"How did you end up with a Depot T-shirt?"

"I found it in the woods on a tree. I never saw her in the woods." She crossed her arms over her chest. "Why are you asking about this now?"

"I'm a writer. I'm working on a piece about the festival. And I want to learn all I can about Patty and the other victims. I keep thinking their stories have the clues that'll help me find their bodies."

"What clues?"

"I'm not sure. But I always know it when I see them."

A slight breeze teased the edges of her gray hair. "You're here because of a T-shirt."

"Sheriff Taggart found you in one of the tents, covered in bruises. Some were old but many were fresh. Taggart assumed Billy beat you up."

"I remember Sheriff Taggart. He reminded me of a boxer. All muscle and frowns. But he was kind when he spoke to me."

"Billy beat you up that night?"

She slid her hands into the back pockets of her overalls.

"Billy is gone. There's no one else to protect."

"I was confused in those days. Those were several lost years."

"Billy told Taggart that someone from the woods grabbed you. He said they beat you up that night. That he saved you."

A breath filled her lungs and then trickled over her lips. "Someone did grab me that night."

"That was true?"

"Yes. Taggart asked me about it, though I didn't have answers for him. But whatever happened that night is embedded in my bones and psyche. It was one of the reasons I had trouble getting sober. But I did. After a few years of sobriety, I reached out to a counselor." She glanced at the clock as if reminding herself how long she'd been sober. "Do you want some tea?"

I wasn't going to push her. "Yeah, sure."

"I have a pot in my little office. I'd feel better not having this conversation out here."

"Right." I followed her, then remembered the dream catcher and reached back and grabbed it.

She vanished around a curtain. I followed, my dream catcher's feathers and beaded cords bouncing around. She filled an electric kettle and then filled two tea strainers with loose leaves.

The space was six by six, and the walls were covered in botanical posters featuring ivy, lemons, wildflowers, and fruit trees. There were seven dream catchers on the walls and dozens of small ailing plants around the room.

"Looks like a plant clinic," I said.

"It is. You'd be surprised how many people return with half-dead plants, wanting their money returned. I always take the plants back and tell them if I can't revive it in thirty days, I'll issue a refund." She poured boiling water into two cups that read "Amy's Garden."

"A second chance, right?"

"We all deserve one."

I didn't like small talk, but I didn't mind trying for Amy's sake. "Anyone take you up on the offer?"

"A few come back. When they see that the plant is thriving, they leave."

"No one wants their plant back?"

"One. I refused." She handed me my cup.

I blew the steam off the top. It smelled like grass. I sipped. It tasted like lawn clippings. "Delicious."

She cradled the hot mug in her hands and held it close to her chest. "In my counseling sessions, I went back to that night."

Memories of traumatic events could be tricky. Old facts sometimes tangled and stuck to other experiences that had nothing to do with the original trauma. "What did you remember?"

She sipped and then set her mug down. "I had to pee. And the line to the latrine was fifty people deep. I decided the woods was the best way to go."

"Where was Billy?"

"In the tent. Doing coke." ˙

"Okay."

"I went to the woods and felt uneasy. I should've left then, but my bladder was about to burst."

Living on the road had put me in uncomfortable circumstances out of necessity. I'd learned to listen to feelings like that. Though the handgun I carried wasn't as effective if I was ambushed. "What happened?"

"I'd finished my business and was zipping up my pants when I heard a girl scream."

"You heard a girl scream? Did you ever tell Taggart this?"

"By the time I'd been in counseling and remembered, Taggart was dead. And no one in Dawson wanted to hear my stories about the Mountain Music Festival."

"Everyone still wants to forget."

She flexed her fingers. "I ran toward the girl's screams. I don't know what I thought I'd do if I found her, but I ran toward it." She traced a callus on her palm. "When I moved past the trees into a small clearing, there was no girl. But someone else found me. Whoever it was came up behind me and wrapped a rope around my waist. I grabbed the rope, but they jerked hard and shoved me forward. I fell face-first on the ground. He straddled me."

"You said *he*. A man?"

"I don't know. Whoever slammed my face against the ground. It felt like my brains were rattling in my skull."

That attack would have accounted for some of her fresh bruises but not her older ones. "Did this person say anything?"

"No."

"And Billy?"

"I don't know where Billy came from, but he pulled the person off me. My attacker took off and vanished into the woods. Billy helped me up, but he was pissed. He'd told me I'd been stupid."

"You had to pee. You tried to save a girl. That's not stupid."

Her gaze grew distant before it refocused on me. "My shirt was ripped, and Billy saw the T-shirt. He scooped it up and told me to put it on. He took me back to the tent and gave me a joint."

"Did Billy say anything about your attacker?"

"If he did, I don't remember."

"How long were you in the tent when Paxton found you?"

"I don't know. The sun was up. When I was in the woods, it was dark."

"What's the last song you remembered hearing from the stage?"

"The Blind Eagles played 'Free Bird.'"

"They were on the stage between three and four."

"How do you know that?"

"I've lived with this story for a while. I know the facts better than anyone."

"My name was never in the paper. How did you know about me?"

"Taggart mentioned you in his police reports. He left his files to me."

"Why?"

"He knew I write about crime. Knew I was Patty's kid. Maybe he thought I could wrap up the loose ends."

"I've thought about that scream a lot over the years. I think that's why I collect the dream catchers. I hear her at night sometimes. I wonder, if I'd been faster or more careful, I could've saved us both."

"You can't play that game."

"Easier said."

"How do you know she was in trouble?"

"The scream."

"Did it sound like a woman?"

"Yes. Why do you ask?"

"There's a theory Colton had help. Everyone assumed a man. Maybe your screamer wasn't a girl in need. Maybe she screamed to lure you deeper into the woods to isolate you."

"Why would you say that?"

"Four women just vanish. No struggles. No calls for help. I'm convinced someone else lured these women away." I had no facts to back it up, but it explained so much.

"I never thought about it like that."

"Think about it. You never found her, right?"

"I thought I ran in the wrong direction."

"Or maybe it was a recording." Colton had had all kinds of access to audio equipment.

"Up in those mountains in the rain?" She shook her head. "I don't think so."

"Women are capable of violence."

"That puts a different spin on it all."

"Did you notice anything about the person who grabbed you?"

"I felt a ring scratch my cheek."

"Right or left hand?"

"The scratch was on my left cheek."

"The ring would've been on a left hand. Anything else about the ring?"

"The edges weren't smooth. Not jagged but rough."

"I've dozens of pictures featuring Colton. He wore a signet ring on his left hand."

"Taggart caught the killer, right?" Amy said.

"Maybe. Or your attacker was a random creep who didn't have anything to do with the case."

"Do you believe that?" Amy asked.

I considered the question. The tents and woods were on the west side of the venue. I'd stared at it from the farmhouse window. "I don't know."

Chapter Twenty-One

SLOANE

Sunday, August 17, 2025, 7:30 p.m.

The dream catcher dangled from my rearview mirror as I parked in front of the Bistro. Inside customers filled small tables, and servers moved around the Italian-style restaurant. It hadn't been open thirty-one years ago, so I'd not paid attention to it. I glanced down at my T-shirt and jeans. Not dressy, but they'd have to do.

I walked up to a greeter. He glanced up from an iPad. A frown suggested he was ready to tell me to hit the road.

"I'm meeting Grant McKenna."

Raised eyebrows and a slight nod. "He arrived about thirty minutes ago."

I followed him through the packed dining room to a table in the back. As we approached, Grant stood. A gentleman. I didn't meet many of those. "Sloane. I was beginning to wonder."

I pulled out my chair and sat. "Sorry. An interview went long."

He sat and motioned the waitress over. "What can I get you to drink?"

When she arrived, I glanced up at her. "A cola. With lots of ice."

"Will do," the waitress said.

"How are your interviews going?" He always stared at me with keen interest.

"Hard to say yet. Everyone has been willing to talk to me. As expected, lots of emotion. Thirty-one years erases as many memories as it exposes."

The waitress arrived with a cola in an iced glass. Condensation dripped down the sides as a thin layer of foam skimmed the top.

"Do you think you'll find them?" he asked.

I sipped my soda, savoring the sweetness. "I'd rather hear about you. What brings you to Dawson? We've established our first meeting wasn't by accident. I'm guessing you didn't happen by the Nelson farm, did you?"

"No."

"Do you work cases like this often?"

"Whenever local law enforcement calls, I try to assist."

"That's your job?"

"I've gotten my private investigator's license. I do this pro bono."

The waitress arrived with a large pizza and set it on the table.

"I ordered," Grant said. "Do you eat pizza, or would you like to order something else?"

"Pizza works for me." The garlic and tomato smelled good, and I realized how hungry I was. "Salads waste my time."

We each served ourselves pizza. I folded my slice like a taco and took a bite. We both ate in silence. Finally, he set his slice down and wiped his fingers on a cloth napkin. His nails were neat and even but not professionally done. He liked order, but he wasn't fussy.

"What do you like?" he asked. "Beyond the work."

"It's all about the work," I said. "That drives me."

"Why?"

"Your work doesn't drive you?"

"It's not the first thing on my mind when I wake up in the morning."

"That's lucky for you." I took another bite. "I go to bed with my stories on my mind. I dream about them, and the ghosts are waiting for me each morning."

"Ghosts?"

I set my pizza down and wiped my fingers clean. "They tend to circle me until I find them or catch their killer."

His head angled. "What if you fail?"

"I've not failed yet."

"Do you have a plan if you do?"

I shook my head. "I never have a plan B."

He drew in a breath. "You're a burn-your-bridges kind of person."

"Yep."

"What about family? Friends?"

"This feels a little like a job interview. If you think you're working with a super-stable person, think again."

That prompted a grin. "I know what I've gotten myself into."

He didn't. But arguing wasted time. "I have no family. And friends are hard to make when you travel all the time."

"Sounds lonely."

"I do just fine." There were times I'd envied families with a strong connection. But I never related to what they felt. The closest I came to that feeling was satisfaction when I finished an article.

"Cabin life still agreeing with you?" he asked.

"My phone is an extension of my right hand. Feels a bit like I'm missing an appendage."

He chuckled. He was attractive. Dark hair, square jaw, and eyes that missed little. He loved the work as much as I did. He could have been retired on a fishing boat. But he was here eating pizza with me, trying to wrap up a case no one cared about. I suspected he was a strong believer in right and wrong. Black and white. Me, I checked ethics and embraced the gray.

Grant leaned forward a fraction. "You're looking at me like I'm a suspect." He wasn't annoyed. In fact, I thought he was enjoying my scrutiny.

"Randomness happens. But circumstances can be manipulated to direct the randomness."

"Meaning I manipulated all this? I intentionally met you at the conference, slept with you, and found you here for a reason?"

"Did you target me?"

He paused. "I did. I knew Colton was on the verge of getting out of prison, and you were also investigating the Mountain Music Festival. Your past articles were effective. For the record, the sex wasn't part of the plan."

I wasn't offended. Like me, he had an agenda and went after it. "Happy accident. Fair enough. How goes my interview request with Colton?"

"He's dragging his feet."

"Why would he rush? He holds the cards. And he likes the game. Likes teasing everyone. The kills were thrilling, but this endless game of 'Where are the girls?' is far more fun. Colton's silence keeps us all imprisoned in some way."

"Interesting way of looking at it."

I reached for another slice of pizza. This was the first time I'd been hungry all day.

"What did Colton do with the bodies?" he asked. "How did he transport them?"

"One of the trailers. And he had help."

Grant stilled. "Taggart believed he stowed the bodies and came back after the crowds cleared."

"Possible. But I don't think so."

"Who?"

"Not sure, but I'm betting this person or persons is still alive. Their existence is another reason why Colton stays quiet."

"An emotional connection to the accomplice?"

160

"No. Colton doesn't want his helper revealing the bodies' location." I pulled off a piece of cheese. "Bodies mean no chance of freedom. Their combined silence prevents mutually assured destruction."

"I'll pull Colton's prison visitor logs and any correspondence for the last thirty-one years."

"I'd like to see those names."

"Consider it done."

"Great." I took a few more bites. "Thanks for the meal and the help."

"You're leaving?"

"I'll catch up with you when there's more to discuss."

"You pissed at me?"

I shook my head. "I don't care enough to be pissed."

Chapter Twenty-Two

CJ Taggart

Saturday, May 21, 1994, 5:00 p.m.
The Afternoon After

After Taggart left the concert site Saturday afternoon, he drove to his apartment. He was dog-ass tired, and a headache pulsed behind his left eye.

He had a small first-floor apartment in Dawson near the office. He'd thought about property in the mountains, but that would take time.

A cool breeze teased his face as he opened the back door. He stepped inside to a small entryway, where he shrugged off his rain slicker, hung it up, and wrestled off his belt holster. He set his gun on a shelf. Sitting, he tugged off his muddy boots.

A sigh leaked over his lips. His back ached, and his knees pulsed. There'd been a time when he worked a forty-eight-hour shift and shook it off. Not anymore.

He stripped and turned on the shower tap. When the water steamed, he stepped under the hot spray. He groaned as the heat burrowed into his bones and chased out the chill. His headache still throbbed, but the drumbeat felt a little slower.

Rafe Colton was a liar and a con artist. It was a matter of time before he was behind bars. And Taggart hoped he was the man to lock him up.

When the hot water turned cold, he stepped out of the shower and dried off. Towel around his waist, he moved into the kitchen and set the coffee maker to brew. By the time the pot was full, he'd dressed in clean khakis, a pressed shirt, and fresh boots.

He filled a cup. As he sipped hot coffee, his phone rang. He swore.

"Taggart," he said.

"Sheriff, this is Brenda in dispatch."

"What's wrong, Brenda?" Since he'd been on the job, she'd not called him once. Not even when a drunk had plowed his red pickup truck into the hardware store.

"Sara Grayson is pacing the waiting area. She's Patty Reed's mother. She said Patty has not come home."

He pinched the bridge of his nose. "I don't know Patty that well. Has she taken off like this before?"

"Not according to her mother. She always hurries home to the baby. She was due home late yesterday."

He thought about the abandoned burger stand that had been ransacked by hungry crowds. "Tell her I'll be there in a half hour."

"Will do, Sheriff."

He hung up and downed the last of his coffee. He settled his holster and gun on his hip. As much as he bemoaned the interruption, a glance at a half-full whisky bottle reminded him he never got along well with extra time.

In his vehicle, he shifted gears and pressed on the accelerator. He didn't slow until he was pulling into the office's parking lot. Inside, he was greeted by ringing phones. Seemed busy for a Saturday in a small town, but this was only his second Saturday in Dawson.

He found Brenda behind her console, scribbling notes and nodding. "Yes, sir. I'll tell the sheriff."

She ended the call and swiveled in her chair toward him. "Sara is in the conference room waiting for you."

"Thanks, Brenda." He stopped at the break room and poured two cups of coffee and then found the small ten-by-ten room that served as their conference space.

Sara Grayson wasn't sitting at the small round table but staring at the old sheriff's picture on the wall. An oversize T-shirt covered her thick frame. Faded jeans tightened around her legs and ankles. She had short graying hair. He saw no traces of the energetic Patty.

"Ms. Grayson."

When she turned, he held up a cup. She accepted it but didn't sip.

"Why don't you have a seat?"

Dark circles smudged under her eyes. "I don't need to sit to tell you my daughter is missing."

He set his cup on the table and pulled out a chair for her. She didn't move. He resisted the urge to roll the tightness from his shoulders. He grabbed a legal pad and pen from a small credenza.

"Please, have a seat. I'm dead on my feet and I won't sit until you do."

She drew in a deep breath and sat.

He angled his chair toward her and lowered into the seat. "Tell me what's happening."

"What's happening? My daughter didn't come home last night. I called the diner this morning. Buddy said she left the burger tent last night and didn't return. He said she's fine and just messing with him. But that's not Patty. She comes home as quick as she can to see the baby."

"Where's the baby now?"

"I left her with Jody, Patty's neighbor."

"Do you watch the baby for Patty while she's working?"

"No. Jody does. They trade babysitting favors."

"What's Jody's last name?"

"Thompson. Jody Thompson."

"When is the last time you saw Patty?"

"When Patty dropped the baby off Friday morning, Jody was out of town. I knew it was going to be almost twenty-four hours watching the baby, but she begged for my help." She dropped her gaze to her calloused palm.

"Are you and Patty close?" Natural for a mother and daughter to be close, but that wasn't always the case.

"Not since she dated Larry Summers. I told her he was trouble, but she didn't listen. He got her pregnant, stole from her, and left her."

He scribbled the man's name on the pad. "When is the last time Patty saw Larry?"

"He left her before the baby was born. But he came in the diner a few months ago. He made a fuss. But a customer chased him off."

"Does he have contact with the baby?"

She straightened. "No. Hasn't sent her a nickel to support that child."

Women fell prey to former boyfriends too often. "Is Patty dating anyone else?"

"She wouldn't tell me if she was. She knew I wouldn't approve. The last thing she needs is a man."

He thought about the young woman who always had a smile on her face when he saw her. "Was she meeting any friends at the festival?"

"She never told me." Sara shook her head. "I need her back. The baby only responds to Patty. She's hard to handle. She doesn't like people. She smiles when she wants something, but she's often very quiet. I think she's got more of her father in her than Patty is willing to admit."

"Can you write down your contact information? Also, any numbers you have for Larry Summers?"

"Last I heard he was working in a garage near Staunton. But you can check Patty's trailer and see if she has any numbers for him."

"Write down her address." Patty was an adult. She was free to take off with friends or vanish for a day or two. If not for her baby, he'd give her a week or two before he chased her down.

Sara scribbled down Patty's address. He recognized the trailer park. It was located on the south side of town. There'd been a report of a break-in there a week ago. It was on the verge of becoming a dive. No telling who lived near Patty and had been keeping an eye on her.

Sara removed a key from her ring. "This is the key to her trailer. I was just there, but there's no sign that she came home."

"You went inside her place?"

"Yes. I needed more diapers and formula."

"You'll need to file a missing person report."

"Why? I just told you."

"We need formal notification. There are laws I must follow."

"What kind of laws?"

"Patty is an adult. She's not broken the law. And I need twenty-four hours after this report is filed before I can open an investigation."

"You aren't going to do anything?" Sara demanded.

Rules like that one irritated him. When anyone went missing, the first hour was the golden hour. The more time that passed, the less chance the missing person would be found alive. He took the key. "I didn't say that. Fill out the paperwork, and I'll call you as soon as I find anything."

"Okay."

"I'll have Brenda bring in the forms."

"Right."

He left Sara staring at her untouched cup of coffee. "Brenda."

"I have the missing person forms," she said. "What else?"

"Where's Paxton?"

"He went home to grab a few hours of sleep. Want me to wake him up?"

"No. Let him sleep."

"Where are you headed?"

"To visit Patty Reed's trailer."

Brenda didn't question the twenty-four-hour waiting window on the missing person report. "Right."

◆ ◆ ◆

Taggart arrived at Patty's trailer, located in a small twenty-unit park on the edge of town. Her unit was simple and didn't appear to have the bells and whistles some others did. She didn't have a front garden or a porch. Though there were rust spots on the siding, the steps were swept and the windows clean.

He pulled on latex gloves and then climbed the steps, inserted the key Sara gave him, and let himself inside. The interior was dark, but the soft scent of baby powder clung to the air. The carpeting looked freshly vacuumed, and the small kitchen was clean. Dishes were stacked in a drainer, and a red washcloth was draped over the faucet to dry.

The living room was picked up. Blankets were folded, pillows fluffed, and a collection of baby toys piled in a small basket. There were several framed pictures of the baby. The child's smiles looked strained and her gaze serious.

The bedroom was at the back of the unit. The bed was made, and the crib sheets smooth. On a small desk, he saw several brochures for accounting classes. Tacked to a small bulletin board was a GED certificate. He opened the desk drawers. They were filled with paper, pens, pencils, a sleeve of condoms, and a stack of letters. He reached for the opened envelopes. They were from several community colleges. The first was a rejection letter, as were the next three. He replaced the letters in the envelopes and closed the drawer.

There was also a brochure for a resort in Colorado. The facility was looking for waitresses and promised twenty bucks an hour. That would have been a hell of a pay bump if it were true.

Finally, there was a stack of photographs taken of Patty and a guy. Tall, with thick, dark hair. Taggart guessed this must be Larry Summers. He stared at her smiling face. A pretty girl with a plateful of responsibilities at a young age. Maybe she wanted to dump this life and find a new one. No college rejections, judgmental mother, abusive ex, or moody baby.

Anywhere else must have looked pretty good to Patty Reed.

Taggart arrived at the festival entrance a half hour later. The muddied hillside had been stripped of ground cover, and the small trees were bent and broken. The field at the base of the hill was a sea of mud. It was disfigured with deep tire ruts, scattered trash, flattened tents, and overflowing trash cans. The stages and trucks were gone, and the vendor who'd brought the porta potties was loading the last of the ten units onto his flatbed.

As he shut off the engine, Brenda came in over the radio. "Dispatch to Sheriff?"

He took the microphone and pressed the side button. "Ten-four."

"Another woman called the station. She says her niece was at the festival, and she's not checked in. It's too soon to file a missing person report."

"What's her name?"

"Laurie Carr. She's nineteen, blond, and petite. She was hoping to sing at the festival."

"I might have met her. I think she worked the burger tent with Patty."

"Laurie was supposed to call in this morning."

He checked his watch. Eight o'clock. "She's overdue."

"Her aunt is convinced she's in trouble."

Many missing person cases resolved themselves. The person in question was either drunk, on vacation, or staying at a friend's house. There were dozens of reasonable explanations. "If she calls back, take her statement."

"Will do."

Taggart walked over to the site where the burger tent had been located. Buddy had cleared out all the equipment and broken down the tables. Waste, embedded in the mud, encircled large green, bulging trash bags.

He moved to where Patty had stood and looked out toward the entrance to the festival. When he'd last seen her, she'd been hustling to work the grill and the register. During the height of the event, Patty wouldn't have seen beyond the crowds encircling her.

His gaze scanned the field. Patty had been working the event with a blonde. Was it Laurie?

The beep of the flatbed drew his attention to the porta potties that had rested near the edge of the woods.

The truck driver lowered a forklift that slid under the porta potty. "Sheriff, you seen Rafe Colton?"

He didn't know the driver. "Not since yesterday."

A frown deepened the man's grizzled face. "He was supposed to meet me here with a check."

"You are?"

"Pete Manchester. I rented him the porta potties."

"Is that like Colton, to be late?"

"I've heard rumors about unpaid bills. But he offered me good money to do the job. He's a hard man to say no to."

Taggart wasn't surprised to hear Colton wasn't here with a check. This festival was proving to be one huge con. "I'll keep an eye out."

"Right."

"All your units were lined up here?"

"Yeah, there were ten of them. They're filled with trash and shit I don't want to know about. It's going to be a hell of a cleanup to get these back into service. I told him he needed more units."

Colton wasn't worried about destruction. His kind created chaos and then moved on, leaving the mess to others.

Taggart walked past the muddy square imprints where the units had rested. "Let me know if it doesn't go well with Colton."

"I will."

Taggart moved toward the woods. During the festival, it had been filled with people who'd sneaked in or needed a place to escape the rain or get high.

Into the woods, the first thirty feet of ground was trampled flat. And judging by the smell, anyone who hadn't been able to get into the latrine had used the woods. He kept walking.

The damage of too much humanity eased. The underbrush reappeared, and soon it looked as if no one had stepped on this part of the earth in a hundred years.

He cut through the thicket and trees toward the fire road.

He still didn't know what he was looking for. Why would Patty or Laurie venture this far into the woods? He looked up toward the sun bleeding through the thick tree canopy. The trees would have slowed the rain, but it would still have been damp and cold. From here he couldn't see the field through the thicket. In the dark, it would have been easy for a woman to vanish.

In the distance, white fabric flapped from a tree. As he moved toward the strip, plowing through the brush, branches grabbed his shirt and pant legs.

When he reached the cloth, he realized it was a T-shirt. Plain and white, it was small and fashioned for a woman. The fabric was ripped, and splashes of brown and red covered the front. He'd seen enough dried blood to recognize it. He imagined a large hand grabbing a fistful of fabric until it ripped. He left the shirt where he found it.

His gaze scanned the immediate area. Ahead, he spotted a single athletic shoe coated in mud and lying on its side. Like the shirt, it was a woman's style. As he studied the distance between the shirt and shoe, he imagined a shirtless woman running in the dark. She was panicked, disoriented. Had she tripped and lost a shoe? Did her pursuer catch her? Did she fight? He couldn't tell if she'd gotten away or if she'd been captured.

Taggart's jaw pulsed. He reached for his walkie and radioed Brenda. "Sheriff," she said.

He cleared his throat. "Brenda, has Sara Grayson heard from Patty?"

"No. And Monica Carr hasn't heard from Laurie."

Tension crept up his back.

"You think they have a reason to worry?" Brenda asked.

His gaze scanned the carnage. "Do me a favor. Call Paxton and tell him to meet me at the concert site at sunrise."

"That doesn't sound good. You find something?"

"I'm not sure what I found. But we need to search this site."

Chapter Twenty-Three

SLOANE

Monday, August 18, 2025, 6:00 a.m.

Since I was a little kid, I'd never been a good sleeper. I'd often wake while my grandmother slept and roam the house. At first, I was content to search Sara's desk drawers. But when that lost its appeal, I removed the contents of her purse, spread them out on the floor, and inspected each item. A few times I chewed her nicotine gum, but I decided I didn't like the way it made me feel. I wasn't a fan of drugs that altered my mind. That explained why Sara's medicine cabinets, chock-full of antidepressants and sedatives, never interested me.

By the time I was seven or eight, I'd grown bored with lurking around my house. I wanted to see more. I wanted to know what was happening in the dark world outside.

My nocturnal field trips were simple at first. They began with me standing in my backyard and studying the cycles of the moon. Less light was better.

I soon was staring into the neighbors' yards and then their windows.

Peering into another person's world was thrilling at first. I watched Mrs. Miller refilling her coffee cup with Jack Daniel's. I observed Mr. Sanders as he stood by the toolshed in his backyard, unzipped his pants, and grabbed himself. He pumped, moaned, and finally rested his head on the metal shed. There was Debbie Gilbert, who rose most nights around 1:00 a.m. She'd sit in her kitchen and talk on the house phone. I knew she dated Jimmy Brown, who'd been arrested for assault. I figured she was talking to him.

By the time I was ten, my neighborhood was no longer interesting. Amazing how predictable people could be. Mrs. Miller died of liver disease. Debbie talked to Jimmy until he went to jail again. And it was a wonder Mr. Sanders still had a dick after all his late-night toolshed trips.

By twelve I was riding my bike a few miles away and breaking into empty houses. Inside strangers' homes, I felt powerful. I could take or do whatever I wanted. A few times, I grabbed loose change, a necklace, and one of two dog-shaped salt and pepper shakers.

My scavenger hunts didn't hurt anyone. And it was odd how easy it was for me to get away with it all. All fun and games until a local girl, Sally Winston, vanished. She was ten years old. I'd been in the Winston house once. It had looked normal, but warning signs weren't always visible.

After Sally vanished, all my nocturnal adventures felt small and stupid. Sally's disappearance reminded me of Patty. Both had been here one moment and gone the next.

Two weeks later the cops found Sally's half-nude body in a ravine. I'd expected them to also arrest her killer. Unlike Patty, they had a body. But the cops never found the killer.

I often rode my bike past the spot where Sally's body had been found. I'd heard killers returned to the scene of the crime. I spent hours sitting in the shadows, watching the ravine and willing the killer to return. But if he did, I never saw him.

Her funeral attracted hundreds of weeping people dressed in black. The police had detained men with criminal records. They'd been interviewed and their DNA collected. The media covered the story for months. But there was never an arrest. All that work for nothing.

The cops had moved on to the next case. And the media found the next bright shiny crime to write about.

I hadn't known Sally, and if she had lived, I wouldn't have cared about her. She'd come from a happy, functioning family. But the injustice of her death landed her on Team Outcast. And I wanted to find her killer. I wanted to see him punished.

By the time I was sixteen, I was working fifty hours a week cutting grass and doing odd jobs. I saved up enough money to buy a 2002 three-speed Toyota Corolla that had a dent on the back bumper but a solid engine. My new wheels extended my hunting grounds.

But the killer never struck again in our area. He vanished.

Sally, like Patty, never received full justice.

The ghosts were circling tonight.

Later, when the sun rose, I sat at the kitchen table. I scrambled eggs while toast cooked in the ancient toaster. When the wall phone rang, I hesitated before raising the clunky receiver. "Hello."

"It's Grant."

Relief now attached to the sound of his voice. "Tell me something forensic."

"You know more about this case than anyone."

"What about Colton's recent visitors?"

"His attorney has seen him a few times in the last five years, but I'll have to pull the visitors' logs for a complete list."

"Can you get it?"

"Sure." And then: "The torn bloody shirt and lone sneaker found in the woods belonged to Tristan Fletcher."

"I know." My toast popped up. "I haven't spoken to her father yet. He's not returned my calls. I hope he doesn't shoot me when I knock on his front door."

"That's not funny."

"It wasn't intended to be. Not everyone is ready to be dragged down memory lane."

"The blood was Tristan's. There was a familial DNA match to her sister."

"Lannie Fletcher. She lives in the DC area now. The mother passed twenty-eight years ago. Mr. Fletcher still lives in the family home."

"When are you seeing Mr. Fletcher?"

"Soon. And then I'm tracking down the festival's security guy."

"Remind me who that was," Grant said.

"Kevin Pascal. He worked for Woodward Security. The firm Colton had hired. The firm sent three security guards to the festival."

"Right. Colton said he hired twenty guys, but the president of Woodward testified that Colton had only hired three."

"Kevin also dated Debra Jackson. She broke up with Kevin a few months before the festival. According to Debra's sister, Kevin still had a thing for Debra." I didn't mention the picture I'd seen of the couple on Kevin's mantel.

"Think Kevin could have been involved in her disappearance?"

"Statistically speaking, women are killed by men who know them." Maybe after this case was done, I'd take a second look at the men who'd been in Sally Winston's life.

"Debra's necklace was with the trinkets Taggart found in Colton's barn."

There had been four incriminating mementos, including Debra Jackson's necklace, Laurie Carr's guitar strap, Tristan Fletcher's ring, and Patty's driver's license. There were also witnesses at the concert who'd seen Colton with the women. Other women testified that Colton could be violent in the bedroom. The evidence was slim, but the will to put a killer behind bars was strong.

I pushed the egg around with my fork. "The partial prints pulled from the buckle on Laurie's guitar strap and Patty's driver's license were never identified."

"I ran the prints again through the national fingerprint database. They're still too smudged for a read."

"Four young, strong women simply vanish." If whoever had helped the killer was still walking the earth, they'd escaped their punishment.

"Any theories on the second person?"

"Someone these women would trust."

"Like a security guard?" he asked.

"Maybe."

"There was no evidence there were two killers. Colton never once hinted that he had help."

"I'm not letting up on this theory."

He chuckled. "Dog with a bone."

"That's me."

"What's next?"

"First, I'm talking to Brian Fletcher. Then I'll catch up to Kevin."

"You think you can solve this, don't you?"

Did no one have faith in me? "I'll crack this."

Chapter Twenty-Four

CJ Taggart

Monday, May 23, 1994, 4:00 p.m.
2 Days After

Taggart and Paxton had spent most of their Sunday walking the woods ringing the festival field. They found discarded clothes, shoes, beer cans, a backpack complete with wallet and identification, condoms, and cigarettes. The woods had been their own party site. Close enough to hear the music but private enough to avoid prying eyes.

They'd found a muddy backpack. It was black, battered, and covered with music festival concert patches. Taggart unzipped the pack and found a worn brown wallet inside. The owner's name was Jim Richards.

He wasn't familiar with the name, and neither was Paxton. But having the guy's name and home address made life easier.

Two hours after finding the backpack, Taggart rolled up on a small house located in Keswick, fifty miles east of Dawson. The one-story brick rancher was painted white, and the garden beds were neat and mulched. Parked in the driveway was a Ford Escort and beside it a red pickup truck.

Out of his car, he settled his hat on his head and walked up to the front door. He stood to the left of the door and then knocked. He settled his hand on the grip of his weapon.

Heavy footsteps sounded in the hallway, and the door opened without hesitation. The woman standing on the other side of a screened door appeared to be in her eighties. She was slender with stooped shoulders and a sharp gaze.

"I'm looking for Jim Richards."

"That's my grandson. Is he in trouble?"

"Not at all. His backpack and wallet were found, and I'm returning it."

"I'll take it."

"I need to give it to him."

"But I'm his grandmother."

"Yes, ma'am. But I need to hand it to Jim."

She drew in a breath. "He's in the backyard. He's fixing the lawn mower."

He could walk around the back, but if Jim didn't want to speak to him and Grandma alerted him, he'd be gone out the front door and in that truck before Taggart could catch up. "Call him to the front door."

Grandma didn't look happy, but she vanished into the house. Minutes later a tall, lean man appeared. He was wearing jeans and a long-sleeve work shirt. Jim Richards's DMV record stated he was thirty-one, weighed 160 pounds, and was an organ donor.

"Jim Richards?" Taggart asked.

"Yeah. You have my backpack?"

"I do."

Jim rubbed his palms down his jeans. "Can I have it?"

"It's in my car. Come with me, and I'll give it to you."

Grandma lurked close, but she didn't speak.

"Yeah, sure."

Taggart motioned for Richards to go first, and he followed, his hand still on his weapon. At his car, Taggart fumbled with his keys. "Do you know where I found it?"

"The music festival. I was wasted."

"We found your backpack in the woods behind the latrines. It must have been a hundred feet into the woods."

"I was trying to get away from the rain. Figured the thick tree cover would keep me dry."

"It must have been pretty crowded back there."

"It was. We were bumping into each other. It was hard to find a tree to lean on. We were all soaking wet."

Taggart found a grin. "Sounds like it was a hell of a party."

Jim relaxed. "It was. We all had a damn good time."

"When did you move into the woods?"

"What does that have to do with anything?"

"Humor me."

Jim shrugged. "I don't know."

"What band was playing?"

"Hard rock. Moody Manic, I think."

Taggart had the band lineup and was using their performance schedules as his base timeline. "About midnight."

"I guess. It was raining. I was soaked."

That fit with the timeline. "So, you're in the woods. How many people would you say were there?"

"Two hundred. Three hundred. I'm not sure. What's with the obsession with the woods?"

Taggart ignored the question. "Did you see any disturbances in the woods?"

"Like what?"

"You tell me."

"A few of the guys got a little rowdy."

"What does that mean?"

"There was one guy who saw a chick he liked. She kept saying no, but he wasn't listening."

"Happen to know any names?" he asked.

"No names. But the chick was carrying a blue guitar. She was in the woods to keep it dry."

Laurie was the Blue Guitar Girl. She'd exited the stage minutes after 11:00 p.m. "Do you know the guy's name?"

"No. It was filled with folks from other places. I didn't see anyone I knew."

"And what happened to the girl with the blue guitar?"

"I don't know."

"You remembered the blue guitar."

"It was different. Hard to miss."

"What did the woman with the blue guitar look like?"

"Pretty. Had a nice smile. Hot."

"Any more of a description?"

"Nice tits."

"And you didn't notice where this hot woman went?"

"She was hanging with another chick. She was cute, too. Spun around like she was a dancer. The two drifted off into the shadows. Thinking about what they were doing made me hard."

"What did the second woman look like?"

"She seemed young."

"How young?" He'd been at this long enough to realize Jim had seen more than he wanted to let on.

"If she said she was eighteen, I'd want to see her ID."

"Blond, brunette, redhead?"

"Dark hair. Kind of wild and curly."

"Did the two women appear to know each other?"

"I don't think they did. I think the younger one offered Blue Guitar Girl a blunt. They went deeper into the woods."

"Did anyone follow them?"

"I don't know."

Jim's testimony wouldn't stand up in a court of law. Any good defense attorney would tear him apart. "Because you were inebriated?"

"That's right."

"Who did you go to the festival with?"

"I have a buddy. His name is Bill. He was there. He can tell you I didn't do anything but smoke weed."

"Bill got a last name?"

"Parsons." He rattled off Bill's number.

Taggart scribbled it in a small notebook he always carried.

"Who else did you notice in the woods?"

A sigh leaked through pursed lips. "It was pretty busy."

"But you had to have noticed a few people."

"The concert promoter was there."

"How do you know this person was the festival promoter?"

"He told everyone. He was a real friendly guy. Smoked some weed. I heard him say that this was his party. He was chatting up Blue Guitar Girl."

"Was his name Rafe Colton?"

"I didn't catch his last name. Light-brown hair. He looks like that singer, Kurt Cobain, if he wasn't dead now."

The description fit Colton. "Did he say why he was in the woods and not near the stage?"

"We all thought he was going to bust us for poaching on the festival. None of us had paid for a ticket. But he didn't care about us."

"You snuck in via the fire road, he doesn't get ticket money, and he doesn't care?" When Jim hesitated, Taggart shook his head. "I don't care about a bunch of guys sneaking into a concert. Or smoking weed."

"He didn't care. He said he needed a break. The rain was beating us all down. He did a couple of lines of coke."

"Did Colton follow Blue Guitar Girl?"

"He watched Guitar Girl and the chick with her real close. He liked the look of them both."

"Did he follow the women?"

Jim sniffed. "I don't know. I was smoking and Bill asked for a toke. I turned to give it to him. We shot the shit for a while, and when I turned back, that Colton guy was gone. So was Blue Guitar Girl and her girlfriend."

Taggart removed Patty's picture from his pocket. "Was she in the woods?"

Jim studied the picture. "Hamburger Girl."

"You know her?"

He handed back the image. "I bought a burger from her. She's a hottie."

"But she wasn't in the woods?"

"Not that I saw. But it was crowded. Why all the questions about these gals? Is there a problem?"

"Might not be a problem at all." He'd been searching for Patty and Laurie. Jim must have spotted Blue Guitar Girl, a.k.a. Laurie, around midnight.

Taggart opened his trunk and removed the mud-splattered black backpack. "If I have more questions, I'll call you."

Jim unzipped his backpack and dug out his wallet. "Yeah, sure, man."

Taggart slid behind the wheel of his vehicle. He'd learned a long time ago that if his gut was tight and he felt edgy, something was off with a case.

Right now, he was working on an ulcer.

Chapter Twenty-Five

Sloane

Monday, August 18, 2025, 8:00 a.m.

The drive to Brian Fletcher's home took a half hour. His daughter Tristan was among the missing from the Mountain Music Festival. Brian wasn't responding to my calls or emails. But I was accustomed to rejection. He wasn't the first person who didn't want to talk to me.

The Fletcher house was a dark-green two-story wood-frame house. Shrubs lined up in single file along the front. A large oak shaded a mulched bed filled with blooming azaleas.

Tristan Fletcher had wanted to be a dancer. She'd been hired as a backup performer for the Roving Rangers, and local media had taped one of the band's performances. The film had captured her petite body moving seductively to the rock music. Her long black, curly hair framed her heart-shaped face.

I'd watched the video a dozen times. When she'd moved to the music, her hair had swung from side to side. She was eighteen when she'd vanished, but she looked a few years younger.

As Tristan danced, I shifted my focus from her to the people around her. A few of the band members tossed her grins, and when one of the guitar players launched into a long riff, he faced her. Smiling, she moved toward him, swaying her hips. The guitarist leaned toward her. She skimmed her fingers down his arm. He wagged his tongue at her.

The crowd cheered at the sexual teasing between the two, and when Tristan moved back to her spot in the background, the crowd was applauding.

I rang the bell. Silence echoed in the house. I glanced toward the four-door car in the driveway. As silence stretched, I wondered if Mr. Fletcher wasn't here. Also not a first.

No one came to the front door. So I retraced my steps and walked down the sidewalk toward a privacy fence. It was locked. I fished a pocketknife out of my backpack and used the blade to wrestle the lock loose. The latch gave way and the door swung open. I pocketed the knife. I listened for the growl of a dog. When the stillness remained, I stepped into the backyard.

A rainbow of flowers rimmed the privacy fence and filled a mulch bed in the yard's center. A children's swing set complete with a yellow slide, tower, and red rings. I knew Tristan was the older of Fletcher's two daughters. I'd not dug into the younger sister's life, but I guessed she'd had a child.

When I rounded the corner, I saw a man hunched over a bed. He wedged a trowel at the base of a weed.

"Brian Fletcher."

When he didn't react or turn around, I noticed his earbuds.

My eye remained on the sharp edge of the trowel cutting into the weed as I approached.

I tapped Fletcher's shoulder. He whirled around, the trowel raised like a weapon. I stepped back, hands up in the air. I waited for him to focus on me.

He yanked out the earbuds. "Who are you?"

"Sloane Grayson. I left you messages," I said. "I'm here to talk about Tristan and the Mountain Music Festival."

He stabbed his trowel in the soft dirt. "We don't have an appointment."

"I've driven a couple of hours," I lied. "Can we talk for a few minutes?"

"This isn't a good day."

I'd slipped my foot into the proverbial door. "I promise to be quick."

He sighed. "Can we do this another day?"

I wasn't leaving without an interview. "I'd like to learn more about Tristan. All my sources are media and old articles. No one's talking about her anymore."

His lips flattened into a level line. A muscle pulsed in his jaw. "I'm not fond of stirring up the past."

"I like to dig into it. I like to see what crawls out of the shadows when I shine a light into the darkness."

"Be careful what you wish for."

My wry smile was calculated. "I've heard that before."

He yanked off his garden gloves and rose as if his knees hurt. "Come on. It's cooler in the house."

I followed him inside. The interior was dimmer, and it took my eyes a moment to adjust. I moved into the kitchen, noticed wood-paneled walls covered with dozens of framed photographs. I was tempted to study each photo, but I was aware he would see my curiosity as a violation of his privacy. All the mementos and photos told me that this room was a memorial to the family he'd once had. An old golden retriever slept on a dog bed by the fireplace. The dog's tail thumped, and he slowly rose and crossed to me. I held out my fingers and let him sniff.

Fletcher washed his hands, dried them, and replaced the dish towel back on the sink. "Can I get you something to drink?"

"Water would be great."

The dog retreated to his bed as Fletcher retrieved a glass from a cabinet and filled it with water from the tap. He set the glass on the counter and stepped back, as if being close to me troubled him. I was the knife poised to slice into old wounds.

I sipped the water, grateful for the cool liquid in my dry mouth. I didn't get nervous when I interviewed anyone. I'd never been afraid to travel into prisons, back alleys, or crack houses. At moments like this, my mouth still went dry. Though I didn't have emotional reactions to tough questions or answers, my body did. Maybe on a cellular level I had a semblance of a conscience. Maybe.

"What do you want to know about Tristan?" Mr. Fletcher asked.

"I've watched her performance at the festival. She was very talented. Did she always want to be a dancer?"

"She was dancing almost as soon as she could walk. Anytime there was a song on the radio, she was moving. Her mother enrolled her in dance classes when she was four. She took to it like a duck to water."

I skipped my questions about Tristan's mother because I knew she had died of cancer soon after her daughter's disappearance. Few writers examined the damage done to family members. Like a bomb exploding, the initial blast killed some, but it also wounded more. Stress had killed my grandmother before her sixtieth birthday.

"She won quite a few competitions," Mr. Fletcher said. Pride blended with frustration in his voice. "She was very ambitious."

"That's what it takes to make it in that world."

"So many prizes I had to build a second set of shelves in her bedroom. She was so proud of all her accomplishments."

"She had plans to study dance in New York, right?"

"She'd earned a slot at Juilliard."

"What was it about the Mountain Music Festival that caught her attention?"

"She heard bands were looking for backup dancers. She wanted the stage experience with a large live audience."

"The Roving Rangers?" The band had broken up months after the Mountain Music Festival. Two of the three members had died, and the third was in his eighties and living retired in North Carolina.

"That's right. They thought dancers would add interest to their performance. She begged me to let her go. She thought real-world stage experience would make her a better dancer."

"But you said no."

"I did. A festival like that promised nothing but trouble."

"She lied and said she was visiting friends."

He shook his head. "Yes."

"Did she lie often?" I asked.

"She was a good kid."

"But a kid. They do dumb things."

He stilled. "They do."

"Taggart interviewed a witness who possibly placed Tristan in the woods behind the venue with another victim. Her name was Laurie Carr."

"I know who she is." Mr. Fletcher shook his head. "Taggart asked me about her, but I never met her."

"Tristan had just performed a routine onstage. Laurie had sung. They had a lot in common."

"Maybe. Why do you care about my daughter?"

"I want to know her story. What drove her? What were her strengths and weaknesses?"

He stared at me, silent. I thought he wasn't going to comment, and then he said, "Tristan called me on that last day. She told me she'd arrived at her friend's house. She sounded so excited. It was her first real outing since her accident."

"Accident?"

"She fell the year before. Broke her ankle bad. It had healed, and she was getting her strength back. She became depressed, and she was desperate to prove herself."

Victims came in all shapes and sizes. Sinners, saints, and all those in between. "Did she mention any problems? Was anyone bothering or following her?"

"No. Everyone liked her."

"Based on the festival timeline, Tristan's performance was at ten. The band finished before eleven. What do you think she would have done after her performance?"

"I don't know. But with all her other performances, she was always full of energy. It could take her hours to come off the high and refocus on the real world."

I waited for him to explain, but when he didn't, I chose not to push. "Did you ever speak to the band members about her?"

"No. I didn't want to see or talk to them."

His lack of curiosity struck me as odd. "Did they reach out to you?"

"The band leader, Brad. He called a few times. I let his calls go to voicemail. There was nothing he could say."

"What about your wife? Did she have questions?"

"She was sick then. I tried to shield her."

"May I look at the pictures on your wall?"

The question caught him off guard. "Why?"

"Helps me understand Tristan."

A muscle pulsed in his jaw. "Sure. Help yourself."

I moved to the largest wall in the den, covered in at least twenty color and black-and-white photos of the Fletcher family.

The sisters looked very much alike, but it was clear Tristan had a dancer's elegance. "Why the swing set in the backyard?"

"The kids next door come by after school sometimes. Their mother works two jobs. I put the set up for them."

"Nice of you."

"Nice to hear children's voices again. I miss that." He met my gaze. "Do you have children?"

"No."

"If you get the chance, take it. It'll make your life better."

I didn't have what it took to care for a child. "You'd say that even after losing a child?"

"I wouldn't wish away the years with the girls for anything."

Fletcher's cell phone rang from his back pocket. He glanced at the display. He frowned and sent the call to voicemail.

"You didn't go to Rafe Colton's trial, did you?"

"No. I didn't have the stomach for it."

Representatives from the other families had all been at the trial at one point or another. Monica Carr and Sara had been fixtures in the courthouse. When I looked back on those days, I realized she enjoyed the trial more than mothering me—the distant, moody child.

But no one from the Fletcher family had attended the trial or the sentencing hearing.

"I don't want you to mention Tristan in your article," he said.

"The focus of the piece is the victims."

His jaw clenched. "Why now? Why after all this time?"

"I want to find their bodies. I want to bring them home." I knew Tristan had a marker in the cemetery, but the coffin was empty. Mrs. Fletcher's grave was to the left, and a marker-in-waiting was there for Mr. Fletcher. None for the sister, but maybe she'd decided to draw the line with spending time with the family in the afterlife.

"Is an empty coffin enough for you, Mr. Fletcher?"

His brow furrowed with a mixture of frustration and surprised anger. "None of it is enough, Ms. Grayson. That festival blew my family apart. And anyone who thinks bones in the ground will fill the hole inside of me is a fool."

Taggart had been a linear thinker. His tunnel vision was locked on finding the killer. He'd found enough evidence to prove his case in court. End of story. But he'd not found the missing women. Beyond the families, the remains were a mild curiosity for the world.

Taggart caught his killer, but he had failed the victims.

I would not.

Chapter Twenty-Six

CJ TAGGART

Tuesday, May 24, 1994, 1:00 p.m.
3 Days After

Taggart tracked down Patty's ex-boyfriend, Larry Summers, to his family-owned business near Staunton, Virginia, about a forty-five-minute drive west of Dawson. Summers had left Dawson, Patty, and his child, but he was close enough to keep tabs on them both.

Summers was in his late twenties and had been paroled after two years for breaking and entering. When he'd been living with Patty, he'd roughed her up when she was pregnant. She'd called the cops, and from what Sara said, she'd left him. He'd cut her off completely after that. She'd sued for child support, and he'd threatened to make her disappear.

And now Patty was missing.

Taggart parked beside a rusted pickup truck.

Out of his vehicle, he settled his hat on his head. A pneumatic drill buzzed. Like Taggart, Larry Summers had been big for his age when he was a kid. Both had worked in their stepfathers' garages by fifth grade.

In the early days, Taggart handed the old man tools and swept floors. But by the time he was fourteen, he was changing oil and transmission fluids, plugging tires, or swapping spark plugs. His stepfather had wanted him to take over the garage, but he'd run off to the marines right before his eighteenth birthday.

And now he was back in Dawson. As the old man used to say, "The farther you run, the closer you get to your past."

He walked into the garage. Scents of oil and grease took him back to a life he'd abandoned. There were two cars on the racks. A Chevrolet sedan and a Ford pickup truck. A mechanic was under each vehicle.

"I'm looking for Larry Summers," Taggart said.

The man under the Ford ducked his head down. Curiosity shifted to suspicion. "I'm Summers."

"Mind if I have a word with you? I'm Sheriff CJ Taggart," he asked.

Summers grabbed a stained cloth from his back pocket and walked toward him. The second mechanic had stopped working and now paid close attention.

"Is there a problem, Sheriff?" Summers was six foot three and had a muscular build. His short black mustache drew attention to puffy eyes swimming in a full face. This was the guy in the photo Patty kept at her trailer.

"I have a few questions." He'd bet money that Summers was hungover. A crushing headache might have slowed him down, but Taggart didn't underestimate the danger. He waited until Summers was clear of the garage and all the wrenches and screwdrivers were no longer within arm's reach.

"About?" Summers asked.

"Patty Reed."

Summers drew in an aggravated breath. "Whatever she's saying about me is a lie. I haven't seen her in over a year."

"She's not saying much," he said.

"Does she want money for the kid? Because I'm barely getting by here."

"When's the last time you saw your daughter?"

"Never have. I told Patty I don't think the kid is mine. She got around when we were together."

Taggart had heard similar claims from other men during his career. It still pissed him off but didn't make him so mad that it clouded his judgment. "You haven't seen Patty in over a year?"

Summers wiped his hands with the grease-stained rag. "That's right. Why do you care?"

"According to the police reports, you threatened to kill her if she pressed for child support. She's also threatened to file a restraining order against you."

"She never did that."

"But she did call the cops. You bruised her arms and her face."

"She fell. She was clumsy."

"I read the report. The arresting officer said you have a history of drinking and getting into fights."

"Sure, I like a few beers after work. That's not against the law."

"When was the last time you were in Dawson?"

"Six months, maybe. There are good bars there."

"And you never happened by the diner where Patty works?"

"I don't give a shit about Patty or her kid. We broke it off over a year ago. Again, why are you here? I've got to get back to work."

"Patty worked at the Mountain Music Festival over the weekend."

"Okay."

"Where were you this weekend?"

"Here. Working. A Mustang with a blown transmission. We playing twenty questions? Or are you going to tell me what's going on?"

"Patty vanished from the music festival. No one has seen her since Saturday morning."

He shifted. "What does that have to do with me?"

"You're the guy on record who beat her up."

Grinning, he shook his head. "You talked to Buddy? He's not a Boy Scout. He has a thing for Patty."

Buddy had been at the festival restocking supplies. He'd driven his van up the fire road and parked on the other side of the woods, where Patty had been last seen. "Did anyone see you working here over the weekend?"

"Sure. Seth over there will vouch for me."

Seth had stepped out from under the car. He was watching them in plain view. Taggart noted Seth was as big as Summers.

"Seth, is that true?" Taggart asked. "Was Summers here all weekend long?"

"That's right," Seth said as if the answer had been rehearsed. "We worked side by side all weekend long. Guy was never out of my sight."

"Even when he went to the john?" Taggart countered.

"You know what I mean," Seth said. "He didn't leave the garage."

For now, there wasn't much he could do. But he was sure that both men were hiding something. "Can I search the garage?"

"When you get a warrant," Larry said.

"I'll call in a request now. My deputy will deliver it."

Both men glanced at each other. Yeah, there was something in the garage neither wanted him to see. He moved to his vehicle and slid behind the wheel. He reached for the radio and called into the office. "Brenda, I need you to call the judge and get me a search warrant." He explained where he was and who he was talking to. When he rose out of the car, both men's stony features telegraphed their anger.

"We have work to do," Summers said. "We don't have time for this."

"The work will have to wait. I want you boys to stay right where you are."

Seth pulled a cigarette from his pocket. He fished out a cigarette and a plastic lighter from the packet. "This is bullshit."

"Boys, I don't have beef with either of you. But I'm looking for a missing girl."

"I haven't seen her!" Summers shouted.

"I'm going to have to be convinced of that," Taggart said. "And it's going to take a search of the property before I'm convinced you aren't part of this."

"Go ahead and search," Summers said. "There's no woman here."

"I'll wait for my deputy and the warrant. I don't want there to be any misunderstanding if we end up in court."

"Look, man," Seth said. "I got weed and some coke. But no chick. Kidnapping and murder are different levels of trouble."

"Yes, they are," Taggart said. "Don't you agree, Larry?"

"I didn't hurt Patty," he said.

"We'll find out."

The three of them sat in the warm spring air. Taggart craved a cigarette. He reached in his pocket and settled a cigarette between his lips. He lit the tip and inhaled. This morning he'd promised himself this was his last pack, but already he'd decided to pick up a new carton on the way home. This case was going to be a ballbuster.

They waited two hours before Deputy Paxton arrived with the search warrant.

Out of his car, the deputy settled his hat on his head. "Larry, Seth." Then he looked at Taggart. "I've known those boys for years."

The community in this part of the world was small and tight-knit. Right now, Taggart was the outsider. "Do you have the search warrant?"

Paxton produced the slim piece of paper. Then in a lower voice, he said to Taggart, "Judge doesn't want you on a fishing expedition. Just anything related to Patty."

The way the law read, anything Taggart saw in plain sight in the garage was fair game. And if he heard or saw anything related to Patty, then he could open a closet door or look in a locker.

"You stay out here with them. I'll have a look around."

"Right."

Taggart walked into the garage and shut off the radio playing an '80s rock song. The space smelled of gasoline and oil. A workbench was covered with all kinds of auto repair equipment. A poster of a blonde in a blue bikini hung on the wall. Miss July 1988 was hot enough to stand the test of time. The sights and sounds brought back memories of thousands of hours working in the old bastard's garage.

He searched the garage bay, the office, and a storage shed out back. It was unlocked. He opened the door. If he found Patty, dead or alive, he would find a reason to justify why he'd searched inside.

The storage shed was crammed full of extra parts, hoses, old tires, and all kinds of crap that ate up almost the entire space. The chances of anyone storing a body or holding a woman here were slim to none.

After forty-five minutes, he conceded that there was no evidence Patty was on the property. That didn't let Summers off the hook, but after this fruitless search, he wasn't getting another warrant unless he had more cause.

Outside, he found Paxton and the boys joking about something. When they saw him, Paxton had the sense to wipe the smile off his face. Seth looked a little contrite. Summers did not.

"Tough coming up empty-handed, isn't it, Sheriff?" Summers said. "I could've told you she's alive and well. Mark my words: She's hanging in a hotel room with someone from the festival. She always liked the artistic types."

The car radio buzzed. Irritated, Taggart grabbed it. "What is it, Brenda?"

"We got another call about a third missing woman."

His body stilled. "Who?"

"Debra Jackson. She never showed up to work or school yesterday."

"Who called in the report?"

"Her younger half sister. Marsha Sullivan. She's sixteen, a minor."

"Where's the mother?"

"Miss Sullivan says their mother is out of town with the stepfather. Debra lives alone in a trailer. Moved out of the family home last winter. The high school called looking for Debra, and the sister covered for her. But Marsha got worried and called Debra's boss. Debra hasn't been seen since she left for the concert late Friday evening."

He rolled his head as tension wrapped around his neck. "Okay. I'm on my way back."

"Another thing. Her unit is down the street from Patty Reed's trailer."

Chapter Twenty-Seven

SLOANE

Monday, August 18, 2025, 3:00 p.m.

Back at the cabin, the afternoon sun had softened. What filtered through the trees didn't quite reach the cabin's interior. And the few table lamps and single overhead fixture didn't brighten the drab room.

I dragged Taggart's recliner toward the window, hoping to see better as I settled in the chair to reread the digitized police reports detailing his visit to Larry Summers's garage.

Maybe most would be upset reading a father's callous words about his daughter. But I wasn't upset. I cared as much about Larry Summers as he did me. I had no feeling for him. In many ways, I was him.

Brian Fletcher had asked if I had children. Said I should grab the chance if I ever had it. But Larry's words were proof I would be a disaster as a parent.

At this stage of his investigation, Taggart had three missing women to find. By the time Tristan Fletcher's report had been filed almost a week later, the case was making headlines in local news. Soon it would go national. Dawson became ground zero for every reporter looking to get an exclusive.

As Larry was quickly cleared, a rush of reports flooded the Dawson sheriff's office. These claims of missing women created lists of possible victims and offenders who all needed to be interviewed. But Taggart's attention never wavered far from Rafe Colton, who remained the number one suspect in his mind.

The landline's ringer echoed in the cabin, cutting the silence. I almost reached for my cell, then realized the phone remained mounted on the wall. This token of the past was irritating. I raised the receiver to my ear. "Hello?"

"This is Bailey from the rental office."

"Bailey. How are you?"

"That's my question for you. How are you doing up there? That place has had its issues over the years, and I'd hate it if you were without hot water, or a toilet didn't flush."

She'd not called about toilets. "There's only one."

"Are you saying it's an issue?"

"No. Everything flushes just fine."

"Good. Good."

"Is that it?"

"How's your story going?"

"Slow and steady."

"No new revelations?" she asked.

"I'm piecing it together."

"What does that mean?"

"Not sure yet." I turned and the cord twisted around my body. "While I have you, I have a couple of questions about the festival."

"Why would you want to talk to me?"

"You were there. You saw it all happen."

Her voice dipped. "I was drunk that night. And don't put that in any article, please."

I took a step toward my notes, but the cord stopped me. "Weren't you friends with Debra? She worked at the dry cleaner's."

"Yeah, sure. She was supposed to meet me at the concert. But we never connected."

"Your dad didn't approve of her."

"Daddy could be a real snob. We didn't see eye to eye on a lot of things."

"Kevin brought Debra to the concert."

"That's right."

"How do you know that? You said you never saw her."

"I ran into Kevin that night. He told me she was at the festival."

The surveillance footage at the dry cleaner's showed Kevin picking Debra up close to 10:00 p.m. "What time was that?"

"About eleven. It started raining harder soon after."

"And you never hooked up with Debra at the concert?"

"Nope."

"Didn't you tell Taggart you walked home? But that wasn't exactly true."

"Once I sobered up, I didn't see the point in leaving. The place was rocking."

"Did you see Buddy?"

"Yeah. He was at the hamburger tent when I stumbled over there to get a burger."

"Was Patty there?"

"She was. But right after she served me, she took her break."

"What time was that?"

"Close to midnight."

"Did you see a blonde working with Patty?"

"I don't think so. But who knows."

Bailey wouldn't have been the type to notice burger-stand workers. "What about Kevin Pascal?"

"Mr. Security Guard. He was around, puffed chest looking like he was it." Before I could ask another question, she said, "Do all these little details really matter?"

"They're filling in pieces of the picture."

"Be careful you don't let the case drive you crazy like it did Taggart. The man was obsessed for the rest of his life."

"How so?"

"He was seen walking in the woods near the farm. He spent a lot of time in the Depot, as if he expected Patty or Debra to return."

"Why do you think he finally killed himself?"

"Lord only knows."

I couldn't decide if Bailey was worthless or lying. "Right. Thanks." I hung up.

Many cops served their entire career and never worked a massive case like the Mountain Music Festival. And Taggart had won the big prize. He had arrested his man. If life were a state fair, he'd have walked away with the giant blue stuffed Cookie Monster.

But he'd not wrapped up all the loose ends. And I'd seen loose ends and unanswered questions lead to obsession and self-destructive behaviors. I'd read about tough-as-nails officers who'd wrestled under the weight of unsolved cases. The burden was especially heavy in child abduction or murder cases. Some found a way to move forward. Others lost their sanity.

Most thought my obsession with this case was fruitless. More about ego and clicks than justice. In their minds, what difference would it make? Yeah, sure, a dying man wouldn't go free, but what harm could a guy like that do now? Even if I hit the bull's-eye, I wasn't winning a first-place prize. My carnival reward amounted to a cheap plastic key chain, or a rubber bouncy ball soon tossed in a junk drawer or the trash.

But I didn't care. The critics could eat it. I was here for the dead.

Chapter Twenty-Eight

CJ TAGGART

Wednesday, May 25, 1994, 9:00 a.m.
4 Days After

Taggart swung by the diner to grab his morning coffee. He glanced toward the counter, half hoping to see Patty. But Buddy was behind the counter topping off coffee for a customer. His smile looked strained. Another customer asked for a refill and another for a menu. Buddy clearly felt Patty's absence.

Taggart spotted the mayor in a booth in the back. He wasn't front and center or shaking hands but lying low. More complaints and questions about the festival were snowballing, and Taggart knew Briggs must be feeling the pressure. When the weekend hangover passed, folks realized the festival might have created as many problems as it had promised to solve.

Taggart crossed to the mayor's booth. "Mind if I sit down?"

Mayor Briggs nodded. "If you've got good news."

Taggart sat. Buddy caught his gaze and then set a mug in front of him. He filled the cup. "Thanks, Buddy. Any word from Patty?"

"Not a word." His brow furrowed. "I stopped by her trailer this morning. Sara was there with the baby, but no Patty."

"Any idea where she went?"

"None. And I've called everyone I can think of."

Taggart thought about the folded blankets in the baby's crib. "She the kind of woman to leave her baby behind?"

"No. Not Patty," Buddy conceded. "She's crazy about that kid."

Taggart sipped his coffee. "Is she seeing anyone other than you?"

Buddy glanced at Briggs. "No."

"Okay. Thanks."

"Sheriff, tell me when you find her," Buddy said.

"Will do."

As Buddy moved to another table, Taggart sat in silence, not bothering a glance toward the mayor. He'd never been good at sucking up to the brass, and civilian life had not changed that.

"Maybe Patty did run off," Mayor Briggs said.

"Along with Laurie Carr and Debra Jackson? I have three missing person reports on my desk now."

"Why didn't you tell me about Debra?"

"I'm doing that now."

"I don't know Laurie, but Debra doesn't have the best homelife." The mayor drummed his fingers against the side of his mug as if flipping through a card catalog of excuses.

"I hear Debra is doing well on her own. And Laurie's aunt said she always checks in."

"Three single women. Maybe they're partying together." The mayor grunted. "This isn't a five-alarm fire."

The mayor's easy dismissal of the women irritated him. "It's a pattern I don't like."

The mayor pushed his half-eaten plate of food away. "Don't get over your skis, Sheriff. There were thousands of people at the event. And the fact that three are missing doesn't mean much yet. They'll turn up. Just you wait and see."

"And if they don't?"

"From what Colton told me yesterday, the festival brought in a lot of money. Dawson's going to see a big check. And he said the music reviews in the papers were good. He said it's a matter of time before other music festivals are looking at us. This is going to be big for Dawson."

Colton said, "Have you seen the money?"

"Not yet. That kind of thing takes a little time." Briggs sipped his coffee. "Don't tarnish Dawson's reputation."

"I'm going to keep looking for these women."

"Try to be discreet."

"That's going to be easier said than done. Sara Grayson called a local reporter. She's trying to get interviewed."

His face paled. "Does she know about Debra or this guitar girl?"

"Sara and Monica Carr spoke at the station."

"Shit. This is a small town, and rumors run through Dawson like wildfire."

"Good."

The mayor tossed his balled-up napkin on the plate. "What's good about it?"

"The more people who know about the three missing women, the more tips I receive. I'm considering a press conference."

"You know that's not how it works. Every nutjob and his brother are going to be calling the station and reporting a sighting. That happened five years ago when the Taylor boy went missing."

The Taylor boy had been a five-year-old who'd wandered off from his parents' campsite. "I heard about that case. One tip from a couple of hikers led to his rescue. That's how it goes. Needle in a haystack."

"That's not very efficient."

"Solving a crime isn't an easy process."

"Crime." The mayor leaned forward and dropped his voice. "We're not talking about a crime. We're talking about three girls out of thousands who got a wild hair and took off."

"Three young women who were known for being reliable. And now they're gone."

"They'll turn up."

Taggart wasn't so sure. He took two more gulps of coffee. Monica had said Debra had broken up with Kevin Pascal. Time to track him down.

◆ ◆ ◆

Taggart found Kevin Pascal working security at the local furniture plant east of town. Rumor had it the company was going out of business and everyone there would be out of a job soon. Kevin had been hired to make sure none of the exiting employees did any damage or hurt the management.

Inside Taggart found a receptionist sitting at a small brown desk. She was in her sixties, and he was willing to bet she'd worked there most of her life. Her smile was tired, as if she knew the job was going away. "I'm looking for Kevin."

Without much fanfare, the receptionist picked up her phone and dialed. Five minutes later Kevin emerged in a security guard uniform.

"Kevin?" Taggart asked.

Kevin didn't appear surprised to see the sheriff as he walked up to him. His hand was outstretched. "Yes, sir. What can I do for you?"

"I got a call from Marsha Sullivan. You know her?"

Kevin cleared his throat. "Yeah. I know her."

"Marsha said her sister, Debra, is missing."

His smile disappeared. "What do you mean, missing? I dropped Debra off at the music festival Friday night. Her car was parked in front of the dry cleaner's this morning."

"You drove her?"

"Yeah. You saw me. I was working the event."

"I saw you."

"You know traffic was going to be hellacious, and I had a parking spot. I offered to drop her off at the front gate."

"What were you doing at the dry cleaner's?"

"Picking up my uniform. The call to work the festival security was last minute."

"Last minute?" Colton had said security was all lined up.

"My boss called and said he had a request for security, and he was rounding up men. I rushed to get my uniform from the dry cleaner's. I offered Debra a ride."

"What did you think when you and Debra arrived at the festival?"

"The event was a crush. Poor borders. A security nightmare."

"Did you and Debra hang out together at all?"

"We grabbed a quick picture together and then I had to get to work. I saw a fight that needed to be broken up. Debra went looking for her sister."

Many guys like Kevin wanted to be cops. Most failed some portion of the entrance exam and often saw their job as a kind of deputization. Taggart found if he treated them as equals, they were very helpful. "Can you give me a report on the event?"

He shifted his stance and hooked a thumb in his belt. "Lots of theft. Pickpockets and snatched purses. I stopped a couple of guys who were getting handsy with drunk girls. And there was a small container fire near the woods."

"Fire."

"Folks filled an old metal drum with wood and set it on fire near the woods. They were trying to keep warm. It wouldn't have been an issue, but the fire was so close to the tents and the trees. We were getting rain, but, you know, it was dry as a bone for weeks. I made them put it out."

"That wasn't the big one?"

"No, that came later. About one a.m."

Taggart hadn't seen the first fire, but there was a lot he'd missed that night. "Anything else?"

"I patrolled. There were kids trying to get on the stage to see the band. Had to chase them away. Then there was the basic urinating in public or indecent exposure."

"Good work. And you never saw Debra?"

He shook his head. "I wished her a good evening, and she vanished into the crowd."

"Was she meeting anyone other than her sister?"

"Yeah. Her friend Bailey Briggs."

Bailey. "Blond. Petite."

"Yeah. She and Debra go to high school together. You know her?"

"Came across her at the event."

"Hard to keep Bailey down for long. She's always on the move."

"Those two tight?"

"I don't know if they are super friendly. But they both love music and wanted to see the bands."

"I hear Debra works pretty hard."

"She's driven. You know her stepfather is a bit of a douche. She moved out last fall."

"When did you two break up?"

"January."

"Can I ask why?"

"I don't see why it matters. She wants to go to college. I want to stay local and keep doing what I love to do."

"You like the security work?"

"It's temporary. I want to get into the police academy."

"Have you applied?"

"Once last year. Blew the shooting exam. But I've been practicing."

"Keep at it. The admissions offices always like the guys who are hard workers."

"Well, I do work hard." He leaned forward as if they were sharing confidential information. "Mind if I ask why you're looking for Debra? I mean, she's over eighteen and is independent."

"Marsha says she missed work and school."

"She's done that before. I mean, Debra is steady about ninety-five percent of the time. But she gets revved up every so often."

"You think she got a wild hair?"

"She's been working so hard. She didn't get into her first choice of college and had to accept her second choice. She was disappointed. I told her I was proud of her, but she was bummed about it."

"When did you have this conversation?"

"On the way to the festival. It was nice catching up with her. We'll always be friends."

"You're not worried about her?"

"No." He angled his head as if sharing a secret. "I mean, if she doesn't show up in a day or two, then I would worry."

"Her boss said she hasn't missed work before."

"Like I said, her not getting into her first-choice college hit her hard. We used to blow off steam together. I know her. She's with a guy. And once she gets disappointment out of her system, she'll be back."

Taggart never liked it when a witness had all the answers. Most were unsure or had doubts. Not Kevin. He was so sure about a girl he'd not dated in four months. A girl who'd broken up with him. A girl who'd met up with an intoxicated classmate.

"Do you know Patty?"

"From the diner? Sure."

He kept his tone light and his stance nonconfrontational. Just two LEOs shooting the shit. "Is she friends with Debra?"

"They live almost next door to each other. I don't know Patty that well, but Debra likes everyone."

"Okay. Thanks, Kevin. Mind if I call you if I have more questions?"

"Yeah. Call me. I'm here to help."

Taggart extended his hand. "Thanks. Nice to have you on my side."

◆ ◆ ◆

Taggart pulled up in front of Bailey's house. She'd been one of the first people detained, and then she'd vanished from the first aid trailer. He'd hoped her case was a one-off, but she'd been the harbinger of the night to come.

He parked in front of the simple white house with a neat front lawn. Her father was the mayor and the primary engine behind the festival. It made sense the girl wouldn't want her father knowing she'd been detained by the police.

He rang the bell and stepped to the side. A dog barked inside. The door opened to Bailey. She looked very different than she had at the festival. Her makeup was subtle, clean, and her blue eyes were clear.

"Hey, Sheriff. What's up? Daddy's not here right now."

"I came to talk to you about the festival."

Her smile faded. "Do we have to do this now? My parents are going to be home soon."

"It's not about you being drunk in public or that you're underage." He wanted her to feel the weight of the charges he could bring.

She glanced around as if she expected a parent to be listening. "Okay."

"It's about your friend Debra."

"What about her?"

"You saw her at the festival?"

"Yeah. We met off to the side of the stage. We hung out for a few hours. Why do you care?"

"She's missing."

Bailey threaded her fingers through her hair. "What?"

"Her sister called the station. No one has seen her since the festival."

"That doesn't make sense. She was right in the center of the action when I saw her."

"Who was she with?"

"A girl. Tristan, I think."

"Tristan Fletcher."

"How did you know?"

He countered with a question. "What time was this?"

"About eleven, I think."

"Why did you and Debra go your separate ways at the event?"

"I wanted to get something to eat. My stomach was a little messed up. She didn't want to leave because a new band was starting to play. When I ate my burger and returned to our spot, she was gone. I was beat and didn't feel great, so I decided to go home."

"Did you see Patty at the stand?"

"Yeah. She looked overwhelmed, but she was there. So was Buddy."

"What time was this?"

"It wasn't quite midnight. And it was pouring rain."

"And Debra has not tried to contact you since the concert?"

"No. But we don't talk all the time. Do you think something bad happened to her?"

"Was she drinking?" he asked.

"Sure."

"Were you drinking more?"

"A little. Like I said, my stomach was messed up."

"What about Kevin? Did you see him?"

Her face crumpled into a grimace. "No. I didn't see Mr. Weird."

"Why do you call him that?"

"Because he's odd. He thought of Debra as a wife. He had their whole future mapped out. He even had names for their kids."

"Kevin said he and Debra wanted different lives. That's why they broke up in January."

Bailey laughed. "That's true. But there was nothing mutual about it. Debra broke it off. He wasn't happy about the split."

"Has he had contact with Debra?"

"Not that I know of." Her head cocked. "Do you think he hurt her?"

"I don't know. I'm just asking questions so I can find Debra."

"If she calls me, I'll let you know."

A silver Ford Taurus pulled into the driveway alongside his car. The mayor, dressed in a charcoal-gray suit, rose out of the car. His serious gaze settled on Taggart.

"That's my dad," Bailey whispered. "Don't tell him what I just told you, okay?"

Taggart didn't make any promises as Mayor Briggs approached him. "Good afternoon, Mayor."

His quizzical gaze turned suspicious. "Sheriff. Can I help you?"

"I'm trying to find Debra. From what I understand, she's a friend of your daughter's."

Mayor Briggs frowned. "Bailey, I thought we agreed you would hang out with different people."

Bailey's smile straddled humor and contrition. "I am, Dad. I told you: Sheila and I were going to the festival. I just ran into Debra there."

Mayor Briggs's jaw tensed. "You were back at Sheila's home by one a.m., correct?"

Logistically, there was no way she could have gotten off the mountain at midnight and made it back to Dawson in an hour unless she had wings.

"Yeah," Bailey said. "I didn't want to wake you and Mom."

Taggart watched the girl. She was lying to her father. "We left way before it started raining."

Bailey was full of secrets. But that wasn't a shock with teenagers. "Mayor Briggs, I'm contacting all of Debra's acquaintances. Bailey is just one of many names on my list."

Briggs glanced at his daughter as if searching for the telltale signs of a lie. The girl's face was unreadable. "If my daughter hears from this girl, I'll have her contact you."

Chapter Twenty-Nine

SLOANE

Monday, August 18, 2025, 5:00 p.m.

I liked cemeteries. I didn't have a lot of bandwidth for the living, but the dead were okay. They were quiet, undemanding, and patient. The four women I was searching for weren't pestering me or calling out for help. My driving force was me. But it always had been.

As I walked the rows of tombstones, I inhaled the scent of cut grass. The land stretched out over the rolling hills toward the mountains in the distance. I guessed if you cared about where you ended up, this place was okay. Me, I didn't want to be in the ground. Who wants to be locked in the same space forever? Nope. Burn me and sprinkle my ashes.

I'd searched for a grave marker on the cemetery's website, but here now, it took me a moment to orient myself. When I spotted a few landmarks, I moved west. It took five minutes to find the right grave.

I glanced down at the brass plate. The marine logo followed by CJ TAGGART, 1944–2020.

"Figured I should stop by and pay my respects. But I'm not sure how me standing here accomplishes that." I knelt and brushed the leaves from the plate. "It's taken me a while, but I'm working the case now. No one wants me here."

Wind whispered through the trees.

"But that pretty much sums up my life." The irony was amusing.

"You talking to him?"

The question came from a man standing at a fancier grave up ahead. He appeared to be in his late seventies. He had gray hair, a weather-lined face, and a thick mustache. He wore khakis and an ironed white shirt.

"I am. Who are you?"

"Mitch Lawson. I come each day to visit my wife." Fresh flowers filled the vase at the grave. Wilted ones of the same variety were discarded on a sheet of newspaper.

I looked behind that to the gravestone of Daisy Lawson. She'd died ten years ago. "Did you know CJ Taggart?"

"We often found ourselves at the diner for supper. You must be the reporter."

I rose. "I'm not a reporter. Just a writer."

"Aren't they the same?"

"Reporters recite the facts. I'm trying to re-create the story."

"What's that mean?" Mr. Lawson asked.

I'd explained this distinction before, but most didn't understand that my work was more of a calling than a paycheck. "I don't want a headline or clicks. I'm looking for the missing women."

"They aren't missing. They're dead."

"Still missing." He was right. Finding bones in the ground wouldn't change much in the grand scheme. But all answers, even the bad ones, were better than none.

"Any leads?" Mr. Lawson asked.

"Not yet." I stepped toward him. "Did Taggart ever talk about the case?"

A hint of shaving cream was smudged on the skin under his ear. Back in the day, his wife probably would have wiped it away before he left the house. "If he did, it was always around an anniversary, when a reporter showed up to ask questions."

"I've read all the articles on the case. The last anniversary article was ten years ago."

"That's right. My wife, Daisy, had just passed about that time. And I was in the diner often. The reporter was interviewing Taggart in the back booth."

The last article had been a predictable rehashing of old facts. Nothing new. "Did Taggart remark on the interview?"

"He didn't like the guy quizzing him. Said he hadn't done his homework."

The reporter had no curiosity about the missing victims. "Did you know any of the women?"

"My daughter went to high school with Debra."

"What was your daughter's impression of Debra? She the kind of gal who would just take off?"

"Carrie said Debra was focused. She had her sights set on college. Carrie always said Debra was going places."

"I've heard that. Did Carrie know Kevin?"

The old man shifted, drawing attention to his bony shoulders under his shirt. "She said Debra could do better."

"Kevin told Taggart he was cool with the breakup. Said he had moved on."

"That's not how I heard it. Carrie was out with Debra one evening. Kevin was following them."

"Following them? Maybe it was a one-off?"

"Debra commented that she was tired of him always being there."

"Kevin was a stalker?" The picture on his mantel proved he hadn't forgotten her.

"I don't think it got that bad. We live in a small town. But Carrie said Kevin tended to be around."

Taggart had pulled Kevin in for questioning. He had been cleared of all charges. "Do you remember where Kevin lived then?"

"Close to the furniture factory—now the computer company— where he works."

"That factory closed, correct?"

"About thirty years ago."

"How many jobs were lost?"

"Fifty or so. It was a hard blow to the town."

Kevin had left town after the trial. Folks treated him differently. Not everyone thought he was blameless. He'd moved back several years before Taggart died. "Did Carrie go to the concert?"

"No. I wouldn't let her go. No good comes out of young people fueled on booze and music." Mr. Lawson shook his head. "She was mad as a hornet."

Patty had been a year or two older than Carrie. She'd been at the festival for work, not fun. Sara, when she drank, grumbled that she'd told Patty not to take the job. But I'd never blamed Patty for chasing the money that could set her free. "Did you follow the trial?"

"Everyone did. Hard not to. That consumed us all for almost eight months. Reporters flocked to town."

"That would've meant a local revenue bump," I quipped.

He grunted. "Mayor Briggs said as much once."

How much money had been made off the backs of those dead women? "Any theories about the location of the bodies?" It was a Hail Mary kind of question. They rarely worked, but every so often I scored.

"I always thought they were close. So many hiding places then. Old wells, rock quarries, sheds, barns."

"The search crews spent months combing the area."

"They didn't start up for a good ten days after the festival. And we were going through a hot spell that year. Human remains don't look human after a week or two in the heat." Mr. Lawson sniffed. "Have you talked to the man serving life in prison for four murders? Rafe Colton knows."

"Working on getting that interview. But I'm not in a rush."

"Why not?"

"Everyone hangs on his every word. And he likes that. I'm in no rush to dangle the bait only to have him snatch it away."

"I'd let him rot. He's been in prison for almost thirty-one years and will die there."

"He's up for parole. He'll get out if I don't find those bodies."

Mr. Lawson muttered an oath. "Wouldn't that be something. He gets out because Taggart didn't find the bodies."

I wondered if Taggart was turning over in his grave. "Colton's aware that I'm working on this article. It's nice to think he has plenty of time in his cell to think about what I'm writing about. I want him to wonder and maybe worry a little longer."

He chuckled. "You don't look troubled."

"I'm not."

"Taggart used to say his greatest wish was five minutes inside Colton's mind."

"Do you think that's what got to Taggart?"

"He never uncovered all his answers, and it really bothered him. Maybe the thinking did him in."

How many times had I wished for deeper insight into a killer's head? Maybe one day, I'd find that insight and still hold on to my less-than-normal life. "Did he think Colton could have had help with the bodies?"

"He never mentioned that until the very end. A couple of weeks before he died, he thought he might have a lead."

"Did he say what?"

"No. Said it could be nothing."

Five years ago, I had Taggart's case files, but I was ignoring them. Maybe if he'd reached out sooner, Taggart might have talked to me. "I'll keep that in mind."

"What do you think the chances of finding those bodies are?"

I wanted to find them, but what I wanted didn't always jibe with what the universe doled out. "Bad odds have never stopped me before. In fact, I like them."

"I almost hope you don't find them."

"Why?"

"They're dead. No unearthed bones will change that. And finding the bodies will tear open old wounds in this town. That case just about did us in. Took years for people to forget."

I had no problem tearing Dawson in two if it meant finding the bodies. "That's what I keep hearing."

"Be careful. A lot of money was lost after that festival, and folks are real protective of what they have rebuilt."

I drove out to where the old furniture factory had been located and found myself staring at PH Puckett Computers, Kevin Pascal's employer. The building was an island of reflective glass and metal. Surrounded by a mile of asphalt parking, it was a guidepost to Dawson's future.

The furniture company had failed, but the land remained in a prime location off Interstate 64 between Dawson and Staunton. Made sense it would get reused.

Kevin drove here five days a week. Time had allowed people to forget an old arrest and the festival, making it easier for his return. He'd come full circle.

I was convinced the abductions were a two-person job. For years, Taggart had not second-guessed his investigation. He'd locked on his target, didn't look left or right, and never considered other scenarios. However, if Lawson was correct, maybe something had changed Taggart's mind.

Whoever had helped Colton had been an unexpected accomplice. There'd been a report of a scream from the woods. Multiple people had seen Colton at one point or another during the evening. There'd not been long enough gaps for him to abduct four women.

I crossed the lot and walked into the glittering lobby. Finding a smile, I crossed to the reception desk. "Is Kevin Pascal here?"

The woman looked up at me. Brown eyes narrowed behind thick lenses. "Who are you?"

"Sloane Grayson."

She nodded. "The reporter."

Writer, but why bother to correct her. "That's right. Is he here?"

"I'm not sure."

I jabbed my thumb over my shoulder. "His car is in the lot."

She glared as if the death stare would make me vanish. When I remained intact, she reached for a pen and pad. "I can leave him a message. He's working now."

"Patrolling the mean streets of Puckett Computers? I'll wait until he can take a break. I'll just sit over there."

She frowned. "I'll call the police if you don't leave."

"Okay. Call them. It'll make for good fodder for my article."

"I'll buzz him again."

Three minutes later, the side door opened. Kevin appeared. He wore his dark uniform, starched and crisp. This close, I could see he was heavier and his hair thinner than the young man in the picture with Debra at the festival. Frown lines etched heavy grooves around his mouth.

"Mr. Pascal," I said. "Thank you for seeing me."

He didn't speak but guided me outside, away from the receptionist. "Why did you show up where I work?"

"It's a good place to find people."

His fingers tightened into a fist. "I don't want any trouble."

I smiled. "Neither do I. I just want to talk."

"I've heard you've been all over town asking about the festival."

"I've been busy, yes."

He slid his hands into his pockets. "I don't have anything to add. Why are you here?"

"You were part of the security team at the festival. You had a ringside seat to the chaos."

"I barely remember the festival."

"And Debra. Do you remember her?"

Hearing her name darkened his eyes. "I'll never forget her."

"When was the last time you saw her?"

"She was by the stage. She and Bailey were drinking and dancing."

"She and Bailey were close?"

"As close as Bailey could get to anyone. Debra thought they were friends. But Bailey hung out with Debra to piss off her dad."

"I thought Bailey was close to her father."

"No. She hated the old man."

"Why?"

He rattled pocket change. "You'd have to ask her."

"You never saw anything suspicious at the festival?"

He looked over his shoulder to the company's front door. "I saw a lot of trouble that night. But I put it all in a report to the sheriff."

"Taggart searched your truck?"

He shoved out a breath. "He didn't find anything."

"That piss you off?"

"I didn't like it, but I knew he'd find nothing. Cops got to do what they got to do. Part of the job."

"What about Colton?"

"Colton. He was charming. Fun."

A car drove past, and the driver glanced in our direction. Kevin shifted, uncomfortable. "I drove Debra to the festival, saw her once at the stage, and then lost track of her. That's all I have."

"Why did you leave town for twenty years?"

"Hard living here after the festival. The festival was a raw wound for a lot of years."

"And you came back when the coast was clear?"

His lips thinned. "Yep. This place is home."

"What's the deal with the barn on Miller Road?"

His jaw pulsed. "What do you want to know? It's falling in on itself. Used to be part of a large farm."

"You used to go there when you were younger?"

"What kind of question is that?"

"Just asking. Did you take Debra there when you dated?"

"Sure. We camped out there a couple of times. Why does that matter?"

"Was it searched when the women vanished?"

"I'm sure it was." He shifted. "I hear the land has been purchased, and the barn is going to be torn down."

"Who bought it?"

"I don't know." He took a step back.

"Seen Marsha Sullivan since you returned home?"

"No."

I enjoyed watching the tension ripple through his body. "I like her. We had a nice conversation."

"Okay. Great. If that's all you got, I'm done. And going forward, leave me alone."

Chapter Thirty

CJ Taggart

Wednesday, May 25, 1994, 6:00 p.m.
4 Days After

Taggart parked in front of the small house that Rafe Colton had rented a few miles from Dawson. Colton had moved in three months ago, when festival planning had kicked into high gear. He'd been a fixture in town offices and council meetings. Whenever there was doubt about the festival's feasibility, he was there to charm anyone who needed persuading.

Taggart strode up to the front door and knocked. Inside, rock music blared. When he didn't hear footsteps, he pounded hard.

The door opened and a bleary-eyed Colton faced him. He flashed a broad, disarming grin. "Sheriff. Hey. The cleanup crews should be on-site any minute."

"I was there midday and didn't see anyone." Four days after the festival ended, the Nelson farm looked like a garbage dump. Trash, clothes, and shoes littered the trampled ground.

Colton's smile softened with contrition. "I know my people have been slow. And that's on me. I've been on the phone with Briggs telling him the same."

Few guys like Colton served in combat, and when they did, men died. "Like the security team you hired for the event?"

Colton held up his hands in surrender. "That wasn't my fault. I had a contract with the company. They screwed me."

"I hear you called Woodward in a panic on Friday looking for men."

"That isn't true. I called months before. They lost the paperwork. That wasn't my fault."

"It was your job to make sure that security was covered."

"I *know*. I fucked up. Buck stops with me. But the festival is over, and there were no major disasters. I'll do better next time. I learned valuable lessons."

"Rapes, robberies, and missing women. I'd say there were several disasters."

"There's always someone that goes MIA after an event like that. Too many drugs or two much booze distorts their brains for a while. Then they clean up and stumble home. Rapes and robberies happen anywhere, anytime."

"These missing women aren't fools."

He grinned. "Everyone has it in them. We all go nuts from time to time. It's being human, right?"

"I looked you up in the system."

"And you found the charges against me. I'm no choirboy. And flirting with the ladies is part of the job when you're in entertainment." The grin returned. "Chicks love music men."

Taggart wasn't charmed. "A woman filed a stalking complaint against you. She said she woke up and found you at the foot of her bed."

"I'm very aware. Her name is Cassidy Rogers. And she's mad because I wasn't faithful to her." He held up his hands. "I have a reputation for being a player. I'm always up front about that." He shrugged. "It pissed her off, and she decided she needed some revenge."

"Cassidy said you climbed on top of her. She said you put your hands around her neck and threatened to strangle her."

"And the investigating officer found no marks on her neck, did they?"

"They did not."

"Because I didn't try to hurt her. She invited me over, accused me of cheating. I talked her down and into bed. And then she lost her shit."

The officer had insisted on executing a rape kit. And Ms. Rogers had agreed. Colton's semen had been found in the woman, but there'd been no signs of vaginal bruising. There'd also been no indication of trauma on her body.

Colton could be telling the truth. Had the woman filed her complaint to get back at him? She wouldn't be the first. Or Colton had been acting out some of his darkest fantasies when he'd put his hands around the woman's neck. Without squeezing, he might've been curious if her pulse would quicken or her breathing speed up. For whatever reason, he could have lost his nerve. That incident had occurred three years ago, and there'd been no formal complaints since. Still, three years was lot of time to refine his fantasies and bolster his nerve to kill.

Colton leaned forward a fraction, as if they were pals. "What do you want from me, Sheriff? I'm not a great administrator. Guilty as charged. I'll get the trash picked up. And we can all move on from this event."

"Patty, the young gal who worked at the hamburger stand, is one of the missing. You met her several times in town, didn't you?"

Colton sighed. "I saw her in the diner when I was hanging up posters. I shot the shit with her for a few minutes there and when she arrived at the festival. She seemed like a great kid."

"She was last seen by the toilets near the woods."

Colton shrugged. "What do you want me to say?"

"You know those woods were wide open. You had lots of people sneaking into the concert."

"It happens at every festival. It's impossible to secure all the borders." Colton shook his head. "Openness is the nature of festivals."

"I was promised the event border would be secure."

He shrugged as he slid his hands into his jean pockets like a chastised schoolboy. "I was wrong, okay? Not the perfect event, but it was a hell of a success. The crowds were a crush. It told me people are hungry for that kind of experience."

"Do you have final numbers on the event?" All Taggart had at this point were estimates.

"We sold all the tickets, but we had twice, maybe three times the estimates."

"You estimated five hundred people. There were at least two thousand at the festival."

"Wow. I didn't realize." He sounded pleased. "I knew we'd done well, but not that well. The bands loved it, and the music producers in the crowd loved the vibe. Great feedback from the trade magazines and reviews in the local papers."

Taggart had read the reviews and newspaper articles. They'd focused on the bands, the music, and the crowd's energy. The rain had been mentioned but not the sucking mud, dwindling food, and troubles in the woods. The entire event had been on the edge of chaos, but the sun had risen, the rains had eased, and people had cleared out. Colton believed he'd dodged a bullet.

◆ ◆ ◆

Taggart had a reputation for being single-minded. When an idea settled in his head, he couldn't let it go. That trait had helped him escape Dawson when he needed to, and later it assisted in solving hundreds of military cases. But it was the same quality that had gotten him drummed out of the marines.

Taggart located Cassidy Rogers. She worked as a waitress in a small café an hour west of Dawson. He'd read her report, and nothing had struck him as exaggerated. According to the responding officer, she'd been shaken but calm and clear.

Taggart walked up to the register. "I'm looking for Cassidy."

The young girl nodded toward a midsize woman with blond hair. "Thanks."

He approached the woman, careful not to invade her personal space. "Cassidy Rogers?"

She turned, her smile fading when she saw his uniform. "Yes?"

He removed his hat. "Mind if I ask you a few questions?"

"About?"

"Rafe Colton."

Her spine stiffened. "What about him?"

"Trying to get some background information on him."

"Why?"

"Is there somewhere we could talk?"

She nodded to the cashier and indicated she was taking a break. He followed her out back to an alley.

"What has Rafe done now?"

"Nothing that I know of. But I want to know more about him."

"He must have done something." She folded her arms. "He's in the center of another shitstorm."

"Why do you say that?"

"You must have an idea of my history with him, or you wouldn't be here." She inhaled. "I read a small article in the paper yesterday. A girl is missing after the Mountain Music Festival."

"It's three girls now."

She rolled her head. "I'm sorry to hear that."

"What's your history with Colton?"

"You read the reports."

"I want to hear it from you."

A silence settled over her. Going backward was never easy for him, and he guessed her as well. "I met him at a concert. He was repping a local band that I liked. We hit it off. We had a one-night stand, and life went on for me."

"But not for him?"

"I kept running into him. He always seemed to be at the café, or across the street, or at the grocery store. Creeped me out. And then I didn't see him for a couple of weeks, until I woke up in the middle of the night and found him at the foot of my bed. He was on top of me in a second."

"The medical report said that you had no bruising."

"He held a knife to my throat. Told me to lie very still. He said we would have a good time like we did the first time. I was terrified. So I lay still and let him do what he wanted. I mean, who was going to believe me, given our history? After, I thought he would leave, and that would be that. But he wrapped his hands around my neck. I felt the power in his hands. I hadn't looked at him before, but now I had no choice. His eyes looked black. He could have strangled me, and I couldn't do anything about it."

"And he just stopped?"

"My roommate came home. We both heard her in the living area, which was off my room. He let go of me and kissed me on the lips. He told me I was special. And he would never forget me."

"And he left?"

"Through the window. Like he'd come into the house." She picked at a callus on her palm. "I went to the hospital. And filed a report. But you know how far that went."

"Did your roommate take you to the ER?"

"No. I drove myself. I had sense enough not to shower."

"Did you ever see him again?"

"No. I made such a fuss, and he sensed if anything happened to me, he'd be on the suspect list. As soon as the charges were dropped, he left town."

"Did he try to strangle you the first time?"

"He put his hands around my neck. He didn't squeeze hard, but he got right in my face. He said he'd dreamed about that all his life."

"But you didn't file charges that first time?"

"No. I'd said yes. And I was drunk. I figured I got what I deserved because I'd been stupid."

"Know anyone else he did this to?"

"I try to stay as far away from him as I can."

"Thanks for your time."

"He liked seeing my fear," she said in a rush. "It excited him knowing he had my life in his hands."

"You mentioned you were aware of the festival."

"Yes."

"Did you go?"

She hesitated. "Yes."

"Why?"

"I thought it would be fun. But when I arrived, I couldn't stay."

"Why?"

"An event like that would be the perfect setup for him. Girls are drinking. Crowds. Music. Like shooting fish in a barrel. Easy for a girl to fall through the cracks."

Taggart drew in a breath. "Do you think Colton had a hand in the women's disappearances?"

"I don't know. But I wouldn't be surprised. A guy like that can't resist the temptation."

"Was he dating anyone? Any friend who helped him?"

"I heard he was dating another girl. Young. A dancer."

"Do you have a name?"

"No. But if you find her, you might get a few answers."

Hours later in the dark, Taggart sat outside Colton's house. The lights were on, and he heard music pulsing. He couldn't identify the song, but it was rock.

Darkness wrapped around him as he watched Colton pass his front windows. Beer in hand, Colton appeared to be singing. He was having a blast. No apparent worries about the wreckage of the festival or the three missing women.

Life was moving on for Colton.

Taggart flexed his right hand as his thoughts turned to Patty, Laurie, and Debra. One had come to the event to make money. One to make a name for herself. And the last for a much-needed break. Cassidy was right. He'd created the perfect event to hunt women.

Taggart pointed his finger at the window. "I'm going to get you."

Chapter Thirty-One

SLOANE

Tuesday, August 19, 2025, 5:00 a.m.

I pinched the bridge of my nose and closed my eyes. It was quiet in the woods. Only the sounds of wind, an owl, and maybe a bear pawing over the front porch. Through the canopy of trees, stars winked.

I'd been rereading the articles the press had written about the Mountain Music Festival. When Patty went missing, the media did not notice. When Laurie vanished, the world yawned. When Debra disappeared, everyone woke up. Three was a pattern. And stories spun around repetition.

Taggart held his press conference on a Sunday, nine days after the festival ended. One day after Taggart's press conference, Brian Fletcher arrived at the police station to report his daughter Tristan missing.

Tristan Fletcher. The dancer. Cassidy Rogers had said Colton had been dating a young dancer. Colton had been around a lot of dancers in the music world. Maybe he liked them in general. Long, fit young bodies were hard to resist. Tristan had been at the festival handing out wristbands. She'd been nearby when Taggart had broken up a fight during the festival.

Two days after Taggart's press conference, Mayor Briggs had insisted to a reporter the women would turn up. *"Estimates placed two, maybe three thousand people at the event. People are bound to get lost in the shuffle. Of course, we are searching. And if any of these women hear this, please reach out to the Dawson sheriff's office. Dawson is a peaceful town, and this festival was a celebration of life."*

The mayor was still spinning his positive story. He was a politician, and his job was to sell the town, but when did a positive outlook become negligence?

Nine days was a lifetime in the world of a missing person. Their golden hour had long tarnished.

My stomach was queasy, and I could feel energy building in me, as if a stopwatch embedded in my brain had sped up. *Ticktock.* Colton was getting out in twelve days, and I hadn't found an answer.

After a quick shower, I dressed and drove into town. I picked up aspirin at the local drugstore across from the Depot.

As I approached the diner, I saw Paxton enter. Sheriff Paxton liked his routine. He worked Monday through Friday and ate his breakfast here Tuesdays and Thursdays.

I walked into the diner and took the seat next to Paxton in the back booth. When he glanced at me, he looked more annoyed than curious. "Still working on your article?"

"I am."

Callie held up a pot of coffee, and I shook my head. "Soda?" she asked.

"That would be great. Thank you."

"Coming right up."

"Found out anything new?" Paxton asked.

"Hard to say." I jostled a couple of aspirin out of the bottle into my palm. I swallowed them. "I stare and stare at my computer screen but don't see the solution. All I need is the one critical piece, and it will come together."

Paxton lifted his cup. "What do you want to know?"

"The blue guitar case," I said. "You found it in the woods."

"That's right."

"Walk me through it." I had Taggart's version.

"After the press conference, the case exploded. Taggart and I knew the clock was ticking louder and louder."

By then the clock had expired. The women were dead. "Where did you find the case?"

"In the woods. It was lying at the base of a tree, half buried under leaves."

"And no one had seen it?"

"No one had looked yet. We all kept hoping the girls would be found. But after the press conference, we rallied volunteers and hit the woods hard. The minute I saw it, I knew it was important. I called Taggart over right away. He radioed dispatch and told them to get the county forensic team over."

"Your prints were found on the guitar case." I let the statement stand.

The fact had been lost over time. "I picked it up and then I put it back down."

"No gloves."

"I wasn't thinking."

"Understandable," I said. "There was a lot going on. When did you learn it was Laurie Carr's guitar case?"

"Right away. Her name was written on the inside."

"Brian Fletcher was the last to file a missing person report." I thought about the wall of photos in Mr. Fletcher's den. The Fletchers' lives had been condensed to thin paper images trapped in black wooden frames.

"That's right."

"Why do you think Mr. Fletcher was so late calling in Tristan's report?"

"Tristan's sister had told her parents that Tristan was staying with a friend. The sister saw the press conference and panicked. She told her parents she'd not heard from Tristan."

"Do you believe that?"

"Sure, why not?"

"Mr. Fletcher didn't realize Tristan was missing for nine days?"

"The wife was sick with cancer. Families under stress miss details."

Mr. Fletcher's wall of photos suggested he was obsessed with details. "Cassidy Rogers said Colton was dating a dancer."

"He dated a lot of women in the entertainment field."

"Tristan Fletcher was a dancer. Ever wonder if the two hooked up before the festival?"

"No way. Tristan was barely eighteen and going to a fancy dance school in the fall. She was too much of a straight arrow to date a guy like that."

"I keep coming back to the fact that Brian Fletcher was so late contacting the police. Maybe he knew something. Maybe he worried what the cops would discover if he called."

"We talked to Brian Fletcher for hours. His story never wavered."

"How do you think Colton got the bodies off the mountain?"

"There were dozens of trailers on-site near the stage. I think he stowed them in there and drove off with them after the concert ended."

"Colton was seen at the location the morning after, right?"

"Showered and clean. Looked fresh as a daisy."

"Does that track with a man who just disposed of four bodies?"

"No one realized there was a problem until three days after the event. Plenty of time to go back and retrieve the bodies." He shrugged. "That's what we thought."

I shook my head. "Did it bother you that no one, and I mean no one, heard any of the four girls screaming or resisting?" I lied.

"It was so crowded. A lot got missed."

"I think someone lured the women to a place where they could be subdued. And I think that person drove the bodies off the mountain for Colton."

"Taggart and I believed Colton was the classic Lone Wolf."

"Colton had a concert to run, but he still had time to subdue and murder four women? That's a busy guy."

"Colton wasn't too worried about the festival logistics. And he was doing cocaine. It can give a man superhuman strength."

"Toward the end of his life, Taggart began to suspect Colton had help." Taggart hadn't shared his theory with anyone other than Mitch. But I wasn't above passing that bit of news around town. "Did he ever run those theories past you?"

"He never said anything to me about it." He sipped his coffee. "Believe me, Colton acted alone."

As I left the diner, I saw Grant leaning against my truck, his arms folded over his chest. His eyes were shielded by Ray-Ban Wayfarer glasses. He wore a black T-shirt, jeans, and hiking boots.

"Your meeting with Colton will be in three days," he said.

I wasn't sure I was ready. There was a big missing piece of this puzzle. And I wanted it when I saw Colton. "Terrific."

He pushed away from the car, straightening to his six-foot-plus frame. "You're getting around."

"That's my job."

"You're onto something?"

"Like what?"

His head cocked. "I'm not sure. But you're getting close to something."

I met his gaze. "I could've stumbled upon a big pile of nothing."

"Paxton looked tense when you were talking to him."

"You were watching us?"

"I was."

I glanced toward my Jeep. "Where's the tracking device?"

A smile tipped his lips. "Say again?"

"There must be one on my Jeep. You keep showing up."

He shrugged. "Don't know what you are talking about."

I'd search the car when I got back to the cabin. "Okay."

"When you go to the prison, I'll be with you."

"Why?"

"You'll need the backup."

"I won't."

His smile broadened. "I'll be in touch with the exact time."

Chapter Thirty-Two

SLOANE

Tuesday, August 19, 2025, 11:00 p.m.

I couldn't sleep. I'd lain down about an hour ago and done nothing but toss and turn as the wind rustled through the trees. An owl hooted.

My tolerance for staring at ceilings was low. The more I willed sleep, the more elusive it became. I tossed back the covers and tugged on my T-shirt and jeans. I moved into the kitchen. Instead of putting a coffeepot on, I grabbed a ginger ale from the refrigerator.

Images of Fletcher's family picture wall kept returning to me. It resembled a shrine more than a memory wall. But snapshots didn't always tell the truth. Anyone could smile for a second or two and create the impression of happiness. I'd smiled for Sara whenever she pulled out her camera, which wasn't often. The muscles in my face had strained as I said "Cheese" and counted the seconds until I heard the camera's click.

Brian Fletcher had waited until after the press conference to report his daughter's disappearance. I popped the top on the soda and sipped as I moved to the window. I stared into the darkness. "Why did you wait?"

Cradling the can, I snatched a packet of luncheon meats from the refrigerator and my keys. At the Jeep, I dumped my backpack in the front seat. I grabbed a flashlight from the glove box and searched under the wheel wells and bumpers. I found a tracker under the right rear bumper. "Grant, don't you trust me?"

I pocketed the tracker. Engine started, I drove down the mountain as my headlights cut through the inky darkness. Gravel kicked under the tires as I skirted curves too fast. When I reached the bottom of the hill, I slowed at the stop sign but didn't stop rolling.

The drive to the Fletcher house took thirty minutes. When I pulled into the quiet suburban neighborhood, I cut my headlights. I wasn't the only night owl in this world, and I'd found in suburbia that when someone saw my headlights, they often called the cops. The Fletcher house was dark when I drove past it and around the corner. I parked across from a small park and retraced my steps back to the Fletcher house on foot.

I slipped through the gate and up to the sliding glass door. There were no signs indicating a security system, but that didn't mean he didn't have one. I tried the back door and discovered it was open. No security system beeped a warning. Why didn't everyone have an alarm and lock their doors?

Inside, I pushed past gauzy curtains and into the cool air-conditioned den. Using the light from the moon, I crossed to the wall of family photos. There were plenty of images of Tristan as a young teenager. And a few looked as if they'd been taken right before she'd vanished. She had a brilliant smile and an almost angelic face.

The years after her disappearance were stark. Dad, Mom, and little sister were all more sober and stiff. And then it was Dad and little sister. No more family vacations, no big smiles that touched the eyes. This progression was normal. The loss of a child and parent gutted families.

And then about twenty years ago, images of the sister appeared with another woman. She was blond, petite, and fit. I thought perhaps it was a life partner but discarded the thought. Both women had long, thin noses, high cheekbones, and square jaws. A cousin maybe?

I snapped several pictures of the sister and the other woman. I removed the picture from the wall and studied the second woman's face. She and Tristan had to be closely related. I flipped it over. It read "Lannie and Susan, 2010."

Paws padded down the hallway. Worried the dog would bark, I quickly removed the luncheon meat from my pocket and walked toward him.

"Hey, buddy," I whispered.

He wagged his tail. Most people thought a dog was protection, but domestic dogs had accepted humans since the caveman days. This fellow was no different. I tore up the meat and laid it out in a line on the kitchen floor. It would buy me enough time to leave the house.

I slipped out the back door as the dog gobbled. I closed the door and crossed the backyard. The back fence squeaked, and as I closed the latch, a light in the upstairs bedroom clicked on. I wasn't the only light sleeper.

I moved down the driveway and street as if I had every right to be there. I wasn't sneaking around or up to trouble. I belonged here. Most people accepted almost anything I did, as long as I projected authority.

In my Jeep near the park, I didn't study the images, because the longer I lingered, the greater my chance of being noticed. Headlights clicked on behind me. A glance in the rearview mirror told me it was a truck, but I couldn't see the driver.

I didn't panic but drove back toward Dawson, maintaining the speed limit. The second driver remained within fifty feet of me the entire time. It was almost 2:00 a.m. when I pulled into the Depot's parking lot.

I waited in my car scrolling on my phone until Callie turned on the restaurant lights and began setting up for breakfast customers. Minutes before 5:00, she flipped the sign from closed to open.

I shut off my engine and retrieved my gun from my glove box. Instead of hurrying inside, I walked back toward the truck behind me. I was more curious than worried.

Grant sat behind the wheel as if all this were normal. He almost looked amused.

I reached in my backpack and held up a tracker. "This belong to you?"

He was nonplussed by my discovery. "You're hard to keep up with otherwise."

If I cared, I'd be annoyed. Or maybe flattered. But neither registered. "You going to stay out here, or do you want to get coffee?" I asked.

"Coffee." He rose out of the truck.

I was tall for a woman, but he had me beat by five inches. I slipped the gun into my backpack and moved toward the diner. Inside, the scents of coffee and cinnamon pancakes greeted me. My appetite flickered but didn't flame.

Callie filled mugs for us. "Toast?"

"Perfect," I said.

"I'll take the pancakes," Grant said.

"Coming right up."

The diner was too quiet to muffle my conversation with Grant. "What do you want?"

He sipped his coffee. "What did you see in the Fletcher house?"

"Why didn't you try to stop me? Breaking and entering isn't legal."

"As long as you're not setting fires, better to let your process play out." He sipped his coffee. He'd been in law enforcement long enough to know how far to bend a rule. "I didn't see you break into the house. The first time I saw you, you were crossing the front yard and headed to the street. That might be considered trespassing, but I'm not a cop anymore."

Aware he waited for my answer, I shifted my focus to Callie and asked for a soda. When she set it in front of me, I took a long pull on the straw.

"What did you find?" he asked again.

I wasn't sure what I'd seen and realized I wanted to talk it through. "I focused on the wall of family photos."

"And?"

I opened the photos app on my phone. "Tristan's younger sister, Lannie, was photographed with another woman about twenty years ago. This woman is either a first cousin or Tristan in 2010."

"Tristan had been dead over fifteen years by 2010."

"I know. So, a cousin."

"Do you have a name for this cousin?"

"'Lannie and Susan' was written on the back of the image. I don't have more than that." I dragged my finger through the condensation on the side of the glass. "Brian Fletcher was the last of the four families to file a missing person report."

"Lannie didn't tell her parents that Tristan was at the festival. When Lannie did speak up, Brian filed his missing person report."

"It makes sense. Kids lie to their parents," I said. "I did my share."

He arched a brow. "No. Really?"

"Shocking, I know."

That teased a smile. "I have a twenty-two-year-old son. There were times when he used disinformation to his advantage."

Grant was in his early forties. He'd been a young parent like Patty. "I don't picture you chasing a kid."

"I did my fair share. So did his mother. For the record, we divorced two years ago."

I liked that he wasn't attached. "Sorry to hear that."

He shook his head. "She wanted a different life. It's for the best."

"Do you want to talk about it?"

"Not really."

"Good." I sipped my soda. "There was a lot of pressure on Taggart to solve this case. Word of missing women spread fast. This was a town where people didn't lock their doors until the festival."

"Within two weeks of the festival, Taggart arrested Colton." That arrest had earned Taggart twenty-plus years' worth of re-elections.

Callie returned with a plate of pancakes and one with toast. She set a fresh soda in front of me. I jabbed the straw into the floating crushed ice.

"Thanks," I said.

"Soda and toast," Grant said.

I always grabbed whatever sounded good. I chalked it up to the story. "My stomach often gets upset when I'm working."

"It's like this on every case?"

"Basically."

The front door opened, and several guys walked in. The waitress grabbed menus and walked toward them. I shifted my attention to the toast. I covered a slice with strawberry jam. The first bite was amazing, but by the third, I was full.

I reached for my phone and opened a social media app. I searched Lannie Fletcher's name. "The sister lives in Washington, DC, and works as an attorney. She's now forty-seven, is unmarried, and has no children."

As Grant sipped coffee, I opened Lannie's profile. "She hasn't posted a lot. Vacation pictures. Cabo. Sonoma. Hiking in southern France."

"Who's she hanging out with?"

"There was a dark-haired guy who was photographed with her a few years ago. But he's vanished from her page in the last year." I flipped through several years. In 2018 I found a picture of Lannie with Susan. The two were at a charity drive for missing kids held at the Dance Studio. The photographer had been about ten feet from the women. A death like Tristan's rippled through an entire family.

Grant took the phone and, with a swipe of his fingers, expanded the pictures. "Lannie didn't tag her, but she did tag the organization: Missing Children Found." On his phone, he searched the group. "Five pages into the Missing Children Found site, there's a photo of them. The tagline says Susan Westbrook."

I searched Susan Westbrook on several social media sites but discovered no profiles. I searched the Dance Studio. It was in Arlington, Virginia. It had multiple five-star reviews.

"Susan doesn't have any presence online. But the Dance Studio does." I studied the image of Lannie and Susan, still wondering if the unknown woman was Tristan decades into the future. "Tristan Fletcher's body was never found. Her high school ring was found in Colton's barn with the other victims' trinkets. Everyone assumed she'd died."

"You think she's alive?" He shook his head. "You're stretching this one."

"Why? Her body was never recovered."

"This means she's been in hiding for thirty-one years."

"It was easier to vanish in 1994."

"I don't know."

"Can you analyze the photo of Tristan Fletcher and Susan Westbrook and tell me if they're the same person?"

"I can do that."

"How long will it take?"

"A day. I still have friends who can push it through."

"That would be great. Thank you."

Amusement brightened his dark gaze. "'Thank you'? Where's the real Sloane?"

"Body snatchers took her yesterday. I'm a simulation."

He regarded me. "Good to know."

His scrutiny was unsettling. He saw something in me. I had no idea what, and I wasn't comfortable with it.

I shifted my focus back to the images of Susan and Tristan. Family genetics were powerful—Patty and I were living examples— but something about these two women set off red flags. My head was starting to pound. I needed a quiet place to process.

"Call me as soon as you have results," I said.

"Will do."

"See you soon."

"Where are you going?"

I tossed fifteen bucks on the table. "DC."

He grabbed my wrist. "Wait."

It wasn't an unbreakable grip. It was a suggestion. *Take a pause.* A comma in a sentence. So, I waited.

Chapter Thirty-Three

CJ Taggart

Monday, May 30, 1994, 10:00 a.m.
10 Days After

Following the press conference, the office was inundated with calls. Taggart recruited a half dozen volunteers to operate the phones so Brenda could do her job as a dispatcher. The office received at least thirty calls a day. A good portion were either crackpots, attention seekers, or the lonely. He'd known when he held the press conference the flood gates would open. But in the chaos, he had the chance for a lead that would help him find these women.

A knock on his door caused him to look up from his case notes. Brenda stood in his doorway. "I have another guy ready to file a missing person report."

There had been four additional missing person reports in the last twenty-four hours. Paxton had interviewed all the family members and located the four additional missing women. In each case, there'd been no foul play. Finding these women gave him hope the others would appear.

"Who do we have?" Taggart asked.

"His name is Brian Fletcher. He said his daughter Tristan was at the concert, and he's not seen her since the festival."

Taggart pulled in a slow, steady breath. "Okay. Show him in." He rose and straightened his tie. The man who appeared at his door was tall, lean, and fit. He had thick brown hair and faint lines feathering from his eyes.

Taggart came around his desk and extended his hand. Fletcher's grip was firm, but his gaze darted down and then back up. Fletcher looked like the kind of guy who didn't like to make waves.

"Mr. Fletcher? You're here about your daughter?"

"Yes."

"Have a seat, and I can get the details from you." He motioned to a chair on the other side of his desk. Both men sat. "Do you have a picture of your daughter?"

"I do." His hand shook as he removed a photograph from his front coat pocket.

Taggart studied the image. This girl had a sweet smile and bright, expressive eyes. The Tristan he'd seen at the festival was seductive and edgy. "I remember Tristan from the concert. She's a dancer."

"That's right. She's a great kid. Loves to dance. Loves music."

His impression of her had not been as positive. "And she went to the music festival?"

"I think now that she did."

"Think?"

"She wanted to go, but I said no. So she went to stay at her friend's lake house."

"But she didn't go to the lake house."

"No. My youngest daughter, Lannie, knew Tristan was going to the concert, but she didn't tell me or her mother. We only just found out that Tristan wasn't at the lake."

Taggart remained silent. Young girls and boys made dumb decisions. He'd seen his share in the military. "When did Lannie tell you the truth?"

"After your press conference. She called Tristan's friend and discovered Tristan never made it back to the lake house. My youngest admitted that Tristan had gone to the concert."

"How did Tristan get to the concert?"

"She caught a ride with her friend Callie. The girls separated at the front gate."

"And the concert was overcrowded. Rain. Mud. They lost track of each other."

"That's what Callie said."

Taggart ran through the standard questions: Did Tristan have a boyfriend? Had anyone been hassling her? Any threats or anything out of the ordinary? All no.

He wrote down a few of his impressions: *Nervous. Fidgety. Tense.* "There's no other place she could have gone?"

Frown lines furrowed Fletcher's brow. "I've called all her friends."

"And everything's all right in the home?"

Fletcher's eyes hardened. "We have challenges, but we're a happy family. My wife has terminal cancer. And Tristan would not run off knowing this."

"But Tristan defied you and went to the concert."

"What the hell are you trying to say?"

"I have to ask all the tough questions, Mr. Fletcher."

"She's a good kid. I know she snuck off to the concert, but that's not like her."

Fletcher loved his daughter but, like many parents, didn't see the truth. "Okay. Let's start from the top, and I'll fill out the missing person report."

"Is anyone out there searching?"

"We have volunteers walking the woods around the concert site. We're doing all we can now."

"How can so many girls go missing?" he asked.

"That's what I'm trying to find out." Phones rang in the background. "All those phones you hear? They're tips called into the office."

Fletcher's brow knotted. "Have you found the bodies?"

"Not yet. But we're doing everything we can." Taggart had learned a long time ago not to make promises he couldn't keep.

◆ ◆ ◆

Everything we can. Everything. Taggart saw a lot of activity, but no results. They were checking boxes. But was that everything?

His own words rattled in his head as he drove to Colton's house. He shut off his lights as he parked across the street. Colton's house was dark, and there was no sign of life.

The concert promoter had screwed up so much, but he'd had the site cleaned. Every bottle, sheet of paper, or discarded piece of clothing was gone.

The spring chill had given way to summer heat in a matter of days. The air in the car grew stuffy, so he rolled down a window. Crickets sang their night song.

He'd been on his share of stakeouts over his military career. He'd never liked sitting and waiting, but he'd learned sometimes patience paid off.

An hour later, headlights emerged in the distance. They grew closer, sweeping the road and slowing. Colton's Jeep pulled into the driveway.

He was alone and carrying a brown bag twisted around a bottle. At the front door, he swayed as he fumbled with keys. After two attempts, the key slid into the lock. The door swung open. He stumbled inside. Lights clicked on.

Seconds later he passed the front window and stopped. He picked up his phone. He gripped the receiver and was soon shouting. The call lasted for over five minutes before he slammed the phone down. He paced the room and then picked up the phone, ripped the cord from the wall, and threw the phone against the wall.

Taggart sat up in his seat. What had pissed Colton off? He must've known by now about the press conference. The media was now paying more attention to the festival. Like sharks, they smelled blood and were ready to paint Colton's day of peace and love in crimson.

Fifteen minutes later, Colton was showered and had changed into fresh clothes. He left the house and drove off in his car.

Taggart switched on his engine. He kept the headlights off as he followed Colton. He maintained a healthy distance and watched as Colton's Jeep took a right at Route 158. The road led away from town toward the concert venue.

Following this late at night was difficult. He had to keep his distance, so Colton wasn't tipped off. The man was edgy, angry, and if he was still buzzed, he could be paranoid.

Colton's next left suggested he was driving to the concert site, so Taggart took a right. He stopped, turned his car around and, after waiting a beat, pulled back on the route to the concert site.

He drove past the entrance and took a right onto the fire access road. His lights off, he drove up the rutted road. His vehicle rocked when the front tire hit a deep hole. Cursing, he righted the car and stopped just short of the mountaintop. He shut off the car and walked through the woods toward the back entrance to the concert site.

As he moved through the woods, headlights washed over the field. The Jeep stopped, and the lights glared ahead into the empty, barren field now stripped of vegetation. Colton got out of his Jeep. He clicked on a flashlight and crossed to where the stage had been. He walked back and forth, flashing his light over the ground. His pace grew faster as he retraced his steps again. He stopped, knelt, and picked up a plastic grocery bag bulging with something.

He jogged back to his Jeep, tossed the bag inside, and nosed the car back toward the exit. Within minutes, the lights of his Jeep vanished down the hill.

Taggart walked through the woods to the spot where Colton had found his bag. What the hell had he taken? Who had called him?

Chapter Thirty-Four

SLOANE

Wednesday, August 20, 2025, 6:00 a.m.

"You look troubled."

Grant's comment rose above the din of the restaurant crowd. "What do I look like when I'm troubled?"

"More intense. Like you're ready to break into a house or steal something to relieve the pressure."

That prompted a nod. "I should smile more."

He looked amused, as if he expected a punch line. "What does it feel like when you smile?"

"Nothing," I said. "It feels like nothing. But I recognize that it's effective. People tend to relax when I smile."

"You were smiling when you spoke at CrimeCon."

"Conference Sloane smiles because people react well."

He sipped his coffee. "When we were alone in your room, were you pretending then?"

Sexual satisfaction was a connection I didn't have to fake. "No."

Grant nodded, setting down his mug. "Why do you break into houses?"

"What do you mean?"

"Does bending or breaking the rules really ease the pressure?"

The question hit close to home. He'd been a cop. He'd interviewed people like me who'd crossed the legal lines much further than I ever had. He had a good sense of who I was. "It can. And it can also be an effective way of gathering information."

"It's not legal."

I grinned. "Trackers fall in a gray area."

He grimaced. "Stick to the stoic face."

I liked him. He didn't judge me or try to change me.

"Why would Brian Fletcher report his daughter as missing if she wasn't?" he asked.

"Taggart remembered Tristan at the festival. She wasn't the prim and proper dancer in Brian's images. She was darker and wilder. He chocked that up to kids and stupid choices. He never expressed any doubts about Brian Fletcher's story in his notes."

"Do you think Colton knew that Tristan was alive?"

"Very good question."

"I'll have Colton's complete visitor logs tomorrow."

"The pictures on Brian's family room wall suggest he knows she's alive." Frustration tinted my words.

"You sound very convinced."

"Even carrying such a terrible secret, Brian Fletcher couldn't resist displaying both his daughters' images."

"The truth finds a way to leak out." He studied me with sharp hawk eyes.

"Did Brian Fletcher have an insurance policy on Tristan?"

"I can check."

I leaned forward a fraction. "I bet he did not. If he lied, he didn't do it for money. His house is a memorial to his family."

"Why lie?"

"There's only one way to find out."

"I'll join you."

I almost rejected the idea but considered his connections might be of help. "You'll have to hold back. People tend to talk more when I don't have a cop standing beside me."

He rubbed the back of his neck. "I'm not a cop anymore."

I shook my head. "Yeah, but you still look like one. That's all that matters." I was anxious to get on the road.

"You're the boss."

The drive took three hours. Grant drove and I scrolled my phone, searching for any trace of Susan Westbrook or Lannie Fletcher. Lannie didn't hide herself from the world. But other than the one picture I'd seen of Susan at a fundraiser, she had no profile. Susan had owned the Dance Studio in Northern Virginia for nearly twenty years. Her studio had an excellent reputation and always had a waitlist. The publicity photo of Susan featured her lithe body dressed in a ballet skirt. Her blond hair was fashioned in a tight bun, and she stood straight and graceful in pointe shoes. But her face was turned from the camera, so anyone who looked at the image wouldn't recognize Tristan Fletcher.

It was late afternoon when we arrived in Northern Virginia. Grant wound his way off the beltway toward the side street in Falls Church. He parked in front of the Dance Studio.

The white brick building had tall windows reflecting the outside world. The facade created an illusion of light and brightness while it blocked out the world. Smoke and mirrors.

A couple of vans parked out front, and two moms helped little girls dressed in pink leotards and tulle skirts. Each wore sneakers, and they all carried little matching bags. One of the mothers opened the front door, and both moms watched as the girls scurried toward the door. They were giggling, laughing at each other's jokes. They vanished inside. For a moment, I saw shiny wood floors, a mirror, and barres. The door closed.

The girls' joy was a curiosity to me. I'd felt accomplishment and sometimes contentment, but joy had always eluded me.

"Did you ever take dance classes?" Grant asked.

"Sara, my grandmother, enrolled me in a tap-dancing class when I was six. But I lasted two lessons."

He shook his head. "Why?"

"One of the girls, Daphne, was the best dancer. And she was good. I was impressed."

"But?"

"She bullied another slower, awkward girl. Everyone acted as if it was a regular thing. It made me mad to watch that little kid doing her best not to cry. So I bodychecked Daphne."

"Good for you."

I shrugged. "That bully lost her balance and hit the floor. Her face smacked the wood hard. The impact bloodied her nose. All the girls freaked out. The teacher was appalled. I was not invited back."

"Did that bother you?"

"No. She had no right to be cruel to that other girl."

"Is there a soft spot in that dark heart of yours?"

I shrugged. "Sara wasn't surprised, but she also wasn't happy. She lost her deposit." The cramp in my chest reappeared. Looking back, I realized how hard it had been for her to scrape together the money for those lessons.

"Would you have hit her if you'd known Sara would lose her money?"

"I'd have been more careful." I couldn't picture any of these little dancers getting into a fistfight. Laughing, smiling, and giggling, they were the picture of happy children.

"If you'd been my kid, I'd have taken you out for ice cream."

Six-year-old me could have used an ice cream that day. I didn't understand how I'd been painted as the bad guy. I'd stopped a bully. Another van pulled up in front of the studio. Another mom and tiny dancer hurried toward the door.

"Time for me to ask a few questions," I said.

"In the studio?"

"To that mother. Stay here."

I rose out of the car, combed my fingers through my hair, and tucked in my shirt. I crossed the street and reached the van as the mother approached. She was short, muscular, and had tied back her blond hair into a dancer's bun. She looked a lot like the other two mothers.

"Excuse me," I said, smiling.

The woman faced me, her gaze wary as she studied me. I smiled and downshifted my demeanor to relaxed. "Sorry to bother you. I'm curious about the Dance Studio. I have a six-year-old, and she's determined to learn ballet. Do you have a moment to tell me about the Dance Studio?"

The woman didn't look convinced. Her fingers tightened around her keys. "It's great. We've been here for a couple of years."

"I hear Susan Westbrook is good."

"She's strict, and she expects perfection from the girls. But she gets amazing results."

"Strict is good. My little girl has lots of energy." If I had a little girl, I couldn't imagine her lasting more than a few lessons.

"She'll learn to channel her energy into dance. Miss Susan runs a tight ship."

Miss Susan sounded a little authoritarian. "That's great. Do you think I could slip inside and watch the class for a moment?"

"They don't like outsiders. The receptionist is a pit bull."

"Good to know." I found my warmest smile. "Thanks."

Some of the woman's wariness eased. "Sure. We'll see you around."

I entered the building and crossed to the reception desk. Beyond it was a large studio populated by a collection of little girls all dressed the same and standing in the center of the room. A woman appeared from the back, and she clapped her hands. Her delicate frame was wrapped in a leotard and a gauzy skirt that skimmed above her knees. There wasn't an ounce of extra fat on her body. The girls stopped talking and giggling. Susan Westbrook.

Susan was petite and lean and secured her blond hair in a smooth ponytail. She lined up the girls in a straight line and walked along the row, seeming to inspect their outfits. She paused to straighten a hair clip or adjust a tutu that had gone askew.

The girls appeared to enjoy her attention, and when she moved to the front of the room and struck a pose, they all mimicked her.

"Can I help you?" The question came from a thin, middle-aged woman with salt-and-pepper hair.

"I've heard a lot of good things about this studio. I have a six-year-old who loves dance." The trick to lying was to keep it simple.

"We have a waiting list. But I can give you an application. We'll add your daughter to the list once we have your deposit."

"Great." I looked at the application as if I cared. "Do you mind if I watch the class? I'll stay back here."

"Just be very quiet. And don't move beyond this desk."

"Of course." For the next thirty minutes Susan led the girls in a series of dances. The tiny dancers' movements were rigid in a *Stepford Wives* kind of way.

A poster advertised a recital scheduled for Saturday. This must be the last big practice session before the show. The receptionist glanced at me several times. In the last thirty minutes, she'd determined that I didn't fit in this suburban world.

I watched for a few more minutes but saw nothing of real interest. As I turned to leave, I remembered manners helped. "Thanks," I whispered.

I left the studio and walked across the street, aware that the receptionist was watching me. I slid into the passenger seat. "Susan Westbrook is leading the class."

He fired the engine. "The place looks legit."

I glanced at the Dance Studio brochure. "It says she trained and danced in Seattle. Thirty-one years ago, it would've been easier to re-create herself across the country. She opened this studio twenty years ago. The kids and mothers seem to love her."

Grant pulled into traffic. "The most we could get Brian Fletcher and Susan Westbrook on would be filing a false report. And after thirty-one years, no one would care."

"Brian is a straight arrow."

"Even straight arrows will lie to protect their children."

"Sara told a few lies on my behalf, but that was more to protect herself than me."

"Many parents will do anything to protect their child."

"Would you?"

Grant nodded. "I would." He parked in front of a place called Presidential Burger. "You look like you could eat. You didn't eat a lot of breakfast."

"Sure."

We both ordered burgers, fries, and sodas, and found a booth in the corner. I focused on the food, sensing it was going to be a late night. I still wasn't sure how I was going to approach Susan, but I needed to wait until the children and parents had cleared out from the studio.

As I sat, I imagined Tristan's father panicking and calling in a false missing person report. I didn't have a lot of stats on Susan yet. She could be a legitimate cousin. But I had serious doubts.

"If I get a DNA sample, can you test it against DNA from Brian Fletcher?" I asked.

He wiped his hands with a napkin. "How are you going to get samples from them?"

"I'll figure something out."

"Gently, Sloane. Adults who bodycheck other adults get arrested."

"I get it." I glanced at my watch. "The studio closes at eight o'clock. I'll be there when she leaves." The burger that had tasted so good now felt heavy in my stomach. "I hate waiting."

"In your line of work, I'd think you'd be used to it."

"I still don't like it." I picked up a fry. "Do you like waiting?"

"I've accepted the wheels of justice can move slow."

"But you hate it?"

"What I hate is when good work is undone, and bad people are set free."

"You have no doubts about Colton? At the trial, his attorney made a decent argument that Taggart planted the evidence."

"Colton is slick. He's a salesman at heart."

"What was he like when you interviewed him?"

"Charming. Almost pleasant to be around. He's popular with the guards and the inmates."

"Are you sure he's guilty?"

He was silent for a moment. "He's never proven otherwise, despite the lawyers who he charmed into taking his case. And until anyone proves otherwise, I don't want him released. His doctors say he's sick, but who knows. He could still hurt someone else if he gets out. He's had thirty-one years to think about what he'd do to everyone who wronged him."

His intensity was attractive. The air between us crackled. At least it did for me. I couldn't read him well, which made him more interesting. "This is a first for me."

"What?"

"I've learned to key off others' emotions. But I can't read you."

Another unfathomable half smile. "Nothing to see here. I'm a simple creature. I want a bad guy to stay in jail."

"You're not simple. Not by a long stretch."

"Is this the part where we talk about feelings?"

My laugh rang genuine. "God, no."

"So, what's the point of this banter?"

"Sexual tension, Grant. You're not feeling it?"

Blue eyes darkened. "The Dance Studio doesn't close for hours. And there's a hotel down the street. That direct enough for you?"

"It is."

The hotel was generic, uninspiring, but it was clean. I let my backpack slide off my shoulder to a chair angled by a small round table. Grant closed and locked the door behind us.

The two double beds were covered in a light green-gray-blue bedcover. The nightstands were polished. But the buttons at the base of the lamp were ringed with dust.

I removed my shirt as I kicked off my shoes. When I faced Grant, he stood still, staring at me. I stepped toward him.

My fingertips skimmed the top of his belt buckle, and I kissed him on his lips. He tasted like the mint he'd grabbed as we'd walked out of the diner.

His hand came to my waist, and he pulled me toward him. My fingers slipped below his belt to his erection. Orgasm was something I could feel. I'd been so stunned by my first, I'd avoided contact with men for a while. Like a drug addict's first hit of heroin, I didn't want to spend the rest of my life chasing the highs.

His hands slid to my breasts and squeezed. Energy shot through me.

He removed his shirt as I unfastened his belt buckle. His pants slid to the floor. He yanked back the bed covering, and I landed on clean white sheets. I shimmied out of my jeans and kicked them aside. The mattress sagged as he climbed on. Hovering above me, he kissed me on the lips. I skimmed my fingertips down his flat belly and wrapped my fingers around his erection. The phantom fist, always in my chest, tightened.

My heart pulsed faster. I could have been speeding down a highway, slipping into a stranger's home, or climbing on a roof as I searched for an adrenaline release. Impatient, I guided him to me. He pushed inside me. My nerve endings tingled.

A grunt rose in his chest as he filled me. I pushed my hips up toward him. He pumped. My fingers slid to my center. Soon we were both panting and riding a big wave.

The crash came, as intense as it would be fleeting. When I came, he came. And for a moment, my heart pulsed. Okay. This was acceptable. This was what people felt.

I rose from the bed and sat on its edge. This was always the awkward part. The part of sex that I didn't connect with.

"You okay?" he asked.

"Yes." I glanced back, smiling.

Staring at me, he rolled on his back and tucked his hands behind his head. "You look upset."

"I'm not. That was great."

"Did you enjoy what just happened?" he asked.

"I did. I find your company pleasant."

"Pleasant?"

"It was intense. Freeing." When I'd orgasmed, the tightness building in my skull had eased.

His expression was hard to read. "From you, that's a ringing endorsement."

"Take the win."

He smiled.

I'd never done a good job of explaining myself to anyone. But I could change that with him. "Sara said that Patty would get frustrated with me when I was a baby. Patty told Sara that I wasn't an easy baby. I didn't act like the other babies."

"Not fitting into the crowd isn't always bad."

"Most people like humans that conform. Humans are pack animals by nature and are suspicious of the lone wolf."

I wasn't sure why I was trying to explain myself. This wasn't like me, and yet, I felt he needed to understand. "I've tracked down several family members of the victims."

"And?"

"They're a little like me. They all have a wound. They see and feel their injuries. Even after thirty-one years, they struggle not to cry. When I watch these folks cry, I wonder what it feels like."

"Does it bother you that you don't cry?"

"No. It's a blessing, given my life and what I do."

"How do you experience the world?"

This was the most I'd ever talked about my lack of feelings. "I'm in a glass jar. I can see the world. I can see sadness and joy. But the glass keeps it all at a distance."

"Do you ever want to get out of the jar?"

"Maybe. I'm not sure I could write this article if I reacted like everyone else. So, like I said, it's a blessing."

He moved beside me. He didn't speak for a long time. "But it bothers you."

"It does. And it doesn't." But pain and pleasure are connected. Hard to enjoy one without the other. "What we just experienced is as close as I come to feeling something."

He kissed me on the lips, his hand sliding to my belly. I closed my eyes because I'd learned when I stared back, my pointed gaze creeped out my partners.

"Do you want to feel something again?" he asked.

"I could be convinced."

He took my hand and pulled me up. "Let's see if we can break that glass jar."

Several hours later, Grant sat behind the wheel of his truck, parked in front of the Dance Studio.

I dug in my purse and pulled out the tracker. "Thought your tracker could come in handy."

He chuckled. "Okay."

I slid out of the truck and jogged across the street. The group inside was breaking up, giving me a few minutes. I dashed down an alley to the small parking lot. There were three cars. A small four-door Toyota, a Kia, and a white van. The van had plates that read "TD Studio." I took that as my hint and hurried toward it. I attached the tracker to the back rear tire well.

I walked back to the front of the studio as the last mom-daughter combo was leaving. Susan was closing the door when I pushed back on the glass. "Susan?"

She hesitated. Her gaze grew wary. "Yes."

"I'm Sloane Grayson." This time I didn't bother with a lie. "Do you have a moment?"

"It's been a long day. Call my front desk for an appointment."

I didn't relax my grip on the door. There'd be no easing into this conversation. "Do you know Tristan Fletcher?"

Susan's face paled. "No. Should I?"

"I think you do."

She stiffened. "Go away."

"I can't. Not until we talk."

"I don't know who you are, but I have nothing for you."

"You look scared."

She shoved me back, then closed and locked the door.

Chapter Thirty-Five

CJ Taggart

Tuesday, May 31, 1994, 10:00 a.m.
11 Days After

The phones had not stopped ringing since Sunday's press conference. Three more women had been reported missing, but all had been found. One caller insisted she'd seen the bodies north of town at the Nelson farm. Another insisted he'd seen Colton with one of the girls, but his tip was discarded when he couldn't prove he'd been at the festival. One woman said she was a psychic and the spirts of the dead were crying out to her.

Through it all, Taggart continued to watch Colton's house. During this time, he lobbied the judge for a search warrant. He kept insisting if he could search Colton's property, he'd find evidence related to the missing women.

Press from around the region had caught wind of the story, and reporters were swooping into Dawson. Taggart had taken a few interviews, reinforcing that the police had no suspects. Despite his efforts to assure everyone they were safe, few believed him. Kids were no longer riding their bikes alone. Girls went out in pairs or trios. The gun store sold out of Mace and handguns.

Taggart's taciturn answers to the media weren't selling enough papers, so a few reporters began interviewing family and friends of the missing women. As profiles of aggrieved families hit the papers, the pressure on the mayor grew.

"What the hell." Mayor Briggs clutched *The Washington Post* as he closed the door to Taggart's office. "That damn story is gaining traction."

Taggart rose, straightening to attention. "I know."

Briggs shook the paper as if it were a club. "What are you doing about it?"

"I've been asking for a search warrant for Rafe Colton's house. So far, the judge won't give it to me."

The direct response caught the mayor's attention. "Why are you so sure Colton is behind this?"

"That music festival was designed to fail," Taggart said. "It was oversold, its borders weren't controlled, and the promised security was MIA."

"Maybe Colton is an incompetent con man."

"Or he set it all up to hunt women."

The mayor's face paled. "Hunt women? Jesus, don't say that out loud."

"Either way, I want to search Colton's property."

Briggs sucked in a breath and blew it out. "I've heard from everyone from Rotary, the church, and the diner. Everyone has a story about how that festival failed."

"There's no downside to searching Colton's house. If I'm wrong, then we'll move on and keep looking for the women. You'll be the first to know what I find."

"What about the tips on the bodies?"

"We've sent volunteers north of the town and festival site. So far nothing."

"Shit. Finding them would help."

"Wishing won't make it so. I need to search Colton's house."

Briggs shoved out a sigh. "If I make this happen, I don't want any of this leaking to the media."

"It won't."

He tapped the rolled newspaper against his thigh. "What the hell is everyone going to say if you prove I brought this to the community?"

"Guys like Colton find their way into places like Dawson. They arrive with a plan to exploit good, trusting people."

He shook his head. "I shouldn't have trusted him."

"He's a hell of a salesman."

"You didn't buy it."

"I've seen his kind before."

Briggs met his gaze. "What if you're wrong?"

"Colton's festival caused untold damage to the Nelson farm. The garbage is gone, but the fields are rutted and worn bare. The roads are so furrowed, they'll have to be regraded. I have seven sexual assault claims, twenty robberies, and twenty mugging charges. I doubt anyone will get that upset if I search his house."

Mayor Briggs rubbed the back of his neck. "The festival was supposed to be a moneymaker. Now we'll be lucky if we break even."

"I need a search warrant. You and the judge are friends."

The mayor nodded. "Can you do it while Colton's not home? I don't want to make a thing out of it in case you're wrong."

"I'm not wrong."

Briggs ran his hand over his thick gray hair. "Why did you set your sights on Colton?"

"It started with a feeling." Before the mayor could rebut, Taggart held up his hand. "And a string of broken promises and a disregard for security were major red flags."

"There's a big difference between 'con artist' and 'killer.'"

"I can't prove anything until I search his house. I must start somewhere."

"Okay, fine. I'll call Judge Owens and tell him to grant the warrant." Briggs ran his hand over his hair. "I don't know if I want you to be wrong or right about this."

"If I'm right, we'll find those girls."

"Think any could still be alive?"

It had been more than ten days. Yes, they could be alive, but his doubts grew each day. "I don't know."

"If you're wrong, we both are going to get roasted."

He'd been hung out to dry before. "It's a simple search. No charges have been made."

"Don't pull in the state police yet," the mayor said.

"It'll be Paxton and me."

"And Paxton can keep his mouth shut? That boy ran his mouth when he was a kid."

"He won't talk. I don't tolerate any leaks."

"Okay. When are you going to do it?"

"As soon as we have an open window."

The mayor shook his head. "I hope you're wrong."

"I hope that I'm not. We have four missing women and a community that's getting impatient. An arrest would help calm nerves."

"Call me when it's done."

The mayor was right. Colton was a con artist and a shoddy promoter, but that didn't make him a killer.

Taggart had nothing solid on Rafe Colton other than a gut feeling that he was tangled up in the girls' disappearance.

He'd watched Colton's house for eight nights, sitting in the dark. Colton usually arrived home about 10:00 p.m., only to leave two hours later.

On the first night Colton was on the move, Taggart had followed him to a ramshackle convenience store. Taggart had sat outside and waited almost thirty minutes before Colton reappeared with a six-pack of beer and a plastic bag filled with VHS tapes.

The next day, Taggart had returned to the store and asked the clerk to tell him what Colton had rented. Twenty bucks later, he'd learned the videos Colton liked to rent were the hardcore kind. Kink. BDSM. Forced sex. Taggart had rented a few himself, wanting to know how Colton thought. It wasn't his first porno, but he'd never liked the added violence.

Taggart got his search warrant quickly.

He knew Colton's pattern well enough to guess he'd leave his home by 1:00 in the afternoon. When he and Paxton had arrived on the property, Colton's truck was gone.

Taggart pulled his Crown Vic around the house, so it wasn't visible at first glance from the street. Out of the car, he surveyed the tall grass surrounding the house and a small barn out back.

"What are we looking for?" Paxton asked.

"Anything tying him to the missing women."

"Where can we look?"

"Open surfaces. But if you have a gut feeling about something, let me know."

Taggart strode toward the back door. The house was a rental, and Briggs had gotten Taggart a spare set of keys to the house. He shoved the key in the lock and twisted. The dead bolt opened.

They entered the residence. The shades were pulled, and the house was bathed in shadows. It smelled of pot and beer. Music posters decorated the walls. Woodstock. Rolling Stones. Bad Company.

"You stay in the living room," Taggart said. "I'll check the bedroom."

"Will do." Paxton moved, his body tense, as if he expected to get caught.

Taggart entered the bedroom. Colton had a large bed with a headboard and posts. The spread was smooth and the pillows in place. Across from the bed was a dresser, and on it sat a television and a VCR.

He pressed the eject button on the machine and a movie popped out. *Bondage Babes.*

He opened the top dresser drawers, filled with concert T-shirts. He searched each drawer until he was sure there was nothing linked to the victims. He combed through the nightstands, the closet, under the bed, and behind the picture frames. A nervous energy tightened his belly as he exited the bedroom and moved past Paxton, who was searching behind the couch cushions.

In the kitchen he opened all the drawers, noting the large collection of sharp kitchen knives. The cabinets were filled with old plates, cups, and glasses.

"Find anything?" Paxton asked.

"Nothing."

Frustration fizzled through him, and he moved back to the kitchen sink and stared out the back window to a barn. It was an old wood-frame structure with a few small windows and double doors.

The barn was fifty feet from the house and in a direct line of sight from the kitchen. "Come with me to the barn."

Paxton joined him. "The search warrant is for the house."

"And all structures."

"I don't think it says that."

"It does." If it didn't and he found critical evidence, he'd talk to Briggs.

Hinges squeaked as he opened the barn door. Inside, light filtered through the roof's missing shingles. Slashes of light cut across the air, catching particles of dust in their paths.

The barn was filled with equipment from the festival. Speakers, dismantled stages, a large banner announcing the festival hung from the rafters, wafting in the breeze that rushed in behind him. A half dozen large trunks were stacked on top of each other. Stage props included rolled-up rugs, a large sparkling globe, and stage lights.

Dust kicked up around his boots as he crossed to the trunks. It was common for killers to keep mementos from their victims. These were often small trinkets. It was clear Colton liked mementos from his concerts, and it tracked he would do the same with victims.

"What did you save?" he muttered to himself.

He flipped up the lock on the top storage box. It opened, and he lifted the lid.

"I think we're out of the safe zone," Paxton said.

"This box is stored in the barn."

"I thought we were limited to the house and what was in plain sight."

"Paxton, do me a favor? I need a flashlight from my trunk."

Paxton hesitated. He wasn't the quickest on the draw, but he understood he was being given an out. He couldn't testify to what he'd not seen. "Will do, boss."

When the barn door closed, Taggart opened the lid. Inside were blankets and folded tarps. He dug his arm into the box and rooted through the layers until his fingertips grazed the wooden bottom of the trunk. Sometimes killers went to great trouble to hide their trophies. Others kept them displayed—hidden in plain sight. These killers liked to have them accessible because the simple act of seeing them triggered sexual desire. Many killers masturbated as they fondled a trinket.

The women had been missing for a week and a half. Whatever had happened at the festival was still fresh in Colton's mind. And with the increasing media coverage, he had plenty to stimulate memories of the event.

Taggart closed and moved aside the first trunk, then searched the second. It wasn't until he opened the third and bottom trunk that he found a dusty brown shoebox nestled in the center of blankets.

He lifted the lid of the box. Satisfaction rushed him. A blue guitar strap was curled into a tight ball and wedged in the corner. Laurie Carr, Blue Guitar Girl. In the space between the guitar strap and the edge of the shoebox was Patty Reed's driver's license. Her smiling face stared up at him. His throat tightened. There were two other items in the box—a heart necklace and an onyx ring. He replaced the lid back on the box and closed the trunk.

A jolt of victory was blunted by the hard truth that these women were no longer missing. They'd been victims. They were dead.

Hinge doors squeaked open, and when he glanced over his shoulder, sunlight silhouetted Paxton's shape. "I have the flashlight."

Taggart's knees protested as he straightened. "We need to talk to the judge and then radio the state police."

Paxton's gaze locked on the trunk. "You found something."

"I'm not sure what I found," he lied. "But I need to talk to the judge before I look any further."

Paxton looked relieved. "Okay."

Outside sunlight warmed his chilled skin. He wanted Rafe Colton to spend the rest of his life in jail, and he wanted to find those women. He would have to tread carefully to accomplish both.

Chapter Thirty-Six

Sloane

Wednesday, August 20, 2025, 9:00 p.m.

Grant and I sat in his truck down the street from the Dance Studio's back parking lot. He opened the tracking app on his phone that he'd used to keep tabs on me.

An hour after I left the studio, the app showed movement. Susan's van was soon headed west. We stayed a good distance from her, letting the tracker do the work. We drove to a suburb outside of Leesburg, Virginia.

He parked in the parking lot of the community's recreation center. "You okay?"

"It's a lot. I never thought I'd find one of them alive."

Maybe on some level, I'd hoped that if anyone had made it out alive, it would have been Patty. Even if her living meant she'd abandoned me, I wanted her to be the lone survivor.

"It's going to take a DNA test to prove it's her," Grant said. "And I'd bet she's not going to give one up."

"Hair or saliva samples are easy enough to get."

"You need to do this part by the book, Sloane. Taggart's search methods were always suspect."

There had been suggestions that he'd planted the evidence. The defense attorney had argued Taggart could have obtained all the trinkets from searches he'd conducted of the victims' residences or from the festival site. Taggart had been alone when he'd made his initial discovery. But when state police arrived, he was waiting outside, and he played it all by the book. It had taken fifteen minutes for them to find the evidence.

"Susan's shocked reaction to her old name was all the proof I need."

"You sound like Taggart. Got to have more than a feeling. The police will require more."

"Is she still in the same place?"

He glanced at his phone. "Yes."

I searched the address on my phone. "She incorporated her business twenty years ago. I would bet her home is owned by the corporation." Hiding behind a corporation was an effective way to dodge searches for a name or Social Security number.

"Layers of corporate identities are a good way to hide in plain sight."

"She's not going to stay in her house long. Her cover has been blown," I said. "Her legal troubles have just begun."

"She's calculating the damage now," he said.

"Taggart voiced suspicions about Brian Fletcher. He always wondered why the guy was so late filing his daughter's missing person report."

"Brian's reasons were plausible," Grant said. "Taggart was in the center of a shitstorm, so he never pressed or followed up. Brian Fletcher never attended the trial. His wife had died. They held a funeral for his wife and Tristan at the same time. Tristan's empty coffin was laid to rest next to her mother's."

"If Tristan survived, her father must have known," I said. "But he deliberately broke several laws and reported her missing."

"He thought he was protecting her," Grant said.

"She was fearful for her life," I said. "Or maybe she knew she could be arrested for helping Colton lure the girls to their deaths?"

"We need to talk to her," he said.

"First thing in the morning."

"We're going to need to find somewhere else to wait. We'll get noticed here, and someone is going to call the cops."

"I want to make sure she's still in her house," I said. "Do you have a screwdriver?"

He reached behind the seat and opened a small toolbox. He handed me a red-handled screwdriver. "Should I ask?"

I shook my head. "I'll be right back."

"Roger."

Out of his car, I walked down the street, pumping my arms as if I were out for an evening power walk. I walked into Susan's cul-de-sac and spotted her van in the driveway of the last house. The lights were on in her home, but I strolled by, keeping my head turned. I circled the cul-de-sac and then approached her car. I jammed the screwdriver into the back tire. Air hissed out.

Standing, I returned to Grant's truck, and he drove. "There's a strip mall a mile from here. We can wait it out."

"Right."

He swung into a drive-through, grabbed a couple of hamburgers, fries, and sodas, and parked in a darkened portion of the lot. I nibbled fries and sipped soda.

"I can take the first shift watching the tracker," he said.

"No need. I'm a bad sleeper."

We both sat in silence for most of the night. I dozed once and found myself tripping into a dream. Patty was there, smiling and holding her arms open for me. I stood stock straight, unwilling to let her embrace me. She smiled, accepting that her daughter had never been one to show affection.

The rising sun leaked over the dashboard, and when I opened my eyes, Grant was drinking hot coffee. There was a fresh soda in the drink container. I sipped. He was a good guy. Generous. "Time to visit Susan."

"Want me to come?"

"No. Better it's just me." I smiled, hoping it looked genuine.

He arched a brow. "I'll be right here."

Grant wove through the suburban streets that all looked alike, and he found Susan's house. In the daylight, I noted her yard was small but maintained. A ballerina flag hung under her mailbox.

He parked behind Susan's white van, a vehicle no one would notice or remember. But that was the point, right? *Don't let your guard down. Always hide.*

I grabbed my purse and walked up the trimmed walkway to the front door. A summer wreath made of fake sunflowers hung from the door.

I rang the bell. When I didn't hear any movement, I rang it again. "Come on, Susan. We need to rip this Band-Aid off."

Seconds later, footsteps sounded in the hallway and the door opened. Her blond hair was pulled back in a tight dancer's bun. Her fitted top molded against a thin frame, and a light skirt skimmed over a leotard.

The instant she saw me, she tried to close the door. I put out my hand and blocked it.

"I don't want to cause trouble," I said.

"Get off my property or I'm calling the cops."

I pressed hard against the door. "Do you really want to call the cops, Susan? I'll get arrested for trespassing, but then I'll start telling the police my story. And it's going to stir up a lot of questions."

"Go away!"

"Do you know that Colton is scheduled to be released soon? The powers that be decided thirty-one years was enough. And he's got cancer. Compassionate release, from what I hear. He'll be interested to see you, I bet."

"I don't know what you're talking about."

"My mother was Patty Reed. She was one of Colton's victims. I'm trying to find her body."

"I don't know her name." She pushed harder.

Irritation snapped. I was tired of reminding people that my mother had existed. "She sold hamburgers at the festival. My grandmother was babysitting me when she vanished."

"Go away!"

I locked my elbow, turning my arm into a rod. "Come on. I bet you know a lot of details about this case. If you didn't meet Patty, you could have bought a burger from her."

Tears welled in her eyes. "Please, leave."

"I can't." I spoke softly but my arm remained rigid. "I must find the missing women. I must find my mother."

"I can't help you."

"Susan, I'm not going away." I stepped back and she slammed the door.

I sat on the front stoop, reached for my phone, and called Grant. He answered, and our gazes locked. "It's her. And it's going to be a while."

"I have all the time in the world."

"Good." I began scrolling. I didn't pay close attention to what I was seeing, but it gave me something to do with my hands while I waited for Susan to chill.

In the distance I heard a police siren and wondered if Susan had called my bluff. The sound grew closer. I kept scrolling. But then the wail trailed off and stopped.

As the sun rose higher in the sky, it grew warmer. I should have packed a hat. Sunburn was always a drag. But I didn't budge from my perch. Grant stood in the driveway, and his stance was relaxed, as if he'd done a thousand stakeouts.

Inside, I heard footsteps pacing by the front window. Curtains fluttered. More neighbors left for work. A few glanced in my direction. But I smiled and waved as if my sitting here were the most normal thing in the world. A smile and an attitude went a long way to dissuading anyone's worries.

Another hour passed.

At 9:30, Susan opened her door. "What's wrong with you?"

"I'm very determined." I didn't glance up from my phone. "My ass is bonded to your front steps until we talk."

"I have to go to work."

"Your studio opens at noon, right?"

"How much do you know about me?"

"As much as a quick internet search could tell me. There's a lot more I'd like to know about you."

"How did you find this house?"

I remained relaxed. She was talking to me. Progress. I skipped the part about the tracker on her car. "I started with your studio, which has a good online presence. Finding your home address took more legwork." The next was a guess. "Hiding your home address behind your incorporated company was a good idea."

"I like my privacy."

I looked over my shoulder. Her face was flushed and her eyes red. "I don't want to invade your life. But Colton is about to be released. And you saw something at that festival that sent you into hiding for thirty-one years."

"I'm not who you think I am."

"I think you're Tristan Fletcher. I'm still not sure if you were Colton's helper or one of his victims."

Her face paled. "I would never have helped him hurt anyone."

Ah, an admission of sorts. But I didn't look at her, fearing she'd lock down again. "So, you did know him?"

She pursed her lips. "The press covered the case extensively."

"I know. I've read all the articles." I shook my head and closed my phone as I rose. I faced her. "Those women were silenced. I want to give them a voice."

"Everyone has forgotten them." The words slipped over her lips like a whispered curse.

"Their families have not. They're still grieving. They can't move on because there's a hole in the middle of their hearts." The words sounded trite, corny even. But the image summed it up. "I'm not leaving for their sake."

Silence ticked between us. And then: "Come inside."

I stepped inside. I didn't glance over my shoulder toward Grant standing in the driveway. Air-conditioning cooled my hot skin. The house was immaculate. A carpet indented with vacuum cleaner tracks, a mirror so polished it cut the light hitting it in two, and kitchen counters behind her wiped clean. I'd hoped to grab a dirty glass or hair from a comb for a DNA test. But there was nothing.

"Thank you," I said.

She closed and locked her front door. "You cannot expose me."

"You're Tristan Fletcher."

"I didn't say that. And if you spread that lie, it won't matter if it's true or not."

"I don't want to go public. But I will if you don't talk to me."

She folded her arms over her chest.

"I don't bluff, Susan."

"Don't you care about me?" Her voiced kicked up an octave. "This is going to destroy my life."

"At least you're alive."

"I can't undo what happened thirty-one years ago."

"You can help me find them."

"Who's the man in the car in my driveway?"

"Former cop. He's been working with me. He's interested in keeping Colton in prison."

"You'll end the life I have." She was a broken record, her fear on constant repeat.

"I don't want to ruin anything." That wasn't true. She'd been hiding for thirty-one years, and her silence had trapped so many innocents in their own prisons. Even her father was ensnared in limbo. "But sometimes you must break a few eggs to make an omelet."

Tears glistened in her eyes. "Can't you just go away and leave me alone?"

"What happened at the festival?"

She closed her eyes, shaking her head.

"Colton kept a ring that your father identified as yours."

Her thumb brushed the underside of her ring finger, as if she could still feel the delicate gold encircling her skin.

"You were last seen near the stage about eleven p.m. on Friday night. What happened?"

She walked into the kitchen, grabbed a glass, and filled it with water. She drank and then washed the glass with soap and water before setting it in a dish drainer by the sink.

Whatever Susan thought about her life, it was clear she'd been in her own prison. She never made a move without fearing discovery. Even drinking from a glass was too much of a risk for her.

"What happened?" I pressed.

She rested her hands on either side of the sink and stared out the window. "Rafe Colton saw me dancing at the festival and told me I was good. He asked if I wanted to dance on the stage when the next band played their set."

"I've seen pictures of him. He was an attractive man."

"And so charming." She shook her head. "I thought I knew what I was doing. I thought I was so smart."

"You were eighteen. I've met very few teenagers who know the world."

She faced me.

"No one saw you leave with him," I said.

"Colton told me to meet him behind the stage. I had to check in with a stage manager and get a pass. I was so excited. I couldn't believe how lucky I was."

Her statement didn't match up with testimony in Colton's trial. The stage manager testified he'd never issued Tristan a pass. I studied her face, decoding her expressions. She'd had thirty-one years to convince herself that this story was true. I took a small step toward her.

"I met him backstage a half hour later. The next band was setting up, and there were trunks and boxes everywhere. Equipment swaps, yelling, and band members scurrying. I think about that moment often when my studio hosts a recital. The girls are running around, and their parents are chasing after them. Like herding cats, but it somehow gets done."

"And then you danced at about ten p.m. that Friday night."

"Yes."

Her long, lean body had swayed like a siren's onstage as she'd moved around the lead guitarist. "Was it amazing?"

"Intoxicating."

"Your performance ended about ten fifteen p.m. From the reports I read, no one noticed you vanish."

"The rain was pouring. Bands and crew were trying keep their equipment dry. Colton was behind one of the tall trunks. He had water bottles and offered me one. As I drank, he drifted off to deal with a band member's issue. I didn't finish the bottle because I was cold and very tired."

"Was the water drugged?"

"It must have been. I felt woozy. I stumbled away from the stage toward the woods. I leaned against a tree and tried to clear my head. As my knees buckled, someone caught me. When I woke up, I was in a trailer. My pants were gone and there was a man shoving inside me."

"Was it Colton?"

"Yes. He had his hands around my neck, and he was choking me. As I coughed and grabbed for air, he slammed inside of me harder. My body felt as if it were being split in two. I'd never been with a guy before that night."

I searched for pity, but all I found were faint hints of annoyance. Why didn't I believe her?

Susan glanced at her hand, tracing a callus on her palm. "I passed out."

"And when you woke up?"

She drew in a breath. "It was very dark. I panicked and hyperventilated. But I knew if I screamed, he'd come back. There was a little light leaking through the door cracks, so I found my pants and pulled them on. I could also make out the form of three other bodies. I crawled to each person and felt for any sign of life. They were all dead." The last few words were nearly inaudible.

"Did you recognize any of them?"

"I didn't know their names until later, when I saw their pictures in the newspapers along with mine."

The first trailers had left the festival site at sunrise. And Colton had several witnesses who placed him on the festival grounds until midmorning. "What did you do?"

"I gathered my clothes and then tried the back door latch, and it opened." Her eyes glistened as if the memory still carried weight. "I got out and closed the door behind me."

"Where was the trailer when you escaped?"

"A field. There was no one around."

"Did you see the driver?"

"No. I ran into the field and hid in the grass. I dressed lying down and then waited until the truck drove off."

"Where was the sun?"

"Above the horizon, but it was still cool."

"What did you see around you?"

"I don't remember much. I was in shock and terrified. I walked for hours and then found a road."

"What road?"

"Two-lane."

"Traffic?"

"No."

There'd been hundreds of cars leaving the site all morning.

"I walked. Finally, I saw a gas station at the corner of Tanner's Run and Sherman Road."

I knew the intersection, but the gas station was gone. "Where was the sun now?"

"It was high in the sky. And it was getting hot. I found a pay phone and called my father."

The intersection was about ten miles south of the Nelson farm. It was also a few hundred yards from the barn that had fascinated Kevin.

"Did you see the truck and trailer?"

"No."

Her story was plausible. Or well rehearsed over the last thirty-one years. She was a dancer, accustomed to finding perfection. "Did anyone see you at the gas station?"

"No. After the call, I hid in the woods until Daddy arrived."

"Whoever opened the trailer must have known you were missing."

"That's why I was terrified. I told my father what happened. He wanted to call the police and take me to the hospital. I begged him not to. Mommy was sick, and I was terrified they'd come after me."

"They?" I asked. "You said Colton raped you."

"There was another person in the trailer. He was watching."

"He? You saw him?"

"No. But I heard the breathing."

"Could this person have driven the trailer off-site?"

"I don't know. Maybe."

Colton had always denied the murder charges and insisted he didn't know where the bodies were buried. "You're sure there was a second person?"

"Yes. I'm positive."

Chapter Thirty-Seven

SLOANE

Thursday, August 21, 2025, 10:15 a.m.

I left Susan's house exhausted. I slid into Grant's passenger seat and laid my head back against the headrest. "She admitted it all. She's Tristan." I recapped what she'd told me. "She convinced her father to report her missing."

"Colton was arrested two weeks later. Why keep the secret for thirty-one years?"

"She said there was someone else in the trailer. She didn't see any faces. Colton strangled her until she passed out. When she woke, she was alone with the three other dead bodies. She feared Colton or this second person would come after her."

"So she played dead until she could escape."

"Yes."

"She couldn't be too worried about discovery. She's living in plain sight."

"She re-created herself thirty-one years ago. By the time she'd returned to the east, she was a blonde and people had forgotten about the Mountain Music Festival."

He sat back and folded his arms over his chest. "Who is the second person?"

"She doesn't know. There are many festivalgoers who are still alive and well. It could be anyone."

"If she'd come forward, Taggart would've had a witness who'd seen the bodies. We wouldn't be in this situation now if she'd been honest."

"Maybe."

"Who drove the bodies off-site?"

"She doesn't know."

"She called her father from a pay phone?"

"At the gas station at Tanner's Run and Sherman Road." This was all assuming she was telling the truth. And I wasn't convinced.

"You think she's lying?"

"Kind of takes one to know one."

"This does support your accomplice theory. When Colton says he doesn't know where the bodies are, I think he's telling the truth. Whoever was helping him never told him." He glared at the house. "She never saw the second person?"

"No."

"But she's certain she saw the bodies."

"Yes."

"She can still testify to the rape and seeing the dead bodies," Grant said. "That'll be enough for the parole board not to grant Colton a compassionate release."

"She doesn't want to go public."

Grant shook his head. "She can be compelled to talk."

"She's been hiding for thirty-one years. She won't be intimidated. She'll run as soon as we leave the driveway."

"Maybe not. She's been here for twenty years. She has a history. She didn't have a life to speak of in 1994. And we're more flexible in our teen years."

"I'll bet she's braced for this moment for thirty-one years."

"The tracker is still on her car?"

"It is."

"I'll call local police. They can watch the house." He dialed and raised the phone to his ear. Minutes later a patrol car pulled into the cul-de-sac.

"Don't expose her. Not just yet. I think she knows more than she's saying."

"Like what?"

I shifted in my seat. "I don't know. But there's more."

His jaw pulsed as he got out of the car and spoke to the officer. When he returned, he didn't look any happier. "They can watch her for a day or two. But they can't watch her forever."

"Understood. My next visit will be her father. She's handled this secret better than he has. He looks like a man eaten up with guilt and remorse."

He drove out of the neighborhood to a small coffee shop in a generic strip mall. "What do you want?"

"I'll take anything."

"Easy enough." Ten minutes later, Grant returned with a soda, a coffee, and two wraps.

Parchment paper crinkled as I lifted a rolled tortilla to my mouth. I took a big bite, amazed at how much I needed food. "Thank you."

"I'll buy you all the wraps after today's break."

"I still haven't found the bodies."

"You're closer than anyone has ever gotten."

"Close doesn't count."

"Close is better than a million miles away, which is where we were two weeks ago."

I wanted to believe Susan was on Team Outcast, but I couldn't make the jump. She wasn't telling me everything. "Who else would keep Colton's secret all this time?" I asked.

"Assuming they're still alive?"

"Let's pretend that this person is alive for now." My thoughts drifted to Kevin Pascal, Sheriff Paxton, and Bailey Briggs Jones. All had been at the festival. All knew Colton. "Colton was a charmer and could convince anyone to do anything."

"Hiding three bodies is a hell of an ask," Grant said.

I understood manipulation. It wasn't hard if you didn't care about consequences. Colton and I were cut from the same cloth.

"You aren't Colton." Grant was watching me.

His ability to read me was unsettling. "I didn't say I was."

"But you're thinking it."

"Did I tell you my old man is in prison for life? He hacked three people to death two years after the festival. The prosecutor reported that Daddy showed no emotion or remorse at his trial. He laughed at sentencing. The media called him a psychopath."

"None of us can pick our families, Sloane."

That prompted a startled laugh. "We also can't escape the genetics they dump in us, either."

"How many violent crimes have you committed?"

"Define *violent*."

"You know what I mean."

"None." I sighed. "I don't feel emotions like real people, Grant. I'm not as violent as Larry, but I'm not even close to the angel Patty was."

"Saints aren't very interesting."

"You don't get it. I don't feel at all." Sensing his disappointment, I added, "I want to. But I don't."

"I think you do care. You care about this case."

"It's a puzzle. I love puzzles."

"You put everything into the cases you report on. I've read your work. There's real empathy in your writing for the victims and their families."

"I'm a mimic. A good one. But a faker nonetheless."

He shook his head. "Not buying it."

A smile tugged at my lips. "I like you."

"I find your brutal honesty refreshing," he said.

"It grows tiring for most."

"I make my living rooting out liars. Your honesty will never get tiring."

I was doing my best to chase him away. Everyone who should have mattered to me was gone. "Okay."

"What does that mean?"

"Did I tell you I broke into the Nelson farmhouse?"

A brow arched. "Did you? When?"

"After I saw you in town. I doubled back."

"Why?"

"I wanted to see it."

"The festival house?"

"Your house." Maybe I'd been as curious about him as I was the house he'd inherited.

"And what did you learn?"

That he had a softness for lost causes. "It's a teardown."

"Maybe." He grinned. "The work is going to take the rest of my life."

"Good to have a purpose."

"Do you break into houses often?"

"Beyond the farmhouse, the Fletcher house, and Kevin's apartment, a few here and there."

He leaned forward and lowered his voice. "You broke into Kevin's apartment?"

"He has a picture of Debra and himself on his mantel. It looks like it was taken at the Mountain Music Festival." I opened the pictures on my phone and showed it to Grant. "A guy in a uniform is trustworthy, right?"

Grant shook his head. "Kevin still loves Debra?"

"Or the idea of her." Sara had professed her grief and loss for Patty. But I sensed if Patty had walked into our house, Sara would have been so grateful that she wouldn't have had to raise me anymore. "Or maybe he doesn't want to forget what he did to her."

Tension rippled through him, but he didn't look away.

I felt the need to add, "My undocumented criminal history isn't violent, but it is long."

He was silent for a long moment. "How did you leave it with Susan?"

"I told her I wouldn't say anything. I left it to her to reach out to the police."

"She won't, will she?"

"No. If she's telling the truth, not until the second person in that trailer is found. She's biding her time for that cop to leave the cul-de-sac."

"And she saw the bodies?"

"That's what she says."

"What about sounds? Smells? Textures?"

"She heard breathing during her assault." I reached back, recalling her words. "The second person was breathing fast."

He turned his coffee cup handle from the left to the right. It was something he did when he was chewing on a problem. "Hyperventilating or excited?"

"I don't know." I used to think memories were concrete, but I realized now that time tended to attach to facts and alter the meaning. I didn't doubt what Susan had heard, but her interpretation at the time could have been off if she had endured a sexual assault. "She has gaps in her memory, but some moments are very specific."

"Trauma can blur or sharpen memory."

"If she's telling the truth," I said.

"You don't think she is?" he asked.

"Look for someone who is the opposite of Colton. Someone who is awkward or nervous. Who would have been too afraid to carry out a crime as the primary assailant. That would explain the breathing."

"You just described Kevin Pascal, Sheriff Paxton, and Bailey Briggs Jones."

"Maybe."

The thought of someone watching Patty suffer in her final moments unsettled me. The glass cracked, allowing frigid anger to rush me. But Grant's steadiness wrapped around me like a warm blanket.

"When do I see Colton?" I asked.

"Tomorrow."

Chapter Thirty-Eight

CJ Taggart

Friday, June 3, 1994, 1:00 p.m.
2 Weeks After

Once Taggart presented the evidence he'd found in the barn to the judge, the wheels turned faster. The state forensic lab was called, and within a couple of hours, they'd dispatched a team to Colton's house. The team had been on-site when Colton pulled into his driveway.

He parked behind a van and rose out of his car. He was confused by the collection of police vehicles, but he made no effort to flee.

Taggart had arrested hundreds, maybe thousands of people during his career. And he'd seen every kind of reaction. Some panicked and ran. And others, like Colton, acted as if he'd made a huge mistake.

Taggart could already write Colton's defense team's argument. They'd insist that their client was innocent. Sure, Colton had been a poor festival manager, but he had no ill intent. He hadn't hurt anyone. They'd also claim Taggart had planted the trinkets.

"Mr. Colton," Taggart said.

"What's going on, Sheriff?" Colton's grin had faded.

"Rafe Colton, you have the right to remain silent." He rattled off the Miranda rights as he reached for his cuffs.

"I'm not sure what's going on here." Colton looked as if he were waiting for the punch line of a joke. "But someone has made a big mistake."

"No mistake." The handcuffs rattled in Taggart's hand. His body braced as he anticipated resistance. The nicest guys could turn violent when faced with cuffs locking around their wrists. As Paxton approached, his hand on his weapon, Taggart reached for Colton's wrist. He clinked the first cuff and secured the second behind Colton's back.

"This is a fucking setup," Colton shouted.

Taggart tightened the cuffs. "We'll talk about that at the station."

"Why can't we talk about this here?"

Taggart wanted him in the interview room. He wanted to control the situation.

"Does this have to do with those missing women?" Colton demanded. "I've been out here searching with the volunteers in the woods. I want them found more than anyone."

Taggart moved Colton toward his cruiser.

Colton glanced toward the barn. The muscles in his body tightened and he braced his feet. The shock of the moment had worn off, and he was grasping what had happened. "You've made a mistake, man."

"We'll see," Taggart said.

"Why do you think it's me?" The veins in his neck bulged as he strained to look back at Taggart. "I'm not your guy!"

Taggart refused to engage.

"Did you find the girls?" Colton demanded. "Has someone found the bodies?"

Taggart didn't respond.

"You can't prove anything without bodies." Colton's expression was bright with worry. "You need bodies to prove there's even been a death."

Taggart shoved him toward the police car. The fucker was guilty. But Colton was right—without the bodies, proving the case would be difficult. Countless volunteers had been searching for over a week around the Nelson farm. But there'd been no sign of the missing women. Taggart didn't need bodies to know the women were dead. The mementos proved the connection between the missing women and Colton, but juries liked to have a corpse.

Taggart opened his vehicle's back door. Colton stiffened. "Do not fuck with me." Tension radiated through the promoter's lean, muscular body. "You're making a mistake, man. I never hurt anyone."

Taggart shoved him into the back seat and slammed the door. Colton stared out the passenger window at Taggart. Brown eyes had hardened. All traces of humor were gone.

"He doesn't act like a killer," Deputy Paxton said.

"Did you expect a confession?" Taggart asked.

"He looked baffled."

"Did he? Confusion can be read multiple ways. My guess is Colton wasn't expecting us. He's doing mental gymnastics. He is wondering about what we found."

Paxton dropped his voice. "Are you sure about this?"

"I sure as hell am."

"Do you think he'll tell us where the bodies are?"

"He has every reason not to."

The Dawson police station was too small for a legitimate interview room, so Taggart had Colton brought from his cell to the conference room. The department didn't have a video camera, so he'd visited the local appliance store. When he'd explained why he needed the camera, the store owner had been happy to lend it to him. The Sony Handycam now sat on the credenza. A glowing red light indicated it was recording.

Colton still wore the clothes he'd been wearing that morning. Dark circles ringed under his eyes and the smirk was long gone. "What the hell is going on? You can't keep me without filing charges."

"I can hold you for twenty-four hours without charges." Taggart pulled out a chair and angled it toward Colton. He tossed a file on the table. "But I bet you know the legal system pretty well, don't you?"

"This is bullshit."

"You've been arrested before."

Colton sat back. "We both know you know that."

Taggart opened the file and glanced at Cassidy Rogers's face. "Tell me about Cassidy."

"Is she behind all this? That bitch has been gunning for me for a couple of years."

The veneer slipped for a moment before Colton caught himself and sat back. "What do you want to know? We went out a few times, and, yes, we had sex."

"You never tried to strangle her?"

He leaned forward. His hands strained against the cuffs. "The sex was always rough between us. She liked it. She asked for it."

"She filed assault charges against you."

"It got kinky between us that last time. In the morning, her roommate showed up unannounced. I'm there in my underwear drinking coffee with Cassidy."

"That so?" He didn't believe a word.

"Yeah." Colton looked a little outraged at the challenge. "The roommate saw Cassidy's bruises and freaked out. Cassidy was ashamed that her roommate got a glimpse of her darker side. They kicked me out. Next thing I know, the cops are arresting me. And those charges were never proven. Cassidy dropped them."

There had been a lack of evidence. Colton's lawyer had brought forward several men who testified that Cassidy liked rough sex. It became a case of he said / she said.

Taggart worried this case would follow the same route. He had trinkets, not bodies. And any good lawyer would suggest Taggart had planted them. He pulled Patty's picture out of his file. "Tell me about her."

"Patty? I didn't know her beyond the festival."

"You met her before, right?"

"I saw her at the diner for a few seconds. I was hanging up posters for the festival."

"Did you suggest the Depot have a booth there?"

"That was Buddy's idea. He saw an opportunity to sell a ton of burgers. And he did."

"Patty did the work at the festival. Buddy showed up at about ten p.m. to restock the booth, but he got stuck working the tent when she vanished."

"I never saw him."

"Did you talk to Patty at the festival? Did you chat her up?"

"Sure. She was cute. Fun. Good sense of humor. I backed off when I realized she had a kid. I don't do chicks with kids. Don't want the complications."

"When's the last time you saw Patty?"

Colton leaned forward. His eyes were strained with the first hints of panic. "I didn't kill Patty."

"I didn't say you did."

"She's one of the missing girls, right?"

"When is the last time you saw Patty?"

"I don't know. At the burger stand. The event was bigger than I'd imagined. I was putting out fires."

"What kind of fires?"

"Band stuff. Equipment failures. Power surges. A drunk guitarist. It's standard for an event like that."

"You've done many similar events?"

"Yeah. Across the state. Not as big but similar."

There'd been chaos at his other events, but no missing girls had been reported.

"I can see how a guy would be attracted to Patty. She's a looker," Taggart said. "If I were a younger man, I'd go after someone like her."

Colton's voice was gravel. "Like I said, I didn't have time for her."

"Because of the band dramas and the festival."

"Yeah. That kind of event isn't easy to pull off."

"And you think you did a good job with the festival?"

"Not my finest work. It got out of hand. I admit that. But I didn't hurt anyone."

"I talked to Patty's mother today." Sometimes painting a victim as a real person worked in interviews like this. "Patty's baby won't stop crying. She wants her mother."

His face remained stoic. "Man, what do you want from me? I don't know what happened to Patty. And I sure wanted nothing to do with that kid."

"Where are they?" Taggart asked. "Where are the girls?"

"You don't know?" Confusion turned to amusement. "You keep acting like you got all the cards."

"I have a lot of cards."

Colton sat back, his grin returning. "But you don't have the bodies. Which means you don't have shit."

Chapter Thirty-Nine

SLOANE

Thursday, August 21, 2025, 1:00 p.m.

As Grant confirmed final details of my appointment with Colton, I drove out to Brian Fletcher's house. I wasn't sure if Susan had called to warn him that their thirty-one years of lies were unraveling. But I was hoping to catch him off guard and willing to talk.

I rang the bell, and when he didn't answer, I went straight for the privacy fence gate. The dog trotted across the backyard toward me, wagging his tail. I pulled a dog treat from my pocket and fed it to him. I rubbed him between the ears, and he followed me, barking as we made our way to the back door. I knocked on the sliding door. As tempting as it was to break into the house, I decided to wait. Brian Fletcher wouldn't be thrilled with me, and I didn't need to find myself at the wrong end of a gun.

I knocked again.

The dog nuzzled my hand. I gave him another treat. When Fletcher didn't appear, I slid the door open a few inches. "Mr. Fletcher? It's Sloane Grayson."

The air conditioner hummed, but the house had an unsettling stillness. "Mr. Fletcher?"

I tossed a couple of treats on the deck, and when the dog turned to eat them, I slipped inside and closed the door behind me. The kitchen was cleaned, the counters wiped, a coffee mug in the dish drainer. An open bottle of Jack Daniel's rested in the center of the counter. No glass. He'd been drinking straight from the bottle.

"Mr. Fletcher."

I glanced at the pictures on the wall. The pictures with Susan were gone. Left behind were the faint impressions of the frames.

The dog barked. He was at the sliding door, pawing at the glass. I turned from the door and walked down the center hallway. As I moved toward what looked like an office, I caught a sick, sweet scent.

When I'd found my grandmother's body, she'd been dead a couple of hours. She'd died in her recliner. The television was still blaring cable news. Later, I learned she'd died of a heart attack. The smell had been the same, and after she'd been taken away, I remembered getting a lungful of it when I dragged the recliner outside to the curb.

I wasn't repelled or nervous but curious as I edged open the office door. The lights were off, and Mr. Fletcher's office chair was swiveled away from the door. His right hand draped over the side, and on the floor was a handgun. I looked around the room and saw no sign of the missing pictures.

"Mr. Fletcher?"

Silence mingled with the hum of the air conditioner.

I moved toward the desk with some caution. The less I disturbed, the better. The wall facing him was splattered with blood.

I stepped close enough to see the blood on what remained of his face. The bullet had traveled up the roof of his mouth into his brain. My stomach tightened, and I backed away.

"Why did you do it?" I asked.

My mind flipped through what I should do next. Call the cops? Call Susan? Call Grant?

I exited the house onto the back porch. The dog greeted me with a wagging tail, but as soon as I reached out to him, he sniffed my hands, legs, and feet. His ears flattened. "I found a big mess, fella."

Sitting in a patio chair, I tugged treats and my phone from my pocket. I dumped what biscuits I had out on the patio and called 9-1-1.

The phone rang twice. "9-1-1, what's your emergency?"

"I'm reporting a suicide. Brian Fletcher shot himself."

"Who is calling?"

I hesitated. "Sloane Grayson. I'm sitting on his back patio now. I just found him."

"Are you sure he's dead?" the dispatcher asked.

"Yes."

"The location?"

I rattled off the address.

"Stay on scene. We'll have a car there in five minutes."

"Will do."

"Are you all right?"

"I'm fine. I'll be on the back porch with the dog."

"I can stay on the line until the officers arrive."

"Not necessary." I hung up. The dog nudged my hand, and I realized his large water bowl was empty. I filled it from the outside faucet and set it down. He lapped and slopped water on the deck.

I called Grant. He picked up on the third ring. "Sloane."

"I'm at Brian Fletcher's house. He shot himself."

"What? You were supposed to wait for me."

"I didn't. And I found him in his study. The police are on their way."

"Any sign of Susan?"

"All the pictures of her are gone."

"Okay."

"Right."

Why would Brian Fletcher kill himself? He'd been protecting his daughter for thirty-one years. She must have called him and told him

I'd found her. But again, why kill himself? Did he think his death would draw attention away from her to him?

I sat back down, closed my eyes, and tipped my face toward the sun. A twinge of remorse for Brian Fletcher snapped my skin like a rubber band.

Did he regret not coming forward sooner? If he had pressured his daughter to talk to the police three decades ago, would Colton's accomplice have been found? His actions had let a coconspirator run free, and families still struggled for closure.

Sirens wailed and the dog lifted his head from the water bowl. He barked and turned toward me.

"It's okay. Just the police." I took hold of his collar and tugged him toward me. Out of treats, all I could do was scratch him between the ears.

The back privacy fence gate opened, and two officers appeared. Their guns weren't drawn, but each had a hand on their sidearm, ready to draw at a moment's notice.

"Ms. Grayson," the first officer said.

"That's right." I moved to stand, but he motioned me to sit.

"Stay where you are. Keep your hands in sight."

"Sure. Fletcher is in his home office. It's on the main floor beyond the den. Door is on the right. I went through the sliding glass door."

"Thanks," the officer said. The second officer disappeared into the house.

"How do you know Brian Fletcher?" the officer asked.

"I'm writing an article. I interviewed him a few days ago."

"You're poking into the Mountain Music Festival."

Small towns were efficient with news. "That's right."

"Fletcher's daughter was one of the victims."

"That's right. And so was my mother."

"Did he appear upset to you the other day?"

"Sure. All the families I've spoken to were upset. He missed his daughter. His life was never the same."

"Did you get the impression he wanted to hurt himself?"

"I didn't," I said. But maybe if I hadn't tracked down Susan, he'd still be alive. I considered telling the officer about Susan but decided to save that for later.

"You need to wait here for now," the officer said.

"Dog and I are going to sit in the shade in the backyard."

"That your dog?"

"Mr. Fletcher's dog."

The officer rubbed the dog and then glanced at his collar. "His name is Cody."

"Right."

"Stay in the backyard."

"Sure."

Cody and I found a shaded spot and sat on the lush, thick grass. The dog lay down beside me, but he kept a close eye on the people moving in and out of his house.

"It's crazy. But it'll be okay." That was a lie. Cody's life would change. "Don't worry, I'll make sure you're okay."

As more personnel arrived, we moved to a lawn chair under the shade of a tree. We were forgotten for the moment. Any communication I made to Susan could be traced through my phone records. That would prove I knew of her existence, and I'd become an accessory to something.

I opened my phone and texted, Your father died by suicide. I don't know what the police will find, but I've said nothing about you. My thumb hovered over the send button before I pressed it.

Cody and I remained on-site for another hour before Grant appeared at the back fence. He scanned the scene, his gaze settling on me. When he seemed convinced that I was in one piece, he ducked under yellow crime tape and moved toward the officer safeguarding the scene. They spoke, another officer was summoned, and within fifteen minutes Grant was motioning me toward him.

I rose. Cody's head perked up. And together we walked toward Grant.

"They have your contact information, and I've vouched for you," Grant said. "You can leave."

"Did you tell them about Susan?"

"I didn't. I don't want it getting back to Colton."

"Good." Cody followed me toward the back gate. I stopped and looked at the golden retriever. Shit, if I left him here, he'd end up at the pound. And at his age, he wouldn't have many takers. I walked to the officer. "I'm taking the dog."

"It's not your dog," the cop guarding the perimeter said.

"We've bonded. I'm not leaving him here."

"You have her information," Grant said.

"If anyone wants me or Cody, they can call. In the meantime, I need dog food." I scooped up the water bowl and dumped out the water. After more discussion between the uniforms, an officer brought out a large bag of kibble and a leash.

"Thanks." Cody looked at me. I hooked the leash to his collar. "Let's go, Cody."

Cody wagged his tail.

I took the dog food bag, and the three of us walked away from the scene. I turned on my Jeep's engine, cranked the AC, and put Cody in the back seat.

"Do you know what to do with a dog?" Grant asked.

"Feed, walk, repeat, right?"

"A little more than that."

"That'll do for now?"

Grant looked past me to see if anyone was watching us. And then: "Did you contact Susan?"

"I texted her."

Grant shook his head. "Why did you text her?"

"She needed to know."

He checked his phone. "Her car is still at her house."

"I never looked in her garage. Is there a second car?"

He frowned. "I don't know."

"I'll keep my eyes open, then. Cody and I are headed back to Taggart's cabin if you need me."

"Are you safe up there alone?"

His question wasn't unreasonable but still felt a tad overprotective. "I have Cody."

"He's ten or twelve years old. And he greeted you like part of the family when you broke into the house. Twice."

I rubbed Cody's head. "He's a good boy."

"You're assuming Brian Fletcher's death was a suicide," Grant said.

"You're saying it's not?"

"The timing is worrisome."

My mind skidded over my memories of Fletcher's bloodied body. I'd not studied it. I'd not lingered. I'd been more worried about leaving my DNA than analyzing the scene. The forensic team was in that room now, studying and photographing blood spatter, analyzing the position of the handgun relative to the wound, and dusting for fingerprints. Maybe my first impression was wrong. Maybe he didn't kill himself.

"You think Susan could have killed him? Her father protected her secret for thirty-one years. But their silence created a lot of suffering."

"Who else knows Tristan is alive?" Grant asked.

"I don't know."

"This second person who was in the trailer with Colton would've realized one of the girls was missing. He would've known all along that Tristan had escaped," Grant said.

"And this person knows where the bodies are buried. Bodies mean Colton never sees the light of day again," I said.

"A devil's bargain."

"What time is my appointment with Colton?"

"Tomorrow. Four o'clock."

I didn't experience fear like most, but the pressure in my head expanded. "Great."

Grant followed me to the cabin. I'd told him I was fine, but he had a bit of a savior complex, which I didn't mind right now. One thing to be brave, another to be foolish. Cody drifted off to sleep until I made the turn onto the gravel road leading to the cabin. He raised his head, looked out at the woods, and sniffed. I supposed the woods had better smells than suburbia.

I slipped Cody's leash on, and we got out of the car. I walked him to the woods, and when he'd taken care of business, I took him inside. I filled a water bowl for him.

I grabbed the dog food bag from the Jeep and filled his bowl. He gobbled, his tail wagging.

A car pulled up outside, and seconds later, Grant's steady footsteps climbed the porch stairs. Cody looked over at him, wagged his tail. "Great guard dog."

Grant scratched the dog's head. "Lucky for you."

"I'm hoping the woods will help him tap into his inner wolf."

"Not likely." He pressed his mouth against mine.

He tasted good. "Has anyone checked Susan's house? Is she there?"

"The local cops are short-staffed. They'll report back as soon as they can."

I wrapped my arms around him. He felt so solid and steady. Grant was proving to be the kind of guy who showed up in a pinch. His hand slipped under my T-shirt and cupped my breast. A twist of a swollen nipple, and I groaned. I was beginning to crave this from him.

Cody barked.

I glanced at the dog. I grabbed a blanket from the bed and laid it on the floor. Cody looked at the blanket as if to ask, *What am I supposed to do with this?*

I went to the refrigerator and grabbed the remains of a sandwich I hadn't finished. I handed it to Cody. He took it and settled on the blanket. He grunted his pleasure, his teeth gnawing the doughy bread.

Grant followed me into the bedroom. I shimmied out of my jeans as he undressed. I pulled off my T-shirt, the cool air teasing my bare nipples. I reached for my thong, but he told me to keep it on. The bed squeaked as I lay back and propped myself up on the pillows.

Grant was very focused. He prowled between my open legs and kissed my belly. Then he slipped his finger under the delicate fabric of my panties. He cupped my face in his large hand and locked on my gaze. I threaded my fingers through his hair and kissed him. Energy radiated inside me, scraping the underside of my skin.

He unfastened his belt buckle and opened his pants. Seconds later, he angled around the small scrap of fabric and then pushed inside me, fast and hard.

The sex was rough, his thrusts aggressive. I liked the way he took me to the brink and then eased up, over and over, before I tumbled. Our bodies grew slick with sweat. My heart pounded in my chest as he again teased me toward climax.

He circumvented my dampened emotions and communicated directly with my body. We both came at the same time, and when he fell on the bed beside me, my heart thrummed in my chest.

That night I slept until about 1:00 a.m. When I woke, Grant was sleeping beside me. Cody was settled on his blanket bed. Shadows danced on the walls like specters. My mind began racing toward the case details.

Why had Brian Fletcher killed himself? He'd lived thirty-one years carrying the weight of a terrible secret. He had a good relationship with his neighbors, had been well liked by his coworkers until he retired, and volunteered in his church. He'd shown no signs of cracking. And just like that he broke like Mayor Briggs and Taggart had.

What had driven these men over the edge?

Chapter Forty

SLOANE

Friday, August 22, 2025, 11:00 a.m.

Susan was missing. The word came in from local police, who'd done a welfare call at her house. They'd pounded on her door, and when she didn't answer, they entered the residence. She did have a second car. And it was gone.

Grant had confirmed my interview with Colton was still a go. And now Grant, Cody, and I were on the road.

The drive to the deepest edges of southwest Virginia was a good three hours. Time to organize my thoughts. I knew this case inside and out, but I would have to pick and choose my questions if I wanted any meaningful response from Colton.

"Do they know when she left?" I glanced in the rearview mirror. Cody was snoring.

"No."

"Why take off?" I asked. "Did the medical examiner confirm Brian Fletcher's time of death?"

"Based on Fletcher's liver temperature, he died at approximately six a.m."

"That leaves a gap between Susan vanishing and her father dying."

He sipped his coffee. I looked out the window at the passing line of trees that were thinning as we hit this patch of I-81 south. "What are you saying?"

"All she needed was three hours to drive from Northern Virginia to Dawson."

"Are you suggesting Susan shot her father? Christ, he hid her secret for thirty-one years."

I shook my head. "And then he made a mistake, and I found her."

"So she drives to Dawson and kills him? That's a big leap."

I sipped my coffee. I didn't feel great. "Maybe."

Grant watched me closely. "You are pale."

"I get this way when I work a story. Mind stays sharp. Body falls apart."

"You were working this case when we met at the conference. You drank coffee like it was water," he said. "What's changed?"

"I've lost my taste for it." Never to this extent, but this case carried higher stakes. "I'm sure it'll return."

"When my ex-wife was pregnant with our son, she couldn't drink coffee," Grant said.

"Pregnant?" I'd have laughed if his comment didn't strike a deep chord. "I don't have a taste for coffee, but that doesn't mean I'm pregnant."

"You're sure?"

"I'm careful." When we'd ended up in my hotel room, the hormones had been raging in us both. We'd not used protection the first time. Stupid, but I refused to worry about it.

He tightened his hand on the steering wheel. "Have you had a test?"

"No. Why would I?" I glanced at his coffee. My stomach tumbled. "I mean, it was only one time when we got a little careless."

"Once is all it takes."

I shook my head. I didn't need this now.

"Sloane, it wouldn't hurt to check."

Pregnant. A baby. My eyes closed. Fear and worry rushed me, knives out and screaming. I wondered if this sense of disbelief was how Patty had felt. Sara said that Patty at eighteen had accepted me onto her ragtag team without question. She'd had no idea how to make it happen. But she had. And if it came to it, so would I.

Damn it. This was the last thing I'd expected today. "Let's talk about this after the interview."

"Is the baby mine?" he asked.

"You're jumping ahead. There is no baby."

He nodded. "But if I'm not wrong . . ."

"Is this conversation really necessary?"

"It is." Dark glasses made it hard to read his expression as he stared ahead.

I plucked at a loose thread on my shirt hem. "Then you would be the daddy."

He drew in a slow breath. "Okay."

"Just like that? You look so calm."

"I am. What about you?"

I sighed and glanced back out the window. I drew in several deep breaths. "Team Outcast might get a new member."

"Okay."

We didn't talk anymore. And did my best to forget about what we'd just talked about.

Rafe Colton was not on death row. Because the bodies had not been found, their absence had planted enough doubt in the jury's minds. They'd sentenced him to life in prison, but not to death. That made today a little easier. Visiting a lifer was difficult, but not impossible.

From the moment Rafe Colton had entered prison, he'd put his charm to good work. He'd been a model citizen for almost thirty-one years, and everyone from the guards to the warden liked him. They enjoyed his easy demeanor, his talent for defusing tense situations, and his ability to mix with any of the prison gangs. His Friday guitar concerts had always been a hit. A few times, visiting artists who'd at one point done prison time paired up with him, and they'd jammed for the prisoners. He was the cool everyman, just like he'd been on the outside. In a world of violent offenders, he'd used his charm to win hearts and minds and whitewash over dead women, rapes, and lies.

Grant and Cody dropped me off at the front door. Grant promised to wait. I didn't know what to say, so I thanked him. As I walked toward the prison gates, I didn't dare look back at him or Cody. This moment was as close to domesticated as I'd ever come. And it scared the shit out of me.

I went through the security routine, and forty-five minutes later, I sat at the small desk on the other side of a glass partition. The seats to my right and left were filled with two women. Each looked as if she was in her fifties or sixties. Gray hair, skin deeply lined, and resigned expressions testified to the weight of having an incarcerated loved one.

My father had been imprisoned in Tennessee since 1996. I had never asked Sara if I could visit him. I knew her well enough to realize she'd have said no. But for all the fights we'd had, that one never came up.

Once, I'd bribed a police clerk to let me read Larry's criminal file. My bio dad had walked into a Chattanooga bar, gotten drunk, and then, with lightning speed, gutted three men with a hunting knife. The patrons had subdued him, the cops came, and his life on the outside ended.

In prison, Larry had a record of violence. He'd never get parole, and he'd never see the outside again. Suited me just fine. I'd never missed him, and the way I saw it, if Patty was dead, he had no right to walk around free after how he'd treated her.

Kids had teased me about not having parents. Their smug expressions and know-it-all tones had pissed me off. Why were they better than me because their mothers hadn't gotten murdered, or their fathers hadn't sliced three men to death?

When the playground turned ugly, I struck back. After I punched the first boy in first grade, I got suspended, but few tested me after that. And for those who did, I found more subtle forms of revenge. I had my faults, but I knew how to protect what was mine.

The door on the other side of the glass opened, and three prisoners were escorted to their seats. Two were hulking men in their thirties or forties. Their arms and necks were covered in tattoos. If anyone conjured an image of a lifer, it would be these two.

The third man was different. He was trim, fit, and his thick hair, now gray, skimmed his shoulders. The gray didn't make him look old but cooler, hipper, in a Bon Jovi kind of way. If he were on the outside, the ladies would still be chasing him.

His gaze skimmed the interview tables and their occupants. Without hesitation, he moved toward the seat across from me. He sat, grinned, and studied me. He reached for the phone on his side of the glass. I did the same with mine.

"Sloane, I feel like I know you." Colton's voice rattled like smooth gravel.

Charm was one of the coping techniques I'd learned on the first-grade playground. And because I didn't feel guilt, I could smile. Hours of practice had forged the perfect grin. "I could say the same."

"I've read all your articles. You're a terrific writer."

"Thank you."

"You do an excellent job of getting into the minds of killers."

"The victims, too, I hope."

"Of course. But all writers start with victims. They gloss over what drives the killers. And let's face it, without the killer, there's no story."

I thought about Patty staring into Colton's eyes as he drove into her while another person watched the scene. "They're people, too. They have needs, wants, and desires."

"Exactly." He threaded his fingers, flicking a thick shock of gray hair off his forehead. "So, after all these years, you're here. What took you so long?"

"I'm writing about the Mountain Music Festival."

"Ah, the Festival Four. The Lost Ladies. A great deal has been written about that case. I've been interviewed by a few writers over the years."

"The story comes and goes in popularity. People are fickle. They care about a case one day and not the next. I try not to chase the trends."

"Most writers tried to link me to the victims. They were very predictable. Finding the smoking gun was their ticket to stardom."

"What brought you to Dawson? What was it about that tiny town that was so appealing?"

He relaxed back in his seat. "Beautiful setting. The mountains are stunning. And it's close to Roanoke, Charlottesville, Richmond, and DC. It made sense."

"You organized other festivals before this one."

"I did. They didn't do as well. But I was learning."

"You don't know what you don't know, right?"

"Exactly. A little like writing?"

I chuckled. "Read any of my early stuff, and you'll see I had a few things to learn."

We chatted about my career. He was interested in the Susie Malone case. He smiled when he mentioned the random fire in the storage unit that had exposed the pastor's cache of trophies.

I shrugged, smiled.

He laughed. "You're a pistol."

"You had casual relationships with the Festival Four, right?"

He didn't shut down but, instead, seemed ready to talk. "I didn't really know these women." He held up a hand. A handcuff rattled. "I'll amend that. I did know your mother. I saw her a couple of times at the diner. And at the hamburger stand. She was always hustling. I admire that kind of work ethic. It's rare. Especially today."

"That's not what you told Taggart."

He looked amused. "Seems fitting I'd tell you more about Patty."

Tell more or lie more. "You'd have to work hard to make it in the music industry."

"You do. That business chews up and spits out people all the time." He tapped his finger to the side of his head. "You also must keep a positive mindset. You let the negative thoughts in, and you're cooked."

"Everyone comments about how positive you are. You're popular here."

He raised a brow. "Not sure if that's saying much."

"It is. Negotiating all the groups is tricky, from what I hear."

"People just want respect and attention." His head cocked. "How do you think that pastor is faring?"

"I'm sure he's made new friends."

His laugh was so natural and easy. "I've always built alliances. Never burned a bridge." His words were softened with a self-deprecating vibe.

"That's what I've heard about Patty. Positive, I mean. I don't remember her."

"She always had a kind word and a smile on her face." He leaned forward. "She wanted out of Dawson. Odds are against girls like her, but she was going places."

Girls like her. Outcasts. The ones no one remembers. "Tell me about her." My curiosity was genuine.

"You look so much like her. The dark hair. The shape of your face." He leaned closer. "But your eyes are different."

My eyes were the same color as Patty's. A bright blue. Sara had said that enough times. But I understood what Colton was saying. When I looked at the few pictures of Patty, I could see they were always bursting with emotion. *She wore her heart on her sleeve,* Sara used to say. Patty could never hide her love, fear, or laughter.

Yeah, I had the same color eyes as my mother, but my eyes never reflected true feeling. I would stare in the mirror for hours, trying to mimic those emotions. I never managed it. My version of happy or sad always looked like a cheap knockoff.

"But you know that, don't you?" he asked. "You know you're different than her." He sighed. "She never could have written the articles you have. The facts of those horrific cases would've crushed her. That's the downside of feelings. They can cloud judgment and weigh you down."

"You should be a writer. You've spun an interesting story around my eyes."

He didn't laugh this time. "It's been a long time since I stared into the eyes of a young woman. Most of my visitors are grizzled cops. They try to hide their anger toward me, but they've never managed it. Like I said, feelings can be a burden."

This intellectual exercise/discussion was not productive. "Tristan Fletcher's father died early this morning." Susan had not called me since I'd texted her. And she was missing. The local police had contacted Lannie, and they'd asked her about her father's mental health. She had been crying by the time the call ended.

"Tristan." No hints of remorse softened his sharp eyes. "The dancer."

"You remember her?"

"I remember the stories I've read about her. She was one of the Festival Four. I read all I could about her and the others." The cuffs on his wrists shifted as he flexed his fingers. "There wasn't much to find about Patty. Your grandmother, Sara, gave a couple of interviews in the beginning."

I steered us back to the topic at hand. "Are you going to ask how Brian Fletcher died?"

"Does it matter? Or do you want this to be a guessing game?" He grinned. "I'm open to anything."

"No games today. His death looks like suicide, but the medical examiner has not issued a ruling." Murder, suicide, undetermined. The *undetermined* always caught my attention. Shouldn't the medical examiner know how someone died? Turned out, it wasn't always so clear cut. Even natural deaths couldn't always be nailed down.

"After all this time?" Colton said. "And he decides to end it. Seems a little foolish." An amused brow lifted. "Say what you want about me, but I'm no quitter."

"Cops are saying you put a lifetime of burdens on the man's shoulders. They say, if Tristan was still in his life, he wouldn't have shot himself."

"Shot? He meant business, didn't he? No false attempts to stir up drama from that old boy."

When I didn't respond, he added, "Try living in a max prison for thirty years. There are lots of reasons to give up here. But I never once considered it. Not once. You can't let those kernels of doubt in your mind, or they root and sprout."

"Positivity, right?"

"Exactly." He leaned forward a fraction. "I'm curious. Why did Brian buckle now? Was he sick?"

"There's a new witness."

"For the Festival Four case?" He looked expectant. "Was it your mother? Did she decide to reappear in her baby girl's life?"

"Not Patty. She's still MIA."

"That's too bad for you. Little girls need their moms."

"This witness says you weren't working alone. You had help."

"I did?" He waggled his eyebrows. "All this time, and now you have evidence that I had an accomplice. Sounds compelling."

"It makes sense, if you think about it."

"How so?"

"You never told anyone where the bodies were buried because I don't think you know where they are."

"Really?"

"Without the bodies, you stayed off death row. You get lots of media and law enforcement visitors over the years hanging on your every word. You stay a little relevant. And I hear you're a big deal here."

He looked amused. "Is this the moment you ask me where they are?"

"You aren't listening. I don't think you know where they are. Whoever helped you knows, but that person never told you."

He grinned. His teeth weren't as white as in his old promo pictures, but the smile was still electric. "Then if I'm so worthless, why come here?"

"I wanted to meet you."

"Why?"

"I'm using every new detail I've learned to find those bodies."

He bunched up his lips as if stifling a laugh. "You're so sure of yourself, Sloane. Positivity is good, even if it's misguided."

"I don't do false bravado, Mr. Colton. This story isn't my first rodeo."

He shook his head. "You remind me of him."

"Who?"

"Your daddy. You don't look like him, but you're as cold as he was. Guy had a lead heart."

"Ah, dear old Dad. Serving life for a triple murder. When did you meet Larry?"

"I was at the diner. The festival was just an idea, and Patty was pregnant with you. Larry came in."

His lawyers had told the story of Patty and Colton's first meeting. According to the defense attorneys, Larry had been harassing Patty, but Colton had come to her aid.

If Patty had been the only missing woman, that tidbit would've helped Colton. But Patty wasn't the lone victim. "Let me guess, he was mean to her." I'd heard enough war stories from Sara.

"She wanted to make it work with him. But he was too nasty."

I let him talk. I knew he was manipulating me, but I was curious about Larry. His DNA mattered more now.

"Did you know I helped Patty name you?"

I still didn't respond.

"I grew up with a kid named Rick Sloane. I liked the guy. But he was a hell-raiser. Anyway, I must have been thinking about him when your mother was asking everyone in the diner for name suggestions. I tossed out Sloane. To my surprise, she grabbed it."

"Good for her."

"Rick died when we were about sixteen. He drove too fast and took too many chances. Took a curve too fast. Hit a tree and died on impact. There wasn't much left of him to bury."

"Burned to ashes."

"That's about right."

The room was warm, but my skin was chilled. I searched for sadness or remorse but couldn't find either. I wasn't so different from my old man. Was I on track to screw up the next generation? Or was there enough of Patty in me to make a go with a kid?

"I watched Patty tell Larry she was pregnant with his child. He showed no feelings. He did not care. His callousness hurt her. She was crying and ran to the back room. He tried to follow her, but I stopped him."

"Hero to the rescue."

"I'm like you. I don't like bullies, Sloane."

Was the emphasis on my name supposed to be a bonding moment? "All the girls were similar. Young. Attractive. Vibrant. You have a type."

"We all do." He sat back. "Let me guess. You go for guys that are sensitive and in touch with their emotions. Makes you feel like you've got a connection. But after a few weeks, you realize that you're incapable. So you lose interest and move on."

The arrow hit the bull's-eye. He was right. I reached for long-term implications but couldn't grasp them.

The woman sitting next to me chuckled softly and raised her hands to the thick, smudged glass. The man on the other side did the same. Their grins were sloppy, but in this moment they felt genuine.

"I love all women," he said.

"You love them so much you hide them and keep them all to yourself forever."

"You just told me I don't know where they are. Which is it?"

"The point is no one else can have them. And one day you believe you'll stand over their remains."

"You mean their naked, stripped bones? I imagine all the flesh is gone and the bones are discolored."

The truth always leaked out. "When you drift off to sleep at night, do you dream about their bones?"

Dark eyes glistened with amusement. "Dancing like marionettes on a clear day in the mountains?"

"I bet it's a rush. To know their flesh and bones are nearly dust."

He chuckled. "You're clever."

"Not really. I tend to be very direct."

"I'm sure you'll have lots of good theories as you hammer out your word count."

"I don't want theories. I want the truth."

Colton leaned forward, closed his eyes, and sniffed. "God, but I wish I could smell you. I love the scent of a woman. Especially after she's had sex. When's the last time you got some?"

Three decades hadn't softened him. He was enjoying my attention. "Do you ever dream about Tristan Fletcher or Cassidy Rogers?"

His eyes brightened. "Cassidy is a bitch. Tristan is dead. I like my women willing and alive."

"You liked Cassidy at one time?"

"Sure. She was hot."

In the reflection on the glass barrier, I caught the deputy's tight-lipped expression. I think the officer's outrage was as much for himself as it was me. Not everyone was charmed by Rafe Colton.

"And you don't dream about Tristan even though she's dead."

He grinned. "Give me a picture of her at the festival and I will."

I reached in my bag and pulled out a picture of Tristan at the festival. "Like this?"

His eyes darkened and he leaned closer. "Yeah."

"She had a thing for you, didn't she?"

"A lot of chicks did."

"But she hung out with you in the weeks leading up to the concert, didn't she?"

"Sure. No law against that."

I laid the picture face down in front of me. "I forgot to tell you. Tristan is still alive." I smiled. "I'm not going to lie. Finding her alive and well threw me for a loop. Who would have thought that one of the Festival Four was alive?"

"Is that the best you got?"

"Tristan remembers the inside of a container and seeing the other bodies. She remembers the second person in the trailer."

"Nice try, Sloane."

I could not name the feeling unfurling inside me. It was acrid and angry. "She said all the girls around her were dead when she startled awake. I guess you didn't strangle her well enough. Oh well. Either way, she's going to testify that she saw the bodies." I smiled. "No release for you."

His grin vanished. But surprise darkened his gaze. "Good story."

Did he not know about Tristan's escape? "All these years the cops were searching for bones. And little did they know that a living witness was right under their noses."

He shook his head. "For a girl who doesn't like games, you're good at it."

The deputy's slight surprise told me he was paying close attention. "I thought seeing you would be interesting. But I'm bored. I don't need the bodies anymore. I have Tristan."

His face hardened. "Why did you come here if you don't need me?"

"To see your face when I told you."

"If I did have a little helper, and I'm not saying I did, but if I did, doesn't that worry you? That person has everything to lose and will be freaking out."

He was right. Coming here could very well have put a target on my back.

"Then I'll have to be extra careful, won't I?"

Chapter Forty-One

CJ TAGGART

Monday, December 8, 2014
Twenty Years After

The community breathed a sigh of relief when Taggart announced Colton's arrest in early June. After Colton's arrest, the commonwealth's attorney had quickly filed charges. At trial, he'd fashioned the portrait of a complicated, dangerous man who should never be free again.

More sexual assault accounts like Cassidy Rogers's came to light. Women told Taggart in graphic detail how Colton enjoyed their suffering as he sexually and physically abused them. Some admitted Colton liked threesomes and got off when one of the partners sat by the bed and watched.

Several town leaders from the region testified that Colton's other festivals were just as poorly organized, and many were plagued by assaults and robberies. An FBI agent searched missing person reports in all the areas where Colton had held festivals. He came up with three missing women. None of them had been found, but there was never enough evidence to link any of it to Colton.

Taggart was more convinced than ever that he'd made the right move.

A few questioned Taggart's luck. Finding those trinkets had been one hell of a Hail Mary. Almost a little too good to be true. There was talk the evidence had been planted, but it was a small sin compared to Colton's greater depravities. Taggart's cobbled-together puzzle pieces created a good enough picture of a murderer.

Bottom line was, the killer had been caught. It was as happy an ending as there could be.

In many jurisdictions, the case would have been thrown out. But there was an unspoken consensus in the Dawson community that Colton deserved prison. His lawyers lobbied for a change of venue, but the judge had refused. The town of Dawson, especially the mayor, wanted a pound of Colton's flesh.

And the town of Dawson got its justice. Eleven months after the music festival, Colton was convicted on four counts of murder.

Despite all the congratulations, Taggart didn't feel the full weight of the win. He'd never found the women, and for that he felt as if he'd failed.

Taggart had thought Colton would eventually break and tell him— or someone—where he'd buried the women. But as hard as Taggart had pressed Colton in the interrogations, the man had never wavered. He insisted he was innocent, and that Taggart was framing him.

Five years after the trial, Taggart had taken the case file records and made copies of them all. He'd swapped the copies for the real files and hidden the originals in his cabin. He'd hoped time and a new perspective would help him see the case in a new light. But the facts refused to lead to the bodies. In his gut, he knew he had the right man behind bars. But the specter of missing remains taunted him more as he got older.

He'd kept tabs on Sloane Grayson, Patty's kid. Sara had moved her to Charlottesville and raised her there. He'd never seen her as an infant, and the first time he'd laid eyes on her, she was six. He'd spent an all-nighter reading the Mountain Music Festival files and the profile on Patty Reed. On a whim, he'd gone looking for her kid.

He'd found her on the playground of her elementary school. Her mother's black hair and angled face made her easy to spot. The kid had been watching a couple of boys teasing another girl. She'd held back, and he'd thought for a moment she was just afraid to confront the older boys. Then she'd picked up a rock, marched toward the boys, and smacked the biggest one. He'd fallen forward. Blood stained the rock, Sloane, and the kid's shirt when the teachers came running. Sloane, who showed no signs of remorse, had been pulled away. Teachers gathered around the crying boy.

Taggart followed Sloane through her time in school. She was arrested several times for breaking and entering as a minor, and she would've ended up in juvenile detention if he'd not spoken privately to the judge. Social workers determined she had sociopathic tendencies. But she wasn't like her father. Though she didn't take pleasure from violence, she wasn't afraid to bend rules to the point of snapping. In his mind, she was a perfect blend of her parents.

It made sense to give her his files. He wasn't sure if she'd tackle the story, but if he'd had to bet, he'd have put his money on her.

In thick black ink, he scrawled the only note to her: "I couldn't find the missing women." Maybe Sloane could.

Chapter Forty-Two

Sloane

Friday, August 22, 2025, 9:30 p.m.

By the time Grant parked in front of the cabin, it was pitch-black on the mountain. The air had cooled, and the wind blew in quick gusts, twisting the leaves and straining branches. A storm was coming. I hoisted my backpack on my shoulder and then slipped on Cody's leash before we got out of the car. Grant followed.

"I'll go to the convenience store and grab a couple of pizzas," he said.

"That would be great. Thank you." I'd spent the drive processing Colton's visit and a possible pregnancy. The two thoughts competed for brain space. The pressure in my head was building, and it was hard to concentrate.

Cody peed, sniffed the wind. His tail wagged.

"You okay?" Grant asked.

"I'm fine. Just processing the day." I met his gaze, feeling I owed him an explanation. "I'm a little overwhelmed."

"I get that." He came toward me and wrapped his arms around me.

I wasn't sure how to react, but some of the stress tightening my body eased. "I'll be fine."

"I know. You're tough." He kissed me on top of the head. "See you in an hour."

"Right."

"Cody, hop in the car, buddy," Grant said. The old dog was happy to follow Grant, with whom he seemed to have already bonded. Me he liked, but Grant he adored.

When Grant pulled down the driveway, I was glad no one was at the cabin. I needed a little quiet to decompress. Lightning streaked across a dark, starless sky.

I pushed through the front door, locked it. My body ached and my head pounded. My stomach grumbled. I lowered my backpack on the kitchen table.

Outside, thunder rumbled.

I stripped and turned on the hot spray of the shower. Stepping under the water, I imagined Colton's grin, the sounds of prison doors slamming shut, memories of Patty, and worries of a baby. They all washed off my body and down the drain. The hot water petered out, so I shut off the tap and grabbed a towel. I dried off and combed out my damp hair. I padded into the kitchen and opened the refrigerator. There was a carton of eggs, a few apples, and bread. I grabbed the bread and fished a couple of slices out of the sleeve. I took a bite.

I glanced at my phone. No Wi-Fi. And data was stretched too thin for a signal.

There was no way of knowing if Susan was still in Northern Virginia. She'd spent thirty-one years hiding and building a lifetime of habits to protect her identity. And now she was on the move? Would she come to Dawson, or vanish into the wind?

I pushed my thumb into the softened bread. Using the landline, I called Grant, knowing he had service at the bottom of the mountain. "Did the medical examiner inspect Brian Fletcher's body?"

My abruptness had never thrown him. "He will first thing in the morning. Fletcher's youngest daughter, Lannie, arrived in town today."

"Where's she staying?"

"Local hotel."

"Which one?"

"You can't talk to her."

"Why not? She was in on the lie with her father. They both knew that Tristan was alive and changed her name to Susan."

"The cops are still interviewing her. They don't need you complicating the process."

"Susan hid from everyone for almost thirty-one years. She knows how to get around unnoticed. If she were going to run again, she'd be smart. She'd change her appearance and ditch her car for another one. I bet she had a go-bag with cash in the house."

"There's a BOLO out for her and her second vehicle, which is a gray four-door sedan."

"The kind of car no one pays attention to."

"They are now."

"Colton turned white when I told him Tristan was alive."

"Good. Let him chew on that for a while."

Susan had said that Colton had had an accomplice. My mind had jumped to Kevin. Was that simply because I didn't like the guy? "Susan didn't tell the entire truth."

"What's she holding back?"

"I keep thinking back to Taggart's impression of Tristan. She was seductive, combative, and high. I wonder if Colton dragged her in that trailer or she went willingly."

"Not a rape?"

"She wouldn't be the first girl to make a bad decision and then turn the tables on the story."

"What about what she saw in the trailer?"

"That was too on point not to be real. That's the moment she realized she'd chosen the wrong guy."

Thunder clapped and lightning lit up the sky. Cody whimpered.

"Cody doesn't like the thunder," I said.

"No, he does not. For such a big dog, he's a baby."

"Maybe he's just wise to the dangers of storms."

Grant chuckled. "You could be right. We have the pizza in hand. We'll be back at the cabin in a half hour."

I walked toward the window, straining the limits of the phone cord. My reflection in the glass obscured what could be out there.

A shifting in the shadows caught my attention. Gaze narrowing, I searched the tree line.

"Did you hear what I said?" Grant asked.

"Sorry, I'm staring at the woods. I thought I saw something out there."

"Are you sure? No one goes up there."

"I know." I moved toward my bedroom to grab my gun, but the phone cord stopped me.

"Can you see anything?"

I shut off the lights and returned to the window. The trees swayed. Bushes rustled in the wind. Through the darkness, I didn't see anything that resembled a person. "No. Must have been an animal."

"We're on the way. And I'm staying on the line."

"You'll lose the signal in about two minutes."

"We'll keep talking as long as we can."

"It could be the wind."

"Since when did you embrace wishful thinking?"

"Never."

I turned from the window and moved toward the dining room. My fingers tightened around the phone's bulky receiver. "I must be a little jumpy after the prison visit."

"Maybe."

He was pacifying me. The trip hadn't rattled me as it would most people, but he knew a possible pregnancy was weighing on my mind.

"Do you think Colton's been in communication with his accomplice all these years?"

"He's received lots of fan mail." Grant's signal was breaking up. "I should have his visitor log by morning."

Colton had been the darling of many online groups. His good looks, which had grown more rugged with his time in prison, attracted lots of fans. "It'll be a deep dive into decades of visitor logs."

"Are you saying that's too much for you?"

I chuckled. "Please. Child's play." The primitive part of my brain that had hummed warnings began to settle.

The line crackled again. "I'm about to lose you."

"I know. See you in a few minutes."

"Great." I hung up the receiver, moved to the bedroom, and retrieved my handgun from under my mattress.

As I sat at the round table, the shadows outside shifted quickly. My body hummed with unspoken warnings.

And then a figure neared the window. The person was dressed in black, face covered with a ski mask. I tightened my grip on the gun.

I stood back, my body tense. Who had tracked me down up here?

A second later a brick smashed through the glass. Behind it was a Molotov cocktail, flaming bright red as it flew through the opening. The bottle crashed against the wooden floor, spreading burning liquid.

I wasn't afraid, but I was hyperfocused. I grabbed a blanket off the couch and tossed it on the fire. The bulk of the flames struggled with the smothering fabric as more fire crept out from under the edges. I stamped my foot on the smaller blazes. The heat burned me, forcing me to pull back before stamping it out again.

A second brick came through another window. This time two firebombs followed it.

Smoke filled the cabin. I grabbed my backpack and raced to the cabin's rear exit. As tempting as it was to rush outside, I didn't. If I were the assailant, I'd have set a trap near the primary and secondary exits. Instead of using the door, I hurried into the bedroom. Smoke choked out the air. I threw open the window, taking a moment to suck in clean air. I shouldered the backpack, hiked my leg over the windowsill, and hoisted up my body.

The drop to the ground was about five feet. The ground below was rocky and uneven. The smoke and flames pressed against my back. I had to jump. I gripped the gun, leaped, and landed on the uneven ground. The backpack threw off my balance. My ankle twisted and I fell on my side. The impact sent a shock of pain up my leg. As I stumbled to my feet, my ankle protested.

Raising the gun's sights, I leveled my gaze on the dark woods, searching for my little pyro friend. The wind rustled in the trees. Behind me the heat of the burning cabin became so hot, I was forced to hobble away toward the woods.

Footsteps crunched over dried leaves, but I didn't see anyone. "Come on," I whispered. "Don't you want to keep playing? This is just starting to get fun."

Silence mingled with the wind.

The flames lit up the night sky, illuminating the forest. I caught a flicker of movement. Footsteps thundered. But this time they were moving not toward the cabin but away from it.

A car's wheels crunched in the driveway, and I raised the gun's barrel. I came around the side, in time to see Grant rise out of his car. The light of the flames danced across his tense features as he stared at the cabin in horror. He moved toward the front porch now crackling from the heat.

"Grant!" I shouted.

He turned. Relief eased deep lines around his mouth. He raced toward me and hugged me close.

I relaxed into him. It felt good to press against solid muscle and feel the tight band of his arms around me. A sigh released over my lips.

"What happened?" he asked.

"Someone tossed a Molotov cocktail in the cabin."

"Who?"

"I don't know. I saw someone running through the woods away from the house but didn't see who it was." I pulled free of his embrace and looked back. Flames were now burrowing through the roof. It was a total loss. I'd saved my backpack, which contained my laptop and wallet. I could keep going.

"We need to get down the mountain so I can call the police and fire department."

"It'll take them at least a half hour from Dawson. I need to move my car away from the flames. There's a spare key under the mat."

"I'll do it. Get in my car with Cody."

I slid into the front seat of his car while he ran to mine. Cody pushed through the seats and nudged me. "It's fine, Cody. Just a little fire." The flames licked high in the trees. Fat raindrops fell.

Grant started my Jeep and moved it to the turnaround, well out of the fire's path. When he jogged back, the center beam of the cabin cracked. Flames hissed. It took seconds before the cabin's center fell in on itself, sending sparks in the air as thunder rumbled.

More fat rain droplets fell as he returned to his car. He opened the front door and slid behind the wheel. I was amazed at how shaken I was. The skies opened, sending rain showers down the hillside. The fire roared and sizzled as rain hit it. It was a beast in agony, drawing in its last breath.

"At least the woods won't burn," I said.

"The rain will also slow down whoever did this," he said. "This mountain will get slick when the dirt turns to mud."

Fire hissed and bellowed as rain fell and steam rose. "It is a good thing." He backed up his truck and nosed the vehicle down the mountain road now turning into a soupy, muddy mess.

He reached the hard service road and was two miles down it when cell reception returned. He called the local police and fire.

"Whoever did this is worried," I said. "I've struck a nerve."

"A Molotov cocktail doesn't require anything high-tech."

"That's what makes it so effective."

"And you didn't set the fire?"

I glanced at my soot-covered jeans.

"I remember a storage unit being set on fire," he prompted.

"I had nothing to do with this fire."

"Okay."

"You believe me?"

He nodded. "I do."

I studied his profile and, finding no hesitation, said, "Good."

"How about you lie low and let the cops see what they can find? It might not be just you anymore."

A baby. That was an unsettling thought. "Maybe. Maybe not."

He shook his head. "You don't have to do this alone."

"Are you going to help me?" It was a half challenge, half joke.

"Yeah, I am."

"Grant, you don't know me. I'm not built to do forever. I can promise you, my brand of seeing the world grows very thin with people."

"I'm more patient than you think."

"I don't want you to tolerate me. I decided a long time ago, I'm okay with how I'm wired."

Frustration furrowed the lines on his brow. "I'm not asking you to change."

"But you'll want me to at some point. You'll see that I can't live a normal life."

"Normal is overrated."

In the distance, a siren blared. "That was fast."

He shoved out a frustrated sigh. "Sometimes we get lucky."

"Maybe."

As the rain fell on his truck, the light from the flames at the top of the mountain faded.

Blue-and-white lights bounced off the tree leaves as a cop car raced through the rain and up the hill. Grant waited for the fire trucks to pass, then shifted into first gear and followed them.

Sheriff Paxton rose out of the car. He was draped in a rain slicker. His boots smashed into the soft earth as he made his way to Grant's driver's-side window. Not like the sheriff to make these night calls. Grant rolled down the window.

"What the hell?" Paxton asked.

"It's a long story," I said. "You were up here fast."

"I was driving home when I saw the flames." He glanced past Grant to me. "Doesn't surprise me to see you."

"I didn't set the fire, if that's what you think," I said.

"Maybe not. But you have a knack for pissing off people who would love to see you burn."

Chapter Forty-Three

SLOANE

Saturday, August 23, 2025, 9:30 a.m.

Baiting a hook was easy. But reeling in a fish required finesse and skill.

I sat in the Depot booth. Cody slept on the floor beside me, unaware of the buzz of conversations and rattle of plates around him. I caught Callie's attention. She was already filling a soda glass for me and a water bowl for Cody.

Cody lifted his head, lapped up water, and went back to sleep.

Grant was working his connections in the medical examiner's office. Brian Fletcher's autopsy was this morning. The consensus was suicide, but if I were going to kill someone, I'd make it look like it was a self-inflicted wound. I thought about Taggart, who'd had a new lead and was "the last man who would kill himself." My thoughts also drifted to Mayor Briggs. Another self-inflicted gunshot wound to the head. Three men associated with the Mountain Music Festival. And all shot dead.

Callie returned with a soda for me. I'd woken this morning hoping my coffee craving had returned. But my stomach refused to consider it. After this case, I'd get tested and confirm if Team Outcast had a new member joining soon.

"You want anything more to eat?" she asked.

"Toast would be great."

"Will do." Callie paused. "I heard about the fire."

"It was an old cabin. Bad wiring, I bet," I lied. "Shame it burned."

"The fire chief was in early. He said there's nothing left but ashes."

"It was a pile of dry kindling ready to go up. Paxton will figure out the cause."

Callie rolled her eyes. "Well, then, you should be just fine."

Callie. Taggart referenced a Callie in his notes. "You were at the festival."

"Yeah. I was."

"What was it like?"

A smile teased the edges of her lips. "Great fun at first. So exciting. Not much happened around here in those days."

"How old were you?"

"Seventeen. Like half the kids in this town, I defied my parents and snuck out of the house so I could go."

"Callie, you surprise me."

"I was quite the troublemaker back in the day. If I wasn't sneaking off to the barn to drink, I was throwing fireballs down the mine shaft."

"Mine shaft?"

"By the barn. Old gold mine." She shifted her stance.

"You knew the victims."

"Sure. I knew your mom. And Debra. Tristan and I went to a dance camp together the summer before." She patted her full hip. "You can see I haven't danced in a while."

"I can't even clap in time to a song. Were you good?"

"Yeah, I was decent. Tristan was super good. She was the star of our camp."

I stirred the ice in my soda. "What was she like?"

"She was nice enough. She always had her eye on the prize."

"Prize?"

"Fame. Fortune. Leaving Dawson." Callie shrugged. "She could be high-strung. But most teenage girls are."

"Did she know Rafe Colton?"

"I don't know how long she knew him, but they were friendly at the festival. But he was outgoing with everyone."

"Was Tristan using drugs at the festival?"

Her gaze grew distant for a second and then refocused. "It was a lifetime ago. Kids do dumb things."

"I'm not judging. I'm trying to understand that day."

"I never saw her using, but she was super agitated that day."

In 1994, I'd bet she'd been using coke. "And she was with Colton?"

"He was with a lot of girls that night. But yeah, she was clearly into him."

Luring her to a trailer for sex wouldn't be a stretch.

"Why are you so interested in Tristan?"

I sipped my soda. Time to bait the hook. "Because she's still alive."

"What?"

Her shock was amusing. "I know. She escaped the festival and has been in hiding for thirty-one years. Crazy, isn't it?"

"Shit. Where is she?"

"She was in Northern Virginia. She has had a dance studio up there for twenty years." The soda slurped as I drained the cup. "Now she's in the wind. I'm not sure where she is. On the run, I guess."

"Her daddy must have known."

I nodded. "Yep."

"Does Paxton know?"

"He will soon enough."

"You're so different than Patty," she said.

I detected no traces of disappointment. "I've heard that."

"But maybe that's a good thing. Better to be tough in this world."

For once, it might be nice to wear rose-colored glasses. But the universe had never delivered my set.

"Do you remember a gas station with a pay phone on Tanner's Run? It would have been due south of the concert."

"Yeah, that was Izzy Bay's gas station. My brother bought bait there all the time. But it's been gone twenty years."

I thought about the old barn on Tanner's Run Road. Kevin had seemed fascinated by the structure. "Was there a barn near that station?"

"Yeah. It was part of the Foster family farm. Quite the spread in the 1930s. The barn is all that's left, and it's barely standing."

"The Fosters are from the area?"

"No. Foster Sr. came from the east. He came to Dawson to mine gold, but that was a bust, so he became a farmer." She shook her head. "I remember Kevin used to talk about the mines. He wondered if he could get rich if he dug in them."

"It's played out."

"That and it's now ready to collapse."

A customer called out, and Callie glanced over her shoulder. "Better get going."

"Thanks, Callie."

Paxton entered the diner, and the instant he saw me, he frowned. I motioned him forward.

To his credit, he crossed the diner, angled past Cody, and sat across from me. "You still smell like smoke."

"I took a shower and washed my clothes." I sniffed my arm. He was right. "Any luck on who tried to barbecue me?"

"We've roped off the area, but the rain wiped away a lot of evidence."

"What about the bottles thrown into my house? Anything special about it?"

"The structure is too hot to investigate now."

Made sense. It could be a day or two before the ashes cooled. "Tristan Fletcher is alive."

He stilled. "Say that again."

I repeated my statement as I pulled up the website for Susan's dance studio. "Alive and well."

He studied the image. "How do you know it's her?"

"I've talked to her." I explained how I'd found her and the main details of our conversation. "Call Lannie if you don't believe me."

He sat back, shoved out a breath, and then reexamined the image. "Susan doesn't look like Tristan in these pictures."

"Thirty-one years and a hair color changes a lot. But it's her. And her father knew she was alive. He had pictures of her on his walls."

"I didn't see pictures like that when I was in the house yesterday."

I leaned forward. If it came to it, I'd text him the pictures I had snapped during my breaking and entering adventure. "Someone took them."

"This is the craziest damn thing I've ever heard."

"I get that. But you need to process this information fast. We're on a clock now."

"What clock?"

I ignored his question. "Was Taggart's suicide a shock?" I asked.

"Hell of a shock."

"And the medical examiner ruled his death a suicide?"

Paxton's face paled. "He ruled it undetermined."

"Why not suicide?"

"Something about the angle of the bullet. I thought the doctor was trying to protect Taggart's legacy, and I didn't argue."

"Did you investigate Taggart's death?"

"Sure, I investigated it. Taggart had high levels of alcohol in his system. But he was a drinker when he was alone. I found nothing else that caught my attention."

I'd bet Paxton was so worried about finding evidence of suicide he didn't look that hard and likely missed other evidence.

"Anything special about his last days?"

"Drove the road between the festival site and the town a dozen times."

I pictured the winding road, the barn, and the mountains. "Did he say why?"

"No. I know the case never let him go."

I understood that. "And Briggs? He shot himself, too?"

Paxton frowned. "Yeah. Why are you so fixated on this?"

"All of these men were connected to the festival. They knew details that could stir trouble."

Paxton shifted in his seat. "Everyone in this town had information on the festival." As I readied to fire another question, he held up his hand. "Back to Tristan. If what you're saying is true, we need to find her."

"Yes, we do."

"Do you think she knows where the bodies are?"

I reached for my phone and texted, I know where the bodies are buried.

Paxton peered over the edge of my phone. "That true?"

"Do you wear a bulletproof vest?"

"Sometimes."

"Might want to strap one on today, pal."

As I drove out of Dawson, the dream catcher dangled from the rearview mirror as I dialed Grant's number. My call went to voicemail. I recapped my conversation with Paxton, the text I'd sent, and my final location.

I turned east on Tanner's Run Road toward the rolling hills. In the distance, I saw the barn's dried, sun-stripped boards.

My phone rang. "Grant."

"Where are you?"

A beat of silence and then: "A mile from the barn on the old Foster family farm. I think that's where the bodies are buried."

"How did you come up with that?"

"The original Foster bought the land to mine gold. It went bust, so he turned to farming. There's a mine shaft on the property. I think the barn is very near that shaft. Thirty-one years ago, someone could have parked a van inside the barn. This person could have gone undetected as they dumped the bodies in the shaft."

"Who did it?"

"That's what I'm about to find out."

"I'm fifteen minutes from you. Can you wait?"

"No." Cody rose on the passenger seat and stared out the windshield.

"Someone set fire to your house, Sloane. Someone wants to kill you."

"Yeah. Not ideal." I knew the road well enough to take a slight right a quarter of a mile before the barn. "I got my man Cody to help me."

He swore. "Do not engage."

I pulled off the road and parked. "I could say okay, but I would be lying."

"Sloane. Just wait."

"No can do."

"Why are you pushing this?"

I hooked Cody's leash on his collar, got out of the car, and helped him to the ground. "I've done this before."

He was swearing when I ended the call. The dog and I moved through the thicket of tall grass. The trees thinned. Cody paused to hike his leg and pee. He was chill, given the week he'd had. I liked that about him. No drama. Just one foot in front of another.

Ahead I heard the rumble of car tires, so I knelt, pulling Cody with me. "Shh," I said.

The dog wagged his tail. I fed him a few treats.

A car drove down the dirt road and parked at the barn. Bailey rose out of it. She was dressed in jeans, a simple pullover, and old shoes. She removed dark sunglasses and surveyed the barn.

An older truck pulled up behind Bailey's car. It was unmarked, but there was no missing Paxton's bulky form as he emerged from it. Bailey slipped her glasses back on and whirled around, her body stiff.

"Bailey, what are you doing here?" Paxton asked.

"Looking at the property. I hear the land might be for sale. You know me. I love me a good bit of land."

"You're trespassing," Paxton said.

She smiled. "I'm sorry. I just wanted to see the barn. Trying to figure out how expensive it'll be to tear it down."

"You going to demolish the barn?"

"Yes. I'll sell it for parts and scrap."

Paxton stepped toward her. Even from this distance I could see his body tense as he studied her. "Remember Tristan Fletcher?"

Bailey took a step back. "You been talking to that reporter. She's dug up all kinds of trouble surrounding the Festival Four."

"That's right."

"What about her?" Bailey walked toward him.

"She's alive. Sloane found her."

Bailey laughed. "She's lying. She's trying to shake us all up so someone says something stupid."

"What kind of stupid things would someone say?"

"Something like this. Sloane is trying to spook us."

"Why us?"

"We were both at the concert. She sees us both as suspects."

Her hand slipped into her purse, and she pulled out a revolver. Without hesitating, she shot Paxton in the chest. The bullet's impact knocked him backward, and he fell to the ground. She moved toward Paxton and stood over his still body.

Bailey was a little more bloodthirsty than I'd imagined. But I only underestimated someone once.

"Come on out, Sloane," Bailey said. "You set this little meeting up, so let's finish it."

I wrapped Cody's leash around a bush and then I rose. My gun pressing in the small of my back, I studied Paxton's beefy frame. His chest moved very slightly. He'd been wearing his bulletproof vest.

I moved toward her, not daring a look at Paxton.

"When did you figure it out?" Bailey leveled the gun on me.

"Takes one to know one, I suppose. I've faked emotions for so long I can spot another faker." I'd learned at an early age to smile or cry when my grandmother needed a reaction. Both achieved the desired effect because I was savvy enough to use my whole body to project the desired emotion. Bailey's smiles flashed bright, but they didn't reach her eyes. A rookie mistake, as far as I was concerned.

"What was my tell?"

I ignored the question. "Paxton was right. Tristan is alive."

Her eyes narrowed. "Right."

"Not joking. And I think you know that."

"If she was alive, how did you find the bodies? She doesn't know."

"Why do you say that?"

Bailey paused. "No one knows where the bodies are."

"I do." At least, I was pretty sure I'd figured it out.

"Bullshit."

"You and Colton must have met during the festival planning."

Her smile faded. "We did. He came by the house often to meet with Daddy."

"He's charming and, back in the day, hot. I could see a teenager falling for him. Did he convince you to help him get the girls?"

She stood still, her stare lingering for several beats. "My goodness, you do have a real good imagination."

"First Laurie, right? She'd have been easy. She wanted into music so badly he could've sold her any story to get her alone. She'd have followed him anywhere."

"Laurie wanted to sleep with him. I saw the way she was looking at him."

"Laurie goes to the trailer with Colton. Sex might have been consensual, but he liked to strangle women. Maybe it got out of hand, or maybe he'd planned to kill that night."

Bailey's smile faded.

"Then Patty, and Debra. They weren't as easily lured. A scream in the woods would've sent both running to help. And then Colton grabbed them. By now, I bet he had a taste for the violence and wanted more. He got them all except Amy. The one that got away. Did he try to take Amy in the woods near the tents before or after Patty and Debra?"

Bailey shook her head. "Poor drunk and battered Amy wandering in the woods. Low-life girls no one would ever have missed."

Anger clawed inside my chest. "Tristan was high during the festival. It wouldn't have taken much to lure her into a trailer."

"But don't let her fool you," she said. "She wanted Colton. It wasn't rape."

"Because you were standing in the corner watching."

She smiled. "She liked it."

I'd sensed Susan had been lying. Did she blame herself for going with Colton all those decades ago? That choice tore her family apart. "Until he strangled her."

"You got it all figured out."

"Did you watch Colton rape Patty and Debra?"

Her gaze grew distant, as if staring back into the darkness. "It was oddly hot."

Disgust coiled in my belly. "You drove the bodies out?"

"What bodies? There are no bodies, right?"

"You must have panicked when you opened the trailer and realized Tristan was missing. And then Colton was arrested."

"I don't panic."

"You lay low. When Colton was arrested, your daddy said he wasn't sure if he'd be convicted without the bodies. Colton knew that, too. So you kept your mouth shut."

"Great imagination."

"Did your father figure this out?" I asked. "Did you shoot him?"

Her smile flickered. "I loved my daddy."

"But Daddy discovered something, didn't he?"

"You don't know anything."

I shook my head. "What did Daddy figure out five years after the festival? Did he find a few mementos from the other girls in your room?"

She stared at me with a steady gaze that felt more detached than connected.

"He freaked out, didn't he? I mean, that festival was a disaster for him. I hope you denied it all. Confirming the man's discovery would have been a final blow for him."

"You have a lot of answers." Her flat tone suggested I'd hit a nerve.

"And then what? You spiked his whiskey. Was he barely conscious when you wrapped his hand around the gun and pulled the trigger?"

Silence settled over her.

"Come on. It's just us girls here."

"Shut up."

"Hopefully the poor old man never felt a thing."

Her eyes glistened.

I kept pressing. "And Taggart? Did he get too close? Did you spike his whiskey?"

She shoved out a breath as she blinked. "He wouldn't let the case go. He was ready to pull in the FBI and run the forensic tests all over again. He was convinced that new technology would give him more precise information."

"You drugged him. Shot him."

Her brow knotted. "He wasn't a happy man. Haunted, really. It was an act of mercy."

She might have seen herself as a sympathetic angel, but I saw the demon scratching under her skin. "And Brian Fletcher?"

"I knew Tristan was alive. I figured with you in town, old memories would be resurrected. It was a matter of time before he told someone about her. And I couldn't trust what she might have remembered."

She'd been waiting for the last shoe to drop for thirty-one years. "You going to keep shooting people?"

"I just might."

"You going to toss my body down the mine shaft?"

Her eyes brightened with interest. "You are clever."

"I like to think so."

"No one will remember it soon. The barn is falling in on itself, so I'll buy the land and bulldoze over it all."

"Sounds almost convincing."

Cody barked. Big paws thumped through the thicket toward me. He'd broken free. As he bounded out of the woods, Bailey shifted her gaze. It was a slight shift, the hint of a hesitation. But it was enough. I drew my gun from the small of my back and raised it in one smooth move I'd practiced at the shooting range a thousand times before. My shooting instructors said muscle memory was critical. *Don't give yourself a chance to think. Just react.*

Bailey and I fired at the same time.

Chapter Forty-Four

SLOANE

Monday, August 25, 2025, 1:30 p.m.

State police crews and vans were now parked off the road by the barn. After locating the mine shaft, the crews created a pulley rig and harnesses over the now-exposed opening. Two cops dressed in tactical gear stood over the vertical shaft with helmets and GoPros. They were ready to lower.

I stood back with Grant, watching. I didn't feel anything as I watched the officers' choreographed actions. But my stomach was so taut I could barely breathe.

We were a tight circle: Grant, me, Paxton, and Cody, as well as assorted police from area jurisdictions. Most were curious and wanted a ringside seat at the conclusion of a thirty-one-year-old mystery.

Paxton's bulletproof vest had saved him. The bullet that should have killed him had left a deep bruise on his chest. Bailey's shoulder was shredded. She'd never regain full use. I wished I'd shot her in the leg, too.

Susan, with her sister's support, had turned herself in to the police. She was ready to relay everything she'd seen in the trailer in exchange for immunity. Frankly, I wouldn't have given her the deal. But Grant said the prosecutor wanted to leverage her testimony against Bailey and present it to the parole board before Colton's hearing. Life was full of compromises.

When cops told Bailey that Susan was willing to testify, she admitted that she'd been drawn to Colton immediately. He was handsome, sexy, and dangerous. And she'd been very willing to help him lure his victims into the trailer, where he'd killed them. At first, she'd thought he'd turn her in to the police, but he'd kept quiet because she was the key to his avoiding the death penalty. Unfortunately, her father had found a love letter from Colton to Bailey in her bedroom almost five years after the festival. It had referenced their secret. He'd confronted her, and one week later he'd shot himself. And then years later, Taggart had started driving by the barn several times a day. He'd talked often about breakthroughs in forensic science. He'd killed himself within weeks. And then Fletcher met with me. How long would it have taken for him to confess all to me? And now he was dead.

Bailey had shot and killed all three men, careful to make their deaths look like suicides.

The odd thing was that Bailey had not spoken to Colton in thirty-one years. In their silence, they'd struck a devil's bargain that had allowed her to remain free and close to anyone who could expose her.

Two days ago, when Grant had met me here at this site, he'd been equally pissed and relieved. Only when he saw that Bailey's bullet had grazed my arm did his pulsing jaw ease. Paxton had begun to rouse. Bailey was gripping her bloody arm and squealing like a little pig.

When we'd arrived at the emergency room, Grant had made it clear to the paramedics that I could be pregnant. He was a good man. A lot of guys would have bailed on me by now.

But he'd sat beside me in the emergency room cubicle and put on his best calm expression. I'd wondered if he used that face while interviewing suspects. No emotion but very focused. It was a good look. "What did the doctors say?" he asked.

"Looks like Team Outcast doesn't get a new member." I studied his face closely, but I couldn't detect any signs of relief or disappointment.

"Okay," he'd said.

"You're off the hook."

"I was hoping I wasn't."

"Probably just as well. I can't keep plants alive."

He studied me, his eyes darkening with resolve. "Why don't you stay in Dawson for a while? My house is big enough for us and Cody. You can write your article or book there."

Part of my guard relaxed. I had been focused on this case for so long. It was solved now. A win for everyone. The article would write itself. And then I'd find a buyer. And then came the in-between times that bookended my projects. Without a story or purpose, I was aimless and embraced dangerous stunts to ease my disquiet.

Grant was offering me a lifeline. I didn't have to navigate the inevitable choppy waters alone. "Okay."

His body relaxed a fraction. "Good."

We stood side by side in silence and watched the first officer lower his camera into the shaft. We viewed the monitor as the camera lowered past old timbered walls, pieced together with wooden pegs and nails more than a century ago. The darkness thickened as if it fought against the jarring light.

The camera and light lowered. And lowered. Timbers creaked. Chunks of dirt dropped and hit what sounded like water. The *plop-plop* sound echoed over the microphone.

The camera hovered over the murky black water and then slipped below the surface. Flakes of debris floated like welcoming specters. The camera dropped farther, and I wondered if this hole had a bottom.

And then the camera kicked up silt, and still waters, not disturbed in decades, swirled.

The camera shifted closer to the wall. The officer had explained he'd map the bottom so that he didn't overlook a section.

And then I saw it. A skull, lying on its side, the empty eye socket staring at the camera. I wasn't repulsed or afraid. I was relieved. Someone who'd been lost was found.

Over the next four hours, the team recovered three sets of remains. It was a painstaking process, bringing them bone by bone to the surface.

After thirty-one years, the lost girls were brought into the light. Uncertainty became what it should have been three decades ago: grief. But, for me, there was no grief. Only a sense that I'd done right by Patty, like she had me.

Grant handed me a soda. "You okay?"

Was I? I stared at the remains, dark and discolored, stripped of flesh. I wanted Susan to see them. Her silence had condemned them and their families to the cold, wet darkness for decades. But Susan or Bailey standing here wouldn't change anything.

"I'm okay."

"Let's get out of here."

"I don't want to leave them."

"They are in good hands now." His strong hand wrapped around my chilled fingers. I didn't pull or tug away. I liked Grant. And I thought liking must be the first step to something more. I hoped. I smiled up at him. "Okay."

ABOUT THE AUTHOR

Photo © 2015 StudioFBJ

Mary Burton is the *New York Times* and *USA Today* bestselling author of more than forty romance and suspense novels, including *Another Girl Lost*, *The House Beyond the Dunes*, and *The Lies I Told*. She currently lives in North Carolina with her husband. For more information, visit www.maryburton.com.